Redemption

I0655243

By Christopher C Hulley

But now faith, hope, love, abide these three; **but the greatest**
of these is love.

To my wife Michelle, and my sons Ben and Tom. Thank you
for making my life a joy.

With thanks to Lin Martinique-Whittaker -
http://www.martiniqueart.com for the cover design.

The author can be contacted at redemption@jera.com.au

Table of Contents

World Map

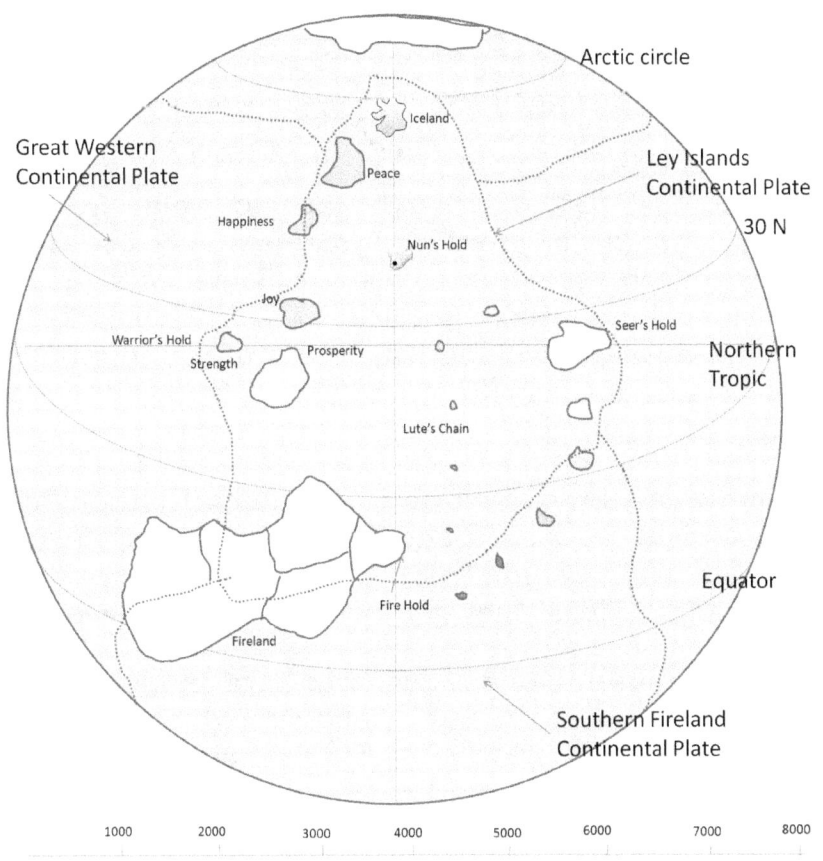

Arctic circle

Iceland

Great Western
Continental Plate

Peace

Ley Islands
Continental Plate

30 N

Happiness

Nun's Hold

Joy

Warrior's Hold

Seer's Hold

Strength

Prosperity

Northern
Tropic

Lute's Chain

Equator

Fire Hold

Fireland

Southern Fireland
Continental Plate

| 1000 | 2000 | 3000 | 4000 | 5000 | 6000 | 7000 | 8000 |

Scale: Miles (approx)

Chapter 1. Tell me what you see

Open up your eyes now, tell me what you see.
It is no surprise now, what you see is me.
Big and black the clouds may be, time will pass away.
If you put your trust in me I'll make bright your day.

Lennon/McCartney 1965

'Sometimes', Bronn thought as he woke from yet another night of troubled dreams and not enough decent sleep, 'sometimes, being a Seer is a right pain in the behind'. He grumbled as he reached for his dream journal, invoking long years of training to stop the fleeting imagery from vanishing, fixing the details firmly in his mind.

Bronn was a bit of a morning grumbler. He thought he had a right to be. He *had* to be a dreaming Seer, of course. Why couldn't he be a trance Seer, or a visionary? At least they got a decent night's sleep.

To be thankful, being a Seer was rare enough, and he was surely one of the best. Good enough that if he had not elected to stay in the Seer's Hold and pursue post-qualification training and a career in the Hold itself, he could have gone to work for any rich lord and lady and had a fine life (for such people had few troubles to send very much sleeplessness to disturb him), or set up his own Dreamshop and have somewhat harder but probably more satisfying work seeing the fates, troubles and best way through problematic times for all and sundry. Either way, he would have succeeded, been rich, and reasonably happy. He knew that, after all, he had Seen the possibilities – for a Seer didn't always see what would certainly be, but often only what the possibilities and probabilities were.

But of course, he would not meet his wife that way. Oh, yes, he would surely meet *a* wife, one who would stand by him, and one who he would love well enough. But only by sticking to the main vision would he meet his true wife, the one whose passion and love would complete his life, make him deliriously happy and raise his Seeing abilities to their ultimate peak. He's Seen that too, of course.

Still and all, he was getting a bit sick of the waiting. It was all very well to know that there was someone out there just right for him. He knew her face well, and the delicious curves of her body, her happy laugh and the utterly gorgeous way her lips would curl up just before she kissed him, but he'd had enough Seeing of all that. He was thirty now, had been Seeing her for four years, and was wanting to do a bit of experiencing. He wanted to hold her, not See himself holding her, no matter how detailed the dreams were.

He scratched the back of his thigh and marshaled his thoughts. Well, there was no doubt that the time had come for action. The same dreams were there every night. Journey to the Nuns Hold, pick up the great Fire Witch. Straightforward enough, mostly the same dream, with so little variation that it could be taken as a prediction rather than as a Seeing of different possibilities. A hard enough task in its own right, but he had Seen the face of the Witch enough that he would know her when he met her. Leave aside the fact that Fire Witches were few and far between outside of Fire Hold, and the Great Ones – level two or higher - would certainly not normally be found with the Nuns of Knowledge.

Then, on to the Ice Hold. A hard enough journey to contemplate, given no-one ever went there, it was not going to be much fun. He grimaced. When he had first started dreaming that journey, five times out of ten it ended with his death, or that of the Fire Witch, or both. A month later, six out of ten such dreams led to success, the next month it was seven, but this month there had been no improvement. He placed another tick in the journal for that dream, under the 'fail' column. He added detail: death by ice bear, ugh, unpleasant. So, now must be the time to go, before the chances started dropping again.

Meet the Ice Witch. Ignore the total lack of any known Ice Witches for the last few hundred years, and the fact that the Ice Hold was a deserted, uninhabited mausoleum according to all reports. On to Warrior's Hold, and then somehow on to Alana's Keep, wherever that was. At least he knew what to do there, to get Alana's Wand. He shivered as the Words rolled around in his head. They wanted to get out, to be said. Words of Command, in his mind! And he had Seen them, not learned them the hard way! They were intricately tied up in his vision of the quest, and surely powerful enough to make the Guardian give the wand up.

And then on, to face Narn the Sorcerer (whose full name was supposed to be Tan'Nar'No) in open battle, and hopefully victory. He glumly noted that the odds, according to his Dreaming, were still no better than fifty-fifty, even if all the preceding quests and journeys were successful.

Groaning, he closed his journal, got out of bed, issued a few orders and made his way to the baths, a delightful series of pools of water, heated to various temperatures by thermal springs, or cooled by the stream from the mountains. He took his time, spending several hours luxuriating in the hot pool, the cold pool, the spa pool and the shock pool. He looked up, as always, in joy and wonder at the caves in which they lay. Vast echoing chambers with stalactites and stalagmites, and artfully carved slots in the hillside designed to maximize the entrance of light, but with shutters that could be closed to minimize the entry of wind and rain. Some of the protective panels were glass, created with great effort by Fire Witches, almost beyond price in value. Seer's Hold traditionally exchanged students and scholars to further knowledge, perform tasks that were needed (such as keeping bats out of the fabulous caves), and to seek brides and husbands to bring fresh blood to the guilds.

He knew very well that there would be few opportunities to indulge himself like this in the coming months or years (his vision was not quite clear there) of the quests, he had Seen the discomforts quite well enough. (Oh, the cold of the far north and the Ice Hold! Ugh! Ugh! Ugh!) Surely Seers' Hold was the most civilized of all the Holds of Magic and learning in the world thanks to these blessed springs. He hoped that his wonderful, beautiful wife would want to come back here to live, when he finally found her. Suddenly, he remembered – a dream from months ago where he found out her name, so brief that despite training it had slipped his mind when he awoke. Kara. That was her name. A lovely name. He hoped his remembering was an indicator that he would meet her soon.

Sighing, he finally rose out of the cooling pool, put on fresh clothes (the last he would get for a while, no doubt) and made his way to the main hall for his midday appointment with the abbot. On his way, he checked in to his rooms, and saw that the preparations he had ordered for his departure were being well attended to. Everything of good quality, but well-worn in for comfort, and to attract as little attention from bandits as possible. A sturdy and reasonably well dispositioned hinny was his for the asking, and a pack mule, and he could see from one glance at the animals that his apprentice had chosen well. He sighed again. He would miss Kev, a quiet, studious boy who rarely had to be asked to do anything twice, and who was at a stage where he would have benefitted greatly from the next few months of instruction. Still, who knew, hopefully Bronn would not be away too long, and there were other teachers.

He walked down the well maintained path that lead to the great hall, appreciating the colorful tropical flowers planted so neatly in ornamental patterns. The warmth of another lovely day beat down on his back, but he shivered. His dreams of the frozen north were all too vivid in his memory. Oh well, at least the first part of the journey was in temperate zones.

The Hold loomed, awe inspiring and magnificent, but not cold and aloof. Seeing, as an art, is mostly about other people, and for auguries to be believed and trusted the oracle must be approachable, empathic, and know how to phrase the frequent ambiguities in Visions in terms the listener can relate to.

Sometimes, the dreams and predictions were good ones, and those were relatively easy to pass on.

But the human condition also involves strife, peril, sickness and death, and a Seer also had to know how to deal with those issues as well, especially when the vision was completely unambiguous. The need for understanding, the need to be close to people permeated all things, and led to a more friendly architecture than one saw at most of the Holds.

The entrance to the hall was high, and wide, to symbolize the breadth of the Seers' vision. But it was made of a pleasant reddish stone, smooth and pleasantly cool in these sub-tropic climes. The hall itself was long, but every effort had been made to make the person walking down it comfortable. There were no suits of armor, no crossed swords on the walls, no solid and locked or barred doors leading who knows where. Instead, there were tapestries on the walls, and not of battles either – pleasant woodland scenes, men and women out enjoying themselves. There were fine tables with vases of flowers, and small alcoves with tables and seating, fruit and water, the whole scene saying 'Welcome, traveler, and if you are weary, rest a while. Be confident that your needs will be met, and do not rush through our halls'.

The Seers did not fight. There was rarely a need, for any such trouble would probably be foreseen. Of course, some sort of defensive capability was necessary. Every now and then there would be someone who was presented with a difficult vision and blamed the Seers, or simply wanted to hit out blindly in anger, fear or frustration. Foreseeing someone with such intent wasn't much help if one did not have the capacity to do something about it! But since Seeing came with implicit empathy, the desire to hit back simply wasn't there most of the time. They did keep themselves in good physical shape (as did all the members of the various Holds), and they practiced a physically flowing form of self-defense designed to clear and harmonize the mind and body and protect the master, but with little of the offensive in it.

There were others in the Hold apart from the Seers, of course, filling many jobs, and one of them was Defender of the Hold. Around the Hold itself lived several tribes, mostly in harmony as they had clearly defined boundaries, and these regarded the Seers somewhat possessively. The phrase 'our Seers' would be heard a lot. Some Seers came from such tribes, and the children of Seers with no inherited ability would sometimes marry into one, as they were not encouraged to stay in the Hold as simple workers once

11

they were fully grown. Strong young men and women would train and vie with one another to earn the right to apply to be a Defender, since they stood a chance of marrying a Seer, holding a position of respect, not having to work too hard, and of course getting a decent bath.

And there were also a few, a very few students – two at the current time - on exchange from Warrior's Hold, just in case. They trained the Defenders and the Seers as needed, continued their studies and practiced amongst themselves. Their pay was invaluable: a Seer would tell them what they needed to know to maximize their talent, whether it was a particular set of exercises, a place to go or the name of a Master who would suit their style the best. They were rarely needed. Just knowing a Warrior was there was enough to give most people pause.

At the end of the long entrance hall, the formal reception rooms began. There was a pleasant waiting room, and a magnificent carpet began inside of it, leading all the way through to the throne room itself, purple, gold and silver in color for healing, wealth and introspection. They called it the 'throne room', because that was where the abbot received people in state, though most foreign dignitaries who visited were at first a little shocked, because there was little of ostentation in it. There were many beautiful things in it to be sure, but it was clear that they had been chosen for no other reason than the abbot liked them. And there was certainly no throne, nothing more than a half dozen very comfortable armchairs and a small table (more chairs could be brought in if needed), and the abbot had no particular chair, he sat where convenient.

This underlined the simple fact that while the abbot was the Seer with seniority and the best record for accuracy, the fact was that Seeing is an imprecise art, and a novice might See a Vision that was not granted to anyone else. The hierarchy was less important than in any other Hold, and men and women lived and worked according to their talent, ability and desire – unlike most of the rest of the world.

Bronn approached the abbot and clasped him warmly by the hand. He was a good friend and a remarkable man. Not only did he see detailed visions of the future with good accuracy, he could see many useful things in the present too –for the future begins just a heartbeat later. But most unusually, he could sometimes See Visions of the past. And while there were always cases where a Gifted person might have traces of other Gifts – Ice Witches were supposed to have included a few Seers, and Fire Witches, Warriors - men who could Project were rare, and the abbot was unique in Bronn's experience in being a male Seer who could project an Avatar, and a Material one at that, as long as it was within sight of the abbot himself.

"So, Bronn, I Saw you were leaving today" the abbot stated plainly. "A good day, to start, I think. I See you coming to the end of our lands safely, though not without incident". Bronn nodded, and spoke his thanks. Visions of one's own life and progress through it were rarer than those of others, and also less reliable as the choices one made had a correspondingly greater effect. As a Seer who had lived long ago said, 'observation changes the event'. It was always good to have the benefit of someone else's Seeing.

"My Vision says that this will be helpful and useful on your journey" the abbot added. "I have had it charged slowly, day by day for months now". He turned towards a Defender standing by his chair, and said "if you please ..." The Defender in turn walked over to a stand, and picked up a staff, and brought it over to Bronn, who took it and looked it over. It looked like an ordinary staff, but the word 'charged' told Bronn it was not all it seemed. He examined a metal band a short way from one end.

The abbot nodded. "Yes, that's it. You slide it down, and twist to the right". Bronn did this, and was then able to slide it further down, revealing a space in which there were half a dozen large rubies, carefully faceted, aligned in a silver lattice. A wire ran from the last one down into the staff.

Bronn whistled softly. Six properly cut rubies of that size, and flawless enough to be used to store Fire Magic were worth a fortune, and not a small one either. "This is a princely gift, Vail" he stated simply. The abbot shrugged. "Not a gift. It's a Hold treasure, of course, and you as a senior Seer are entitled to use it if you need it. And while I haven't Seen too much beyond your leaving this land, you will need it. Mind you, I'd quite like it back, if possible".

Bronn nodded. "Of course, Vail, if I can" he promised. "And the trigger?"

Vail instructed Bronn in the staff's use. "Slide the band back up ... good. Now, one turn to the left and it's locked, in off-mode. Another, and you're at level one, then another to two, and another to three. You press the button you feel there. You get one level-three shot, or four level-twos, or sixteen level-ones".

Bronn knew that the levels corresponded to the power that a Fire Witch of the corresponding grade would be able to generate in a bolt of offence. But the process of storing power was horrendously inefficient. The abbot must have devoted the time and energy of the two Fire

Witches in the Hold, practically continuously for months.

"Wouldn't it have been easier to send a Fire Witch with me?" Bronn asked. Vail shrugged. "We don't have anyone over grade one with us at the moment" he replied. "High grade Fire Witches are rare enough, and what with those Narn has suborned and those who defend Fire Hold to stop him stealing more, I doubt if there are three level twos at large in the whole world right now. And they wouldn't be much use against Narn himself if he came here. At least this way you have one good shot at him, he wouldn't be expecting it – the skill needed to create a new firestaff only crops up every few hundred years or so, and there are very few left at the moment. I doubt if there are five firestaffs still working in all of the world, and as far as I know this is the only one left capable of a level three bolt."

Vail frowned. "My Vision fails me at this point ... I sometimes see myself sending a Warrior with you and sometimes a Defender, and sometimes I see you going off alone. I just don't know ... what have you Seen?"

Bronn shrugged, in his turn. "Nothing, Vail. I haven't Seen anything of my travels in our land. Probably because they are not important and hopefully because they will be relatively safe".

Vail nodded. "I thought as much, and in that case, I'm going to play it safe, and send someone with you who is both a Warrior and a Defender. Satro is his name. He came from the Eastern tribe, the Sori, and showed such promise that we sent him off to Warrior's Hold as an exchange student, and they accepted him for training to full Warrior status. The first one, according to our records, for over fifty years. He graduated but chose to return here, and has been a senior Defender for two years."

"But he has a questioning mind, and now that he feels he has repaid us for our investment in him, he wants leave of absence to travel to the Nuns of Knowledge, and find answers to questions that have been perplexing him for years. I have ordered provisions and a pack mule for him, and they will be ready when you are."

Bronn nodded his thanks. "I'm sure of getting to the Nuns, then" he said. "The journey should be relatively straightforward anyway, barring a storm at sea, and there shouldn't be anything a Warrior can't handle."

Chapter 2. Departure

There is no easy way but there is a way
We both could use some understanding, trust would help
And the journey of a thousand miles begins with just one step

Willie Nelson 1987

Satro greeted Bronn with the easy manner of a man who is completely secure in his own body and mind, who knows exactly what he can do and what he cannot. That was typical of a Warrior, years of training raised his physical skills to a very high level indeed, and just as importantly and at the same time disciplined his mind.

It would be easy to dismiss Warrior training as nothing more than selecting the most physically gifted young boys and training them to a peak. And certainly that was a major component of the Way. But there were four important facts that said there was more to it. Firstly, magical theory *required* there to be four Gifts, and *required* them (secondly) to be at the four corners of the Ley supercontinent, mostly submerged but with the archetypal islands directly South (Fire Witches), North (Ice Witches), East (the Seers) and so to the West.

Thirdly, since the Seer's Gifts related almost entirely to things outside of themselves, those at the Western reaches, being on the opposite side of the great North-South Ley line which drove the Witch magic, naturally related to things inside them. Being internal in focus, direct evidence was sometimes harder to see. Nonetheless, the simple fact was that while there were other places which trained people to fight (like the Seer's Hold Defenders), no place and no one got results like Warrior's Hold in pure, simple fighting ability, and

17

a Warrior's intuition of danger and perception of attack could not be explained any other way. And, of course, there was their shielding ability. Every Gifted person could mount an auric shield to some extent, but the Warriors were better at it, as good as Fire Witches – though projecting an Avatar was as rare for them as in the general population and they showed no greater aptitude in other areas of Witch magic.

And no Ungifted man or woman could detect a well-fletched arrow flying towards them, or really hope to deflect or stop it with a material shield unless that shield was already in, or nearly in position. But a Warrior would turn around and pluck one out of the air as it sped towards his back. He just Knew it was there. There were not too many Warriors, especially over Bronze grade, perhaps just as well as otherwise they would be a major dominating force in the world.

Bronn saw a man perhaps five years younger than himself, of medium height and unobtrusively muscular. It would be easy to say he moved like a cat, or moved with deliberate grace, and he certainly could do so. But usually he moved in a deceptively normal way. Disguise was a part of Warrior training, and they were also taught how to fit in, how to look like everyone else. A Warrior would occasionally lose or drop things, or stumble – when it didn't matter, and when people were watching. But there was no disguising that there was a young man in front of him who was not going to be fazed by stepping out of Seer's Hold and into the semi-wilderness of the Hold tribes, the rigors of the true wilderness beyond them, or whatever the coast and coastal tribes might present them with.

Satro, on the other hand, saw a tallish man, in good shape, but (with a Warrior's trained ability to read others) apprehensive about a long and arduous

18

journey. His first words were friendly. "Don't worry" he grinned. "By the time we've been going a fortnight, you'll be as tough as nails and ready to handle anything our land throws at you."

'Spot on', thought Bronn gloomily, a Seer could have done no better. Amazing how the various Gifts often operated to the same effect, despite their highly different nature. Oh, well, best to be civil. More than best, really – his nature, and his training made it second nature as well. He grinned in return. "I know, Satro. I've Seen it. Unfortunately, I've also Seen myself lying on hard ground and groaning like an old man for those two weeks."

Satro laughed. "I'm sure we're going to get on just fine, Bronn. Pleased to meet you." He held out his hand in the universal gesture of greeting, and Bronn shook it. It felt just like any other man's hand, perhaps a little strong and firm. But as so often happened when two Gifts came close together, Bronn had a little Vision of what could happen if Satro chose to grip hard. He vowed never to put himself in that position. Satro in his turn looked at him, his head tilted slightly to one side and smiled slightly, in a pensive sort of way. "You know, Bronn, you could fight if you had to. I can see it in you. Under extreme duress, you would See what was going to happen, and react to it well in advance. Well, that's good to know."

He looked around, and saw everything was in place. The four mounts were ready, three mules and his hinny tied to a post, Kev standing by. They had minimal supplies, for at first they would expect hospitality from the Hold tribes, and then they would live off the land, and finally buy provisions when they got to the coast. They had Satro's sword, a bow each and a few other assorted weapons, Bronn's staff, emergency provisions and cooking gear, water of course, a small amount of wet weather protection, some spare clothes, medicines and not too much more.

Bronn nodded approvingly. "I See that the time to leave will be in about ten minutes" he said. Satro pursed his lips. "Really? You See that fine a degree, that you can time it to within minutes to get the best outcome?"

"Yes, indeed" Bronn replied with a smile. "Not too hard in this case, mind you – Kev knows me and I him, and unless I misjudge him greatly he has a flask of ale in that basket and three tankards. I'd say ten minutes is about right.

Satro threw back his head and laughed as Kev smiled and started to get the tankards out. "Oh, yes, wise Seer, your vision is clearly correct" he chortled. "Well, I'd not normally drink while on duty, but the chances of some sort of problem so close to Seer's Hold are pretty low." He accepted his tankard with thanks, and the three of them drank a toast to departure and safe journey.

"So, Bronn, there is only one path away from the Hold of course, but after that which way do you favor?"

Bronn took a deep pull from his tankard, and mused. "Well, I've not really Seen anything about the actual path of the journey to Carm" he said. "Usually, that's because it doesn't really matter, or someone else will make the decision. I had simply planned to take the middle road straight through our lands and over the Dragon's Back rather than either coast road. What's your advice?"

Satro pulled at his chin as he hesitated in thought, a habit Bronn would see often. A small beard would come naturally to him with time to aid and abet that habit, Bronn thought. "The middle road is certainly the shortest" he replied with some hesitation. "Yet ... I have a feeling ... I think I'd prefer to go on the northern coast road. I don't know why. But Narn's name has been heard muttered about; yes even here in Seer's Hold. I'd rather go to the Sori, my home tribe first. At least there I am sure we will be welcome by right of kinship."

Bronn stared. "Surely you're not serious?" he exclaimed. "You're not saying one of the Hold tribes would even hinder us, let alone attack us? Why, that would be unheard of for even a traveler seeking a reading, let alone an actual Seer. And with a Warrior escort?"

"Yes ..." Satro mused, finishing his ale and handing the tankard back to Kev with thanks. "Unthinkable. And yet ... I have a feeling that the north road will be the best."

Bronn shrugged. "No point travelling with a Warrior and not listening to his intuitions about safety. The north road it is."

And so, after a brief farewell to Kev, they set off on the road out of Seer's Hold. With only five dozen or so Seers, as many in training, and as many again novices (a lot of Seers left the Hold after qualifying, to work where they were needed), a half dozen other Gifted people on exchange, and about twice as many supporting staff, spouses and children, the land belonging to the Hold was not very great in extent. There were perhaps ten times as many again in the periphery and performing services not directly related, but many essential services and products such as clothing were simply purchased from the coastal cities rather than made locally – they had to do something with all the money those who came to consult the

Seers paid. The Seers charged quite a high rate, because otherwise they would be flooded with folk seeking a cheap answer to trivial questions, and their Visions would not be valued. The rate would normally be tailored to the wealth of the visitor, and while some people always tried to pretend poverty the Seers simply Saw right through them. This meant that a relatively poor person who had a truly perplexing problem could afford to consult the oracles. Still and all, it was mostly the wealthy who came to Seer's Hold because while the fee was usually reasonable, they had to get there. Those who could not afford to travel, or didn't want to, would consult their local Seer. Every major city had at least one graduate from Seer's Hold who had left to set up shop, and quite a few smaller towns as well.

Bronn got some idea why such a valued resource as Satro was being released so readily. He questioned Bronn endlessly about the supporting staff, the nature of the crops, what was done with the Hold's wealth, how Seeing worked and the quest ahead. Bronn patiently answered where he could, but had a sinking feeling that Satro's questions well and truly exceeded his ability to answer, or indeed his desire to speak.

They passed fairly quickly beyond the houses and workshops of those who did the mundane things necessary to support everyday life, and then the farms where food was raised. In the warm climate there was not much need for firewood – some for cooking of course, but not for heating, even in winter, nor for heating water for washing in the Hold – people or clothes were all washed in the warm water from the wonderful thermal springs.

They soon came to the point where the three paths branched from the one entrance to Seers Hold Town, and set off on the northerly one. Satro advised Bronn to dismount and walk or trot for a while every half hour or so, to vary the muscles being used, to stretch, and avoid saddle-soreness. He himself mostly walked, or ran ahead out of desire for exercise or simple exuberance, rejoicing in the smoothly flowing machine that was his body – on that first day, he rode no more than an hour at most.

Towards nightfall they found a small clump of trees in an otherwise unrelieved plain, several of them copses where other travelers had had a need for timber, but with a fair amount of deadfall that made an easy fire, and they settled down for an uneventful night. They did not keep watch – Satro's Gift would alert them well before any danger came along, not that there was much danger out on the plains. The stars were magnificent of course, and the trees blocked what little wind there was very nicely, and they made the most of the perishable provisions they had brought, but it wasn't a cheerful evening of brilliant repartee. While they had got to know each other during the day, the experienced traveler soon learns to put themselves into a bit of a trance, alpha-rythming the day away, allowing the boring bits of travel to pass unnoticed.

The second day was a continuation of the first, but much longer. Despite Satro's warning and his own Vision, Bronn was unrealistic about his own capabilities, and pushed himself too far. A whole day's travelling is very different from the easy start they had on the first day, no more than a handful of hours and with fresh, well rested bodies. He didn't really begin to feel it until nearly the end of the day, when they found a little shelter in the lee of a small hill. After a little food, his body decided it had had enough. He was dog-tired, and they went to sleep early, planning on early rising to start travelling in the cool of the morning. Even as he dropped off to sleep, Bronn knew that was a bit unrealistic. His last thought was that he missed the hot pools dreadfully.

He passed an uneventful night, with no memorable dreams. Besides the tiredness, it was often so – once one set into motion, actions that fitted in with a Seeing, the dreams subsided a bit. But the morning was eventful enough, if only in a localized way. There is nothing quite like the feeling of waking up after a day's travelling, when one has the skills to do it but the body is no longer trained in the right way. Bronn had riding skills, but they were little needed at Seer's Hold. In some ways it would have been easier if he had been a novice, he would not have tried to use muscles which were no longer there. When he tried to move, there were aches and pains and stiffnesses almost beyond belief. He literally could not move for several minutes, and then only like an old man, as he had seen in his Vision.

Bronn then had a very rare experience. With the great strength they all had in their arms, and their intimate and detailed knowledge of how bones, muscles, ligaments and tendons all work together, no-one could give a massage like a Warrior. Besides their spouses, few ever got to see that skill. But Satro stretched him, kneaded him like dough, wrung him out and left him to dry. It was agony, but in a good way. It would be too much to say that at the end of it he felt as good as new, but at least Bronn was able to continue. He let himself be guided by Satro that day, he walked when Satro said walk, rode and rested, stretched and drank when he was told, and as a result after stopping early that day and sleeping well, he was in much better shape to continue the next morning.

That day was enough to take them to the borders of the Sori tribe. There, they saw from the top of a hill what must have been the whole massed tribe of the

Nari, camped in a very warlike gathering. There were only a small number of support retinue with them, and Satro's evaluation was that they were set up as a quick, decisive strike force. There were even a few of the Turi among them, a great rarity for there was little mingling of the three tribes except through the Seers territory itself – there, anyone could get together and marry if they would. Satro recommended circling them and keeping well away, which they did, and found the Sori themselves camped in a defensive position not far away.

Bronn shook his head a lot that day. What was going on? The three tribes kept to themselves. Yes, they did not mingle, but there was no enmity; they were united in the common purpose of keeping Seer's Hold isolated and safe. That was their primary duty, purpose and privilege.

Satro soon found an open path that allowed them to approach the Sori encampment in a clearly visible way that allowed for plenty of warning. No point risking a nervous bowman while trying to get themselves introduced. And so, as they approached the camp, there were a good half dozen men and women with arrows at the ready, waiting for them to ride up – wary, but not at all worried. Satro sat proudly, and announced them as soon as they were in comfortable earshot.

"I am Satro Sori, son of Natho and Elana Sori, protector of Seers and Defender in my own right" he announced. Bronn noticed that he kept the fact that he was also a Warrior to himself. "I travel with Bronn, Master Seer, to Carm. We seek passage and the right to hunt for our daily needs."

The archers were nonplussed. Finally, after some fifteen seconds of thought and as much of muttered talk, one of them sent a rider off, and addressed them. "Please wait awhile, then" he offered, with at least some courtesy. "We have sent for Natho Sori, for he is alive and well, and when he comes he will surely be glad to see you and make you welcome."

Satro sat for a moment, taken aback, a rarity in a Warrior to be sure. "Surely, things have not come to such a pass" he inquired, incredulity in his voice. "To claim to be one of the Sori, that is enough for welcome by kin-right in itself? No-one would make such a claim falsely save by madness or great need, and you must know that Bronn here is a Seer. You see his clothing, his accoutrements and his talisman."

The self-nominated leader of the small band had at least the grace to lower his head. "I am sorry, Satro Sori. But these are strange times. Never before have the Nari gathered against us. Never in the oldest tales have we fought our brother tribes. But there are strangers about, who speak powerful words, who stir the people up, who sway people's minds. The Turi have been changed, and they have swayed the Nari. They dream of uniting the tribes, by force if necessary, and then there is talk of ... talk of ... I cannot bring myself to speak of it. But a change in our relationship with the Seers. We have rejected these words, but we have seen their power. We will not risk an outsider coming into our midst and corrupting our ways. And so, you must be vouched for. Again, I am sorry. But I fear there will be more sorrow over the next few days, that will make this inconvenience a minor matter. The Nari say, join us or fight. But we will not join them. If you are truly who you say you are ... you will be welcome indeed. A Defender and a Seer could be a big help."

It took little more time before the rider had had time to go back to the main camp, and find Satro's father. He came riding up at speed, and stopped short. He leapt

26

off his horse, with the energy of a young man, and gave Satro a bear hug. Satro responded as joyfully, and powerfully. "Yes!" he shouted in delight. "This is my son, Satro! I vouch for him, and anyone with him. And for sure, I know who is with him anyway, for I have seen the Seer Bronn several times before. Welcome, welcome indeed! Come, please come to the camp. And let us tell you of the sorry state of affairs."

Natho Sori turned his horse, and the guards parted and let them through. Although obviously glad to see his son and respectful of Bronn, he would not give much information on the short ride to the camp, saying only that these important matters needed full attention and could not be dealt with while on horseback. He did, however, stop short a little before a small rise that clearly led to the camp. "Satro, I must tell you that your arrival is not as much a surprise as it might have been. Although the last time you passed through here was four years ago, as you know Nadia has a little Seer's talent. She saw you returning today, in a dream. She still pines for you, though she has been courted by Petro for nearly two years now. I am pleased to see you returned, so very much grown to a man, but I must tell you that I think she will be very glad too, and has dreams and expectations of her own. You will have to think carefully how you will handle yourself, and her."

Satro's shoulders sagged a little, and his face became troubled. "Still, after all these years" he mused. "Ouch, not good. I had hoped that as we were so young when I left, and that because I had been gone for so long that she would have moved on. I still am fond of her – but ... I am a Warrior, now, father. Yes, a full Bronze Warrior. I will not have a settled life for a long time to come. I don't think she would be happy coming with me, nor I to stay here ... though I know that would please your heart, father."

Natho shrugged. "A Warrior, indeed. I am proud of you. I had heard rumors. A wise father wants nothing more than to see his sons grown, and on their proper path. Your brother and sister are happy enough to live with the old ways, and both have provided me with a grand-child to charm my heart as I grow old. As long as you visit every now and then, tell me tall tales of faraway lands that I can be proud of and exaggerate to my friends, and bring me little souvenirs whose use I cannot fathom, I will not ask for more. I knew from an early age you would not be content with the life of a Hold tribesman. But Nadia would, I think, follow you to the ends of the earth if you let her. Though I agree, I don't think it would make her happy."

Satro nodded. "Yes, Petro would be better for her. In fact, Petro would be good for her – I remember him as a fine boy. Well, perhaps his love will be enough for him to challenge me if she shows an obvious interest in me."

Natho snorted. "That she will. And aye, he might – while he's a good man, he does not look much outside the tribe, and has a high opinion of it, and himself. But even so, he knows something of what it means to be a Defender, and would be uncertain of victory. And I, who know considerably more, that you are a Warrior, and know what *that* means, know that he could never win."

"No, father" Satro replied. "But," he added after a second or two, "I might lose."

Natho looked at his son appraisingly, made a little "hmmm" of acknowledgement and thought, and they turned together and rode over the rise.

Natho and Bronn both gasped as they reached the top. "Great God of Heaven" Bronn breathed. "The whole tribe is here. Has it really come to this, and so quickly?"

Natho nodded somberly. "Aye. We are at an impasse. In a few hours, we have our final talk. Neither side expects a resolution. And then, later today or tomorrow at the latest, we fight. And fight to win, or die as a tribe. But first, the elders of the tribe will talk, and right glad I am to have both of you to take to that meeting."

As they rode down to the camp, they saw that someone else had ridden out to greet them. She was a woman of perhaps twenty-three years – old to be unwed by tribe customs, but truly beautiful, dressed in a simple but soft dress of light brown. Everything about her was brown, her hair, shining tawny eyes and her skin, and she wore a necklace of fine amber, which sometimes washed up on the shores of the island. She looked to be in glowing health, and very happy. "Satro" she smiled. "Welcome home. I dreamed two days ago that you would return today … and that I would rediscover love."

Satro replied thanks for the welcome, and remarked that she was even more beautiful than the last time he had seen her, for that was tribe courtesy. But when he went to say more, Natho raised his hand, and interrupted. "Nadia, I am pleased for your vision, and hope you come to this, and more. But we have a great urgency, and must settle the matter at hand – I must immediately take Natho and Seer Bronn to the meeting of elders, otherwise …, well, two hours ago I would have said there was little hope for your vision, as I feared that we must fight, and I feared we must lose."

Nadia's face fell, but she did not follow them as they rode on. With all of the talents of magic there came a degree of wisdom, and she knew all too well that the seed of her vision might fall on barren ground, and there might be no men of her tribe uninjured the next day, and few women for they would mostly fight as well. As so often happens, the course of love must wait on the course of war.

There was not much to be said about the camp they rode through. There were tents. The river was not far away. There were fires, and cooking stations, and people breakfasting. But there was little memorable about the temporary accommodation, for it was a workaday setup, housing those who meant to either move back home the next day, or lie there forever. There was little there that did more than meet the immediate need.

They rode on to the simple cover that protected the meeting of elders from the sun, and the unlikely event of rain. The island, being almost tropical, had weather patterns that were so predictable they could almost be used as clocks: if it was raining, it must be the afternoon. While their arrival was expected, there was nonetheless a small stir as they arrived: they were a new factor in what had seemed a hopeless situation, and because of simple human nature, all there looked to them for a rebirth of hope.

Introductions were quick. Most there remembered Satro from four years previously, and many knew Bronn, having visited the Hold. All were glad to see a Seer, unexpected because they either usually stayed at Seer's Hold or, rarely, passed through on their way out into the world – but those would be new graduates; to see a senior Master away from the quicker central route was rare indeed.

One of the first questions was an expected one, bitter though the question was. "Why has this happened?

Why have the Seers not told us of this disaster, and planned for it?"

Bronn had been thinking of an answer for some time, as he knew it would be asked. "You must understand", he replied, "there are many reasons why we Seers might not See this happening. One is, the Angels has decided that we should not. Another is our powers are not enough. A third, simple chance – we do not See everything. Fourthly, though the situation appears critical, there may be a simple solution that eases it. And finally, and I fear this is the true reason, there is the Law of Opposing Power. The four Gifts are useful, subtle and strong. But when one Gifted group opposes another, the Gifts tend to cancel out. And I have heard that strangers have been talking with the other tribes – and with you, though you have stood faithfully. For an outsider to change a Hold tribe against tradition, their words must be powerful indeed, and I suspect Narn the sorcerer, or more probably his Avatars. We – certainly I – had no suspicion this conflict was building up. You say it has happened over a few days?"

One of the elders nodded. "Two weeks" he replied. "Strangers appeared in our midst. They spoke heresy. They spoke of rebellion against the Seers, that they should serve us, who protect them, rather than to exist in mutual co-operation. They spoke of advantages refused to our young people, of the way all could live if the wealth of the Seers was distributed more freely."

He grimaced in disgust. "I am no expert in the ways of the Gifts, but I know rubbish when I see it – or hear it. And many are like me. Though there was some trouble at first, it was sorted out fairly quickly, and we set about rounding up these strangers, with a view to expelling them from our hospitality, sending them in chains to the Seers, or perhaps some punishment more immediate and simpler – we had not decided. But they vanished away. As you say, Master Bronn, they must have been Avatars. And busy ones too, for they had visited the Nari and the Turi. There, sadly, their evil words fell on more fertile ground. And so the Nari face us on the field of battle, their numbers increased by perhaps one in eight of the Turi, or outnumbering us two to one. They came to us four days ago, offering us the choice – join them, or fight. Well, we will fight, if we must. But, we sent runners to the Seers. Has our message been received? Are you an advance party, with aid?"

Bronn shook his head, sadly. "You must not hope for great aid from Seer's Hold" he replied. "Firstly, your runners would only have got to the Hold shortly after we left, and the Masters would have to consider what to do. Certainly, they would do nothing without trying for a Vision. And then, what. Yes, there are about five hundred people at Seer's Hold, and ten times more in the surrounding areas. But that includes women, children, Seers, cooks, cleaners, farmers and the elderly. Most of them would never have held a weapon other than their fist, if that. Seer's Hold relies on the Tribes for defense rather than the other way around. Certainly, there are those who could fight. Perhaps a few hundred. But without a Vision to support it, the decision to strip the Hold and leave it defenseless would not be made. You can imagine. What if everyone rushed here to fight a pitched battle, and the Turi sent in hardened warriors from the south? Seer's Hold would then fall to a force of thirty such, and winning here would mean nothing."

"Secondly, even if the decision was made, and quickly, such a force couldn't get here. There aren't enough horses and ponies. It would take days to get food together, and I doubt there are enough weapons to arm them all. It would be a rag-tag force, with no training, arriving hungry and tired."

"No, your best hope would be that the two Warriors, the best of the Defenders and perhaps a few reasonably young Seers and workers might be released, and get here soon enough. But even then, though the Warriors could obviously run the whole way here and still fight, the others could not. And strong though Warriors are, two would not be enough to make the difference. Especially if Narn has sent Warriors of his own."

The elders stirred at that. It was not a pleasant thought.

"What shall we do, then?" another elder plaintively asked. "It's our duty to protect the Hold. If we don't fight, they will march on the Hold. If we retreat ahead of them, they will harry us, flank us and get there before us. If we run ahead, it will be chaos and they will win anyway. We have no choice but to fight here, on the ground of our choosing, or violate every one of our oaths. Any ideas you have will be welcome; I am not afraid of dying, but I'm not in love with the thought either."

Bronn paused for a few seconds, and slowly shook his head. "I'm more sorry than I can say, for we Seers do not like to let people down when advice is called for. But at this time, I have nothing to suggest. However, we do have a Warrior here, and this is a conflict. What do you say, Satro?"

Satro looked down briefly. And then he looked up again, and thoughtfully said, "Single combat. There are many precedents. Rather than lose many lives, if both parties agree, two champions may fight and settle the matter. I do not believe the Turi and Nari could be so corrupted that they would not hold to the agreement if that was set up, and you won."

The elders nodded, but one of them replied, "Yes, we thought of that. But we know the Nari have a champion, a great fighter and a mountain of a man, hard, skilled and immensely strong. It would be a violation of our oaths in all but name, a coward's way out. We're sure they would agree, as they have no more desire to die that we do, but who would we put forward? We have no-one who could stand against him for more than a minute, let alone have a chance of winning. I have seen him myself."

"Well," Satro replied, "there's always me."

The elder replied, "No, outsiders are not allowed of course, the champion has to be a member of the tribe by bir ... ah. You are, aren't you? But you left, and became a Defender. And then a Warrior. Hmm. Gorgo is a giant, fully seven feet tall and with arms like a strong man's legs, but you a Warrior ... I've never heard of anything like this. What if the Nari object and say you're disqualified?"

Satro spoke musingly. "A Defender is still a member of the Tribe. That much is clear, I think. And though I went off for Warrior's training, I am not Bonded to any city, man or army. I am a free agent. Since being released by abbot Vail to go my own way – I am travelling back to Nun's Hold at the moment – I am my own man. I travel with Seer Bronn as a courtesy to the abbot. And, if a man is not Bonded, employed, apprenticed or anything else, surely his attachment is to his Tribe of Birth? If they object, they would have to say what I am, if I am no longer a member of this tribe, and explain how I have lost my birthright. I think they will have difficulty ... as far as I know, such an issue

34

has never come up before, and therefore, surely the weight of tradition would apply."

Bronn nodded. "Yes!" he agreed. "I have no Vision of this, but I know men. They will be unsure of themselves, for what they do is far, far from tradition. They will be feeling guilty in their hearts. And the natural reaction will be to hold more firmly to other aspects of tradition. If they agree to single combat – and they may smell a rat – then they will be bound by the result, I am sure."

And so it was agreed. A herald, a witness and an envoy were sent. Bronn went as the envoy. The Turi were suspicious, and argued against it on the basis that they were sure of winning if they turned the challenge down. But The Nari responded that it was all very well for the Turi to say so; they had only one in eight of their Tribe on the field. But the Nari would take many long years to recover if the Sori fought. And the herald was careful to insinuate that the Sori knew they would lose either way, but single combat would only mean one man risked.

"It is better this way" the representative Nari elder said. "Elder Natho's son you say? I heard he had gone to be a Defender. A strong fighter, then. But you know our man. We're sure of winning in either case, and there will be less loss of life. A wise decision, and typical of Natho to risk his son. Hmm. I respect him, even if we disagree. I will tell Gorgo to spare him, if possible. So, we are agreed."

"And then, ah ... and then, who knows what the future will bring?"

"Well, I do of course" Bronn replied. "Is that a request for a Viewing? I can try for one if you wish."

The elder shook his head. "No, we have no need. We know what we want, and why."

The three returned, with the good news that at least all would survive. There was general unrest, because many knew of Gorgo and could not see how a win was possible – the elders did not say who the champion would be, planning to keep it a secret as long as possible. The general feeling was that the elders had sold the tribe out, opting for capitulation by putting forward a champion who was bound to lose, rather than extermination. Still, many were glad.

There was yet an evening and a night to pass, and Nadia, happy at that the next day would at least see people still alive, sought Natho out. But as she came into the small area with the tent that had been set up for Bronn and Satro, Petro strode in from the other direction, a tall, well favored man with short cropped blond hair, a keen eye, and at this time a face like thunder.

"Nadia" he snapped. "What are you doing here? People are beginning to talk. They know you and this outsider have a past. It reflects badly on both of us for you to seek him out. Please come away, and return with me."

At least he had the sense to say please, Bronn thought. But still, Nadia was not happy either. She raised her chin, and replied, "Petro, we are but courting. You have no right to say where I should go, or when. I have feelings for you, but I must be sure who I choose, and I have the right to be here, to visit my old friend."

Petro had a slight touch of arrogance about him, but it lessened slightly at these words. Bronn thought he looked the better for it. There was a little of desperation about his manner when he retorted, "Well,

I will fight for your favor and my honor. I don't fear this outsider, even if he is a Defender, what do you say, do you have the guts to face me?" He truculently thrust his chin and chest forward, looking if only he knew just slightly ridiculous. He was just a fraction too young to know how to strike the right pose, and looked more like he was a strutting cock than a fighting man.

Satro looked at him, and seemed to fold. He looked up at Petro briefly, and seemed taken aback. "Nay ..." he said after a pause, but speaking quickly. Then another pause, and "ah, nay, I have no stomach for such a fight ... Nadia, it is unfair of you to put me in this position. You did not tell me you had suitors, and I, I am just passing through ..."

Nadia also seemed taken aback, her mouth opened but no sound came out. Weakness was not well-regarded in the Tribes, there were many, many ritualized fights. Rarely permanently injurious, for there was no sense in weakening the Tribe, hence the need for the ritual.

Bronn noted with approval that Petro also had the sense not to crow or gloat. He nodded in an almost dignified way, and said "It is well, then. If you have no designs on Nadia you are welcome in my tent, as Natho's son, Nadia's friend, and truth to tell I remember you myself, though I was just a boy when you left."

And he and Nadia left together, and Bronn and Satro ate a silent supper and went to bed at nightfall.

Then next day dawned bright and clear, just enough breeze to make things pleasant. A truly lovely day, as though nature was putting on a show for the events to come.

Single combat was another ritualized tradition, so everyone on both sides knew exactly what to do. This was true over most of the world, and for good reason. Who could fight, and how, was well defined, because it was not good to lose a Gifted person if two of them came into conflict (there were few enough of them as it was), and unfair if a Gifted person opposed an Ungifted with no restrictions. And the Gifted were respected (and envied), and their ways and agreements tended to be copied in the dealings and interactions of the ordinary people.

After breaking their fast, both camps came together, arranged on two ends of the combat ring. Four marshals stood at each corner. The Sori, as challengers, issued the formal challenge, the tribe's senior elder speaking loudly and clearly: "The Nari have come to our lands, and propose the joining of the Tribes, to stand against our traditional relationship with the Seers, seeking to forsake our sworn duty. The Turi have come with them, and stand as allies. As the Sori cannot countenance this violation of our sacred trust as a Hold Tribe against all the teachings of our forebears, we must stand against it. However, to prevent the disruption of all tradition, the destruction of the Tribes and great bloodshed, we issue a challenge of single combat, in accordance with our ways."

The Nari elder stepped forward, and also declared according to the formula: "The Sori are our brothers, and therefore though we are in disagreement on this issue, we too wish to avoid bloodshed. We accept the challenge of single combat, the outcome to decide the Tribes' paths. Representing us will be Gorgo, son of Gortho, blacksmith by trade and undefeated champion of the Nari. The terms of the challenge shall be: to the death, or until it is clear that one party can no longer continue, or until one party surrenders."

And the Sori elder spoke again: "The champion for the Sori will be Satro, son of Natho, Defender of Seer's Hold and Unbonded Bronze Warrior."

For three seconds there was silence as the Nari elder stood openmouthed. A susurrus of sound came from the assembled Nari ranks, and a few sounds of discussion from the Sori ranks, too.

The Nari elder said, in a much lower voice that only the two elders and the four marshals could hear: "This cannot be. This is trickery. The Tribe will not stand for it. *I* will not stand for it. You *cannot* bring an outsider in to fight for you."

One of the marshals stepped forward. "I am Natho, and I know you, Eturio. And you know me. You know my honor. I say this man we put forward is my son. Not an outsider, not a recent adoption. Born to my wife on Tribe lands. Raised by my own hand for sixteen summers, till he went to Seer's Hold to train as a Defender, a great honor. You know that does not mean loss of tribe kinship. While there, the Seers saw great potential in him, and paid to have him train in the Warrior school. Another great honor of course, and never heard of in my lifetime, but it is not unknown. And then, he returned once he had passed through the Orange to the Bronze, and resumed his post of Defender. But he is now released, and Unbonded. His blood is my blood, his flesh is my flesh. Who calls him an outsider? I will challenge him myself!"

Eturio looked at Natho a long while. His mouth worked, as at a bitter taste. Finally, he replied: "I do not doubt your honor, Natho, for I know you. I for one would still call it trickery of a sort, for to ask any man to face a Warrior ... I must take this back to the Tribe."

Natho replied in his turn: "Perhaps. I might not have put him forward, as he has truly been absent from the Tribe for many years, but ... you ask a man of ours to face Gorgo. We put forward the best man we have, as did you."

Eturio turned, and left, with his marshals. The discussion took a little while, but it was only minutes before they returned.

"Gorgo will fight your man" he formally replied. "The council stood divided initially, three for, three against. But the Tribe has heard the challenge and its acceptance, and the argument is that we cannot in honor back out. Eventually, argument swayed the council and we voted five to one that Satro's kinright must be recognized."

It was not even mentioned that Satro would not be allowed to use his auric shield; that was implicit in a Gifted person fighting an Ungifted in such combat. Not that most there would know much about it, still they would recognize such a shield if they saw it.

Natho nodded. "Still one council member not satisfied. Might I guess that is the Turi delegate?"

"Indeed" replied Eturio. "It was certainly not me. I am uncomfortable with this whole affair, and I will violate no more customs than I have to. After the initial surprise, it is clear your son has the right. I must warn you, though, that the Turi delegate has urged Gorgo to fight to the death, and he is a mighty fighter, Warrior or no. Still, Gorgo will make his own mind up there, for though he is a giant he is not slow of wit, and is his own man."

The marshals reassembled, and the combatants made their way to the arena. The elders announced that the

40

challenge had been made and was accepted, and the Nari elders introduced their man, Gorgo, naming him and his father and mother, as was called for.

There were gasps from many of the assembled Sori. Gorgo was indeed over seven feet in height, and towered over everyone beside him. And his muscles bulged. He was, frankly terrifying to anyone who considered fighting.

Bronn, standing beside Satro, murmured concernedly to him: "God in Heaven, he is a true giant. I've never seen anything like it. He must weigh over four hundred pounds and scarcely an ounce of fat on him. And I've not Seen a result – Narn involved, for sure. Can you beat him?"

Satro shook his head dubiously. "I've never seen the like, either. He is two inches over the seven foot mark – and I can tell you by my sure knowledge, that is the greatest height a man can have, without there being complications – much taller and the heart is too weak to drive the body. Certainly, my fighting skills are the greater, and pound for pound I am stronger – but there are so very many pounds there, the result is in doubt if he gets a hold on me, or manages to land a solid blow. It depends on the weapons he chooses. If the sword, then yes, I can win, but probably only by killing him. Quarterstaff would be my ideal choice. But ..."

Satro had to stop as he was introduced. His kinship to the tribe was also described, as was his title of Defender. There were murmurings from both sides when his title of Warrior, Bronze Grade was also announced, and Gorgo gave him an appraising look, and appeared to take him seriously for the first time. Not a surly giant, he grinned and rubbed his massive hands, and said a few quiet words to his marshals.

As the challenged party, Gorgo had the right to choose the weapons, and it was announced that he had chosen bare handed combat. The marshals read the agreed rules: no striking while a man was down, no gouging, especially of the eyes, and no scratching. Genitals were well protected by fighter's boxes, but there were few other rules. Either party could call a rest break, and each was allowed to call three, though more could be taken if both men agreed.

The bell rang down: three rings, a pause of ten heartbeats, two, a pause again, and one to start. The two men circled one another, both warily watching to see how the other moved. Then, slowly, closer together – and the first pass was made. Satro moved in, looking deceptively slow, like a dancer. And suddenly, he struck, like a snake – one, two – blows that landed hard on Gorgo's raised arms that shielded him – with no visible effect. Gorgo was surprisingly quick, but not quick enough – he was slightly out of place, and that was enough for Satro. He darted in, and threw a lightening punch at Gorgo's face. Gorgo ducked, and moved away, and the blow did not land full on – but it still cracked against his temple, with a sound that echoed across the ring.

It would have been enough to end any other fight – perhaps with the death of Satro's opponent – but Gorgo shrugged it off, and came back with his own flurry of blows. Satro blocked them early and expertly, of course. But still, they were heavy blows, heavier than anything he had ever faced, and he had to give way and be careful to make each strike a glancing one – blocking one of those hammer falls directly could numb and bruise even his hardened muscles.

Satro saw an opportunity, and lashed out a leg. A solid, expert kick that would have felled a small tree – and Gorgo moved, and robbed it of a lot of force. But

42

still, it took him hard in the side, and he grunted at the impact – and struck back like lightening. Satro pulled the leg back as a part of the strike, but incredibly, Gorgo seemed almost unaffected, and moved forward to land a glancing but solid blow on Satro's thigh.

The leg collapsed, but as Gorgo moved forward to take advantage, Satro flipped back on his hands out of the way, and onto the uninjured leg, and away again. He stood, furiously massaging the leg as Satro advanced again, and called his first time-out.

The bell sounded, to announce a two minute break. Satro limped over to his side, and to Bronn, as fast as he could. He shook his head at offers to rub his leg down – he could do that better himself, and set about it. But he could talk as he did so. "Fast" he stated simply, "Fast, experienced, and unbelievably strong. Five minutes into the match, and already I'm injured. I landed a good one on his head, but it's like a rock. I'm not sure, even, if it's affected him."

All too soon the two minute rest was over, and Satro made his way back to the ring. It was clear he was favoring that leg.

Satro set about rhythmically punching, trying to beat Gorgo down. Some blows landed, most were blocked, and it was a dangerous strategy. Sooner or later, it was inevitable – Gorgo got his hand in exactly the right place, at exactly the right time, and clamped a hold of Satro's wrist.

Before the pressure of his grip could get too strong, Satro made the counter-move, to break the hold – but could not. For an ordinary fighter, that would have been the end of it – he would have surrendered then, or somewhat later as Gorgo crushed his arm. But

Satro didn't even think, for that was the benefit of rigorous training – he quickly braced with the other arm, pulled the gripping hand away from Gorgo's body, and flipped his body over in a cartwheeling motion. Gorgo had to let go – not even his strength could hold over two hundred pounds of spinning muscle with one arm.

And while halfway round, with Gorgo off balance, Satro lashed out with one leg, and once more landed a kick on Gorgo's head. Again, barely enough to stagger him, but this time enough – Satro landed, and danced forward. Too late, Gorgo saw that the injury to his leg was largely feigned, as Satro feinted twice, and then threw a perfect kick-punch.

No slight stagger this time. Satro's foot knocked him flying, as the blow landed with a solid crack. It was a miracle of human endurance that Gorgo did not go down. And Satro followed it up with another to the gut that knocked the wind out of him. Gorgo could not now call time-out. Satro feinted again, and Gorgo blocked, weakly – for him.

And the opening was there, and Satro delivered a straight-edged hand blow across Gorgo's throat, with a precisely measured force, and then stepped well back.

Gorgo's eyes bulged, as he tried to draw breath, but his throat had closed. Only the tiniest whisper of air made its way in. Having had the wind knocked out of him, this did not leave enough air in his lungs to serve his massive frame, and within a minute he was on his knees, clutching at his throat, and thirty seconds later, he was unconscious.

Satro rushed forward, and rolled him over. In a ringing voice, he shouted: "I say Gorgo is defeated. I beg of you, grant me the fight, and that quickly, so I can save his life." Without waiting for an answer, he knelt down, and began gently massaging Gorgo's throat. Swiftly and surely, he rolled the windpipe back and forth, flexing the skin and kneading the muscles, and then began to compress the massive chest. Before a minute had passed, and before the Nari representatives had recovered from their shock at the loss of the fight, it could be heard that Gorgo was starting to get air into his lungs again.

The Nari slowed in their approach, as even they could see Satro was working to save Gorgo, and that his efforts were effective. Before long, Gorgo was breathing on his own, and Satro left him, to go over to the marshals and judges. "Well", he said sharply but not unpleasantly. "Do you agree I have won? Or do you insist I go over and slay that great man?"

The judges hesitated but a moment. It was clear that Satro could return and put an end to Gorgo, although he was showing some signs of returning to consciousness. "The fight is won" one of them muttered, and shortly after, the others all nodded and agreed. Eturio turned, and spoke to the waiting crowd in a ringing voice: "the fight is won, and the cause of the Sori is upheld. We will leave, and resume our ancient ways – for now."

And so it was, of course. The fight of the day was for the problem of the day. The Nari and the Turi could, and probably would, continue to press their case, and could, after a decent interval, seek to raise the tribes up again. So, the next day, Bronn, Satro and Elordo, the senior Elder of the Sori went to discuss matters – with Gorgo first.

They found Gorgo seated at his ease by a tent. He showed little sign of the battle of the previous day, unlike Satro who sported a fine collection of bruises.

45

He rose courteously, laying down a large thin board on which there appeared to be a sheet of parchment. Satro went to shake his hand. "You fought well" he said simply. Gorgo grinned, apparently without any rancor, and replied "You fought better. Never have I been served such a thump. It's enough to make me consider going for Warrior training myself."

"Are you serious?" Satro asked. "I shudder to think of it. If accepted and qualified, you'd be the premier fighter of the world. If ... if you are truly serious, I will sponsor you."

"Nay, but I thank you" Gorgo replied. "I was only joking. Truth to tell, I do not actually like fighting all that much. I'm just good at it."

"What *do* you like to do, Gorgo?" Bronn asked curiously. "I know that you are a blacksmith by trade."

"Aye, that I am – a man must do something, and I was so trained and apprenticed. It is a trade, and it brings in my living, and I am well suited to it, I do my work as well as any, and better than most. But as to what I *like* to do, well, there's not much call for it to be sure. It's but my fancy, my time waster. But ... well, since you ask, and are a Seer, I like to draw. As you came, I was drawing a flower of the fields ... I had never seen the like." And he turned over the board, and showed them.

It was the flower of the vine they called Climbing Jana locally. A large bloom, nearly as big as a hand, with petals of alternating size, and long stamens with a visible hook. Gorgo had drawn it accurately and with feeling, showing both the flower and the supporting vine.

Bronn took the board, and examined it closely. "This is fine work, Gorgo – as good as any I've seen from an amateur. Have you ever thought of doing it for a living, if you love it?" he asked.

Gorgo laughed. "Oh, I've heard there are those who do such things in the cities. But for one such as I, as simple tribesman? Where would I go? How would I get started? I know nothing about such things."

"Well," Bronn replied, "surely you know about the funds the Seers keep, as scholarships for anyone of true talent. You would apply at Seer's Hold, and if accepted – and there is no surety there of course - we would put you in touch with the appropriate schools, see to your training and find the right Master for you to train with. And, assuming you continued to show promise, why the fund would set you up, of course."

Gorgo looked somewhat perplexed. "But I thought that the Seers would only pay for tribesmen to become Defenders, Seers or sometimes Fire Witches? That's the common knowledge that the elders tell us ..."

"You're not serious" Bronn said. "How can you think that? No, the Seers have a Bond, a Trust with the Tribes, of course. We value and support anyone of true talent. Yes, of course, Seers are our primary concern, Defenders the next, and we value the Gifts highly. But what of Satro, here? We paid for him to become a Warrior. And only five years ago, Artro of the Sori became the finest silversmith in all of Camazar. Why, I'm no keeper of the records, but over the last fifty years I know of at least three Sori who have ... who have ... the Sori ... oh, dear God in Heaven, can it be? I know only of Sori ...."

Gorgo, Satro and Bronn looked stunned. Finally, after a pause of some seconds, Satro said, "This sounds like something that needs to be sorted out, and right quickly. Gorgo, can you get us a meeting with the elders of the Nari, and any of the Turi who might be about?"

Gorgo looked a little thoughtful, and shook his head a little. "Yesterday, I would have said yes, with no problems. Today, after losing that fight, I'm not as welcome in the high tents as I was, and they might refuse. Still, if you come with me, Satro, and you too, Bronn, they might well think twice about refusing all of us."

And so the party went to seek the elders of the Nari. Not all of them could easily be found by any means, but they found Eturio, one other, and an elder of the Turi, who were arranging the decampment. They were not particularly pleased to be interrupted, but somewhat grumpily agreed to a short meeting.

"I will make it as short as I can, then" Bronn began. "However, if after I've spoken, you want to hear more, I am at your disposal. The crux of the matter is this: The Seers will sponsor and provide funds for any young man or woman of the Tribes who has true talent, in any field of endeavor – not just Seeing, Fighting, and Magic – and will see to their needs in training."

Eturio was greatly surprised, but an experienced leader, and quickly retorted: "So, do the Seers seek to buy us now? After all this time, when finally we realize our true worth, rise up and become a threat, you finally loosen the hold around our throats? Well, if you are in earnest, I will take it to the tribes, and we will speak again. Perhaps something can be done ... but I warn you, many will feel it is too little, too late."

"No, no, *no!*" ejaculated Bronn, in exasperation. "This is not something new! It has *always* been thus. Over hundreds of years, the Seers have sponsored scholarships for those born in Seer's Hold, and those born to the Tribes, with no distinction or prejudice. If you come to Seer's Hold – or rather, I say, go, for I am outward bound – you can consult our records, and we can tell you the names and lineage of everyone so helped."

"Yes, but only to become a Seer, a fighter, or very rarely a Fire Witch" Eturio stubbornly replied.

"Noooooo! Bronn almost yelled, a rarity in a Seer. No! *No*! We recognize, and have *always* recognized *any* real talent. The Tribes and Seer's Hold are family! Not immediate family, but you are our cousins, often in reality as well as by trust. Of course we support our own! The Sori know this. As I said to Gorgo, I myself know of three Sori who have been sponsored over the last fifty years, a silversmith in Carm, a writer and a historian who lives at Nun's Hold. As well as numerous Defenders, at least a dozen Seers and a pair of Fire Witches. The Nari and The Turi should *know* this, it has always been so, for as long as the Tribes and the Seers have been associated, from before the time of the sorceress, Sha'Lin'Tra the Great!. How can this not be known? The elders of the Tribes meet with the Seers twice a year!"

Eturio was greatly taken aback at Bronn's obvious frustration and sincerity, but replied "but I remember well, fifteen summers ago, when one of our Tribe wanted to be a professional dancer. The Seers rejected her out of hand, and two of the elders of that time, said it was always so. I didn't even bother asking, when my grandson proved a prodigy with numbers, nor did elder Franko when his granddaughter showed such promise, learning three languages from travelers seeking the Seers."

"Well, of course, we're not going to sponsor every gumbah who shows some small talent in some field or other" responded Bronn. "Although much gold comes the Seers' way, we spend a lot on one thing or another, and help many people. Just *wanting* to do something isn't enough, there must be a true talent there, enough to make a living in a valued field. And sometimes, the answer may be no, even then, because we *are* Seers after all. Sometimes, we can See that the person wouldn't be successful, or happy, or might die pursuing a dream. But that's no reason not to *ask*. Sometimes, as the Sori well know, the answer is yes. Gorgo is a case in point – his drawing is fantastic, and we'd give him a scholarship, quick as a bowshot. And your mathematician and linguist too, if they really do have talent. And assuming we don't See any Visions against it. But even so, I don't *understand*. The rights and duties of the Seers and the Tribes are surely well known. How has this been lost? What *else* is lost?"

"I ... I don't know" replied Eturio. "When I first became an elder, we had lost four of the Tribe's elders in a sickness. The remaining two were ... well, elderly. But it never crossed my mind that they had not passed on everything we needed to know."

"A generation lost" mourned Bronn. "Well, nothing to do but pick up the pieces, fix things where we can, and move on. You must, must, *must* go to Seer's Hold, and sit down for a long talk and re-establish the Bonds between Tribe and Seers. And even if this ... this incredible thing has come to pass, what about the Turi? It beggars belief that they have lost this knowledge too."

The Turi elder mused a while. "I'm not sure" he replied finally. "We have had our share of Defenders, of course, and a Seer or two. But that's all I can remember. Certainly no Witch, in my memory. Nor ...

nor for that matter do I ever recall any special talent coming up, in my lifetime. Well, we have a Healer with some talent, and I remember a cousin who was an extraordinary shot with the bow, but they were happy in the Tribe, and their skills were much needed and valued. Our Tribe is the smallest, and our side of the island sparse and hard ... we're herders, and life isn't easy. There is little time for ... hobbies. We value storytellers, of course, and send those with such skills to Seer's Hold and the other Tribes, Carm, and to the Nuns of Knowledge to gather more tales to tell around the campfires. I have been to Seer's Hold myself, twice a year, for twenty years, and I think that the matter has simply never come up. I did not know of this Bond, and will go, too, to the Seers and find out what else we don't know, but should. Maybe ... maybe Narn's Avatar would not have found such ready ears, if we knew what we should know."

"I knew it! Narn is on Seer's Island, for sure, you say – do you know if he himself is in Carm?" Bronn sharply questioned.

"No, I don't think so" the Turi elder replied. He has talked with us for many months, and recently with the Nari. That's how all this got started. But I think only one of his Avatars is on Seer's island. He himself is still on Fire Island, campaigning against the Witches there. He said, when we asked for more direct help, that he could operate in Carm, but only barely here."

Bronn looked at the Turi elder open-mouthed. "Are you seriously telling us", he asked in disbelief, "that Narn is holding an Avatar projection across nearly three thousand miles, with the Eastern Sea in the middle of that? Our abbot, a great man, can project an Avatar, but only a hundred yards or so! I thought it was impossible to project across open water like that?"

51

The Turi elder shrugged. "I know little about such things" he replied. "We've had a few in our Tribe who could project a ghost Avatar – useful, that is for scouting – and one or two who could project a Material one when young, though they lost the knack for it as they grew up. But Narn is a sorcerer – master of a Gift at level three, and able in at least one more. Who knows what such a one can do? Why, they said Sha'Lin'Tra, who you spoke of a minute ago, could project six of them, while dancing the Warrior's sword dance."

"Yes, yes, and they said she ruled the whole world, knew all four Gifts and could fly. They also said she was immortal, but, strangely, we don't see her floating about the sky these days nor ruling the world – that was eight hundred years ago, and people tell tales that grow in the telling. But we're not talking about legend now. We're talking about a living man, and you *can't* project across the open sea. And how could he hold it together when he goes to sleep?"

Satro stirred. "Bronn, little point arguing it. Either he can, or he can't and his Physical is somewhere near. But what's certain is, his Avatar is on Seer's Hold. What can we do about that?"

Bronn shrugged, in his turn. "Little enough, unless we can find it. Then, it might be overcome, unless he dissolves it. But I think we've given his cause a good hard knock, today. If the elders go to Seer's Hold and our Bond is reinforced, I doubt his words will be able to stir up much trouble. Otherwise, despite his opposition, we would have Seen *something.*"

The three elders swore to pass on the word to the others, and Bronn, Satro and Elordo made their farewells, and walked slowly back to the Sori camp.

As they walked over a small rise and down into the lower ground before the next rise that led to the Sori camp, they found a man waiting for them. He was tall and spare, though he could not be called thin. He kept his dark red hair long, and after the mode of the male Fire Witches, bound at the back in a silver fillet. His skin was somewhat darker than most, but strangely his eyes were a very pale blue, almost faded. And he did not look happy.

"With care here," Satro said, "that is an Avatar." "Indeed" commented Bronn, "I feel the pressure. I'll wager this is Narn's Avatar."

The dark man smiled, or rather quirked his lips into something that might be called the beginning of a smile. "Well spotted. And to show you I am observant as well, I see a Master Seer, a young Warrior and an elder of the Sori. Very different folk, yet united in several things – you have all thwarted me, annoyed me, undone months – nay, over a year of preparation, and as a result are all now going to die. With you out of the way, perhaps all is not yet lost. The Warrior first, I think."

And without more ado, he swung into action. His aura flamed red about his head, cascading down his back, and a red and orange nimbus flared up around his right forearm. He raised it, cast it back, and then forward to throw a firebolt at Satro. He was forced to block, which he did, and the bolt shattered on his auric shield. But it hammered him, forcing him back.

"A good block, Warrior, but not enough. I can wear you down before I expend my energies here. If I wasn't working at a great distance and limited to barely level one, you would even now be a corpse on the grass. So, to it." He gathered his offensive aura again, and prepared to strike. Almost as an afterthought, he shot a much smaller lightning bolt with his left arm at Elordo, who had drawn a knife and was rushing to the attack. Unlike a Warrior, Elordo had no ability to create an auric shield, and this minor force was enough to knock him to the ground, out of the fight.

Narn turned to Bronn, and sneered, "So, Seer, do you want to try your luck too?"

Bronn shook his head, and lent on his staff. "No, I have no skills in such matters. I can barely project a shield. It would be foolish to try. I will wait my turn, for I do not believe you will win out against my Warrior friend."

Narn laughed, though, he used his left arm, the shield arm, to raise a shimmering sphere of force to block the knives Satro had thrown hoping for a quick win while Narn was distracted talking to Bronn.

"Again, nice try Warrior – a pity I don't have the time or the local energy to convert you to my cause. Ah, well." And again he threw a bolt, which Satro was forced to block. "I'd say you have about four more such shields in you, Warrior. Time to say your pray -"

And that was all he got out, for Bronn, while Narn's back was turned, had armed his staff, and pressed the fire button.

A firebolt, quite a lot brighter and more powerful than the ones Narn had cast against Satro shot out of Bronn's staff and caught Narn squarely in the unprotected back. The Avatar screamed, and shattered like glass, and the pieces melted like fog.

Satro rose up from his crouch, and looked at where Narn had been, and then at Bronn. "Well, that was impressive" he remarked. "And helpful, too. I fear Narn was right, I wouldn't have lasted much longer. I was never very good at shielding. I ... never picked that for a firestaff. And a mighty powerful one, too. That will have hurt Narn. Not as much as if you destroyed his Avatar at close range, of course, but he won't be raising that one here again for a while."

Bronn nodded. "And we'd better be on our way, and not go on the main road. I would say he couldn't raise another and have it here in any short amount of time, but I'd rather not risk it – I took no chances, and fired all the energy in my staff, and have no way of recharging it at the moment."

Satro nodded. "Not through the mountains, then" he said. "The Northern Fens?"

"No" Bronn replied. "The marshes, I think."

"Oh, Hell's Bells, not the marshes ... that's Turi territory. And hot, we get a sea breeze in the Fens. And mosquitos ... sodden boots ... leeches ... at least there are real paths through the Fens!"

"Well, yes" Bronn agreed. "But the Turi will be a bit disorganized, with many of them over here at the moment, and they are herders. They'll not go into the marshes much. And with so many canals, and so much water, Narn will be hard put to find us again, even if he can project another Avatar to the island. And the mosquitos ... well, we're both Gifted, and it doesn't take much of a shield to keep them at bay."

"Not much" Satro glumly agreed, "but it has to be up all the time."

"Don't worry" Bronn laughed. "A week or two, and you'll be tough as nails, with a shield twice as strong from practice."

But before they left, Satro had another duty to attend to, a painful and difficult one. Nadia came to him, after the evening meal and after the many who wanted to had congratulated him on the fight, and renewed their bonds with him as a Tribe member. Petro trailed after her, no longer sulky of arrogant, more desperate than anything else. It was clear that he would have liked to forbid her to come, but there was no way that could be done. The Tribes were a bit more male dominated than the Seers, but not by much.

She, too, was full of relief and effusive thanks, and seemed still more attracted to Satro, yet also a bit in awe. She said, however, "Now I understand why you refused the fight with Petro! You could not reveal you are a Warrior, and had to cry craven, because if you fought, then it would not be a fair fight!"

Satro shook his head sadly, and replied, "Yes, Nadia, there is some truth in that. I could not reveal my true skills, and not to do so would be unfair."

Petro interrupted, with something between a sob and a shout – "I do not care!!! I will fight you anyway! I will not let you take Nadia, and live!"

Satro bowed to Petro. "Your courage does you credit. But … I was truthful also. I have no stomach for such a fight. If you challenge me, I will yield."

Nadia was crushed. "But why?" she cried. "Am I not fair? Am I not desirable? Do you not love me? What, what is my fault?"

Satro looked at her for a long moment, and then he replied. "Nadia, you are fair indeed, and desirable. And yes, I love you. But as a friend, as I would a sister. And even if it were otherwise, I must leave this place. We travel across the marshes, to Carm, then to Nun's

Hold, Warrior's Hold and then who knows where? I do not know when – or even if – I will return."

"I don't care! I will come with you!"

"You cannot. First and most simply, Seer Bronn has Seen only the two of us going on, and our quest is hard, and by no means sure of success. We must follow his Vision. Second, our way is no place for a woman such as you. There can be no romance between people travelling in such circumstances, and we cannot afford delay to care for your needs, tough tribeswoman though you are. And thirdly, as I have said, I am perhaps crazy to reject you, but it is not what I want."

Nadia wept. "It is not fair, not fair that you should treat me thus and scorn me so!"

Satro replied. "Nadia, you asked what is your fault ... well, it's not for me to say, really. But I will, harsh though it may seem. If you have a fault, it would be this: that you yearn after a man who does not want the same things as you do, yet reject a fine man, a brave man, a man who would fight for you knowing he cannot win because he loves you more than his life. You say it's not fair for me to scorn you – but I have never promised you anything. I have never sought anything. When we parted years ago, as far as you knew, you would never see me again. On the other hand, you have been courted by Petro for many months, over a year as I understand it. You have not rejected him, no not until I returned. And now, *you* scorn *him*, in the way that you say is so unfair."

Nadia stood, with her head bowed, and tears dripping. But after a long moment of silence, she slowly turned her head to Petro, raised her eyes, and looked at him strangely. "Is it true, Petro? Do you indeed love me? More than your life?"

Petro threw his arms wide, and said, loudly and intensely, "Yes! Of course! Have I not said so, these many months?"

Nadia replied, "No, Petro. Not once. You have told me about your skills, and shown them to me. You have told me how pretty I am. You have followed me about, you have eaten with me, you have danced with me. But you have never told me you love me."

"Well, I do. Of course I do. I love you, truly, fully, wholly. You are my night and day. I delight in being with you, and I hold the memory of you in my heart when we part. My life will never, never be a whole and happy one without you."

Nadia turned, and said, "Satro ...." But he had already gone, melting into the night like a shadow. So, she turned back to Petro, looked at him speculatively, took his arm, and they went their way, too.

Bronn, hiding behind a large tree, heard Nadia's voice saying, "You know, Petro, a woman likes to know these things. Why haven't you used these words before? And why don't you tell me more, now?" and smiled to himself. And jumped, when a shadow next to him said, "Ooof. That was hard".

Bronn, his heart pounding from Satro's sudden appearance beside him in the dark, said "Don't *do* that! Make some noise when you sneak up!"

"Sorry Bronn, force of habit – I'll try my best. I would just about rather face Gorgo than go through that again. Still, it seems finally to have gone right. Petro will be good for her. Thank God he had the sense to tell her he loves her. Will they be all right"?

Bronn nodded, probably a pointless exercise in the dark behind the tree. "Yes, of course. I Saw it. I Saw that she would find love this day, as she did. But neither of us Saw with whom. And, we can't have predictions like that going wrong, can we? So, I had a good long talk to Petro about women, what they like to hear, and how you should treat them if you love them, and want them to love you. He seemed to catch on fairly fast, and based on his performance tonight, I'd say he will do fine."

Satro gave his little bark of laughter. "A prediction going wrong? No, we couldn't have that, of course you had to say something and I'm glad you did. Ah, Gifted and skilled. Bronn, you are truly a Master Seer." And together they walked back to the camp, carefully avoiding the path Petro and Nadia had followed.

Chapter 3. Marshes and Carm

We need the tonic of wildness, to wade sometimes in marshes where the bittern and the meadow-hen lurk, and hear the booming of the snipe; to smell the whispering sedge where only some wilder and more solitary fowl builds her nest, and the mink crawls with its belly close to the ground.

Henry David Thoreau

For a day or two they journeyed at night. The moon was bright, and lit up the Turi plains when they came to them well enough to see by, for they were flat grasslands with only the occasional hill. By the third day, however, when they had not seen another soul for a day and a half, they thought it safe enough to travel by day and sleep at night.

There was little enough game to eke out their limited provisions. They saw a few moor hens, tough and stringy, which would have been improved by stewing. Satro's arrows brought them down unerringly, but they had to eat them roasted which made them tough, rather than stewed, because they had left a lot behind including most of their pots. They had gone on with only one hinny and mule, which would be hard enough to deal with in the marshes. There were wild herbs and edible plants enough to keep them in good health, and every so often a stream running down from the mountains off to their right – the Dragon's Back range. One evening, all they had managed to catch during the day was a large lizard, which Bronn thought and Satro said made the most cheerless meal he had ever eaten.

Going through the mountains would have been much more pleasant – there was a halfway reasonable road, or a very good path depending on how you looked at it. The air was cooler, and better for travelling. At the wrong time of the year there were biting flies, but rarely mosquitos. And travelers were so regular that various merchants from Carm went up and down the trail, selling anything a traveler might need. And the view would be magnificent. All this, Satro said, and often. But Bronn didn't mind that so much, it made a welcome break from the questions he couldn't answer. Where did the quest lead? Who else would be in it? What was Satro's role and how could he fill it if he was at Nun's Hold studying this and that? Why did they have to travel so far, why were the Holds built on the extreme edge of their respective islands? That at least Bronn could answer: because the Gifts were polarized by their position on the north-south Ley line. Witches to north and south, Warriors and Seers to the west and east. And the further along those directions, the greater the effect of being born there. But the fact that Bronn could only answer about one question in ten didn't stop Satro from asking.

As the streams got bigger and more frequent, Satro got gloomier and gloomier. Hardy as Warriors were, he took to muttering to himself as the ground got softer and mosquitos more frequent. From Seer's Hold to Carm was less than five hundred miles, but as Satro said, the last few hundred were not going to be much fun. In fact, he remarked he didn't see how they were going to get through at all.

"Not to worry" Bronn grinned. "I'm sure something will turn up." And something did. About the start of the second week, when the occasional pools of water had started to join up into a true marsh, Bronn took a right hand turn, heading to a prominent outcrop of rocks and boulders that seemed to come down a bit further from the distant mountains than usual. Satro could see he had something up his sleeve, and hoped it was a secret way up into the mountains, and that they would travel the last hundred and fifty or so miles to Carm on a decent path.

But what Bronn had in mind was to walk in through a maze of boulders. And there, well hidden where in all probability no-one came more than once a century, hidden under covers, was a well-built canoe and paddles, and some other useful articles such as dry-as-a-bone firewood, fishing lines, wet weather gear, a variety of boots and other items. There was even, buried underground, a little wine, some oil, some wheat in sealed jars, salt and sugar so it was possible to make bread.

Satro was astounded. "How did you know this was here?" has asked.

Bronn replied, "Because we, and I mean we, the Seers, have arranged for it to be here, of course. We have a handful of caches about the country, just in case. A friend told me about this one, just before we left."

"But why? Why are they here? And why did someone tell you about it?"

Bronn looked at him puzzeledly. "You *do* know we're Seers, right? And you know what Seers do? He Saw that I would probably need it, of course. And years before that, we Saw that we would need the caches sometime. Every year, we send parties out to refresh the stores and replace anything that is too old."

Satro nodded, as the light dawned. "I see, of course! But it's a pretty specific prediction that we would need a canoe! Not that I'm complaining, mind."

Bronn nodded, and smiled. "It's easy to get confused between Seeing and plain old common sense. It's not out of the question, of course, that someone would See we need a canoe. Seers have had far more specific Visions than that. But in this case, someone Saw a cache of supplies would be needed here. Given that, it means people would *be* here, and the only reason why they would be *here* would be if they were trying to get to Carm through the marshes. I mean, there's nothing else in this wilderness to attract anyone, and no-where else to go! So, a canoe would most likely be useful."

"Of course, we're not going to be able to put Peto and Peta on the canoe" he added, indicating their faithful mules, "so we'll unload them, and bid them a fond farewell."

Satro pursed his lips. "Will they be alright?"

Bronn nodded again. "Of course! There's no shortage of grass, plenty of water, and they are fine, clever beasts. Most likely, left to their own devices, they would make it all the way back to Seer's Hold unassisted. But probably, they will be discovered by the Turi, who will see our mark on the saddles, and take them home. Or if not, well – we look after our own. Sooner or later, someone will See where they are, and we'll send for them."

The going was easier after that. One person could paddle the canoe and avoid sandbanks, watch out for floating obstacles and look for the proper way through – largely a matter of watching which way the water was flowing. The other could concentrate on maintaining a shield – practically essential, as they were on the water. The mosquitos were so numerous, they would have swelled up like balloons from the bites without one. And one of them could do it, if they were just sitting there. Of course, a Witch could have paddled *and* maintained a shield, but that was beyond either of them for any significant amount of time. With practice, however, Satro soon improved to the point where he as shield caster could also keep a watch out for anything edible that could be shot with a bow and arrow.

Thanks to the Vision of the Seers, or again common sense, they had a simple wet-weather cover for the canoe, and also a mosquito net so they could both sleep at night, a good thing because maintaining a shield while asleep was well beyond either of them. Often, a loose, irritating mosquito or three would get in while they were putting the net up, but Satro could hear the annoying insect and pluck it out of the air with two fingers. The Gifts have their uses in the humdrum of everyday life, of course.

Travelling through the countryside is always interesting. You never know what you will see over the next hill, and there are streams, birds, assorted wildlife, and different kinds of rock and so on. But travelling on a slow winding river through marshlands is not. The marsh birds are much the same from one end to the other, and the marsh grasses do not vary. Water is water everywhere. There are different kinds of fish, but the differences are really only interesting to an enthusiast; the average traveler does not need much more knowledge than which ones are the good ones to eat. The most interesting thing that happened to Bronn and Satro in an average day was to find a bit of ground solid enough to get out onto, make a fire and cook their fish or bird. Drinking water came from the rain, gathered on the canoe cover. Perhaps one day in three they were able to find a bit of land large enough and dry enough to sleep on, which was luxury. The rest of the time they slept in the canoe, which was only just possible.

Slowly, the stream got faster and wider, and finally turned into a true river, broad and flowing and they made real progress. They could get out on the banks at some point in the day, and the fish were better too, bigger and less muddy in taste. The river wound its way down to Carm, splitting into the three branches that divided the city into four parts, linked by many bridges. A day or two before they got there they started to pick up other river traffic, and were glad to lose themselves in the anonymity of the crowd. A dealer in boats took the canoe off their hands for a reasonable sum, and agreed to send word to Seers Hold to ask if they wanted it back and if so to ferry it around the coast the next time a ship came. He was only a local dealer, however, and could do nothing for them in terms of booking passage to Nun's Hold other than to direct them to the right area of the city, and give them a name.

Carm was a big city for the two men. Nothing compared to those on Fire Island, of course, but still, big enough – many thousands of people, though most of them spread out into the surrounding countryside. They ran the businesses of handling and shipping livestock from the three Tribes and their own herds around the city, salting and pickling meat for shipment, dried fish, preserved tropical fruit, and some fresh produce that could take the ten to thirty days trip to the various islands. Many of the people ran supporting industries of course, everything from ship repair to taverns.

Carm was a gem of a city compared to the much larger ones on Fire Island. Small enough, and rich enough thanks to the Seers and Carm itself, it had good sanitation, and true sewers leading out, away from the city, and to a discreet outfall several miles away. A fortuitous current carried the waste away to the south, out into the deep sea. Only very rarely did any wash back the other way due to a major storm. And crime was also rare, mostly due to the somewhat higher than usual number of lesser Seers who had decided to set up shop there rather than leave the island entirely.

As a result, Seers were well known, respected and well regarded, though perhaps not revered with the anxious respect given by those who did not understand the Gift properly. It was more the respect one craftsman gives another. And so, it was a bit of a shock when the shipping agent kept them waiting, seemed indifferent to their needs and offered them passage at an over-the-top rate with a take-it-or-leave-it attitude. Of course, Bronn was not short of coin, and was well able to pay the fare, but even then the agent seemed less than pleased about the whole thing. Bronn would have simply shrugged and gone on his way, but Satro was less inclined to put up with it.

"A moment, if you don't mind, agent. We've come a long and weary way, and have paid a high price in good coin. And yet, you seem less than courteous. What have we done to you? Surely, you cannot fail to see that my companion here is a Master Seer?"

The agent glowered at Satro, who he had not really paid much attention to until now. Then, he noted the Warrior's insignia on his belt, and modified his attitude somewhat. One didn't go around picking fights with Warriors. But still, there was not much friendliness in his voice.

"Well, that's part of the problem, you see. You're expecting automatic subservience just because he's a Seer. For too long, the Seers have been skimming off the cream of our profits and giving little in return. Well, times may be changing soon, and I've no longer the mind to truckle."

"What?" Satro exclaimed incredulously. "Have you gone mad? The Seers *bring* the custom to this island.

66

They are the only reason there *is* any trade, and any profit for you! And giving little in return? You live and work in safety because of them! Try living on Fireland! You'd be paying someone like me a fortune in silver every month just for peace of mind. Their skills are recognized the whole world ov … oh, wait a minute. I see. We've seen this before, not so long ago. Narn's Avatars have been here too, haven't they? And you've been listening to them!"

"Well, what if he has? And what if we have? He speaks nothing but plain, common sense! With his help, alright, yes, with his help, we plan to make some long overdue changes in Carm!"

Satro snorted in disgust. "And tell me, friend, what does Narn get out of these changes?"

The merchant looked at him in puzzlement, very much as the Turi had looked at the two of them. "What does Narn get? Why, he gets nothing! He helps us simply because … he …" – his voice trailed off.

Satro snorted again, with his bark of a laugh. "Friend merchant, you are too good for this world. Blinded by the open-handed generosity and altruism that is no doubt so much a part of your nature and everyday business dealings, you forget the rest of the world is not like you."

The merchant looked at them, and tried to interject. "But," he began, but Satro interrupted and continued: "Most folk do not strive and moil with no thought of recompense other than the pleasure of helping others, they seek gain and advantage as a result of their labors. Particularly something as hard as driving an Avatar halfway across the Eastern Sea."

The agent just looked at them for thirty seconds, obviously thinking hard. Then, a sort of horror came over his face as the implications sank in.

"What ... what you say is clear, now, Warrior ... but I can't imagine how I haven't seen it before. Of course, it's obvious ... Narn is here, stirring up trouble, dividing us against the Seers ... I don't know when my thinking changed, or why. It's like a cloud drawing away from my mind. I know, and have known all my life that the Seers are the primary drivers of business on the island."

Bronn added his own thoughts at that point. "Don't feel too bad about it, friend. Narn is a very powerfully Gifted man. He can turn the minds of others. The more talented a person is, the harder it will be for him, but he is also subtle. Still, once the truth is pointed out, a strong mind will swing the other way again. And you may be no Seer, or Warrior or Witch, but you are a talented merchant, and that counts for something."

The merchant smiled somewhat. "Well, I thank you Seer Bronn" (he knew their names since he had booked them on the ship), "I think the thing that jarred me the most was your friend's talk of generosity, something I've rarely been accused of. But now my mind is cleared ... I have some seniority in the movement that is getting under way in Carm. I'm not one of the leaders, but I have their ear, and I will be putting your arguments about, both on the streets and at the next meeting. I think you will find a change in the will of the people this time next month. At least, I think most have the wit to see that if there were to be changes – and now, to be sure, I'm not so certain about that – then it will be for our own reasons, and our own advantage, not someone else's."

He paused, obviously fighting something inside himself. "I ... I suppose I should refund you something on your tickets ... the price is too high, higher than what I would normally charge a Seer. I ... perhaps, two gold pieces ... ?"

Bronn shook his head, and laughed. "I can see you're upset, friend – I have accepted the price, high though it is, and have no desire to take advantage of your confusion." The agent enthusiastically withdrew his half-hearted hand, and Bronn went on. "But, I will ask that you earn the difference. And I ask nothing more than that you *do* go to those meetings, and speak you mind. What you now have in your thoughts is nothing more than the simple truth, and if you speak it ... well, the Seers value the truth, and we will be well repaid."

The agent bowed, and said in a voice from which all doubt had gone, "Thank you Seer Bronn. It will go as you say."

And so it did. Satro and Bronn had only a week to wait, for ships were fairly regular across to Nun's Hold, and elsewhere for that matter, though Satro had been forced to wait six weeks when he went to Warrior's Hold for his apprenticeship. They kept a low profile, but wandered the city freely. Indeed, they wandered a good deal more freely than Bronn would have dared on his own, because like any city there were places that were less safe than others. But with Satro at his side, he had no concerns. They only had trouble twice, in well separated parts of the city, and the Warrior barely had to exert himself – he was able to let the small gangs off with very little damage, no more than a few bumps, bruises and a cracked rib or two, and nothing permanent. But still, word got around. They had no more trouble, other than one or two people who, having had a drink or two more than was good for them in a tavern, took leave of their senses and thought a fight with a Warrior might be a good idea.

The agent's word got around, too. By the third day, it was not uncommon to find a public speaker fervently spreading the word, and it was discussed in the taverns, the shops and casually by the man or woman in the street. Like a solution crystallizing, the natural caution and suspiciousness of a city of merchants solidified around the obvious truism Satro had pointed out, that Narn had agendas of his own. Bronn mused that Narn's cause had well and truly been set on its heels in Carm, and he hoped Narn did not manage to trace the source back to a certain Seer and Warrior.

Bronn also spent a considerable amount of gold tracking down a Fire Witch. There actually was one in the city, waiting for a ship to Fire Hold, and she was quite happy to earn a fee for working rather than spend money doing nothing. She agreed to come with them to Nun's Hold, and wait for another ship to go on from there to Fire Hold. She would spend hour after hour every day recharging Bronn's staff. It was easy enough for her, she could output enough energy virtually on auto-pilot. Going flat-out would not get it done much faster and would exhaust her, but an easy trickle over ten or more days would at least get some power back into it. Probably no more than one level one shot, but at least that would be something.

And, Nun's Hold was not known as a great center of commerce, so Bronn looked around for cold weather gear. There was little enough of it on the island, semi-tropical as it was, but he managed to outfit himself with enough to keep himself warm, and he also bought outfits for the Fire Witch of his Vision. When Satro asked about similar clothing for himself, Bronn was forced to tell him that he only Saw himself and the Witch continuing on from Nun's Hold.

70

"Well, I'm quite happy about that" Satro replied. "I wanted to go to Nun's Hold for knowledge. I don't like the cold much. Warrior's Hold is right on the edge of an Arctic current, and quite a lot colder than Seer's Hold, even though they're at the same latitude. I never cared for the winter there."

Bronn agreed fervently. He still had Visions of what it was going to be like – snowfields feet deep, huddled meals over meager fires. He spoke feelingly on the subject, and Satro became even more smug about not going.

"You can pick me up on the way back if you like, after you're out of the icebox" he grinned.

Bronn looked at him somberly. No easy way around it, he hoped Satro would not be too affronted. Still, Warriors were trained to service. "Actually, Satro, my Vision doesn't see you continuing on this quest. I have to go, I am critical. The Fire Witch I hope to find on Nun's Hold is essential, too. And we must together find the Ice Witch. After that, I do see us picking up a Warrior … but I see a very specific one. A young Warrior … Gold level, or at least capable of Gold."

Satro whistled. "You don't want much, do you. A Fire Witch from Nun's Hold. There aren't any. Trina here (he indicated the Witch they had hired, whose full name was Shi'Tri'Na) will have to stay outside the Hold walls, by convention since she doesn't want anything from the Hold. An Ice Witch, when none have been seen for hundreds of years. And a young Gold Warrior. None of them, either! There are only a handful of Gold Warriors in the world, and all of them past middle age. While such a rank can be granted for pure ability, it hasn't been done for … well, almost as long as the Ice Witches have been gone! Silver, yes, though they are few enough – I am proud, and rightly so, of having achieved Bronze! But Gold these days requires great service to Warrior's Hold rather than martial skills."

Bronn nodded. "That's why I'm the critical resource. I alone have the Visions to seek and find these people, and I need to find them all before we have a hope of defeating Narn in direct confrontation. But I'm glad you don't seem too upset about it, and I'll be sorry to part. You've been a good travelling companion, and a good friend."

Satro shrugged. "I wanted to journey to Nun's Hold, to learn, to ask my questions. I didn't particularly want to wander the globe on what look like impossible tasks. I trust you Seers to see the way, and if I'm not a part of it, well, that's all right with me, as long as the job gets done. You can call on me if you need me, of course, and I can't see how you could defeat Narn without an army – and a big one, to invade the vast territories of Fire Hold, you may need me again, then – but if not, I have my own dream to pursue."

And so, they continued in friendship. The days passed, and Bronn contentedly saw the pro-Seer anti-Narn feelings in Carm strengthening and consolidating. Nothing was certain when it came to dealing with a sorcerer of course, but Bronn was happy that Narn and his Avatars would face an uphill battle to even regain some of their lost ground.

Finally, the day of departure came. Bronn and Satro stepped aboard the ship, 'The Light Spirit' with pleasure. She seemed to be a well-built vessel, almost dancing at anchor as if eager to be on her way again. The high price they had paid was for the best cabin aboard, and while necessarily small it was well laid out and more than sufficient for their needs.

Trina was also pleased, but not really happy. Her cabin was just fine, but Fire Witches have a natural antipathy to large volumes of water, and most of them dread long sea voyages. The fact that she would be spending longer at the mercy of the waves oppressed her, and she would not have done it for twice the money if a Seer had not been involved. But a Seer was, and Bronn could tell her that he Saw no problems on the trip, nor on her subsequent voyage in the lee of the island chain extending from Nun's Hold to Fire Hold – Lute's Chain, named after the approximate correspondence of the islands' positions to the resting position of the fingers of a lute player. He had that Vision five days ago, and her natural fear of sea voyages had made her willing to take a longer voyage with a Master Seer's vision of safety rather than a shorter one with no such assurance.

She could see that the ship was a good one, and she had the anticipation of a safe passage, and was earning her way besides. But, still ... two weeks in a fragile wooden box floating above miles of cold, deep water ... no, she was not very happy. She was glad to have something to do, to pour energy endlessly into Bronn's staff, and in fact she worked hard at it, tiring herself out deliberately so that she came to the end of each day exhausted, and dropped off into a dreamless sleep. Far better than tossing on a bed at night, listening to the strange sounds of the sea and the ship, and worrying if the noises meant some kind of horrible cold, watery problem was developing in the darkness.

Bronn took the time of inactivity to go over his dream journal and review the various Visions he had been granted over the years, and write up any new ones he had on board the ship. Twice he had the same one, which he had also Seen before: Seeing Ice Hold as though from the top of a very high mountain, laid out

73

below him, but drifting past. He wondered what it meant.

Satro spent the time as he did every voyage he had had – two in total before this, one on the way to Warrior's Hold, and one on the way back. He exercised, on the deck and in the rigging. He trained a few on the ship who had a desire to learn better swordplay. And he spent endless hours gazing out in fascination at the ever-changing seascape, lost in the wonder of the waves, the burgeoning clouds, the flying fish and dolphins, and the endless blues of the water merging into the sky. As he remarked to Bronn, the life of a sailor would suit him very well. More, he expanded, he hoped that when he had set himself up in life there would be money and opportunity for him to take many, many sea voyages.

Bronn heard him rhapsodizing, but also saw Trina give a little sigh of discontent at these words. He had noticed Trina noticing Satro, despite the fact that Warriors and Fire Witches only occasionally got on romantically. But Satro was captivating in his own way – a trim Warrior's body of course, but a broad, honest face, and when one of his little smiles appeared a very handsome one. Surprising that Satro didn't seem to spot how many girls and women cast glances his way. A determined woman could have just as much impact on a man's life as a determined enemy, in some ways, and Bronn thought that Warrior's Gift would alert Satro of that too. Or, perhaps it did, he concluded. Certainly, the thought of having to accompany Satro on endless sea voyages had dampened Trina's designs.

The days passed, with no serious weather threatening the ship as Bronn had foreseen, much to Trina's relief. She seemed to relax a little, and spend less time energizing Bronn's staff. Bronn suspected that she had come to a personal compromise, and had decided that while a long term relationship with Satro might not be viable, a short-term one might have some advantages. None of his business, of course.

Chapter 4. Knowledge

Knowledge is a deadly friend
When no one sets the rules

King Crimson

The dock of Nun's Hold, more than any other of the Holds showed neglect. Perhaps because Nun's Hold was a far smaller island than any other, no more than twenty miles in any direction, and much of that uninhabitable land, mountains so steep as to be nearly un-climbable. The little land that could be used was all used, and dedicated to the needs and purpose of the Nuns. And that purpose was knowledge. Anything else was given second or third priority, and so the dock was kept in repair, but more reactively when something went wrong rather than proactively. The farmlands were neat and tidy, because it made sense to grow as much food locally as possible. But everything else had the look of lick-and-a-promise care.

Bronn and Satro and several others from the ship who were in search of some question that needed answering with facts (rather than tendencies and predictions, which was the province of the Seers) made their way up to the Hold itself. It was typical of the Nuns that there was no generally available transportation for the two miles from the dock to the Hold itself. Too difficult to organize, and anyone who wanted knowledge badly enough would walk. To be sure, for the elderly and infirm there were horses and carts for hire in the tiny village that surrounded the docks, where a few families eked out a precarious existence supplying such services.

Trina would make use of some of those services, staying at an inn which had a few rooms for rent. For, while a Fire Witch was not exactly unwelcome – anyone who needed to know something that had been discovered and written down was welcome at Nun's Hold – if they were just passing through, it made sense to keep someone who could throw fire (and came from a Hold noted for the impulsive and emotional nature of its people) away from a place containing vast quantities of highly flammable books, scrolls, manuscripts, folios, papers, maps and drawings.

There were lots of such careful thoughts. The kitchens were separated from the rest of the Hold by stone passages ten yards in length with nothing flammable in them, and sealable at either end with iron doors. What little heating was necessary was provided by hot water in pipes, and no candles or fires were used anywhere other than in a room that could be sealed off from the rest of the castle – fire-safe lanterns were used where needed. And even so, the rooms where books were stored were many, independent, lit from the outside by windows and had buckets of sand and water easily and regularly available.

When Satro and Bronn entered the Hold, over a very solid drawbridge (for the Nuns were not impractical, and the Hold well protected), the nature of the place was immediately apparent, as it was at Seer's Hold. It was clear that some attempt had been made to make the castle impressive, as it had wide doorways and noble proportions. But the effect was somewhat spoiled by the tendency that books have, to expand to occupy all space capable of holding them. Despite the fact that there were many Stacks for rarely accessed books, libraries and reading rooms for the more useful ones, and display rooms for rare and valuable items, there were also indexes and compendiums, bookcases, racks and tables stacked with books, maps, parchments and workbooks – everywhere, with a fine disregard for style, convenience or any other concern.

Most of the travelers were met by Nuns whose job it was to receive supplicants and find out what they needed, and what they were prepared to pay, because of course knowledge has a price. It was almost free for someone to come to the Hold and browse through the libraries looking for what they wanted, and almost useless. It cost more to get someone who understood the various catalogues and indexes and knew where to look, and had the experience to improvise if the cross-references fell short.

But Bronn, as a Seer, was entitled to special treatment. Seers, after all, were also seekers of knowledge, and complemented the Nuns. They had added many facts and discoveries to the libraries, and there were always one or two Seers in the Hold, helping fill out holes in the fabric. Seers who could see into the past, like the abbot, were particularly valued. And Satro, as a Gifted person was also valued and welcome, for what they could learn from him. And so, Bronn's request to see the Mother Superior was not dismissed out of hand or diverted to a lesser worker, but considered, passed on, and eventually granted. In time, of course. They had arrived mid-morning, but did not get to meet until after lunch. The Hold had many needs, the Mother Superior had her own interests and tasks, and she was getting older.

Bronn and Satro saw a well-preserved woman of over eighty, perhaps becoming a little frail, but still full of energy and with all her faculties intact. She was easier of manner than some of the senior personnel they had encountered on the way up through the hierarchy of offices and waiting rooms.

"Seer Bronn" she greeted them "and Warrior Satro. We know of both your names from the rolls of graduation and seniority from both your Holds, of course. And we have heard of your exploits and clashes with Narn the Sorcerer's Avatars as well. You are welcome in our Hold, and we will do whatever we can to aid you in the desperate struggle that is inevitably coming in the next year or so."

She smiled at their somewhat stunned expressions, and laughed a little. "Ah me, I still take such delight in parading my little gems of knowledge before people. A weakness, perhaps – the ideal student should be concerned with knowledge as a pure abstract of course, but we use such aids, tendencies and tools as we are given. Let me explain. We have two of your brethren currently resident, Seer Bronn, and they foresaw your arrival, and are beginning to See the possibilities of coming conflict. And, naturally, every ship that lands on our shore must, as a part of its contract, tell us of all news they know – and your stories have reached my ears in the few hours you have been waiting. And, so you are here, now, and not some time tomorrow as might otherwise have been."

Bronn laughed in delight, as he always did over such things. It often happened that a Seer appeared amazingly prescient, but simply knew something by direct experience or report, and the contrast between the perceived omniscience and the humdrum fact of everyday experience always tickled his funnybone. But he soon sobered.

"You, too see the coming conflict with Narn, Mother Superior?" he inquired quietly. The Mother Superior nodded, and replied, "Of course. Analysis of trends, projection and comparison to history are corollaries of knowledge. We can, of course, see things that appear obvious to us that may be hidden to others. And we have reports of Narn's Avatars stirring up trouble all over the known world."

"Even here, Mother Superior?"

"Seer Bronn, you are a Master Seer. It is appropriate, and I would enjoy it, to use less formality. Please call me Intira, if you will. And yes, even here. Or at least, he tried. Our Gift - if you don't mind me calling it that, for it is of course not a formally recognized Gift – of knowledge allows and forces us to see clearly. Narn uses misdirection and befuddlement to steer minds to his desire, but such things do not work well with us at all. We are concerned with fact and clarity, and his techniques clash with ours head-on, rather than gradually and subtly as he usually works. And, though it took us a long time and much searching, we found a way of at least restricting an Avatar's movements. An Avatar can be trapped in an iron mesh cage, energized with a form of captured lightning. Not easy to set up, and the Avatar can still be dissolved. But it was enough to, with time, make Narn give up the effort."

"Useful. I don't suppose it would be possible to set such things up everywhere?"

"Not with the world as it is today. It is a two level technology change to get the – ah – lightning generators out into the general world, and the world is not ready for such a momentous release of practical knowledge. The cure would be worse than the disease. But come, you have urgently sought a meeting with me. What can I do for the two of you?"

Bronn went to reply, but Satro was quicker. "If you please, Mother Superior, my request is the easier one, I think, so I will go first. I want to study here, to learn."

The Nun smiled, and said, "I think, Satro, as a companion of Master Bronn, that you should call me Intira also. And what, may I ask, do you want to learn, and what do you want to study?"

Satro answered eagerly. "I thank you, Intira for the honor. As to what I want to learn ... Why, the same as I wanted to learn since I was able to think. Evcrything! Why is the sky blue? Why is the sea blue, too, and why is it wet? What is air made of? Why are people born, what keeps them alive, why do they die, and where do they go when they do? What are the stars? How do birds fly? And so on! Everything! And if I can't learn everything, then as much as I can."

Intira leant back in her chair. "Satro, you are welcome. The force of your thirst for knowledge is obvious, strong and delightful to see. And genuine; I think I am old enough and experienced enough for that to be clear. You may stay as long as you like, and no charge will be made on you. If you wish to expand our library with knowledge of the ways and techniques of the Warriors, we will be glad to have it. And while no-one has thought to attack Nun's Hold for hundreds of years, the advice of a full Warrior will make many feel more secure in these troubled times, and that alone would earn you board and lodging."

She smiled again. "I will impart to you a little secret that is ... not generally known. We are known as the Nuns of Knowledge, but that is a bit of an affectation. While our inner core is mostly women, it is not a requirement, that much is known – we have many men as well ... but neither is chastity. In fact, we encourage our younger Sisters to have children, because it is a simple fact of inherited traits that if we required all true seekers of Knowledge to remain chaste, in a few dozen generations we might well breed such tendencies out of the human race. Many marry, but keep on working. I tell you this because you are a handsome man, but you do not know our ways, and you should be prepared for .. ah .. helpers."

"And now you, Seer Bronn. What can the Nuns of Knowledge do for you?"

"Intira, I have Seen a Vision, many times. It tells me that I am crucial in the fight against Narn the Sorcerer, in finding the right people and bringing them together. Otherwise, the path I see is the world being laid waste through war – war everywhere, something not seen since the days of Sha'Lin'Tra the Great. After that, I don't know. But I must seek out a Fire Witch. A powerful one. At least ... I think that is right. Sometimes, she seems young and less powerful, I do not fully understand that."

The Nun nodded, and leaned forward a bit. "It seems to me there must be more to your request, Bronn. A simplistic answer would be that Fire Hold would be the most logical place for you to search, but I am sure you are well aware of that, and there must be some reason why you have come here, other than that there are sometimes Witches temporarily living in the port village. Indeed you brought one here yourself."

Bronn nodded in his turn. "As you say, Intira. My vision shows that the one I need is one of your Nuns."

Intira leant back again. It is a measure of how clearly the Nuns think that she did not exclaim "that's impossible!" She would not have such an emotional reaction, of course. Instead, she spoke in measured tones: "You surprise me, Seer Bronn. It seems unlikely. I do not know of any such person, and I have been here for sixty five years. In that time, I remember five Fire Witches coming into the castle, and we were most cautious with them – they were vouched for as being exceptionally even tempered for Witches, and even then we were careful." She stroked her chin in thought. "I suppose it is possible that one could live amongst us and not declare herself. But she would have to be extraordinary, and I cannot for the life of me think why she would choose to do so. Fire Witches are typically more people of action, and regard knowledge as a tool rather than an end in itself."

She mused for a moment or two.

"Hypothetically, taking your Vision as a simple representation of truth, how would you go about finding your Fire … Nun? Heavens, that sounds strange …"

Bronn had the answer ready there. "I have seen her face many times in my Dreams, Intira. I will recognize her easily, if I can see your Nuns lined up in one place."

Intira nodded. "That is easy enough. By convention, we dine before sunset, to make as little use of candles and lamps as possible. There are three sittings for supper, and in the ordinary course of events one would expect all Nuns – acolyte, full Sister and Senior to go through the great hall, unless there was some long running experiment going on, and I know of none such at the moment. Except Sister Bertia, who is observing the setting sun and the early twilight, but she is nearly as old as I am, and not the one you seek. At least, she could not travel with you. I am guessing here, but you said you would be looking for a young person?"

Bronn agreed. "Yes, I think so. In my Vision she appears young, middle twenties to at the most early thirties. She does not look old, but there is the feel of some age about her. I see fair hair, and a pleasant face, a well-proportioned physique, neither short nor tall."

"Well." mused Intira. "No-one springs to mind. Though to be fair, I mainly deal with the Seniors. I know most of the Sisters by name, but there are nine and ninety of them, some with duties that mean I do not see them often, or indeed at all. And then there are the novices and acolytes, and of course the support staff, spouses, children, retired people and so on – but you said, a Nun. Still, no point in speculating just yet, we may as well see what simply looking will give us. If you join me in the great hall in three hours, we will see what we can see."

The three hours passed slowly for Bronn. Satro had gone away, to be assigned a room of his own, and to go on a guided tour of the castle. He was eager to begin learning answers, and Intira's warning looked like it should be taken to heart, for once it was found out that he would be staying, there seemed to be rather more Sisters who were eager to show him around than one might expect. Bronn was extended the offer to be shown the castle, but it didn't need a Seer's wisdom to see that the offer was half-hearted, and was not offered a second time when he politely refused, and let them take Satro off alone.

No reasonably intelligent person could be bored in Nun's Hold. One only had to mention a field of interest to the catalogue and index specialists to be guided to more information on the subject than one would have believed existed. And Bronn did spend over an hour reading about the nature of the Gifts, famous Seers and famous predictions – usually from a different perspective to the somewhat technical records of Seer's Hold, and quite often in more detail. But fascinating as it was, he could not hold his mind to it. Events were rushing to a major node in the chain of his Visions.

Instead, he found some pleasure and relaxation in wandering the heights of the castle, looking alternately over the fields and meadows where crops grew and cattle and sheep grazed, down to the port and out to the blue, blue sea, or inland to the towering crags and volcanic peaks, some so high they were permanently encrusted in snow and ice.

The first sitting for dinner came, but he was not successful in finding his Witch. He, Intira and two attendant Senior Sisters went early, and took a table near the entrance, where Bronn could easily see the people streaming in to the evening meal. The Nuns were strictly egalitarian when it came to seating and company. By rule, pre-arranged groups and favorite dining companions were frowned upon. You walked into the hall, went to the server and took your choice from the limited but very well prepared and tasty selections; you walked to a table at random, and sat with whoever happened to be there. Talking about your main area of work or investigation was encouraged, but not in detail, and not exclusively. Silence was not encouraged, for the idea was to exchange ideas and knowledge, and to get to know others as much as possible. A few tables were reserved for special purposes: there was a 'silent' table for those tired at the end of the day, who just wanted to rest. There were a few small tables, where people who had something specific they wanted to discuss could go. But they were special, and not to be used every day. And, to a large degree the system worked.

The people came in, and passed Bronn's table. Many of them nodded politely to Intira and the Seniors. A few times, Bronn's heart jumped when he saw a light head of hair or a young face, but as they came closer it was clear they were not the one. For the sake of appearances, Bronn had a bowl of soup – very good soup it was, too. Intira ate a simple salad, explaining that this was her usual way, as her body did not respond well to a heavy meal at the end of the day. One of the Seniors displayed talent as a trencherwoman, and Bronn surmised she must have an unusual metabolism if she ate that way every day and still remained fairly slim. And the last ate little, for she was busy. It was her job to mark off those they had seen on a list. All the Nuns had a good memory, but she was exceptional – names and faces remained fixed in her memory, and once she saw someone again, she knew their name straight away.

It was a simple process of elimination, Bronn mused as the first sitting came to an end, and the Sisters (and companions) filed out in an orderly fashion. The Sister with the memory for faces, Sister Sesura, marked off three or four names on the list that she had missed when everyone came in, two and sometimes three abreast. She had also marked off a few, just looking around the room. They waited as the last left, and the Sisters on kitchen duty and the permanent staff came in and cleaned up spills efficiently. Sesura marked them off the list, too, while Bronn looked them over in a leisurely way. And then, there were a few minutes before the next bell rang, and he gazed around the room. Pleasant, and well lit.

There were three large fireplaces, the chimneys clearly stone all the way around. The roof beams, far overhead, were covered in thick beaten copper. Still, there were many things in the room that would burn, and a kitchen and dining area would be a danger zone for those so afraid of fire. He mentioned as much to Intira. She smiled, and told him the danger was not as great as he thought. The doors to the room were lined with a light material derived from a peculiar fibrous type of stone that was completely fireproof, and also covered with copper. The tapestries that hung on the walls were themselves woven out of metal fibers. The tables, benches and chairs were wooden, true enough, but had been treated to be as fire resistant as possible. They would burn, but only just. Little was left to chance.

The bell rang, and the second sitting came in, but with no more success. After well under an hour, they too departed, and the process was repeated for the third and last sitting. This was for people who worked late, preferred to eat late, or simply preferred to spend longer at the table, eating slowly and talking with no thought for time, unlike the first two sittings that had to be out of the way for each following one. Before it was ended, bright safety lanterns were lit, for although it was early, it was winter and the sun had set. And again, no success. There had been two good candidates, and Bronn had hesitated, having to fight his natural desire to find a match. But they just weren't right.

When it was clear no more people were coming, Bronn and the three Sisters left the room, and he, Intira and Sesura went into a handy annex where there was a table, some comfortable chairs (and of course many bookcases). Intira asked how many of the roll they had seen that night. "Nearly everyone, Mother Superior" she answered. "There are a few in sickbay." And so, they went up to sickbay, and paid a visit to a half dozen Sisters, some patients and some nurses, none of whom fit the bill. That left very few, and Intira reduced the list even more, disqualifying most of them such as Sister Bertia. She had been grumbling about the stairs, being tired at the end of the day, but when the third-to-last name was mentioned – Sister Sheena, who looked after the novices' needs – she frowned suddenly, and said: "Sister Sheena? There is a Sister Sheena looking after the novices?"

"Yes indeed, Mother Superior. A very dedicated and friendly woman. Many a novice – myself included, not so long ago – has been made to feel at home here through her caring ways."

"Sister Sheena" Intira muttered. "Surely a coincidence." And yet ... we must see her, of course, so Seer Bronn can see her face. I am tired ... but I will walk with you, I think. Sister Sheena. Well, you are looking for an unusual Nun, and if she ... well, well, we will see. But if I were a betting woman, given we have seen nearly everyone else ..." she fell silent, and walked on through the corridors with Bronn, and Sesura for a guide and help, for though they were lit, the Sisters used as few lamps as possible even though they were safety lamps, each with an attendant bucket of sand.

She stopped suddenly, and turned to Sesura, and said in a voice that brooked no debate: "Sesura, I am sorry. But I must ask to go on alone here. Seer Bronn can see to my needs. If what I suspect is true ... well, I promise you, you will hear the truth, and that right soon. But not now." Sister Sesura looked at the Mother Superior for a long moment, then curtsied, turned and went on her way.

The novices' quarters were at the northern end of the castle, the more comfortable end. Unlike many institutions, the novices had a reasonably easy life. There was no desire to mortify their flesh, quite the opposite because joining was voluntary and everyone wanted them to stay. The novices had been to their own little dining room where they could be a bit more exuberant and enjoy themselves (although they could go to the main dining room if they wanted to, and usually did so more and more as they got older), and they had returned for some after dinner homework, and had now retired to bed. There was also a section for adults not directly working with the library, and for children, and also a section where retired folk could take things a bit easier and more slowly.

Sister Sheena was just finishing up in the large common room. As they entered through one door, she turned to go. A suspicious person might have said she saw who had come in, and instantly turned away as though to avoid them, but it would have been a hard call; it all looked very natural. She was nearly out the door, but Intira seemed to have been expecting something, she had a breath drawn already, and before Sheena could take another step, her voice rang out: "Sister Sheena! Your Mother Superior says stay!"

Sheena took the next step, but there was no way any reasonable person could say they had not heard. With a slight slump of the shoulders she stopped. Intira continued: "Sister Sheena, please come back into the room. We would like a moment of your time. This is important, anything else you have to do can wait." Sheena backed into the room, and turned around. Bronn caught his breath, and cried in a choked voice: "that's her!" And, at the same time, Intira said exactly the same thing.

Bronn frankly stared at her. His Vision had not done her justice. She was attractive in an unassuming way, the sort of attractiveness that people see, say "oh, she's pretty" and then think no more of it unless they see her often, when one day it dawns on them that in fact she is beautiful. She was tall for a woman, perhaps a fraction below average for a man's height, she had brown skin, golden-red hair of a medium-short length, with some natural waving in it. While she would not be called slender, she was well proportioned and curved in all the right places. She looked strong but not stocky, very fit and healthy. She had a sweet oval face, perfectly regular, wide but clear eyes, and a curve to her lips that would make people naturally assume she was kind to one and all, and probably animals as well.

Intira stared at her too. It would be going too far to say that a Nun of Knowledge, particularly the head of the Hold, ever looked at anyone or anything in disbelief. But, she came close. Finally, she spoke. "Sister Sheena, Sister Sheena. We lost contact over the years. But I have never forgotten the kind, patient, beautiful Sister who welcomed me as an eager but scared novice sixty-five years ago. In this strange and wonderful world a Seeker of Knowledge is often surprised, but I have never, I think, been so surprised as to see you here, doing the same job, and not a day older than I remember you. I really, really hope I get to hear some of this story, before Seer Bronn takes you away."

Sheena looked at the Mother Superior, and made a little moue of chagrin. "Oh, dear. I seem to have been caught out." Then, she smiled, and any previous thoughts of beauty went out the window. She lit up the room. Her physical presence filled the space between the four walls, and left Bronn breathless.

"Oh well, no point in trying to convince a knowledgeist that I just look like your Sheena, or am her daughter, I suppose. Hello, Seer Bronn. You have come to take me away? It sounds like I have little choice, but I warn you, I am not easy to persuade. And Mother Superior Intira ... I remember you, too. I thought you had great potential as a novice. I am glad my high hopes were not disappointed; you have been an exceptional leader. I'm proud of you."

Intira nodded. "I have done my best, these forty years. And I thank you, for it occurs to me that if you were young then and are young now, you may have seen a few Mother Superiors in your time. But come, my child, I am old, and have had a long day. I need to sit down; is there somewhere nearby we can sit in comfort?"

Sheena nodded. "Of course, Mother Superior. My little office is just around the corner, and has enough chairs for all of us. Please come, it is just this way": and she turned, and walked slowly through the door. Bronn and Intira followed.

The little office was a typical room in the Hold. Built to a common architectural pattern, perhaps five paces by four, tall ceilinged, but with a large window to minimize the need for lamps. And decorated to the individual's taste, which in this case seemed to be dark reds, a little gold, a touch of purple here and there, and of course the brown of many, many books. There were several very beautiful paintings and sketches on the wall, which Bronn suspected were Sheena's own work.

Sheena bade them be seated and offered water, wine or a mixture. Intira said she would be grateful for a glass of water, hesitated, and then said, "On this extraordinary night, it seems right to do something extraordinary. And so, I will have a little wine and water, something I have not done for twenty years." She nodded her head, and pulsed her mouth out and in, in the manner of an older woman than she seemed. Clearly, the meeting had been a shock to her. But, she took a healthy sup of the wine, when Sheena brought it, and rallied.

"It seems to me" she said with a rueful smile "that though I called you 'my child' not so long ago, I should probably more rightly call you 'mother', for all in all I suspect you are older than I, am I not right?"

Sheena nodded. "Sadly, you are right, Intira. But, as I said, you have my respect. You may call me anything you like. I would be honored if you would call me Sheena." She lowered her head, and seemed to shrink in herself. "I suspect, however, before the evening is out, you will call me other names. But, perhaps that need not happen. Perhaps, we should start with Seer Bronn telling us what he wants of me, what has been important enough for him to disrupt a secret I have held for ... a long time."

Bronn had been ready for this moment, if nothing else. He spoke about Narn, and the danger the world faced, with the first sorcerer for hundreds of years spreading his influence and control over the world. He got up, and paced the room, throwing his hands around as he spoke, the words flowing out of him. How his Vision saw Narn ruling the world, if he was not opposed, after a long war. What that would mean for the various branches of the Gift. How he had been granted a Vision that he was a key man, a crucial resource to bring together a group of people, and that his Vision had shown he must come to Nun's Hold, and find a powerful Fire Witch as the first part of the quest, and he had done so, and she *must* continue with him.

He paused. He was going to continue, but Sheena held up her hand. "Seer Bronn, I hear what you say. I believe your Vision. But tell me, do you really believe the world will change so much, if one person of power rules it? Perforce, he must, *must* rely on the continued flow of the direction that the world and society is moving. He can rule, but he cannot direct. He may well affect the lives of a few people who are rulers, and powerful. But the lives of the everyday folk must continue pretty much as they do today. Whatever we do, it may change who rules. But is it worth it? What will be the cost in lives? And, a mighty Fire Witch. Well, I am a Fire Witch, to be sure. And mighty? Not me. My abilities are limited." Somehow, there was a capital L in there. "With the best of intent, I don't know how much help I can be to you. Certainly, I can in no way stand against Narn myself, and my long experience tells me there may be little point in it. It would be a far better thing to simply give him what he wants. At the very worst, he will die eventually, and things will soon return to a balance."

Bronn looked at her, astonished. He had never thought about such a thing, never thought someone could see the world in such a way. Empathic by nature and training, though, he had to admit there was logic in what she said. No sorcerer, however powerful, could direct the whole world and all the people in a direction it did not want to go. Capable of destroying a hundred, a thousand people, or a hundred times as many with his armies, still, the weight of humanity was a mighty force, not easily to be guided. And, not a powerful Fire Witch? His Vision had seen otherwise.

"Still, and I must say though I have not thought about that aspect very much and I have to say that you speak a very telling point ... I have Seen this Vision. I think it has been granted to me for a reason, to save lives. Find the mighty Fire Witch ... and with her, find the great Ice Witch. And then, on to ..."

But he got no further. Sheena gasped in shock, and fell into a chair. It is often talked about, to say someone went white as a sheet. But it is actually very rarely seen, and they would not have suspected up till that point that it would be something Sheena might do. She had seemed totally self-contained, totally controlled, despite having been discovered. But she looked as though she would faint. The blood drained out of her face, lending a sickly green and grey cast to the brown of her skin, despite the warming effect of the sunset and candle flames. Not horror, but something to the same effect. She was totally disrupted. She looked at Bronn, her hands clasping her face, and Bronn and Intira looked at her.

Finally, she spoke. "Are … are you serious? Do you really mean to tell me that your Vision says we shall leave this place together, travel, and find an *Ice Witch*?" she asked, with a kind of desperate yearning intensity that Bronn found hypnotic and unsettling.

Bronn nodded, nonetheless. "That is what I have seen. In fairness, probability about seventy-five percent, with a total likelihood of success in facing Narn about even."

Sheena looked at him with a kind of naked hunger he found disturbing. Seers liked to know what was going on, and he had no idea why Sheena had changed her mind. But, she continued, without giving him much time to think further. "I will come with you, Seer Bronn. With all my heart, one hundred percent. The quest will not fail for lack of my commitment, and I will do whatever else is needed to bring success, to find this Ice Witch."

Bronn could do no more than nod his acceptance. But Intira spoke for the first time in a while: "I am glad that mighty plans seem to be coming to fruition. And I know they will not include me much, for I am an old woman. But first and foremost, I am a Nun of Knowledge. And I beg you, from the bottom of my heart, tell me what all this means, tell me who you are, where you come from. I will swear secrecy if it must be, but please, *please* tell me."

Sister Sheena looked at Intira soberly. She bent her head, and said, softly, "I am afraid … I am afraid and ashamed. But, I will tell. You have the right to ask."

She raised her head, and again made a little moue, not of chagrin this time but of apprehension.

"My name is Sister Sheena. But, that is not the name I was born with. Sheena is a contraction, a simplification of my birth name … which was Sha'Lin'Tra."

Intira looked at her blankly. "You were named after the great sorceress? But that name has been cursed; no-one has named their daughter thus, for … oh, surely not. No. It cannot be."

Sheena nodded, and hung her head. "It is I. I am the sorceress, Sha'Lin'Tra. Or once was. What I am now, I do not know."

Intira made as if to rise. "Cursed! Cursed, your name is, down the ages! We …" and her voice trailed off, as she looked at Sheena, and saw her, a vision of misery incarnate. And she sat, heavily.

Finally, after about ten seconds of pause, she spoke again, in a heavier and deader voice. "And yet, and yet, and yet … we teach that none is beyond redemption." Her voice gained in strength and purpose: "We teach that with understanding and learning, the worst can become the best … and I remember, yes, I remember, sixty-five years ago I found nothing but kindness in your words and your smile. You held me as caringly as my mother, when I was homesick. I am ashamed … Forgive me, for much must have changed. The days of Sha'Lin'Tra the Great are eight hundred years and more in the past, and you are not the same person, otherwise you would want to rule, and you would be Mother Superior, and not I."

Sheena looked up, with a tremulous but beautiful smile through incipient tears glistening in her eyes. "I have tried, Mother, I have tried."

Intira spoke strongly again. "Eight hundred years! What you have seen, how much is lost! I ache to hear the story! I beg you, please, tell me!"

Sheena spoke again, drying her eyes. "Mother Intira, I thank you from the bottom of my heart. For you have upheld the finest principles of the Nuns of Knowledge, against natural sentiment, and I am so very, very grateful. Few have known my secret, and none have forgiven me. Well, perhaps you will change your mind again before I tell all. But you have the right to know, as I said. And Seer Bronn needs to know." She paused a while, gathering herself together, and with a deep breath began again.

"I was born a Fire Witch, more than nine hundred years ago" she began. "In those days, the four Gifts were more a part of the world. They are less so today, because of the loss of the Ice Witches. My fault, but we will come to that."

"My mother was a Fire Witch, but my father was an Ice Witch. Even then, that was most unusual: Fire Witches, as now, were more often attracted to Seers, who balance out their impulsive nature, or occasionally to Warriors who do the same due to the discipline of their training. And often, of course to men born into the Hold, sometimes rarely such men are Witches themselves, or simply to non-Gifted people. It was a bit more common in those days, Ice and Fire often worked together because such a pair can be extraordinary Healers, and despite being almost opposite in nature, very occasionally they might marry."

"Also unfortunately uncommon was the practice of student exchange. It is bad for any Gift to become isolated; their characteristics become more pronounced and eventually, at least for Fire Witches, debilitating; they need interaction and melding with others. And, as I was born a Fire Witch but of an Ice Witch father, I was a natural candidate for an exchange. My mother would be put out of place, sent to the icy north, but it would be home to my father, and so we went as a family, and I was a talented Witch. When we went, at age thirteen, I could already project two Avatars, one of them Material."

Sheena stated it as a matter of fact. But Bronn's mouth fell open, as to a lesser extent did Intira's. Few people ever projected an Avatar before puberty, and Bronn had never heard of anyone of that age projecting a solid, material one. Nor, more impressively, had Intira.

"I hated it. Well, some take to the cold better than others. But, I studied. Talented as I was with Fire, I was not much good with Ice Magic. It came to an unpleasant end … I had to leave; under as bad a set of circumstances as can be imagined. Both my father and my mother died. I never forgave them, the Ice Witches."

Sheena looked down. Both Bronn and Intira could see there was more to the story than was told, but didn't press her. Plainly, after nine hundred years it was still unbelievably hard. Bronn could not imagine what that would be like. Nine hundred years. His own childhood hurts and emotional abrasions were long ago forgotten, even longer ago resolved and that was only decades.

"I returned to Fire Hold, with a burning hate in my heart. They took me in and my training continued.

After three years, I asked for and was granted leave to go and study at Warrior's Hold, and graduated from there." She looked up, and nodded, "Yes, in those days they were happy to train women as well as men, though they may deny it now."

"And then, I returned to Fire Hold, and studied and practiced, studied and practiced. By the time I was twenty-five, I was the most powerful Fire Witch in the Hold, by an order of magnitude. And they all knew it. When I challenged for Prime Witch, it wasn't even commented on that the one who held the position surrendered without a spell being cast or a fireball thrown, though often the stubborn pride of Fire Witches meant a fight to the death."

"And still, I studied, practiced and grew. And one day, it came to me that there was no-one who could stand against me in the whole world. No ten, nor even any twenty. And with the power that my Prime position gave me, I could raise an army, and the world could be mine."

"But, I was cautious. I didn't want to move until there was no chance of meaningful opposition. I had pushed the boundaries of Fire Magic, now with what little I knew of Ice Magic and the ways of the Warriors, I began research into ways of blending and merging the Gifts. And I found many strange and wonderful things."

"Then, I made a mistake, as so many have before me. I fell in love with a young Seer. Like me, he had also trained as a Warrior, which is where I met him first. A most unusual man. In all the years I have been alive, I know of no other Seer who trained as a Warrior, nor vice-versa. Ungifted people born in the Holds, yes, but not a true Seer. A little overlap of talent, perhaps, but the two Gifts are regarded as complementary – either side of the north-south Ley line, you understand."

She paused for thought. "Well, no. I think perhaps that love is never a mistake. My mistake – or foolish, prideful arrogance if you will - was to assume that as he loved me, he would fall in with my plans, be guided by my needs, my hate. But he would not. He said it was wrong to aspire to rule the world. And wrong to vow vengeance on all Ice Witches. He begged me to change, but said if I did not, he could have no part of it and must leave. I didn't believe it, but he did."

Sheena bent her head in pain, and Bronn could see her hands clenching each other, white with strain. "I had discovered powerful new magic, magic that can change minds. With it, one can even change one's own mind, if one is unwise enough. Fire Witches are naturally hot-headed and impulsive, which is not a good combination with power. First, I used this new magic on my lover, to make him an unthinking slave to my will. That lasted about two days; I couldn't bear the result. I freed him of the magic, and once again he left. I took vengeance for his betrayal. And then, in my rage, despair and hurt, I cast a new spell … I burned love out of my mind."

"The pain of loss was gone. Knowing only relief, I laughed at what I had been. And I worked further on my magic, going down stranger and stranger byways. I didn't know it then, but I was able to do so only because I had altered my mind strangely and horribly with that burning."

"I found a class of spells of the mind that spread like an infection. I cast a light but powerful one on a few of my Fire Witches, and watched as it spread like a plague. Prime Fire Witch is normally an uneasy position: rivalry and rebellion, aspirations and hopes lead to a roil, an undercurrent of dissention that has to be watched like a hawk. No-one was going to be foolish enough to challenge me, of course, but assassination is always a possibility. But not now. They were bound to me, bound to my will, and I used them. In six ships, with a hundred Witches under my firm control, we set off for Ice Hold. A simple journey – with that much power at my beck and call, and no concerns about my personal safety I could set up otherwise dangerous mind-links, joining dozens of Witches together in orchestras, concerts, where the power of the group was greater than the sum of its parts. We ran into three storms, and we flattened them out to still water. The winds ran to our order."

"We came to Iceland. We marched across the way to the Hold. The cold meant nothing to us, we heated our immediate environment with trivial effort. The Hold Tribes parted as we came to them, getting out of our way, or dying, it was up to them. And finally, we came to the Hold itself, and the Ice Witches opposed us, for they were strong and able to work together naturally. Not for long. I spent vast energies concentrated in one little area, and captured an Ice Witch. I infected her with one of my mind-control spells. No light one as I had used on my Fire Witches, this was a harsh spell, with no limits. And I let her escape, and of course she infected all the others in the Hold."

Sheena breathed jerkily. It was clear this confession was taking a lot out of her. Intira held out her hand, as if to offer some comfort, and haltingly began, "my child ...." But Sheena stopped her. "I beg you, Mother Superior, hear my confession. Even after all this time, I do not know if I could start all over again ..."

"The Ice Witches were mine. The effect of the spell was, each must express all her (or his, more rarely) Avatars. And the Avatars were mine to control. And, if the

Avatar was lost, destroyed or dissolved ... the Witch could cast no more."

Bronn and Intira stirred. This was unknown! "Yes, though normally the destruction of an Avatar is painful, a Witch can recover can cast a new one after a few minutes or hours, but such was my spell. And, by my edict, they must all leave Icc Hold, which would be abandoned. And so it was."

"I took the Avatars and the Witches back with me. I stacked the Avatars in the holds of my ships, like so many pieces of wood. Avatars need no food, water or even air of course, though they can be destroyed and feel discomfort and, and that discomfort is felt by the Witch who projected them. I didn't care, of course."

Sheena had recovered control by now, and continued in a flat, unemotional voice. "We went first to Warrior's Hold. Warriors are fierce fighters, but a possible disadvantage is that though they can see how to win if winning is possible, they also see clearly when they are fore-done, and will not fight a lost cause if there is no reason. I told them what I wanted: absolute power, unquestioning rulership over them. I would not be unreasonable; their lives would go on mostly unchanged. Pragmatists to a man, they agreed."

"Not so the Seers. They fought. The few Witches they had, that I had not suborned, fought valiantly against us, and they used their Visions to mount physical buffers against our ships' landing; catapults, nets, heat rays produced by mirrors and driven by the sun. To a large degree, they were successful, and would have kept us off despite our magic. But I had my Ice Avatars."

"I drove them mercilessly. They built a bridge, or rather a pontoon of solid ice, floored with rubber, and we marched a quarter of a mile over the sea to land. My Fire Witches, melded mind to mind, protected us. We burned whatever the catapults threw at us out of the sky. Freezing the sea took vast amounts of power, of course. More than three-quarters of the Avatars burned out before we made it to shore, and the rest were shaky. But I threw them against the Seers and the Hold Tribes, and when the Avatars were nearly gone, I brought in the Fire Witches. It was a rout. Within the day, Seer's Hold had surrendered, and the world was mine."

"Like Warrior's Hold, I punished no-one. I required nothing more than absolute obedience to my every word, but made it known to them that my hand would rest lightly. I had enough to do, ruling Fireland. Fire Hold is a tiny bump on the vast expanses that are there, and ruling the Ungifted was hard enough."

"And so, my ambitions realized, I went home. A few Ice Witches I left on Iceland, to stop anyone who tried to make it to the Hold itself. Anyone of any talent was infected by my spell, and exiled. And suddenly, I found myself with little to do."

"I consolidated my magic. With the handful of the Ice Witches that were left that still held power and the best of the Fire Witches, I built a group who knew more about magic and its effect on the body and mind than had ever been built before, or since. I dedicated them to the study of my mind, my body. And, slowly, over four years, we advanced. I learned how my body might be changed. In vanity, I altered the basic parameters of my form, to make myself beautiful. In arrogance, I learned how to control the functions of my various organs, and modified them where necessary. And finally, I learned the ways to put a stop to aging in my various parts, and achieved qualified immortality, and my folly was complete."

"A qualified immortality?" questioned Intira. Sheena nodded. "Yes. I am hard to kill. My body will repair most hurts. I am immune to most poisons, and shrug off disease. But, cut off my head and I would be as dead as anyone else. I would not survive an arrow through the heart."

Bronn asked: "You say, your folly was complcte? In what way? You sound as if you had achieved what many fantasize about."

Sheena sighed. "Yes, of course. But what then? When you have conquered all the lands, when no-one dares dispute your lightest word, when you can do anything you want and go anywhere you wish, when all your revenges are complete, what do you do then? I became aware of a discontent. Then, of something missing. There was no joy in my life. The deep changes I had made to my body meant I would have no children, and there was no possibility of going back, there. I adopted a few, but ... but then, they meant little to me. There was no love in me for them, or for anything else. I had burnt it all out with my magic."

"I knew nothing else to do but continue my studies. For years, decades, I pursued the borders of knowledge. My rule lasted fully one hundred years. I mastered level four magic. The last of the Ice Witches died, with their Avatars and that spell burned out. And finally, finally, just before the time, I think, when I would have wearied from it all and terminated my miserable existence, I found a new ambition. I knew of the Angels of God, of course. I had spoken with one after I had burned my mind. A story for another day. But they can be contacted in other ways, if one knows how. They can be contacted ... and it is possible to ask to become one of them. They could not be forced, not even by me, their powers are of a level beyond what we can muster. Their responsibilities and limitations are just as great. But for someone as fascinated by power as I was, to join their ranks would be ... well, it would be an escape from the hole I had dug myself into."

"And, I managed it – the contact and the question. It was the most terrible experience of my life. They were not angry, or contemptuous in their refusal. That I could have handled, fought even. They were sorrowful, with a depth of sorrow that humbled my loss of my mother, all those years ago. They pitied me, for what I had done to myself. They explained that an Angel lives in a continuous state of love: love for God, love for His works. They loved even me. But I, having burned love out of my mind, could no more join them than a tree could run a race. They made me aware of what my mind and soul was missing, and for the first time I truly felt the damage I had done to myself. I bent my head and wept. Finally, I raised myself and looked them in the eyes, hard though it was, and asked: is there no hope? I was prepared for a 'no' answer and that would have been it. I would have bowed out of this life quietly."

"One of them looked at me, long and hard. I felt his mind probing mine, and subjected myself to it. Finally, he or she spoke to me. 'You have cast your spell strongly. Yet, perfection lies only in God. Though you have scarred yourself, burned your mind, and used your will to damage yourself deeply, you have not fully succeeded. Almost, you understand. What is left is tiny, hurt, hiding deep inside you. If you are successful in getting that little desiccated seed to germinate and grow, it will be a hard journey, and a long one. And understand, when I say a long one, I do not mean long as people normally use the term. I mean long as one such as you understand and experience it, one who has made themselves less than mortal."

"'What must I do' I asked, for I have never been afraid of doing what is necessary."

"The Angel replied, 'for you, the beginning will be to learn compassion. Then, remorse and sorrow for what you have done, and a seeking of forgiveness. It will be hard, and you will never achieve it as the Prime Witch of the world. You will have to cast another spell, a self-limiting one. You will need magic, but you must limit yourself to no more than that of a level one Fire Witch, until you rediscover love. Not someone else loving you, you must learn to love someone else, but not Eros – not the love of simple physical attraction. Unselfish love. And I must warn you, there is no guarantee. It may be the task is beyond you."

"And so, I made a beginning. Over years, I teased apart the empire I had built, rebuilding the Holds and re-establishing their hierarchies, traditions and structures. I was ready to drop everything, but I knew doing so would create chaos in the world, and I felt the Angels would not like that. It would be selfish. I knew that as an intellectual thing; but I did not yet feel it."

"That is, I rebuilt almost all the Holds. It was too late for Ice Hold. The spell I had used could not be undone, and I had burned out most of the Ice Witches, and as I said the rest slowly faded away, and when the last one died, the infection spell ended. That is why, Seer Bronn, when you say we seek a real Ice Witch, a great one, and you have Seen us finding her, I am your companion without argument. You offer me hope, not to undo what I did, but perhaps to rebuild Ice Hold, and at least bring a balance back to the Gifts which has been absent these eight hundred and more years."

Intira stirred. "And what did you do then, Sha'Lin'Tra?" she asked in a heavy voice. It was clear that she had been greatly affected by the story. And, for a Knowledge Nun, horrified. The stories of Sha'Lin'Tra's wars and sorcerous rule were bad enough to have lasted eight hundred years. But to have caused the loss of an entire Gift, the Knowledge of the spells, the capabilities of those people was as evil a thing as could be thought of.

Sheena sighed, understanding full well why Intira had used her proper name rather than the name she had known her by, while a Nun. "I set about the program the Angels had outlined for me. I freed the Fire Witches from my control. I could do that, for the plague spell was much simpler than the absolute one I had cast on the Ice Witches. I created a spell, to limit my own abilities to that of a level one Fire Witch. I can project a single Avatar, manipulate fire and cast many simple fire related spells. But though I have a great deal of knowledge in my head, that is all – I cannot use it."

"I set off into the world. There was no need of disguise; who would suspect Sheena, level one Fire Witch, was once Sha'Lin'Tra the Great? Few had seen my face, after all. I worked. I used my level one powers to help others, those in need, the poor, those disrupted by the changes. There was no shortage of them. And, compassion came easily to me. It was a revelation, the sufferings and problems that everyday folk have. I did what healing I could – little enough; a level one Ice Witch would have done more there, but I had done some study in that area and so could help a bit. For decades, I wished I had not cast my power limiting spell, I could have done so much more to solve their problems. But finally, I came to understand that solving their problems was not what was best. Best was, to help them understand how to solve their problems themselves."

"Remorse and sorrow developed slowly out of that. For hundreds of years, I whipped myself inside, and sometimes outside, thinking on what I had done. Many times I nearly took the easy way out, but the Angels had said I must seek forgiveness. That implied it was at least conceivable. But that's about how far I have come, in these eight hundred years or so. Several times, I have scoured the lands, seeking people who have some talent in Ice Magic. A few arise spontaneously in each generation. I had set some gold aside for such needs, and thrice I sought to re-establish Ice Hold. It didn't work. Once, we kept on going for eight years, but finally, the cold, the lack of sufficient talent to work with, the hostility of the Hold Tribe, and the complete lack of facilities other than the great stone halls was too much."

"Still, I have done my best to atone. I have helped where I could. I have built things, worthwhile, lasting things. And finally, I think, I came to a stable state, where I could work with the world, hoping for some further slow progress towards the next step, forgiveness. But you, Seer Bronn, have completely turned me upside down and inside out. To find a real Ice Witch! I would have said it was impossible. But, a Seer's Vision is a Seer's Vision. And where there is one, there may be more. I am trembling inside, eager and fearful, in a way that I have not known for many hundreds of years."

Intira stirred again. The urge to Know was too strong not to ask further questions. And there were, to be sure, the signs of deep regret, a lot of hard work and personal change. "In eight hundred years, you could do much. You say you have built lasting things. What things have you built ... Sheena?" she asked in a less heavy voice.

Sheena smiled in gratitude that Intira had gone back to using that name. She looked at the Mother Superior steadily; she was already gaining back some of her self-control. "Um." She began. "I will tell you some ... I don't know if you will thank me for the knowledge. You must prepare yourself for a shock. If you will tell me when you are ready?"

Intira looked at her. "Very well ... I think I am prepared. Knowledge must not and cannot be avoided, of course."

Sheena nodded. "Of course, Mother Superior. Well, one of the things I did not want to happen was that much useful information I had learned should disappear, if I was unable to bear the continuance of my life. Many things have been lost, of course, and better so. My plague spells. No-one else learned them, and I have done my best to forget them. Narn has certainly not rediscovered them, though I have heard rumors that he has mind techniques somewhat related. But rest assured he could not use them, even if he did rediscover them, unless he was willing to mutilate his mind as I did. God grant for his sake as well as ours that he's not foolish enough to do so. But so, the knowledge. Before I fully dissolved the empire I had built, I gathered the library and the staff who maintained it, and arranged for it to be moved to a little island in the middle of the world. I paid much gold for masons and carpenters to build a secure building for it, and ..."

Intira gasped. "No!" she exclaimed. "Not ..."

Sheena nodded. "Yes. I am sorry, Mother. And, I named it the Hold of the Nuns of Knowledge."

"But our records, of the earliest times, say it was a woman of vision but Ungifted, who worked valiantly

108

and tirelessly across the years to set this fortress up, and became the first Mother Superior ... oh, no. That was you again? Have you lived in this Hold for eight hundred years?"

Sheena slowly shook her head. "No, Mother. I was indeed the first Mother Superior, hiding my magic. And, at need, I have been others. The sixth, the eleventh and the fifteenth, at times when I felt the vision was faltering and there was really no-one else who could do the job. But not by choice. I had no more desire to lead, to gain power. And no, while I have often returned to the Hold as a refuge, most of the time I have been out in the world. Trying to help. Searching for Ice Magic. And seeking forgiveness."

Intira sat back again. She sat, motionless for a quarter of a minute. And then, weakly, she began to laugh. "Oh, dear!" she exclaimed. "So much going on that I, that we did not know. Eight hundred years of precious knowledge in your head, that I would give much to find out. And now, Seer Bronn will take you away. I see and know the need, but I feel like crying."

"Well, Sha'Lin'Tra the Great. Many stories have come to us, over the centuries, of your rule. Many exaggerations as well, no doubt, but likely many truths. For what it may be worth, the hurts and evils of the past have little direct impact on me, but Nun's Hold is a great good in this world, at least I feel it to be so. And your sincerity and repentance is obvious, and we say, as I said before, that all can change, that no-one is beyond redemption."

Sheena bowed her head. Intira reached out, and touched Sheena's shoulder, and said, "For my part, at least, you are forgiven. I hope you find what you seek. What is it you seek?"

Sheena spoke, in a soft, aching voice: "To re-establish Ice Hold. And, forgiveness. Forgiveness from God. Forgiveness from myself. And forgiveness from the Ice Witches. The last, I never thought was possible, but now I have at least a glimmer of hope. And then, to rediscover love."

Intira spoke again: "These are worthy ambitions. May there be a blessing on your path, that you may achieve them. And may you save us all from Narn the Sorcerer in the process!" and she removed her hands. Sheena sat back once more, clearly much affected.

"I thank you from the bottom of my heart, Mother Superior" she said. "Your words are the first formal forgiveness I have ever had. The first in eight hundred years." She raised her head, and smiled. "And since I have been found out, and must leave these walls with Seer Bronn, and I do try to improve things wherever I go, and being at heart a Nun of Knowledge ... Intira, if you go to the third basement of the Northern Tower, storage area two, and carefully push the bookcase that holds the biographies of the Mother Superiors of this castle, behind it you will find my private library. I had it built when I was supervising the construction of this Hold. There are one or two books you will find no-where else, and my personal records. One must do something with one's time of course, and I have tried to keep a journal of my existence since the beginning of the Hold. There are many things in there that would otherwise be lost ..."

Intira's eyes lit up. No one person could master one hundredth of the contents of the Hold's libraries, of course. But some things were more interesting than others, and the possibilities of the course of history observed by a single person over the centuries were obvious. And then, she made a little sigh of exasperation. "I will read what is there with pleasure, of course. But I hope ... I hope enough time is granted to me to read it all. I must say, Sheena that at the end, I am impressed. You are a true Nun of Knowledge to have seen the need to write your observations down so faithfully. Of course, as you founded the Hold, it might be said the Hold reflects your nature rather than the other way around ... oh dear, I will have to think about this."

Sheena smiled again. "Seer Bronn, do you have any Vision of when we must leave, where we will find this Ice Witch, when we must get there, or how we must travel?"

Bronn scratched his chin, and told her of his recent Visions, of Iceland, Ice Hold, winter, and of seeing the land laid out before him as on a map. Sheena frowned, and then nodded reluctantly, as if a private thought had been confirmed. "It's past the end of winter there now, and starting to be spring. No ships travel regularly to the land of ice now, of course, let alone to the northern end, and by the time we chartered one, fitted it out and provisioned it, spring would be gone and perhaps it would be summer, even autumn before we got there. And I think that *next* spring will be too late. I think you have foreseen us travelling by a quicker but riskier method ... we will have to fly."

"To fly?" asked Bronn, startled. "There are legends that Sha'Lin'Tra could fly ... is it possible?"

"Yes, I could fly ... it was one of my great pleasures, one of the few things I really miss. It was not easy, even with the powers I had. Certainly, as a level one Witch I can't do it today, and even at the height of my powers I wouldn't have tried to carry myself, you, and what provisions we will need across the Northern Sea. But, there are other ways, and we might do it by balloon."

111

Bronn looked at her aghast. Every few years people tried new ways of making balloons work – the legend of ancient ballooners was persistent. The best ones, fabric lined with paper, could stay aloft for hours, though their cost was vast. Trials with oiled and waxed cloth had been made, but a few spectacular disasters had put an end to their popularity. To consider crossing the ocean in such a firetrap? His looks might have been enough, but Seers are good with words, and he spoke eloquently about his concerns.

Sheena smiled again, and said: "Seer Bronn, trust me – I am over nine hundred years old, and have flown balloons many times. I have never fallen into the ocean yet, and as a Fire Witch, if I'm prepared to take that risk with the cold, watery deeps, you should realize the risk is low. In any case, it is late, we will not fly tonight nor yet tomorrow, and Intira is tired. We should continue this discussion tomorrow. Though truth to tell, my mind is a-whirl with the thought of finding an Ice Witch, and I am fearful for my ability to sleep."

Intira nodded. "I am, as you say, tired. But I am fearful for my ability to sleep, too. However, I know my cause and my cure. I will not sleep tonight unless I see your treasure of books, get my hands on one of them, and begin to read. And yet, I know that once I start, most likely I will drift off in under an hour. I must ask, nay beg you, Sister Sheena, to take me to your hideaway, and let me choose something to read."

Sheena nodded. "It will be my duty and pleasure, Mother Superior. Seer Bronn, if you come with us, I will find you someone to guide you to your room. If you will, come here again tomorrow about the ninth hour, and we will discuss what must be done."

And so, they left. Sheena, no longer constrained by anonymity projected a soft light that lit the halls far

112

more effectively than the sparse lamps, and took Intira's arm to guide her. Bronn went to his room, prepared himself for sleep, and lay down on his bed. Mother Superior Intira might have to fight a battle between staying up to read the first words of the precious new store of knowledge that had been revealed to her, and Sheena, or Sha'Lin'Tra might have to balance her need for sleep with the eager anticipation of the re-awakening of a hopeless hope dormant across the centuries, but he, Bronn, knew he would sleep well tonight. The relief of having reached a crisis node and held the Vision, the relaxation of the psychic stress held so long was well known to all Seers of talent. Tomorrow might be the beginning of another stretch of difficult times with their own challenges, but he had met the needs of today. Nothing more was required of him right now. He fell asleep almost as his head hit the pillow, and passed an untroubled night of deeply restoring restfulness.

Two floors up and a hundred yards along, Mother Superior Intira also slept well, cradling in her arms a large, leather-bound volume with a fierce possessiveness and tender care normally reserved for a lover.

And further to the north in the castle, an ancient Fire Witch stayed awake far into the night, totally unbalanced from a calm serenity developed over hundreds of years, alternatively crying with her head in her hands, kneeling to pray with an expression of ecstatic thankfulness on her face and in her words, and hugging herself with a tremulous, hopeful anxiety that had not been a part of her emotional expression for a very long time. In the end, she sank into a troubled sleep, visited by dreams many a Seer would have been glad to have known, but which she was too disoriented to remember, despite training, experience and talent.

Chapter 5. Fire and Ice

Some say the world will end in fire,
Some say in ice.
From what I've tasted of desire
I hold with those who favor fire.
But if it had to perish twice,
I think I know enough of hate
To say that for destruction ice
Is also great
And would suffice.

Robert Frost

Bronn rose early, and breakfasted with the first sitting. Seemingly by chance, Satro was also at that sitting, though as he explained it, it was choice rather than chance. He had spent most of the previous day in an ecstasy of discovery, reading, questioning, and learning. But it had mostly been sedentary. It was not in his nature or training to neglect the physical side of life, and he had gotten up before dawn, run for miles, swum (despite it being winter) and done various routines of calisthenics, and of course gone through the various practice forms of the sword, and his favorite, the quarterstaff. He also admitted that several of the novices and younger Sisters had indicated that other physical activity was likely to be available if he was of a mind, and that he was not at all averse.

"So, all in all you are settling in quite happily here" Bronn remarked. Satro replied that indeed, the Hold was a realization of his dreams. The only lack was that there were few if any people there who could give him a serious workout on the practice floors, and while he could see himself living at Nun's Hold, to keep his skills on edge he would have to travel periodically to Warrior's Hold, or perhaps Fireland. Still, as he had said previously, he loved to travel on the sea, so it would not be a great hardship.

Bronn invited him to the meeting with Sheena. He told him only that Sheena was a Fire Witch, but limited in ability by a spell until certain conditions were met, but that she was the one he had been seeking. Although his Vision didn't see Satro continuing with them, a wise Seer knows he does not see everything, and things can change. Also, he valued Satro's wisdom and Warrior skills. They might have to deal with Ice Hold Tribes.

Intira was present as well. How could she deny herself the luxury of seeing how this saga would develop?

Bronn introduced Satro to Sheena. He shook her hand in greeting, and then his mouth fell open. Bronn had never seen him so perturbed – it would not be going too far to say he was shocked. For ten long seconds he looked at her, and then spoke, with wonder in his voice: "You have a strong grip. A fighter's grip. I would even say … no, I will hold judgment, for … it is not truly relevant here."

Sheena smiled, and they sat. She asked if Bronn had had any Vision of when they should best be on their way.

"I slept deeply" Bronn replied. "Yet in the early hours of this morning, I Saw mixed winds for two days, then clear weather for one. After that, I cannot say at the moment."

Intira added that she had consulted Sisters who specialized in weather observation and prediction, to much the same effect. They concluded that a couple of days for preparation should suffice, but everyone was keen to know what Sheena had in mind by way of a balloon.

"In my private hideaway, besides the many books, there are a few things I have gathered together that I thought might be useful, that were rare or even no longer reproducible. And one of them is a balloon made of this" she said, offering for their inspection a small offcut of a strange material. They examined it in turn.

Bronn felt it, marveling. It was smooth, smooth as silk, but with a finer weave. In fact ... he examined it more closely. It had no weave at all! And strong! He pulled it as hard as he could, to no effect. He passed it to Satro, who applied his own considerable strength, and was able to make the material give, which it did reluctantly, by pulling on one edge. Finally, he asked- "what *is* it?"

Sheena replied, "It's an artificial cloth, made by Ice Witches. They spun it by their magic, which is highly creative, out of oil. They rearrange ... I don't know how to put it. They rearrange the basic nature of the oil, the smallest parts that it can be divided into, and join them together, and cross-link the threads they make, to fashion long sheets of it, optimally aligned for strength. It is hard to describe – I know the words in technical Ice Witch talk. Perhaps the library has the knowledge somewhere to describe what I mean, better."

"Sheets of this were sewn together with thread of the same material, and the seams sealed the same way. The upper half of the balloon was somewhat stronger, to take the strain, and the mouth sealed with very flame resistant material to minimize the likelihood of fire. Balloons like this can hold hot air for hours, and rise above the highest peaks."

116

Intira asked: "And the material is still sound? No natural cloth could last the hundreds of years since it was made." She was careful not to say "since you have had this" as they had not told Satro her true nature.

Sheena nodded. "No insect can eat this fabric. It is prone to decay if exposed to the sun for too long – over a period of months – but it has been sealed away in an almost airtight box. Under such conditions, it would last thousands of years. It will take only the two of us and our immediate needs, but I know that if we rise high enough there will be winds to drive us to Iceland, and across it. I don't know what good that will do, for I've been there before and I would swear there's nothing there, but I trust Seer Bronn's Vision."

Satro stirred. "And will it bring you back?" he asked.

Sheena shook her head. "Not if we find Bronn's Ice Witch – the balloon would not lift three. Not unless we dumped everything we could of any weight, and she was very light. And not at this time of the year. Not unless we care to try going around the world, which would be a mighty adventure. We'll have to rely on someone here arranging a ship. By the time we fight our way back across Iceland, which will take several weeks, it should be possible for one to get there in late spring."

Satro questioned again: "When you say fight your way across, you mean … ?"

Sheena replied: "Ice. Snow. Winds in our faces." Bronn shuddered. Just as he had foreseen. "And yes, perhaps, truly fight. The last time I was there, the Hold tribe was not very friendly. It would be better if we didn't meet them."

"Hmm" Satro replied. "Perhaps I should come with you after all ... no, impossible, as you say there is only room for two. How will you fight a whole Tribe if you meet one? And I must ask, for this is my area of expertise, where I can help you the most. Seer Bronn could fight at a pinch, and has a fine firestaff. But I'd like to know more about your capabilities, Sister Sheena ... or should I say, Sha'Lin'Tra?"

Sheena turned to Bronn, but before she could say anything, he spoke: "No, I didn't tell him, nor did Intira. He must have worked it out for himself."

Sheena looked at him, and asked "How could you know?"

Satro said, wonderingly. "So, it is true! I thought there could be no other explanation, strange though the thought is. You have a private storeroom in the Hold. You have things from the ancient past, a balloon made by Ice Witches. Seer Bronn spoke of finding a powerful Fire Witch hiding here, unusual though that would be. And you've been to Iceland, to Ice Hold itself, and met the Tribes. We Warriors do tend to focus mainly on our own particular areas of skill, but we would have known of any such expedition in recent times. And ... you are a trained Warrior! Not someone trained by a Warrior away from the Hold, trained in the Hold itself! I knew as soon as I tested your hand and your strength. But Warrior's Hold has not trained a woman for hundreds of years."

Sheena nodded her head down, and raised it again and looked at her hand, as if to try to see what Satro had discovered. "Yes, that's true. You have done well; most people would dismiss the idea as impossible despite the evidence you saw".

She gave Satro a brief synopsis of her history, reasons, and current limitations, leaving out a lot he didn't need to know.

"And, as to your question, I gained the rank of Red Warrior. I have done my best to keep my skills up to par, but it's not easy in Nun's Hold, nor as a woman. Mostly, it's been actual combat when travelling and someone tried to rob me – or worse - rather than proper practice."

Satro nodded. "Red. Well, good – better than Bronn could have hoped for, of course. My mind is a bit easier, but still, I doubt you'll have an easy time of it."

Bronn queried – "Red? I don't think I've heard of that grade. What does it mean?"

"It means that the trainee has passed Orange, the minimum grade, and has mastered the skills for Bronze, but does not meet all the physical requirements of that grade. It's very rarely awarded – usually to someone who was an outstanding student and would have passed easily, but was seriously injured in training. There's another, after Bronze, for someone who aspires to Silver but can't quite make it – Green. It's not often seen outside the Hold, because most often the person can't be fully effective; usually they are offered a teaching position. It recognizes their achievements and gives them status in the Hold."

Sheena replied, "Yes, though in my case it wasn't an injury. It was just that my form was too slight to hold enough muscle to meet the raw physical strength requirements. I'm more agile than most, and my skills are good, and pound for pound I was as strong as any but there were simply not enough pounds on my frame. They told me that this would most likely be the case, but encouraged me to continue past Orange as, of course, they like to see any student achieve to their ability. I think they expected me to take a teaching position."

She paused for a moment. "You wanted to know my skill level, Satro. Well, you are a part of this group, and Bronn and Intira already know this. Some time after graduating, I used magic to alter my body. I altered the basic structure of my muscles, and am now quite a bit stronger than I was. Not as strong as you, I'm not much over half your weight, and there is a limit to what bone and sinew can do, but not too far short, I think. If I went to Warrior's Hold, and they were prepared to test me, I would have little problem qualifying for Bronze, I believe."

Satro grinned. "That is good to hear" he replied. "Of course, while one's own evaluations are important – a Warrior should always know their own capabilities – there's nothing like an independent opinion to give one true confidence. I would be very pleased to stand with you on the practice floor before you and Seer Bronn go."

Sheena rose and bowed, and replied "I would be honored, of course, Bronze Master."

She sat again, and said, "Now, to the business of travel. We seem agreed we will start in three days. Early in the morning is best, very early, before dawn, to get the most travel in the light hours of the day. Of course, we'll travel full time – we won't come down at night; there's only one tiny island in the sea on our route, and that very close to the Iceland. The balloon can carry both of us, and we should take observing in six hour shifts. We will take warm clothing, food, water – plenty of it there, for we shall take it as ballast – weapons, and little more, mostly a few items to help us in the cold lands, and various bits of equipment for determining our position. We can't take everything I'd like – or even everything I think we'll need, there just isn't room, nor the lifting capacity in the balloon. It will only hold a certain amount of hot air."

Bronn stirred. "I don't understand that part. It seems to me that however much we fill the balloon up with hot air when we start, it must cool fairly quickly. How will we carry enough fuel to keep it aloft for ... how many days?"

Sheena replied: "We must allow for three full days, though I hope to do it in under two, and the winds are usually reliable at the height we will rise to. But as to heat, I have a container of highly volatile liquid and a burner designed to fill the balloon, but that's really for emergencies, and if I'm tired. Under ordinary circumstances, the heat will come from me. I am a Fire Witch, after all."

Bronn's face cleared. "Oh, of course. But ... forgive me, can a level one Witch truly put out that much energy? Our companion, on the voyage over, was hard pressed to charge my firestaff up much, and she tired easily. That is, I'm sure you know what you are doing, but I've no more desire to end this quest in a cold, watery grave in the middle of the ocean than you do, I'm sure."

Sheena smiled again, and Bronn mused that she had surely done a workmanlike job with her Witch crew those hundreds of years ago, it was a truly lovely smile. Satro, not knowing those details, just privately thought her dimples should be outlawed.

But when she spoke, it was all business. "Well, Seer Bronn, I have to say you're mostly right. I'm self-limited to the abilities of a level one Fire Witch, but the energies that burn in my soul are much higher. It's a bit like walking and running. An ordinary person might be able to walk all day, jog for hours, but run at full speed for only a few minutes. And, the difference might not be so great – running at full speed might be only a little faster than a jog. And so it is with me. I can't do much more than your companion Witch, Trina her name is, I think, can do – but what would tire her out in a few minutes, I can do for much longer, and enough of it while resting to keep the balloon afloat. I hope. But if not, I'm sure that I can stay awake for long enough to ensure we reach land."

And so it was. A few senior Nuns were taken into confidence, more or less. Intira, with Sheena's blessing, updated a scroll to be read on her death, detailing all the knowledge and the location of Sheena's store room. There was only a small chance she might die in the next few months, but to lose that Knowledge was not a chance she could take. The various needs were all gathered together – Sheena was quite impressed that Bronn's Vision had been accurate enough to size her cold weather clothing well enough to fit her with only a few alterations. Sheena and Satro spent many hours on the practice floor: Sheena was keen to pick up new techniques, and Satro fascinated by how effective some of the older ones that had fallen out of favor were. He nearly always won with the quarterstaff, his favorite, and Sheena often won with the sword. Hand to hand they were fairly evenly matched – Satro was quite a bit stronger, but Sheena was faster.

Nun's Hold had many practical people, for knowledge can be theoretical or knowledge about the world. Sheena found someone who knew a lot about firestaffs, and took Bronn and his for evaluation. The Nun – a courtesy title as it was actually a man – gave a low whistle as Bronn presented it. "Hell-lo! What have we here! Oh, I'd like to have this in my collection!"

Sheena smiled, and said, "Yes, it's a beauty no doubt. A Kil'Ton'Ra I think, Tonno?"

The man pursed his lips. "Well, you know something about firestaffs, I think. But that's never a Kil'Ton'Ra. Where's the stippling on the release band? No, it's a Shi'Ri'Tra, I think, though the wood's a bit dark ... no, maybe made by Shi'Ra'Tra, her daughter? She made some fine staff."

"I don't think so" Sheena mused. "It's a three level staff. She really only did two levels."

"Three levels?" he marveled. With a practiced twist he opened the inspection chamber, and whistled again. "They don't make them like this any more" he said. "Look at that wiring! Solid silver, and thick, too. They'd use silver plated copper these days, to cut costs and corners – if there was a Witch able to make them, of course. And those rubies! Massive, and flawless! I didn't think there was a working level three staff left in the world!"

He paused, thinking. "I tell you what this is, I think ... this is a Mal'Ta'Shra custom job, with aftermarket modifications. The size of those rubies gives it away."

Sheena pursed her lips. "Do you really think so? They're pretty rare, aren't they?"

"Rare? I should say so. I've only ever heard about two before, and neither in working condition – rubies burned out and cracked. But it's easy to tell – there should be a plaque at the back – look, there it is."

Sheena nodded. "Oh yes, I see! Mal'Ta'Shra was one of the best, you're really lucky, Bronn."

"Yes indeed. Worth a fortune to a collector as it stands. We could build a better one today with those rubies if

123

we stripped the parts out, but this is a classic. You want me to tune it up? I can do that, though of course without the right Witch I can't make a new one. My dream is that within my lifetime, someone with the skill to sensitize the rubies will be born. Still, not our problem today. Our problem is your staff: What are you going to do with it?"

"We are going to use it – fine piece of work though it is, it's a tool for us."

Tonno winced. "Well, needs must, of course. If I could have a couple of days, I'll re-polish the rubies and true any facets – we've got much better equipment than they had. That'll help prevent burnout. I'll bore out the shaft and put in a long rod of top quality garnet from a light-staff I've got – I've got a contact, a Witch on Fireland who can sensitize garnet; that can hold charge just as well, though it can only trickle out. Still, that would give you two shots at full power, though you'd need a ten minute pause to let the garnet recharge the rubies. I'll add an alternate release, here, Bronn, so you can use the light function – it'll act as a torch, though for emergency use only; for although I'll tune it up and recharging will be easier, it'll still be a long job."

Intira and Satro spoke about the best way to get a ship organized to meet Bronn and Sheena at the southern end on Iceland after the sea-ice had melted and travel was possible. Intira said that she could release some of the Hold's gold to help, and Sheena said she had a local cache of coins that would help a lot too. Satro said he would be happy to stay on Nun's Hold for two or three weeks, and then make his way over to Warrior's Hold for a bit of training, to keep his skills up to par. He could look around for their young Gold Warrior too, not that he held out much hope, but it would be far easier to find a ship to do the journey to

Iceland there, at a major port rather than a transit harbor like Nun's Hold. They agreed on a planned meeting time of two months.

The days passed, the weather settled, and before they knew it, they were on one of the high yards of the castle, sheltered from what little wind there was. Not shivering in the pre-dawn chill, for there was a roaring fire in a big boiler, heating the air above it and all around it. That had been going on for some time, and the balloon was starting to take shape. Sheena decided it was all going too slowly, and exerted her own powers. Muttering the words used to aid specific concentration, which many mistook for spells, she projected pure heat over the broad mouth of the filling funnel. Everyone else backed off as it became too hot for comfort, the balloon began visibly to swell faster, and in ten minutes was fully supporting its own weight, and in only a few more it was straining at the ropes.

Sheena muttered to herself: "Phew! I must be out of practice! I wouldn't like to have to do *that* all day!" In response to Bronn's alarmed concern that she might well have to, she reassured him that it was mostly a matter of practice. Higher levels of Witchcraft used different and more effective techniques that were harder to master, but which she was no longer able to use. What with one thing and another, she had not needed to do a simple high-volume heat spell since before the days when she ruled the world, but in any case, once aloft she would not have to do it anywhere near so forcefully.

Bronn clambered awkwardly into the basket, which was just large enough for one to stand and one to curl up for a sleep, or both to stand comfortably. Most of their gear was strapped on the sides, or even below. He reached a hand out and clasped Satro's in friendship, while Intira blessed their vessel, their quest, and Sheena by giving her a kiss on both cheeks. Sheena vaulted easily into the basket, the holding knots were released and the balloon rose quickly in the cold morning air.

The castle, with the roaring fire, faded away below them, and everything became quite dark. Bronn had an uneasy feeling that perhaps it was better so; he was unsure of how he would have taken to the sight of the earth falling away below them. Even now, though there was no physical way of sensing it, he still had a queasy feeling of nothingness below his boots. He gulped, and held onto the railing just a bit more firmly, just in case the floor suddenly gave way. It quickly became colder, and he was glad he was well dressed in his snow gear – Sheena had said he would need it. Perhaps it would be a bit warmer when the sun came up – as they rose, he could see some signs of the glimmering dawn to their left, as the castle slowly fell away in front of them.

Hang on. The sun was rising on the left. The castle was in front of them – he could still just see the fire. That meant ... "Sheena! We're going backwards! We need to change direction, and go north!"

Reassuringly, Sheena's voice spoke from just two feet away. "It's all fine, Bronn. The wind is blowing south, down here. But as we get higher up, we will get into another wind, which will be blowing north. Not to worry."

Bronn worried, anyway. "Um. How *much* higher?"

"Not too high. A few thousand feet. No more than ten at the most, at this time of year I should think."

Bronn thought sadly of the cold. He knew how it got colder as one went up the mountains. He was already dressed very warmly, but wondered if he should have gone all out and worn everything he could.

As the balloon rose, Sheena continued to pour heat into it, though at a lower rate than when they were launching. Bronn wondered where the heat was coming from. It couldn't be coming from a normal biological process, otherwise Sheena would have to eat her own weight in food every couple of hours. Since they were standing together in the quiet dark, with nothing to do but wait for the sunrise, he asked. She explained that though she did have to use some energy to make things happen, and would eat far more than normally, most of the work was moving energy from one place to another.

There were rules, or rather, laws. Some things could be done with transferred energy, but some things had to be done with energy from within. Easy to learn when young, to do it with something like a candle that was close by. Then, with refinement, to do it with things further and further away. She explained that while Levels of Fire Witch attainment were most easily judged by the number of Avatars a Witch could project (up to level three, anyway), true ability lay in the ratio of internal energy expenditure to external energy result, and the techniques used to do it. Usually, the two went together as the balancing skills necessary were closely related. Rarely, someone might be able to project two Avatars but be poor in energy skills, or vice-versa, but it was very rarely indeed. What most people called spells were no more than verbal ritual to guide the mind in the appropriate channels and ways. That was why Ungifted folk could speak the spells till they were blue in the face, with no result. And past level two, Witches didn't usually bother with the words.

Most Fire Witches used a connection with one or more of the volcanoes in Fireland. Somewhere, she explained, a small patch of lava was cooling a bit more quickly than it otherwise would, and a bit of air in the balloon was heating up.

"I don't suppose you could heat *me* up a bit" Bronn grumbled. Sheena replied that she could, but it was a very hard thing to judge. It was all too easy to overdo it, and broil the person. It was a last resort sort of thing; it took tremendous control and concentration to do it just right, and that meant generating a lot of the energy herself, rather than using external sources. The easiest way to do it would be if they had a fire close by them. "But then, of course, you could just move a bit closer to the fire yourself, and the whole thing would be unnecessary" Bronn replied. Sheena agreed that sometimes the simplest ways were best. She added that Ice Witches were much better at the fine control of personal magic, a survival mechanism – they could usually manage with only simple clothing, walking in the snow perfectly comfortably.

The dawn broke unnaturally quickly, because they were still rising. Soon, the balloon and then the basket were in the redness of the morning sun. The land below was still dark. Or, more correctly, the water below, because they had been blown well to the south. Ahead of them, they could see the mountains of Nun's Hold lit up by the rising sun. Bronn could see they were still far higher than the balloon.

They could see the light creeping across the water to the west of them. While Bronn was inexperienced with flight, Sheena was not, and told him that they were now in a still zone of air, and still climbing. Soon, she expected to hit the northbound air stream, and even Bronn would know when they did – the balloon would tend to be pushed forward above them until they reached the same speed as the airstream. Sheena used a compass to see where they were pointing. She frowned, and said that they had been pushed west a little, but not too badly. She hoped, though, that they would not be pushed much further, or would encounter something with a bit of an easterly component. Still, there was plenty of time for that.

Bronn guessed they had been aloft for about a quarter of an hour, and were now half as high as the peaks. He had long since surrendered to the cold and pulled the flaps of his hat over his ears, buttoned everything up that could be, found and wrapped a scarf around his neck, and in short covered everything that could be covered. The only thing exposed was his eyes. He was already becoming miserable. Sheena was not wrapped up as much as he was, and he asked how she could stand it. She replied that the work she was doing was like exercise, and heated her up quite a lot. She said that she had never flown with anyone who wasn't a Witch – Fire or Ice – and had not really properly considered how cold it would be for a pure passenger.

She looked at Bronn thoughtfully, and then changed her stance. Bronn could see her concentrating, and felt the immediate surroundings getting a bit warmer. Sheena relaxed with a sigh, and explained that what she had done was to heat the basket. Being dead cane, and made as fireproof as the Nuns could make it, it didn't matter if she heated it a few tens of degrees more than she intended. The hard part was not heating things that didn't need it, such as food and Bronn. It certainly helped, for about ten minutes, but then things started to cool down again. Reluctantly, they both agreed, Bronn would have to haul in the bag with their warmest clothes and put on everything he could. It would make it even more crowded in the basket, but keep him alive.

By the time he had done so, the sun was shining full into the basket, bright but not really very warming yet. Dawn had just come to the water below, and to Nun's Hold, only barely visible now a long way to their north. Sheena returned to keeping the air in the balloon hot, and the craft rising, while Bronn looked out in wonder at the blue ocean all around them. There was really too little variation, too little to see for him to feel vertigo – their situation was so strange that there were no reference points for his brain to attach to. The sun became brighter and brighter, and the constant reflection off the water started to hurt his eyes. Sheena noticed, and rummaged in her own bag, bringing out two pairs of glasses, like large reading glasses but dark. He put them on, to his great relief. Not only did it make the sun bearable, but in some strange way they almost completely cut out the reflections from the waves far below.

He asked Sheena how they worked, but did not really understand her explanation, that light vibrated horizontally in all directions, but the waves tended to reflect vibrations in one plane only, and there were stretched crystals in the lenses that stopped transmission of the light in that plane. "Relics from a past age" she smiled. "The frame and the lenses are made from a similar substance to the balloon, from oil, by Ice Witches. I know how to make similar lenses from certain crystals from Fire Island, but it's much harder. So much lost, the skills if not the knowledge, that this quest may return."

As she spoke, Bronn felt the balloon lurch. The basket tipped forward to the north for a little while, and he felt an icy wind blowing, which slowed and then stopped as they rose into the fast blowing air, and quickly were blown up to the same speed. Sheena nodded with satisfaction. She leaned over the basket, and tried to make out their heading, but it wasn't easy. She threw her hand down and released a narrow jet of fire that went down, far down, little flickers of red aura flaming about her as she did. The jet flamed red and blossomed in to a fireball, below the level of the northerly wind. She watched as the balloon rode on, then went to the back of the basket and observed the remnants of the fireball and its smoke, and finally gave her opinion. "Pretty much straight north, as far as I can see" she said, more to herself. "We've been blown a bit off course coming south. Nothing to worry about yet, we've got over a day to correct it."

She relaxed a bit, though Bronn could see her concentrate every few minutes, pumping heat into the envelope. Sheena explained that they were not at their ceiling, but there was no call to go that high. It would be hard enough to cope with the cold and thin air at their present height for the days it would take for them to cross the northern ocean. "As I explained, I use up quite a bit of energy doing this work, and I'll need to eat regularly. And from the look of you, Bronn, you wouldn't say no to some warm soup, I suspect." Bronn agreed that it would be nice, but said that he could see no way it could be done.

"That's quite easy" Sheena replied. "The soup is over there, in that waterbag" she said, pointing to one of the ballast containers, made of course of the same material as the balloon. "It will last a good long time up here in this cold, but no reason not to use it. Dip a pan in it – you can undo the top – and fill that boiler, and bring it to me. Then, find two cups."

Bronn fiddled with the ballast container for some time, but eventually figured out how to open it. It was sealed with a kind of watertight seal that could be opened or closed by pulling a tag around the top. He stirred the soup up with a spoon he found, and scooped a good amount out into the thin saucepan as requested, and resealed the top. He passed the boiler to Sheena, and found two mugs, thin hammered tin for lightness, enameled on the outside and painted in pleasing patterns. Sheena was holding the saucepan by the handle, with her other hand underneath it, frowning in concentration. Finally, she slowly opened the hand underneath the boiler, and Bronn could see the soup was starting to heat. Surprisingly quickly, it began to bubble, and Sheena stopped whatever she was doing, and poured soup into each mug. It was a bit too hot to eat, but Bronn happily held it between his two gloves, and let the warmth flow into his cold hands.

Bronn asked Sheena if she knew how high up they were. Sheena looked over at a small instrument on the basket, and said they were 10,355 feet up in the air, far higher than balloonists normally went on a pleasure ride. She added that she did not have an instrument to tell how fast they were going, but they were going north quite a bit faster than they went south, perhaps sixty miles an hour. Assuming the wind kept blowing at the same speed, which it might, and they were lucky enough to travel in a dead straight line right over the Hold, which they probably wouldn't, and she was prepared to let the balloon fly north in the dark all the second night, which she certainty wasn't, they could be at Iceland in a little over two full days, but would have to come back down out of the wind and hover in the dark as best they could, with the aid of the moon to see by. Sheena explained that Ice Hold was right on the northern most tip of Iceland, and there was no way they would be travelling north all night. They might see the next dawn and find they had overshot the end of the island, and as far as anyone knew there was no other land this side of the pole, and no-one knew what was on the other side, and she didn't care to find out.

By now, they had been blown back to their starting point, though perhaps ten miles to the west, and Bronn looked down on Nun's Hold in awe. The mountains of Seers Island looked out over marshes and plains, and there were few high observation points. Seeing the checkered fields laid out neatly below, the dock with two tiny ships looking like chips of wood, the vastness of the castle reduced to the size of a model was a unique experience for him. The balloon was a cheerful red and white in color, but they were so high up that Bronn doubted anyone would see them. The mountains mostly looked like brown corrugations in a field of white, except for the three main peaks, which towered up and up, nearly to their present height, though Bronn could see they would clear them by a comfortable margin. Despite the cold, which had been temporarily pushed back a bit by the excellent soup now warming his insides, Bronn mused, this was without doubt the most pleasant part of the quest so far. The silence, the land drifting past below, the feeling of being on top of the world.

Sheena had another cup of soup, and then another, and then a large slab of bread, with butter, and a thick piece of ham, and a substantial piece of cheese. She washed it all down with a whole bottle of wine. She offered some to Bronn, who shuddered a bit, it was way too early for him, though he did take some bread and cheese. Sheena explained that the alcohol was useful fuel, and the nature of her altered body and metabolism was that she could pretty much drink wine all day long without becoming intoxicated. But she had to eat like this to refuel her internal energy, which was being burned up at a prodigious rate to drive the energy transfer that heated the balloon.

They watched as Nun's Island drifted by in the very early light. They were well to the west of the Hold itself, and past the cultivated areas, and into steep hills and valleys with rocky slopes well covered in bushes, grass and trees – a lot of rain fell there as clouds dropped excess moisture upon being forced over the mountains by the prevailing winds. There was also a fairly significant river, which drained naturally to the east, and a somewhat smaller one which ran due south to the Hold and was used to water the fields, and supplied the Hold itself by way of a finely constructed viaduct.

Within twenty minutes, they approached the slopes of the westernmost mountain. Soon, the land was close enough below that Bronn could see some of the inhabitants, mostly hardy, sure footed mountain goats who could climb just about anything other than a vertical cliff face, and once a rather splendid large cat, whose big paws and strong claws helped it to climb almost as well, though it could run much faster for short distances. Although it hunted the goats and could catch one every now and then, mostly it subsisted on the large, fat rabbits that lived on the beautifully lush grass. People on the island sometimes hunted the cats if they had a population burst, but not otherwise because if they did, the rabbits would take over. Sometimes, there were too many rabbits, and then the hunters culled them. Man acted as a better balance than a boom and bust population cycle in both species, and the fur of both creatures was highly valued, being very warm and beautiful. The goats were mostly left to their own devices, as they were hard to catch, made poor leather, were practically inedible unless they were stewed for hours, and far too bad tempered for domestication.

The slope rushed up and up. They were pushed slightly to the east, as the wind funneled between the western and the middle peaks of the Three Sages. It was only a small course correction, but still useful. Finally, they were over, clearing the valley by over two thousand feet, and the peaks by several hundred. A few goats noticed them, but were clearly not very impressed by the tiny red dot drifting past in the sky. The wind kept the snow swirling at this height, over a base of hard packed ice that melted reluctantly during the summer, and never completely. A half-hearted glacier wound its way down the valley, melting well above the ground level, splitting into two tongues to feed the two rivers.

And then they were over, and could see the much steeper northern face of the mountains, in the rain shadow. Almost bare rock, too steep even for the goats, and descending almost to the sea. If one wanted to walk around the island, which was just possible, at that point it was best to walk on the relatively flat beaches and reefs exposed by low tide. A few miles drifting took them over to the sea again, and that, Sheena remarked, was that. No significant land now for six hundred or so miles. The wind had slackened off after coming past the island. She said that it might be as low as fifty miles per hour now, perhaps less. They would be hard pressed to make land before nightfall, and there would be little to see, though for the sake of safety, someone should be on watch at all times. She added they could rise even higher, for the balloon was not at its limit, but it would be even colder, and become hard to breath. Bronn quickly replied he would take his chances with the dark.

He also wondered, if there was no land between where they were and Iceland, what they had to keep watch for. Sheena's reply was brief and succinct: "storms."

Bronn did not know all that much about ballooning, but anyone with an ounce of imagination would wince at the thought of this fragile craft in the middle of rain, lightning and gusting winds. Sheena said that since she had to stay awake to keep feeding heat into the envelope above them, she would take first watch. Bronn could lie down and rest, even fall asleep if he wanted. It would be warmer, because he could wrap himself in a blanket, and wrap that in a swathe of spare balloon fabric, which would make it airtight. Bronn had to reply that rest wasn't what was becoming uppermost in his concerns. When he mentioned his issue to Sheena, she replied that it was an easy one to solve. There was a seat, and a bucket lined with a bag of the same material. The other occupant of the balloon would simply look over at the horizon, which would have to do for modesty. Once done, the bag was simply dropped over the side, with a weight in it so it would sink in the ocean.

Bronn settled down in the bottom of the basket, and was able to get properly warm for the first time in hours. Although he wasn't expecting it, the silence broken only by a few gentle noises from the basket and a slight swaying motion was hypnotic, and he drifted off to a dreamless sleep.

He woke several hours later, ravenously hungry. Sheena told him he had slept nearly four hours, and it was past midday. He rose, a little stiffly, and they repeated the soup heating exercise, and Sheena ate another enormous meal washed down with another full bottle of wine, while Bronn ate a more moderate amount, consistent with his relative lack of activity.

Sheena then sat down at ease in the bottom of the basket, and rested somewhat, though of course she could not sleep. Bronn stood and watched the horizon, glad of the sleep as the watching would zone out anyone who was not alert. It was really very pleasant. The sun was now high in the sky and no longer shone in their eyes, being shielded above by the balloon. The air was a little warmer, and some heat radiated down

136

from the balloon itself. Bronn even stripped off a couple of layers.

The sky was no longer clear, and often Bronn saw thunderclouds and storms off to one side. Several times, they went over low-lying clouds, and Bronn got to see clouds from the top for the first time in his life. He gazed at them, spellbound, for ages.

And so, the day passed, uneventfully. Like walking or riding, Bronn soon got used to the balloon, and slept several times, though he did spend quite a bit of time talking to Sheena, and just looking.

Two six hour watches saw the day nearly over, even though they got a bit more light at altitude. It soon started to cool down again, and Sheena said Bronn should take the first evening and night watch, so she could take the second when it was really cold. She took the balloon down, to keep it just in the current of wind going north, and they ate a hearty meal (or at least, Sheena did) and settled in for the night.

Bronn fairly quickly started putting on all of his gear again, but managed reasonably well. Still, he was glad when his watch was over, and settled in to the bottom of the basket, wrapped up and with only a small breathing hole exposed. He slept soundly and easily, despite the almost eerie silence.

Sheena let him sleep well into the next morning, it was already starting to warm up when physical needs forced Bronn awake and up.

Sheena told him she had used an instrument to see how much they had drifted. She said, they had gone a fair bit to the west, and throughout the rest of the day she periodically took the balloon up or down looking for a correcting cross-current, without much luck. As the day slowly faded, she said "I can't see us missing Iceland, but I wouldn't be surprised if we had to walk a bit to get to the Hold, at the moment."

Just as the sun swung low enough to clear the edge of the balloon, setting to the south of west, Bronn was sure he saw a dark patch on the horizon. He called Sheena's attention to it, and she nodded. "That's Iceland, sure enough. And, by my reckoning, about a hundred and eighty miles away, or three hours, maybe a bit less. And, my best guess, the sun will set in three hours, maybe a bit more. It will be a close thing."

Bronn was relieved. He said that if they were close enough to land at sunset, all they had to do was go on a bit, and they could then descend, and be sure of landing on solid ground. Sheena shook her head. "Or a tree, or a river, or on rough terrain, or deep snow, or the middle of a Hold Tribe. I want to be able to see where I'm landing, because I want to be able to take off again in the morning. If I can't, we'll hover. Otherwise, we'd have to slog it over the whole length of Iceland, and that's not much fun in winter. Doing it once on the way back will be bad enough. Of course, I can cast fire downwards, and that will give some light. Quite a lot of light, in fact, if I use the right spell, but still a tricky proposition of balancing. Or, there's the moon. But in truth, that's not the thing that is worrying me most, at the moment."

Bronn made the natural inquiry, and Sheena pointed. "That" she said, succinctly, pointing to the west and north. Bronn had to shield his eyes a bit, but he could see another dark patch on the horizon. "What is it – is that Peace Island?" he hazarded, referring to the outlying and northernmost island of the Warrior's group. Sheena shook her head. "Too far away. No, that's a storm, a biggish though localized one, and it is travelling due east." She paused. "My guess is, it will

138

hit the southern end of Iceland in about three hours ... perhaps more, if we are lucky."

Bronn looked at the two dark patches, the balloon, and Sheena. "I ... I saw us travelling in relatively calm weather" he mused.

Sheena nodded. "I hope your vision is correct, Bronn. And what sort of weather did you see us landing in?"

Bronn shook his head. "I never saw us landing at all, in my dreams. But ... I did see us travelling at a great height, the whole of Iceland laid out before us as if from a great height. I do hope that was prophetic, and not just a probability dream ..."

Sheena nodded again. "And so do I, Bronn. So do I."

They waited tensely, the minutes ticking by. Then, because no-one can stay in that state while nothing much happens, they perforce relaxed a bit. Sheena poured more heat into the balloon, lifting it two thousand feet higher, nearly to its limit, trying to find quicker moving air. Bronn really felt the lowered air pressure and the cold, and within half an hour was feeling dizzy and had to sit down and wrap himself up. Sheena became concerned, and lowered them a thousand or so feet, which helped a lot.

Over two hours passed, and Iceland was now clearly visible as a grey and white featureless plain, stretching off into the distance. Sheena explained that the featureless look was misleading, there were plenty of hills and valleys about a two thousand feet high in places, to make the going difficult. Sheena estimated they were about a hundred miles away, and hoped they would make it, though it would mean landing in the dark or twilight – although the storm was obviously closer on their left.

Suddenly, the basket gave a lurch to the right. Sheena blanched, and looked ahead, to the right, and the left, and then said "I was afraid of that. The wind driving that storm has caught up with us. It's just the forefront – where the clouds start, it will be much stronger. But it's enough to blow us off course. I don't know by how much, but I think we'll be thankful for the wind that blew us to the west during the day."

She sighted using an instrument unfamiliar to Bronn, tracking their movement against a small island a little to their right, and ahead. She explained this was one of the five tiny outlying islands off the south coast of Iceland, called The Toes.

After half an hour, even Bronn's untrained eye could see that they were drifting east at a fairly high speed. Sheena bit her lip, and turned to Bronn. "There is a hope, but it's dangerous. We're not going to make it to the mainland" she said. "The wind will blow us along the shoreline, which extends to the east and north. But we will end up several miles offshore, going north and east in the dark, in a storm. Our only hope is to try to land on Big Toe and weather the storm, and it's not a very big target to hit. Fortunately, the light will last till we get there, or miss it. Bronn ... I'm going to do my best, but it won't be easy. If I get us both killed trying, ... I'm sorry."

Bronn grinned, with gallows humor. "That's allright Sheena, I know you'll do your best. I forgive you in advance, if that happens."

Sheena nodded. "Thanks, Bronn, I appreciate that. Now, I need to show you how to use the emergency ascent and descent. We have perhaps fifteen minutes."

She explained how a cord, when pulled, would release hot air and the balloon would go down. And how a

140

burner attached to a cylinder of gas would boost the balloon with far more heat than she could put out – for a short amount of time, no more than ten minutes. She asked Bronn to be careful with it, there was no way of refilling it anywhere in the world. She would look over the side, and call to Bronn when to release air or boost.

She asked him to look over the side. Big Toe was clearly visible to the right and ahead, though in the fading light and at their height it looked small and dark. She asked his opinion about whether he thought they were heading straight for it, and agreed when he thought they were going faster forward than sideways.

She pulled the release cord, and lowered the balloon several thousand feet, out of the northerly stream, but still in the westerly wind from the storm, and held them there for several minutes, and then rose again. After five more minutes, she judged they were almost parallel with the island, and got Bronn to practice releasing air. They dropped five thousand feet in a few minutes. The sun was now nearly on the horizon, and the storm not far to the west, but Sheena had judged it beautifully. Bronn could see the wind was now driving them almost due east, rising in intensity as they dropped. Bronn reckoned they would just float over the island and land in the sea beyond, at their current rate, and said as much to Sheena.

She nodded, and replied "Landing at this speed would be a disaster. I've never been to Big Toe, but I have heard it described. There are a few rises in the middle – foothills, hah! and I plan to try to land in the lee of them."

They descended steadily, Sheena occasionally calling for release of air, occasionally boosting the balloon herself. As the land approached, she turned on the gas from the cylinder, and lit the pilot flame with a quick gesture of one hand. She got Bronn to try it out. He pulled the cord, and a huge jet of flame sprang up above their heads with a mighty roar. He could feel the balloon lift.

The ground was rushing past below them now, perhaps forty miles an hour and a few hundred feet below. He saw mostly grass, few trees, which was good. Before he knew it, they were approaching the slopes of the hills, and Sheena called "Boost!." He released the flame, and Sheena added her own fire. Then, "Stop!" and a few seconds later, "Boost again! Hard!" Bronn held the cord down, and the fire roared into the balloon. Slowly, too slowly it rose – he could see they were not going to clear the cairn of broken granite that topped the ridge.

But somehow, they did. The wind flowed up, over the crest, and took them with it. Sheena cried, "Yes!" with relief.

However, there really wasn't all that much island left, and it was going past with some speed as they passed the receding slopes on the other side of the hill. "Down!" Sheena shouted. "I mean, release! Release! No, not that much!" she cried as Bronn overdid the air release. "Boost! Boost!" The ground rushed up at them again, and once more the flame roared overhead. "Stop!"

And finally, they seemed stable. They were clearly still descending, but the hills were dropping away to sea level, too, and their ground speed was dropping rapidly. As the last bit of light faded, blocked out by the coming storm, Sheena dropped them down to the ground, and, shielded by the hills, they were being blown along at little more than a fast walk. It was still going to be a bumpy landing.

It was impossible to see anything. But Sheena had an answer to that too, she projected an Avatar which jumped out of the balloon and down to the snow. Sheena's skill meant it could independently cast light, which it did as it ran, oh so fast, over the snow.

Sheena lowered the snow anchors. Shaped like ploughshares, they were designed to ride through the snow about a foot down, neither rising nor sinking, but providing a lot of drag. It couldn't have worked on bare ground, of course – that would have been an uncomfortable landing indeed. But they were attached to the load ropes rather than the basket, and although the gondola was tilted off the vertical as the balloon slowly came to a halt, things were not too bad. Both Bronn and Sheena did their best to keep the basket upright, and the snow out. Sheena pulled the air release vent to full open, and the balloon sank to the ground. They were down.

But not done. Sheena had explained that they would have to get out and secure the balloon; otherwise the wind would blow it about as the storm hit, and perhaps drag it away. There was now no light at all other than the twin glows from Sheena and her Avatar (each enough to light up a circle perhaps ten yards in diameter), and snow was starting to fall, and the wind to rise. There was no time to roll the balloon up, even if they could. They took down the ring that kept the mouth of the balloon tensioned and open, so it lay flat on the ground. And then, they went around the edges that were exposed to the direction of the wind, heaping snow over them with a shovel, Sheena and her Avatar keeping the light spell over their heads, to allow them to see while they worked.

It was hard work. The snow was somewhat compacted – just as well, otherwise the wind would have blown it away – and hard to shovel. Bronn worked as long as he could, and then took a break while Sheena shoveled. He and the Avatar took heavy things out of the basket and put them on the flattened balloon, to weigh it down in the middle wherever possible. And Sheena shoveled, and shoveled, and shoveled some more. She worked like a machine, going on three, five times as long as Bronn, and faster, and still she worked. Bronn offered to take over again, but she shook her head, and said "Modified body! I'm not tired yet!" Bronn let her work a bit longer, but then asked to take over again. He needed the movement to stop from freezing, and she nodded when he said so.

She held up a hand, because with the rising wind it was not as easy to talk. Moving to one side, she raised her arms, and called forth heat, directed downwards. While Bronn shoveled, she melted a circular patch in the snow, which proved to be only about four feet deep, to a width of perhaps three yards. It takes time and energy to melt snow, but she was done by the time Bronn could shovel no more. She called him over, and said, "Rest in here for a minute. I've warmed the ground, too. When you're able, keep weighting the balloon down with any rocks you can pick up." Bronn gratefully sank to the ground and lay down, and let the warmth seep into his clothing, turned over and baked the other side. Useful to have a Fire Witch about, he thought. After five minutes, he groaned, and raised himself, and set about his work again. There were a surprising number of large, smooth rocks about, and he and the Avatar carried them till his arms were sore again. He could see, just, because Sheena was working on the nearby edge of the balloon.

Finally, Sheena came into the melted circle, and lay down. She recalled her Avatar. The light went out. "I'm done" she said, and she certainly looked it. Bronn knew she had expended vast amounts of her own energy. He went to the nearby basket, using the light

144

function of his staff – it seemed close enough to an emergency to him – and gathered what food he could. Bringing it back, he offered it, and Sheena ate and drank, slowly at first, then ravenously. Bronn returned to the balloon, and got a swathe of the incredibly versatile balloon cloth. Securing it with snow at the leading edge of the sunken circle they were in, he propped it up as best he could with stones, forming a crude lean-to. He wasn't confident it would stay up, but it would keep the snow that was now falling thickly off for a while.

Sheena had recovered enough by now to throw her light spell again, and got up to help. They fetched what blankets they had and made the lean-to as comfortable as possible. It was now freezing cold, even colder than it had been in the balloon. They huddled together in their little nest. Sheena, Master Witch, could set up and maintain a small shield of protection even while asleep, and that was enough to deaden the flurries of snow and wind as the storm swirled around the indentation she had melted in the snow, and keep the fabric of the lean-to from dropping onto them. His last thought as he dropped away to sleep, which took about ten seconds, was that this was one of the few times he had been in a bed with a woman, his arm around her, and felt no stirring of any interest whatsoever. This icy hole could not be considered a romantic situation, she was not the wife he had foreseen, and truth to tell, he was more than a little afraid of this Fire Witch.

Chapter 6. Iceland

Come with me, come let us flee
My snow princess and let us be
Happy and warm, away from this ice
Somewhere sunny, that would be nice
But she said with a smile, too true, for you,
But to go from the snow would make me blue
Though you go blue with the cold, for me
It's where I live; it's nice you see.
To run barefoot through snow
Is no hardship, you know
For a snow princess the cold has no fear
And if you would woo, you must do it here.

Anon

The storm howled about them for the whole of the night, and the next day. They were sheltered by the hills somewhat, and somewhat more in the four foot deep burrow Sheena had created, and which she kept reasonably free with her protective shield and by melting the snow that accumulated. But they were running low on food, and Sheena kept her magic to a minimum. Bronn grumbled to himself: this was exactly what he had foreseen, huddled miserably in a freezing cold hole for endless hours in the near-dark. Being human, the fact it was a validation of his Gift and Seeing ability didn't make it any easier.

They passed the time in talk, for there was little else to do. Bronn expanded on his Vision, though truth to tell there was not too much more at this stage: a flight to the Hold itself, and then find the Ice Witch. Then, nothing more till Warrior's Hold. Sheena found this highly encouraging, and speculated in shivery excitement that it might mean a whole community of Ice Witches, their concentrated talent masking Bronn's Gift of Vision. Bronn expanded further, and gave some detailed description about the intricacies of the Seer Gift, how some Visions seemed to be absolute, and some mere explorations of possibilities, and some in-between, and how Seers told the difference.

Sheena, in return, told him much he did not know about Witchcraft, how it was purely an exercise of the mind, but that the Fire and Ice variants were similar yet complementary. Fire magic was more external, elemental, rough, powerful and harder to control, and dangerous to the Witch without extensive training, mostly to stop them doing something stupid in a flame-up of emotion. "As my own history shows all too well" she added ruefully. Ice Magic was more personal, internal, constructive. An Ice Witch could balance hot and cold, but could never drive a balloon across the sea, as Sheena had done. Nor could most Fire Witches, to be fair. A Level Three Witch could do it, but they were rare. However, an Ice Witch could stroll across Iceland in light clothing, carrying a little food, balancing her internal temperature with a skill no Fire Witch could hope to achieve. At this time of the year, anyway – in full winter that might be too much to ask, except from the very best. Sheena hugged her knees to her body. "And to think that after all this time, we might find them again!"

Bronn remarked he found it amazing that after eight hundred years and more, Sheena was still so excitable. He would have expected a serene wisdom, not easily disturbed, after all that experience. Sheena shook her head. "Not me" she replied. "First of all, I'm a Fire Witch, and that's not our nature. And to gain that serenity, you must have inner balance. I am not balanced, as there is so much I seek, so much I want, need to find, be forgiven for. It is true that one can meditate, and achieve inner peace through contemplation. That is one way to God. But that is not the way to the Angels, and I couldn't do it because that would leave all my sins and faults unresolved. If you had known me a year ago, you would have found me serene enough, mind you. It's the possibility of achieving some atonement for guilt carried for so long that has unbalanced me."

The day passed, and the night, and they woke to a clear morning, bitterly cold. While they called it morning, it was quite late in the day. Winter was nearly past, and while they were not yet so far north that the sun ever stayed set all day, they were not far from it and there were few hours of sunlight to be had. At ground level, there was no wind, but looking up, Sheena could see, high above them, that the few clouds were moving north but also east, not what they needed. "Anyway, first we need to get the balloon up again" she said, glumly. Bronn looked out across the land, and could see what she meant. A lot of snow had fallen. It was light and fluffy, to be sure, but there were drifts, and four inches of snow times the surface area of a balloon was no joke. Sheena had no hope of melting it all, there was too much danger of damaging the balloon.

At least there was light. They began by working around the edge of the balloon with the shovel, to remove the heavier ice they had put there in the first place. Working at a slower pace than the day before, they found they could keep going, though it wasn't easy. They took turns finding the rocks and other heavy objects Bronn had used to hold it down. Once most of that had been cleared, they found it was actually feasible to remount the tensile ring that kept the balloon open, and for Sheena to walk inside. She could lift a small part of the fabric using her shield to help, and slide and roll the snow to the edges. Bronn walked on the outside with her Avatar, shoveling where needed, such as when there was a drift, or removing any heavy objects they had missed. It took all the short day, but finally it was done, all except a small strip near the top, which Sheena said would help hold the balloon down if there was more wind, but would roll off when they got it inflated again. If.

All too soon it was dark again. They both continued to work inside the balloon, Sheena casting light, Sheena's Avatar working on the outside in the cold. The deflation panel had to be reattached, fortunately an easy task. A few tears caused by Bronn's boots, the shovel or some of the rocks were patched. But finally, Sheena declared the balloon was ready to fly again. As they closed the tensile ring again and settled down to an evening meal from their reduced supplies, Sheena said she hoped it wouldn't snow again that night. The thought of having to do all that again the next day nearly brought tears to Bronn's eyes, he was so tired and cold.

But the night stayed clear. The moment some light showed, they both rose and grabbed the first thing they could find to eat, some rather hard bread. Sheena muttered to herself, and put the loaf down on the ground, and summoned heat. It wasn't a bad job for early in the morning, the bread was certainly warmed up, and most of it wasn't burnt too badly; certainly the inside was fine. Sheena sighted, and said that the wind low down was now due north. Not ideal, but it would get them onto the mainland, albeit somewhat to the east of where the Hold was. They would just have to hope they could find a bit of easterly wind to blow them west, or they would have to walk.

In the icy cold they remounted the tension ring, and Sheena began to cast heat. The balloon was of course still horizontal, and Bronn stood as near to the opening as he dared, to get the benefit of the passing warm air. It was hard work to fill the balloon. Although it hadn't snowed, there was a thin film of ice rime on the fabric, which both tended to hold it closed and cooled the air in it. After half an hour of slow progress, Sheena finally decided to use the emergency burner. With the basket lying flat, Bronn could only use short, sharp bursts of flame, for fear of melting the fabric. Slowly, the hot air entered the balloon, raising it in a hemisphere, and things moved a bit faster as the ice melted or fell off. With Sheena putting out all the heat she could muster and the flame from the burner, slowly the envelope rose tentatively off the ground, and finally hung over their heads, none too enthusiastically as if it was unwilling to get up so early in the cold morning air. Sheena said for Bronn to stop burning – the cylinder was near empty - while she continued to do what she could. Finally, the fabric was rigid, and the basket starting to lift with Sheena in it. Bronn clambered aboard, they dumped half of the ballast, and after a few more minutes they slowly rose, steaming in the dawn light.

Water continued to drip off the balloon, and as that weight was lost, and though Sheena continued to boost at a lower rate, the balloon rose faster. The air got even colder, and Bronn covered every bit of skin he could with a scarf. But at least they were in the light again, and going somewhere.

Soon, they bid a grateful farewell to Big Toe, which had saved their lives. It was a scant forty miles from the coast, so close had they come. An hour's flight at no more than two thousand feet saw them paralleling the first part of the coast of Iceland. Sheena explained that the coast went due north for sixty or so miles, and then curved to the east. If they continued due north they would soon be over the inland part of the island continent, but still far to the east of the Hold.

And at last, as the day began to pass, Bronn saw his Vision made reality. A great expanse of virgin white snow, with the occasional brown peak of some un-eroded hill or even mountain poking through and them high above it. Bronn could see no way that they could possibly come back through it, and Sheena agreed it was impossible. However, a hundred miles to the west there was a continuous series of ridges that were navigable, provided the weather was reasonable and you knew where you were going. The trick was going to be getting over to the west. She experimented with different altitudes. The wind dropped off to nothing at about five thousand feet, and resumed again at about eight thousand, but with a bit of an easterly vector rather than westerly. Sheena took them right up to fifteen thousand feet. Bronn crouched miserably in the bottom of the basket, and thought he was going to die. But to no avail. She dropped them down all the way to two thousand again: due north was the best they could get, at the moment.

They ate a second breakfast, Sheena eating enough for two big men as usual. She noted soberly that they had enough food for five days, two if she had to keep the balloon aloft. The daylight passed quickly, as they were heading ever further north, closer to the point where there would be no sun over the horizon at all. It wasn't as far to the Hold, and the wind was blowing faster, but still they would be lucky to make it.

After midday, Sheena looked thoughtfully up into the sky. She took the balloon up four thousand feet - and there it was, a westerly airstream, and not a moment too soon. Cold though it was, Bronn endured it, even looking over the side frequently to see how they were drifting to the west. A bit later, Sheena laughed happily, flinging her hair back in relief. "We're going to make it! Easily! We'll be at the Hold before the sun goes down!" She looked at Bronn, and then said, much more soberly, "And then, of course, Bronn, it's up to you."

The last three quarters of an hour passed quickly. After a while, Bronn could see a massive stone structure in the distance, larger even than Seer's Hold. Sheena explained that was because it had to house every living thing on Iceland in the winter. It was built on the top of a rise, with very steep roofs that blended into the rise itself, so that the snow slid off and did not pile up beside it. There was a very large overhang at the front, so that the entrance should not get blocked up either. It looked old, cold, and dead, dead, dead. The windows were almost all shuttered with some strange, durable substance – even after eight hundred years, few of them had surrendered to the elements, but in those few black holes no flicker of light showed. Bronn's heart sank. Was this the end of their quest, was his Vision in error, and they condemned to waiting out their remaining days in the freezing empty cold?

Sheena expertly maneuvered the balloon down to ground level, where the air was nearly still, in front of the enormous structure. There was a wide causeway leading to the front door, flanked by large blocks of stone with large steel lampposts. Sheena muttered to herself, "Rust free steel. They'll do" she explained that they would firmly tie the balloon to one of the posts, and then she would fill the balloon with as much hot air as she could. That would hold it up for a good half hour, during which time they could look around. That done, she used the emergency gas flame for fifteen long seconds, and then shot a jet of fire up into the sky from her own resources. When Bronn looked at her, she shrugged and said they might as well try to attract the attention of anyone who was there and get them to come to the two of them, rather than try to find them in the enormous echoing dark mausoleum in front of them.

She didn't sound very hopeful. She had explained that over the centuries, the only time she had found anyone in there was when she had brought them herself, for her failed repopulation attempts.

But, while she was still pumping heat into the balloon, wonder of wonders, someone did come out. A young girl, somewhere in her teens, dressed in a shortish dress of dark green, not very heavy material, with three-quarter length sleeves. Her legs were not covered, and her feet were bare, and she made no impression on the snow as she came towards them, completely unafraid. "That's her" breathed Bronn, for again he recognized her face, as he had Sheena's. "But so young! She can't be much over eighteen!"

"About fourteen, I'd say" Sheena replied in a wondering voice, full of aching hope. "The people of the north grow up quickly, it's a protective thing – to gain body weight, to protect from the cold. But an Ice Witch for sure. For one thing, look how she's dressed. And for another, that's an Avatar, not the girl herself."

The girl walked slowly over to where they stood. There was almost no wind, but a few tentative flakes of snow fell around them, enhancing the magic of the moment. She looked up at the balloon, straining at the ropes, in wonder, and then at Bronn and Sheena. "Who are you?" she asked. "Why are you here? In all the times I have come, no-one has ever been here."

Bronn smiled and spread his hands in a gesture of peace and welcome. "I am Master Seer Bronn" he said simply. "I have come, pursuing a Vision, seeking, well, seeking *you*. I have Seen you helping us, helping the world. I have come to lay our cause at your feet, hoping you will join us. I am very, very glad to have found you."

The girl nodded, and did a small curtsey, and spoke again. "Seer Bronn, welcome to Iceland. My name is Kira. I will of course listen to what you have to say. I've heard lots of stories about the Seers, and always they were kind folk, friends to us, and my aunt is a Seer in our tribe." Bronn was impressed with her poise and charm, and that she had welcomed without committing anything.

She turned to Sheena, and said "And this pretty lady, is she also a Seer?"

Sheena looked at the girl for several seconds, but before the pause could become awkward, spoke. "Kira, I am so happy to meet you. More happy than I can say. I am no Seer; I am trained as a Warrior, and also … well. I see you are an Ice Witch, and a gifted one at that, for you have cast not only an Ethereal Avatar, but one that can speak. That isn't easy. Can you do a truth spell?"

Kira looked at her warily. "The Warriors were also our friends. And yes, I can do a truth spell – I'm not very good yet, I can't make it work if the person I cast it on fights me."

Sheena smiled, and her beautiful face and smile seemed to reassure Kira a little. And she then said, "Then cast a truth spell on me, please. I will not fight or resist. I want you, so desperately, to believe me when I say something."

A little doubtfully, Kira extended her crossed hands towards Sheena, and spoke the keying words under her breath. Then, she nodded. "The spell's working. You're not fighting it at all."

Sheena nodded, and then took a deep breath. "I swear that I am utterly delighted, happy and relieved to have found you. I swear that I will do no harm to any Ice Witch if I can possibly avoid it, unless in extremity to save my own life or Bronn's. I promise that if I can, I will do everything possible to see to it that Ice Witches return to Ice Hold."

Kira smiled, and replied "You speak the truth. I feel nothing but good will from you. But the Ice Witches returning here? Many times it's been said, but our leaders always say, no, it's not the time. So, a Warrior and a Seer? I don't really know what to do. I'm quite forbidden to tell you where my people are."

Sheena looked down at the snow. "I must tell you something else, Kira, and I know you will know I am still speaking the truth, because I can still feel your spell on me. I must tell you, because I have not only sworn not to harm you or your people by any action, but also not by concealing anything either. Yes, I am trained as a Warrior. But that is not my first Gift. I am, by birth, a Fire Witch, but only a level one at the moment."

Kira put her hand up to her mouth, and gave a small scream. Her Avatar wavered, and it looked like she was going to dissolve. Sheena dropped to her knees, and in a pleading voice, called: "Please! I beg of you! Do not go, not now! You know, by sure magic, that I mean you no harm!"

Kira had both hands up to her mouth now. Although Avatars do not breath, they are driven by the mind that projects them to appear human, and her chest heaved in reaction. But as neither Bronn nor Sheena moved, and knowing that her Physical form was safe, by degrees she calmed a little. "It ... I feel it is true what you say. But we have a rule, not to reveal our existence, and most especially not to Fire Witches. There are also stories ... I cannot say. It's too much for me, I must return and tell my grandmother about you. She'll know what to do."

Bronn nodded, and smiled at Kira again. "Kira, please do go, tell someone who can make a decision, and please return and tell us. But please, also tell them to hurry. We are not Ice Witches. We can't live here, and have food for only a few days. If they hold a lengthy debate, the question may become moot and us a pair of icicles."

Kira nodded, and turned, not dissolving but travelling as an Avatar can, running over the snow effortlessly and quickly. She vanished through the walls of the Hold.

Sheena spoke to Bronn, wonderingly. "Look at her go! A powerful Ice Witch, to be sure – look! She's going over twice as fast as a person can run! But ... an innocent child, still. She's going home, and hasn't thought to dissemble, to show us a false trail. She's going directly home, rather than dissolve her Avatar. Her home is directly north of here. Directly north, and there's nothing there. Nothing that I know of. But there must be ... there must be another land north of here. That's the only explanation. But how?"

Time passed. Sheena said she knew for sure that in a little shed to the left of the main entrance, well out of the way, there was firewood. She knew, because she had arranged for it to be there herself, last time she was there, a hundred years ago. They built a good fire, and heated what food they had, and were warm. Several times, Sheena returned to the balloon to re-inflate it. It was much easier, with a fire burning nearby; redirecting some of that heat was a simple matter.

156

Hours later, when Bronn was nodding off, truly warm for the first time in days, Kira returned. She came slowly up to the fire, and holding her hands in front of her, spoke what must be semi-memorized words.

"My people, the Ice Witches, will receive you. If you can, you must travel due north from here, from the Hold, out to sea. There is a small island. Do not miss it, for there is no other land."

Having delivered her message, she relaxed. She smiled, and said, "You're lucky, you know. No-one's been invited to our island for, well, forever. After I told them about you two and what you're like and what you said, my grandmother, who's the tribe elder, said no at first. My uncle, Marko, who's in charge of the men and the hunting said no, for definite. But my aunt, the Seer, wanted to know more. When I described you, Seer Bronn, as best as I could and told her your names, she said a strange thing. She said, 'Oh, that's alright, they can come – he's my husband.' Is that true? And how can it be, you've never been there before, and she's never left?"

Bronn looked at Kira, taken aback, but not flabbergasted. He had Seen, after all, that he would meet his wife soon. But he had never Seen her to be an Ice Witch. Well, so be it, that didn't really matter. "Kara? Your aunt is Kara?"

"Oh, you *do* know her, then? Yes, she is. We're named similarly, in families, I'm Kira, she's Kara. My grandmother's Kala, and my mother was Kora. Are you really and truly married? And how?"

Bronn shook his head. "We're not really married yet, Kira. I hope we will be very, very soon, though. But we're both Seers. We've Seen each other in dreams, often enough to know each other's names, and we know we are meant to be together."

He turned to Sheena, and asked: "Well, we're on the path once more. When should we go? I'd like to go as soon as possible, of course ..."

Sheena looked around. "We could stay here all night, with me pumping up the balloon. But it would be tiring, and use up energy I may need later. I don't think we can afford to let the balloon down, we might never get it up again. And if I read the signs right, the weather is worsening. There may be snow tomorrow, and it may be impossible to fly. I'm pretty sure there will be fog. Of course, there's a little snow right now, but the clouds are high. We could go under them, and low down the wind is still due north. If there's some light on the island, it might well be easier to find it at night. Kira, you came over the ice as an Avatar, didn't you?"

Kira nodded. "Yes, the ice is thin now, especially near here, but enough for an Avatar of course." Sheena muttered to herself, "Fourteen, and projecting out of sight over ice! And an Avatar that can speak, and cast a truth spell!" But aloud she said, "What will work best is if I project my Avatar, and we walk together. My Physical in the balloon will know exactly where you are then, and we can hopefully find winds to blow us the right way."

And so it was. Sheena split out her Ethereal Avatar, and it and Kira went away, through the Hold and off to the north. Bronn and Sheena got into the basket, untied the rope, and Sheena went about the business of re-inflation. It only took a few minutes; she had kept the balloon well heated and she had the nearby fire to work with. They rose slowly in the air, the breeze carrying them towards the Hold, up and over.

Like all Holds, Ice Hold was built at the extremity of the island. There were no more than a few dozen yards to land's end, and then they were over the sea. They rose, and the wind caught them, and they sped on into the north. There was almost no light, due to the clouds and the falling snow. The occasional break in the clouds and the shafts of bright moonlight showed a dark surface some hundreds of feet below. Sheena's Avatar was casting light, and Bronn could see her as a small glow far in the distance.

Kira's Avatar knew where her Physical was of course, and she returned in a straight line. And Sheena's Avatar followed, and Sheena knew where *it* was, and the balloon went very nearly due north. Kira had said that it was a little over an hour's travel for her Avatar, or, by Sheena's reckoning, over forty miles, perhaps an hour and a half in the balloon in the mild wind at their current altitude. Kira had been to Iceland several times, and sometimes had dissolved her Avatar rather than walk it home. But she'd had this Avatar for some time now, and had become attached to it. Dissolving an Avatar meant building another one up from scratch, which took some time. Every Avatar was different, Sheena explained to Bronn, and the longer they were "alive" (for want of a better term) the more the personality developed, and the harder it was emotionally to dissolve them.

They were blown very nearly due north, but Bronn could see they were very slowly drifting away to the west as well. After ten minutes, Sheena's Avatar was a faint glow off to the right and ahead. Sheena estimated that after an hour and a half, they might be as much as two miles off course. She glumly said that Kira had guessed they would miss the island. Bronn thought that this would be a major problem, but Sheena reassured him. The end of the Hold was past the range of where the sea froze in winter, and going forty miles

159

further north they could be assured of solid ice that would easily bear their weight. She would know when they were parallel to the island – her sense of her Avatar would swing around – and they would land. If the wind was low enough and the ice flat, they might even be able to drag the balloon over to the island. Otherwise, they would let it down and simply walk. Barring a snowstorm or bears they should have no problems, and Sheena could handle the bears. Hopefully, someone would go out with a sled and bring the balloon back; she would hate to lose it.

She experimented with different heights, but there was rather more westerly wind than less, higher up. She didn't want to go even higher, for fear of making things worse. Still, her Avatar reported that the ice looked very solid below, so there should be no problem.

After they returned back down, Bronn could not see either Avatar. They had been going an hour, and when Sheena pointed to where the Avatars were, it was well off to the right. A few minutes later she reported that the Avatars had made it to the island. In the limited moonlight, Sheena guessed it was no more than three quarters of a mile across, and Kira's Avatar said it was perhaps two miles long. A fairly big island compared to the Toes, but not much to support a tribe of several dozen Ice Witches. She was surprised no-one in her day had known about it, but supposed that few ships went further north, and rarely by choice.

Sheena couldn't make her Ethereal Avatar speak, that was a level three talent for Fire Witches – though level one, for Ice Witches. In any case, she wanted them both to be physically present when meeting and talking to the Ice Witches. Slowly they drifted further north, until Sheena took them down and they had an uneventful landing, the snow anchors on the ice bringing them to an easy stop. They climbed out stiffly, and, pulling a rope, slowly dragged the balloon behind them. But it was too much work. They let the envelope down and rolled it up as much as they could. Then, they raised a pole with a flag so that hopefully it would be easy to find, and carrying everything they could they marched across the ice towards the island. Sheena grumbled that the carrying would have been easier if they had her Avatar as well, but of course it had to be on the island as a directional guide.

Half an hour's walking saw them close to the island. Sheena periodically closed down her light projection to see if they could spot the torches that were alight, waiting their arrival, and finally they could see a glow in the distance. Sheena called her Avatar back, and merged with her once again, then projected a Material Avatar, who could help with what they were carrying, a welcome relief.

They walked on, to what would be a very small natural harbor on the island. It felt strange to Bronn to be walking across the sea, towards the land. Strange, and of course, incredibly cold. He was wearing everything he could – wool undergarments, hose, shirt, sweater, trousers, coat, overcoat, shoes, overshoes, hat, scarf and thick gloves, and still despite carrying a pack, with many sundry items, he was none too warm. Still, at least the end of this particular part of the journey was in sight.

They walked across the tiny bay, and to a pier, and climbed laboriously up a ladder. At the end, lit by torches, a small reception committee waited for them. Not very many people, it was after all deep into the night, and snow was falling, with a relentless, steady increase that suggested the weather was settling in and planned to show them what it could do. There was an old, old woman, with two canes and a supporting Avatar who was surely Kira's grandmother, a stocky, powerful looking man who was undoubtedly the head of the hunters and her uncle, several men who looked like hunters themselves but were probably there as bodyguards or muscle as needed, and a few women who looked like Kala's helpers. Kira was among them.

Bronn searched eagerly among the faces. It was hard, in the limited light. Several of the women were talking, and hadn't noticed their approach, for they hadn't said anything and the snow muffled most sounds. But as they climbed the last few steps, one of them looked over, saw Bronn, and her face lit up. "Oh, there you are" she exclaimed, and came running over. Like Kira, she was dressed in green, but a long dress, with full sleeves, of much thicker material. And she wore shoes of leather and fur, also green, but with thick socks, gloves and a scarf, and a warm hat. Bronn supposed that if Ice Witches could use their Gift to keep warm, she had less power, though she was dressed scantily compared to him and even Sheena. She sped over the snow quickly, while Bronn stumped towards her, weighted down by clothes, burdens and tiredness. She threw her arms around him, and tried to kiss him. It was just barely possible, but he couldn't put his arms around her – there was just too much clothing in the way. She looked like a child being embraced by a bear. "Oh my goodness, you're so tired and cold. Come on, we'll get you warm. Kala and Kira, you'll take care of our other guest, of course."

Marko interrupted with his own agenda. "Hang on, we've much to discuss" he began. But Kara detached herself from Bronn's arms, and rounded on him. "For goodness's sake, Marko. I don't know why you wanted to come out, anyway. Whatever is to be done can wait till tomorrow. And, I've told you who this is. If you think I'm going to stand out here in the snow while you blather on for hours, think again. I have other plans."

162

Marko replied, annoyed, "Don't you think we should at least find out why they are here, what their journey and quest is all about? Surely he can rest in a little while? It's the middle of the night, what difference will another hour make?"

Kara laughed. "Well, really. You never cease to amaze me, Marko. And you a man, after all. Do you not *understand*? This is my husband, Bronn. I've never met him before, but have dreamed about him for four years. I'm taking him to the hut. And, he's not going to get any rest, not for a while yet. Don't even think about disturbing us early in the morning, we'll come out when we are good and ready. Until we do, you can question the Fire Witch till you're blue in the face if you want. But leave *us* alone."

And leading Bronn by his unresisting hand, she walked off across the snow into the dark, holding a torch. Bronn lifted his staff, and called forth light, to make their way easier. Kara looked up appreciatively as the spell-light made their way much easier, "Nice!" she murmured, holding his arm around her as best she could. "Well, it's only supposed to be used for special occasions" Bronn said to her. "But this is about as special as things get, I think, Kara my darling. Oh, how long I've wanted to say that." And then they walked off into the night, a flaming torch in one hand, and a steady orange glow in the other.

She led him to a very small house, or a quite large hut, and quickly opened the door and pulled him inside. It was surprisingly warm; there was a fire burning in a metal box, or rather cylinder, banked low. The chimney, also of metal (it looked like copper) wound around the room instead of going straight up. Bronn could see that the heat from the fire would go around the whole room that way, and be far more effective than any fireplace he had seen before. There was a bath behind a screen, and Kara remarked that she had thought he might like a bit of a wash and a warm-up; she had dreamed that, and had got Kira to heat the water. She hoped it was still warm enough. She herself unwound her scarf, took off her gloves, kicked off her shoes and socks, and undid the stays of her dress, allowing it to simply fall off, and removed her undergarments in the unaffected way of a woman who knows her lover well and is comfortable with him, and walked over to the bed, lifted the cover and slid herself into it. "Don't be too long, Bronn my darling" she suggested. "I don't want to fall asleep, waiting."

Bronn went behind the screen and started removing his layers. He didn't worry too much about neatness, though he did keep the clothing well away from the water. He slid into the bath, made quick use of the soap – the best soap he had ever used – and was out in a minute or two. While he was washing, he called out to Kara: "Kara my love, I've seen you in my Visions of course ... but the reality is far, far better. You enchant me." Kara chuckled, and replied "Hurry up and come over here and enchant *me* please." Bronn came out from behind the screen with the towel wrapped around him. "Drop the towel please, lover" Kara breathed. "I, too have Seen you, but want to see the real thing." Bronn complied, and she murmured, "my, oh my ... come on, it's cold out there, and warm in here."

Sheena and Kira and Kala walked over to the main area. Marko, with perfect courtesy walked with them, though anyone could see he was more than grumpy about the whole thing. Still, he accepted that the next day would be soon enough to sort things out. Kala explained that Bronn and Kara had gone away to a small, self-contained house reserved for newlyweds, but they would stay in the communal hall. It was almost too small to qualify as a Hold, but they called it so. It was too dark and too late for much explanation, so Sheena accepted it for what it was. Kala took them slowly through the halls. There were strange, eerie lights that seemed to be globes filled with a green-white glowing light. It was reminiscent of glow-worms or fireflies, but far brighter, bright enough to see dimly by. Still, Sheena's light was much brighter, and helpful. Kala remarked, "That's good magic. I wish we could do that."

They came to a suite of four rooms. As tribe elder, Kala merited and needed so much room. There was a bedroom each for Kira and Kala, a lounge room, and a formal reception room where Kala could meet and talk with such people as requested her time. Kala said that if Sheena didn't mind, she would share a bedroom with Kira, or if she did, Kira and Kala would share a room and Sheena could have the other to herself. Neither Sheena nor Kira minded. Kala remarked that was probably just as well, as in her old age she had developed a tendency to snore.

Like many older people, Kala had a tendency to fuss. No reasonable person could complain in any way that the lounge room they sat down in was untidy. But Kala sat down, and projected two material Avatars, who went about the room, lighting several oil lamps and straightening things, picking things up and generally organizing little things unnecessarily. Kira, obviously used to this process, busied her physical self, making a cup of herbal tea. Sheena admiringly remarked that while she might be able to produce a good light, she wished she had the fine control to heat a cupful of water so quickly and easily.

Kala nodded. "Ah well, we all make do as best we can with what we have, when we have it. I make do with two Avatars, and that only when I am seated – I just don't have the internal energy these days, but when I was in my prime I could manage three Material and an Ethereal, and dance the whirligig at the same time, if the mood took me."

Sheena asked how old Kala was. With the pride of one who has achieved a fine old age with most of her faculties intact, she said that she was one hundred and fifty one years old. "As you know, powerful Witches naturally live somewhat longer than ordinary folk."

Sheena nodded. "And Ice Witches live longest of all. A protective mechanism, for life in the cold north is harsh, and there is a need for the wise to live long enough to pass on all the complexities of Ice Magic to the next generation, and many of the ones after that."

Kala showed that while she might be old, and need two canes to walk with, her wits were still sharp. "They do indeed, young Fire Witch, and for precisely that reason. But how do you know it? There are no other Ice Witches in the world, and no-one comes here. I would have thought that knowledge would be long-lost."

Sheena sighed, and looked down at her hands in her lap. She raised her head, and looked steadily at Kala, but not defiantly, and replied: "I have sworn to do no harm to the Ice Witches to your grand-daughter Kira, and I always keep my word. Neither by commission nor by omission will I do any ill deed. Even if I must tell you things I fear may turn you against me. And, at the end, you have the right to know."

She drew a deep breath, and continued. "I know, because I have met Ice Witches before, and studied Ice

Magic. I am ... I was the Fire Witch known as Sha'Lin'Tra."

Kala showed her wisdom and poise by saying nothing. She sat for over a minute, digesting the words and thinking what they would mean. Kira was obviously concerned, but trusted Kala, and sat, patiently watching her. To be sure, she had the direct knowledge of her truth magic, that whoever or whatever Sheena was, she had no desire to harm any Ice Witch.

Finally, Kala stirred, and spoke. "Are you. Are you, indeed. I am right glad that Kira has truth-spelled you and swears you mean us no harm, otherwise I must confess even I would shudder at the thought that our great enemy, who we have remembered down the generations is in our midst. I must tell you, however, that though Ice Witches are naturally cool-headed, if this news gets out there will be many who would panic. This island is our home, and has been for hundreds and hundreds of years, but we still remember Iceland. The stories have changed in the telling, and most believe it to be some sort of paradise we left because of *you*. In truth, compared to this little island, it probably was, though not the fantasy some believe. I for one have sent my Avatar over there to take a look, as Kira did, but most of my people don't have that level of skill. Hmm. I must ask you. What is it you seek? Why are you here? What do you want from us?"

Sheena replied, calmly looking Kala in the eyes. "I seek forgiveness. I am here, accompanying Seer Bronn who seeks – was seeking, I should say – your granddaughter Kira, to aid him in the quest to defeat the sorcerer Narn, who is looking to repeat my mistakes and rule the world. He has seen her in a Vision. I came with him, because he had Seen an Ice

Witch, whereas I thought none still lived. I am very happy to be wrong."

Kala thought for another long pause. "And if forgiveness is not possible. What would you then?"

Sheena's gaze dropped, and a sadness entered her eyes. But she spoke again: "Then I would like to help. I would like to see Ice Witches return to the world, the rebalancing of the Gifts. I would like to see you to go home, to Iceland."

Kala spoke again, more sternly. "And if we want no help from you, and will not take it, what would you then?"

Sheena sank a little in her chair. "Then I would seek atonement."

Kala sat back. "Atonement?" she queried. "Do you mean you will subject yourself to my judgment? Our judgments? And accept whatever punishment we decide on?"

Sheena raised her head again, and again looked Kala calmly in the eyes. "Yes. If forgiveness is not possible, then that would at least be something. I have been seeking and trying for a very long time. I think I am nearly at the end of my strength. The Angels warned me that what I seek may not be possible, and if all I can do is to offer myself up for punishment, then that is what I will do."

Kala nodded. "I have enough years and experience to not need a truth spell to know you are at least sincere. But you say, the Angels. You have spoken with Angels? I think ... I think that at least you must tell me your full story. And then perhaps we can decide what must be done. I must warn you, if I feel I cannot decide for our people, I will open the question to all, and many are likely to be harsh. But let us hear what you have to say."

Sheena nodded. She told the story, as she had to Intira, at Nun's Hold. A difference was, when she came to the part dealing with Ice Hold, she expanded the story, as it materially concerned Kala and Kira.

"When we came to Ice Hold, I hated it. Talented as I was with Fire Magic, Ice Magic was hard for me. The two are complementary, of course. It was probably unrealistic to expect much of me, but the guilds were desperate for reconciliation. I was a willful child, full of pride in my own achievements. For years, since the time when at age eight I projected my first Ethereal Avatar (Kara and Kira stirred at that), I had been told how clever and special I was. Suddenly, I was the dunce of the class. I was cold all the time. The more talented an Ice Witch is of course, the easier it is for her to keep warm, but I had to rug up like a baby or an Ungifted. Yet obviously Gifted I was, and the support staff did not – could not – take to me either."

"I persisted in using Fire Magic to accomplish the tasks I was given where that was possible. The only thing I excelled at was Avatar projection. Some other things I could do well enough, because there are several ways of doing things. But I could only manage the simplest of creation and re-arrangement magic. While my classmates swept ahead of me and made thread, then cloth out of wood, grass and the like, and then strange things out of oil made solid, I struggled to soften leather. Then too, they grew and matured, whereas I stayed a little girl. Fire Witches do not grow up early."

"My parents were sorry for me, intervened where they could, and of course I realize now that my teachers did the best they could. They too were keen for the experiment to work. I was the problem. Perhaps a less Gifted student would have been better. Perhaps my talents would have overcome the problems with time."

"But, it was not to be. The ice can be cruel. When I was fourteen, my father was killed in an accident. A part of a cliff gave way, and he and three others fell into a ravine, and were lost. My mother was with them, but she survived. With a presence of mind that amazes me even now, my father and one other man used their Avatars to grab my mother and the cliff edge, form a chain and throw her to safety."

"It's easy, and human, to blame, of course. Two of the wives of the men who were lost blamed my mother, though there was no possible cause. They stirred up resentment amongst the others, and the tribal elders decided that since my father the Ice Witch was dead, it would be better if my mother and I returned to our own kind."

"They waited until spring was well begun, and organized a guide to take us across the island to the southern port. No ships would brave the reefs and storms and dock at the small Hold wharf until mid-summer, let alone earlier when the sea was ice, but the journey should have been easy enough. We had a sturdy donkey, and more than enough food."

"But winter still had one more snowstorm up its sleeve. When we were two weeks along our way, the weather turned foul, and dumped several feet of snow on us. Up on the ridges, there was little in the way of protection. With the storm at its height our guide found a tiny cave, more a hollow in the rock than anything. We three could huddle into it, but there was no chance of properly sheltering the donkey. Our guide explained that he would hold the halter until the donkey lay down in front of the cave, and that it would help shelter us from the storm. A tough little beast, it would most probably survive, but we would all huddle up together to generate the maximum amount of warmth. My mother would help, of course. She was a full level one Witch, a bit more really but she had never mastered projecting a second Avatar. Still, she could keep us warm by periodically going out to the front and heating the ground in front of us, and by shielding."

"But, it was not to be. Our guide, getting my mother to hold the donkey's halter, started to clean out some of the rubbish in the hollow. Unfortunately, there was a previous occupant – a snow scorpion. It stung him, and he leapt screaming out of the cave, knocking my mother over. The donkey bolted into the snowstorm, and there was no chance of finding it."

"We did what we could for the guide. My mother called forth flame, and sterilized the cave, for where there is one snow scorpion there is likely to be another. We laid him down, cut open his wound, and tried to suck the poison out. I know now that would never have worked, but it was all we could do. We had some wine, and gave it to him for the pain, but somewhere in the night he passed away."

"The storm raged for days. We had been unloading the donkey for the night, so we had food. My mother would every now and then go and warm the ground, but of course she needed a lot of food for that, so we did it as little as possible, holding each other for warmth until we could do so no more. Our shields helped, of course, as long as we could keep them up, and I helped with projecting heat, though my control wasn't really fine enough yet."

"Finally, the storm was over, and the sun came out. And what a difference! The trail on the ridge was under feet of snow. We could not see the way ahead or the way back past the first branch in the path. Our guide would have known. Anyone who travelled the route would have known. Our donkey probably knew, and made it back to the Hold. But we did not. We stayed two more days while the snow slowly melted, but my mother was afraid that if we stayed our food would run out. So, we pressed ahead – and ran into trouble straight away. It took us another two whole days to get back to where we started from. By then, most of the snow had melted and we could see where we had gone wrong. But it was still not easy. We took many wrong turns – what looked like paths petered out after a few miles, or if we were unlucky, a few dozen miles. We carefully marked where we had gone wrong. It would have been impossible without Avatars, We never came near a Hold Tribe or anyone else on the trail that might have helped us, though periodically my mother and I would send a fireball up into the sky."

"And so the days passed, and we made progress. We could sometimes see far ahead a distant blue of the sea. But one day, finally, the food ran out. Water was no problem, of course. We hunted rabbits, because there was little else. I was actually better than my mother at it, I could shoot a firebolt with good accuracy and from a long distance. But they were few and far between, and lean after a long winter. We were hard put to find enough to eat, but we managed. But then, my mother became sick, falling ill with a fever. With her body and mind weakened by sorrow, worry, cold and not enough food, it went quickly, and in a day she was delirious with a high temperature. She quickly got thinner and became weaker. I kept her going as long as I could. At night it was often necessary for me to project heat, and it drained me. In the end, it was too much for her, and she passed away one night. A large part of it was, I'm sure, sorrow at the loss of my father."

"We were not actually all that far from our destination, and the day after I was forced to bury her – I could do no more than pile rocks on her body – I saw the port in the distance, perhaps three day's walk, and the clear path in front of me. I swore vengeance against the Ice Witches that had made all this happen, and with that fire burning in me I slowly walked down from the heights."

"I actually ate a bit better, enough to keep body and soul together. The rabbits were no more numerous, but each one had only to feed me. Cooking them was no problem of course, but I ate some of the meat raw, living with the Ice Witches had taught me the value of raw meat in providing nutrition normally got from fruit and vegetables."

"I walked down from the mountains, and finally came to the port. Numbly, I made my way to the shipping office. They turned me away, for I had no money. We had not fully unloaded the donkey, and one of the things that had gone with it was our gold and silver. Not knowing what else to do, I went to the ship, and spoke to the captain, saying I was a Fire Witch and wanted to go home. Someone would pay him when I got there, I said."

"He was a practical man, but not a nice one. He said, he never took anyone on the ship for credit, unless he knew them. And then he leered at me, and said I looked like I might clean up well under the dirt of my weeks long trek, and perhaps I would like to work out my passage?"

"I knew what he meant. And perhaps I should have just looked around the town until I found an Ice Witch or a representative. Someone would have looked after me, I'm sure. But what happened was, the rage and fury and frustration that had been building up over the weeks since I left Ice Hold – yes, and before that too – boiled over."

She paused. Kala was listening intently. Kira was also listening, with a mixture of pain and empathic sorrow on her face. She too had lost parents.

"Fire Magic is not like Ice Magic. Emotion drives it, not the cool thoughts you know so well. Stress can be an enhancer for us, though it never is for you. Not a reliable enhancer, sometimes the Witch will break, so we don't use it as an educational method, it's too cruel anyway. But sometimes, instead of breaking, the Witch breaks through. In an instant, I broke through the barriers and limitations of level one Fire Magic, through level two, and into level three."

"Levels in Fire Magic are about the same as in Ice Magic, and the other Gifts. Perhaps one in a hundred thousand people naturally achieve the first level. More in the Holds themselves, of course. And maybe one in a hundred of them achieves level two, one in twenty of them level three. Higher levels are possible, but so rarely seen that they can be mostly ignored. The captain had of course never seen or met a level three Fire Witch – a Queen. Screaming in rage and loss and frustration, I cast a huge fireball a few dozen yards above the captain's head. He flinched from the heat, and I yelled at him that if he didn't take me home to Fireland and give me everything I wanted on the way that I would burn his ship down to the waterline, and him along with it. He agreed fairly quickly. As it turned out, he got a bargain – we encountered pirates along the way. When I heard the crew getting ready to sell their lives dearly, I came up on deck. The captain told me to get below, and I told him not to be a fool.

Despite getting my own way, I was still fuming and simmering inside, and was consolidating my new level two and three skills. I blew the pirate ship apart with a terrific release of energy and emotion, and went below again, leaving the stunned crew to decide whether to pick up a few survivors or let them try to swim to land."

Sheena continued with the rest of the story, as she had told it to Intira and Bronn. And then, she sat with her hands in her lap, and waited Kala's judgment.

Kala sat for a long, long time. But finally, she stirred, and shaking her head, said: "What a sad, sorry tale of prejudice, arrogance, bad luck, bad judgment, evil acts and suffering." She paused. "I am, for my part, truly sorry on behalf of my people for such unfeeling treatment of a suffering mother and a young child. I know from Kira's truth spell and my own skills that, finally, you came to the realization that you did wrong, and great evil. But still, nearly all the Ice Witches wiped out and hundreds, thousands of others, and for what? Simple revenge."

Again, she paused for a long time. "Despite my people's part, I would condemn you without further thought, for yes, even I have my weaknesses, and resent the limitations of the life I have been forced to lead on this forsaken island, even though I have known no other. If not for three things. Firstly, you have spoken to Angels, and they have said that your redemption is possible, and who am I to disagree with them. Secondly, you have carried your burden for a long, long time, and seriously tried to make amends. Few know better than I what a weight the years can be just by themselves, let alone carrying your immense burden of guilt. And thirdly ... have you been told yet how we escaped your net, and are here today?"

175

Sheena shook her head. "No, though I am very glad you did."

"In my family, as far back as we can remember, we have had a tendency to produce Seers. Kara is a good example. Few of them great Ice Witches of course, two Gifts are very rarely highly developed in one person. We do also produce talented Witches. I am one, and Kira will be another – greater than I, if she can keep her mind to her studies. A long way back, perhaps at the time you left Ice Hold for the first time, one of my ancestors had a Vision. A great and detailed Seeing. She Saw a great danger coming to our land – that would be you. She Saw that we must flee if we were to survive. She Saw this island, to the north in the uncharted seas. And she had the skill to motivate others with her words. Twenty Witches she convinced. Whether it was part of her Vision or some other Gift she had, she convinced every one of the twenty she spoke to, and their spouses, and she spoke to no others. In secret, they obtained a ship, and stocked and provisioned it in a bay not visible from the Hold and never visited. They took everything they could possibly think they would need and could get away with. And then, they waited. When they saw your armies were less than a day's march from the Hold, they left in the confusion. No-one missed them at first, and when your mind magic took hold, no doubt no questions were asked."

They fled here, fifty-two of them, twenty female Witches, nineteen men – eleven of them with Witch talent, and thirteen children. Three of the Witches were pregnant. Our great leader and founder Saw we would be safe here. And she said ... she said, we would never leave and be safe – unless the one who drove us away came to take us back."

Sheena's head came up sharply, and she looked at Kala, as did Kira, both their mouths open in amazement.

Kala nodded. "Yes. I am surprised too. After a few generations, we came to believe that this meant we would never leave. While there was still activity on Ice Hold, every now and then a Witch would send an Ethereal Avatar across the ice, to listen and hear what news she could. And so, close to the end we heard that you had disappeared, your empire was broken up, and we assumed you were dead. We never tried to go back, because of the strength of the Vision."

Sheena looked troubled. "There is nothing I would like better than to lead you all back to Ice Hold, and see the Witches re-established there. But if that were to happen, I fear you'd fall prey to Narn. He is seeking to rule the world as I said. We know he has re-discovered some mind-control magic. Nothing like mine, thank God, but enough in its own right."

Kala nodded. "I can see that we cannot go right now. And so ... Sheena, come and kneel before me."

Sheena looked at her steadily. "May I ask why?"

Kala's voice steeled. One could see she was the tribe elder, and a true leader, not a sinecure. "You may not!" she snapped. "You will do what I say, because I have the right to demand that you do it!"

Without another word, Sheena rose and knelt at Kala's feet, and bowed her head.

Kala's voice softened. "That is better. Now. Do you swear to continue this quest that you and Bronn have started, and do your best to rid the world of this sorcerer, Narn?"

Sheena responded, "Yes, I do."

"And will you take my granddaughter Kira with you, and protect her with your life if necessary? And train her as best you can with what knowledge of Ice Magic you have, and other skills if you can?"

"I will protect her with my life, and train her as best I can."

"And if your quest is successful, will you return here and lead my people back to Ice Hold, help them to get re-established in their rightful home, and see to it that my Kira holds her rightful position?"

"I will swear to do this, if I live and it is in my power."

"And will you do all this willingly? Do you agree that I have the right to demand this, and give you nothing in return?"

Sheena dropped her head. "I will. I do" she said, sadly.

"Then on behalf of my people, the Ice Witches, I command you to go forth and do these things. And on behalf of my people, and in recognition of your genuine repentance for your deeds, I forgive you for what you have done."

Sheena raised her head, and stared at Kala in unbelieving hope.

"Up you get my girl. That's enough formality. Eight hundred years of repentance should be enough for just about anything. The past cannot be changed, but the future can be. High time to be moving on. Come and sit down again, and let us discuss the next steps, for there will need to be next steps."

Sheena got up and sat. Kira could see that she was trembling in reaction. She understood from Sheena's story that a burden she had been carrying for most of a millennium had been unexpectedly lifted.

"I must tell you that I will not live to see my people returned to their land. I know, and have told Kira that I have a final illness, and don't expect to live another two years." She raised a hand as Sheena made to speak. "I am content! I have lived over a hundred and fifty years, and that is a target I am happy to have hit. I have outlived three husbands. We call Kira my granddaughter because it's easy, but in truth I am her great, great grandmother. Enough is enough."

She paused again. "The strongest Witch on the island, who would be the next leader, is of course Marko. The first time for a few hundred years it has been a man. Kira will be stronger still, and I had hoped to live long enough and train her well enough so that was obvious to all concerned and she would have her chance, but I thought at the end of the day it didn't really matter, and if the timing meant it would be Marko, then so it must be."

"But it is in his nature to oppose. He would oppose Kira going away. He would oppose our returning to Iceland. He would, and will oppose your forgiveness. What he will do is, he will challenge me. He will say I am old, too old to be leader and make these decisions. Although no leader has been challenged for five hundred years, he will do it. And the reason for this is guilt. He was in the whale hunting party that went out and where Kira's parents were lost, and it weighs heavy on him. For no reason, there is no doubt of his courage, and if anything could have been done, he would have done it. But, he will oppose. Saying 'no' in his mind about his failure makes him want to say 'no' about other things too."

"Twenty years ago, it would have been easy. He can raise only two Material Avatars and I could show three. It would all be over in a few minutes. But now, I can only manage two, which would engage his two, leaving his physical body free to battle mine. No contest there, of course."

"But you are here. And I have read the old books. An Ice Witch can support another with channeled energy for a few seconds, perhaps a minute or two. But the old books say that Fire Witches have more effective support magic. It is said that a level one Fire Witch could provide energy to sustain an Ice Witch for an hour, or more. And you, although you are self-limited to level one magic, still the full strength of your will burns inside you. Could you support and energize me for long enough to win my battle?"

Sheena mused for a moment. "I could do it, yes, Kala. But it puts a tremendous strain on both Witches."

Kala nodded. "Yes, I know that when you withdraw your spell, I will die. But it will have been worth it."

Sheena dropped her eyes. "This is not what I wanted, Kala. Not at all. I have killed enough Ice Witches, I can't bear to kill another."

Kala spoke with a gentle voice. "I know, and I understand. But there is no other way. And so, I command you again: you will do this for me, and you will feel no guilt." She smiled. "That's an order, young lady. Or, I suppose I should say, old woman. Don't worry, it will be good for Marko as well; I will see that his issues are resolved also. And now, it is late enough. Time for bed."

Kira took Sheena and showed her where she could wash a little and rinse her face, absent-mindedly warming the jug of water for her with a wave of her hand. And so, they got ready for bed, both of them tired.

Kira noticed that Sheena seemed sad and depressed. There were the beginnings of tears in her eyes. "Why do you cry, Sheena?" she asked. "Surely, you must be happy, to have the forgiveness you have sought for so long?"

Sheena raised her head a bit, but it sank down again, hopelessly. "Oh, Kira, I am, to be sure. But it's still so hard. I have to re-find love to heal my damaged mind, I know not how. And before that, find forgiveness from God."

Kira replied, "But the Angels have said it may be possible for your mind to be healed. And surely, nothing is impossible for God."

Sheena nodded miserably. "Yes, it may be so. But how, oh how, can I forgive *myself*?" she asked appealingly of Kira.

A bit of the Seer blood awoke in Kira at that moment, and she had a Vision of a tired soul, wearied to the point of collapse bearing a great burden too heavy to contemplate down the centuries, with little hope.

The cold north is harsh. There are few chances to learn compassion. Mistakes are either recovered from or are fatal, there are few in-betweens. And the survivors and those left behind have to get on with the needs of everyday life, with little time to mourn. But the young Ice Witch did what she could, holding her and murmuring soft words of comfort and hope as the most powerful sorceress in known history wept like a little girl whose heart is breaking, crying bitter tears of sorrow and remorse and shame deep into the night.

Chapter 7. Conflict

When the fantasy bells
Of the universe ring
You can fly through the sky
On a dragonfly's wing
There is magic within
There is magic without
Follow me and you'll learn
Just what life's all about

Kate Bush

*Do not meddle in the affairs of wizards, for they are subtle, and
quick to anger*

Tolkien

Sheena awoke, and for a moment did not know where
she was, so disorienting had the emotions of yesterday
night been. She cast a small light, and looked at the
room in puzzlement, turned, and saw Kira sleeping on
the other small bed in the room, and remembered. Her
face lit up as she recalled the wonder of Kala's
forgiveness, and somehow this morning the other
steps on the way to her redemption didn't seem so
impossible. After all, two things that she had thought
to be impossible had happened; why not others?

She turned off the light spell again; there was no need
to wake Kira. With sensitive vision and perhaps a little
imagination, it was almost possible to see the faintest
dark red of approaching dawn through the triple-
glazed imperfectly transparent window, and she knew
that it meant the day was already somewhat advanced.
Winter was over and spring well started, but this far
north the sun still rose late. She quietly rose from the
bed, intending to go out into the living room, and see if

Kala was awake. But the slight movement and perhaps her earlier light woke Kira. She stirred sleepily, and bade Sheena a good morning. Then, with the energy of youth, she sprang out of her bed, stretched, and with no more ado made to leave the bedroom.

Sheena stopped her. She was going to wait until Kira was fully awake, but it seemed she was already mostly there. "Kira, thank you so very much for your comforting words last night. But I must apologize. It was not fair for me to dump all of that onto you. My only excuse is that I had been carrying that burden for a very long time, and it was removed very suddenly, and unexpectedly. I am ... better this morning."

Kira hugged her in the simple, unaffected way young girls can have, smiled, and said "You're welcome. I'm glad you're feeling better."

They left together. The Hold had some form of heating; it was nowhere near as cold as the outside. But it was cold enough. Sheena was comfortable in her warm nightgown and a wraparound soft coat called a housecloak in Iceland, and house boots, all thoughtfully provided by Kala, and her modified metabolism. The boots were beautifully made and tooled, furry and warm, and the housecloak a rich red on the outside but lined with a darker material, intricately embroidered. All signs of a people able to work with leather and material and colors because of their magic, and lots of time to make things beautiful. Kira wore her nightgown, also wonderfully embroidered, which served the needs of modesty but little else. Her arms and feet were bare, and she looked warm as toast.

Kala was seated in the living room, with a few candles for light. She wore a bit more than Kira – a wraparound gown and soft fur slippers, but her Ice

Magic was also keeping her comfortably warm. "Welcome and good morning" she greeted them. "I have been awake for some time now, thinking over my life. I sleep less these days than I used to, for sure. I have been out, and spoken to the circle of elders. We will have a general convocation in the Great Hall later today, at noon, and then we shall see what will be. Sheena, as I said last night, you must be prepared at that time to lend me your strength. So, you must make whatever preparations you need for it."

Sheena nodded her acceptance. "You have so commanded me, Kala, and it shall be done. It is best if I start before the meeting, though no other preparation is really necessary. But what if it is not needed? What if ... Marko, his name? Marko does not challenge?"

Kala shrugged. "Then, you will release your support, and I will live till another day. I am ready to go, but not eager – I wouldn't mind that. I would like to see you and Kira return victorious, and formally hand over leadership to her, but all my instincts and experience say it will not be so. Still. Nothing is certain. Well then, if you have no other task or preparation, breakfast. And then, would you like me to show you the Hold, what we have wrought here in this wilderness?"

Sheena nodded. "I would like that very much" she said. "But, won't it tire you out?" "Not at all" replied Kala. "I will stay here, in my rooms, and send an Avatar with you, to show you around. It is of course best and easiest to project an Avatar as much like oneself as possible. The dichotomy between one's image of oneself and one's Avatar should be kept to a minimum, to avoid burnout. But, I don't think of myself as an old woman, and so my Avatars aren't. Self-delusion, the key to happiness in old age, my dears!"

Sheena laughed. "I don't think you are an old woman, either, Kala" she said. "And I should know."

They dressed for inside the Hold. Kala was not going to show them around the outside until the sun was well up.

They left Kala's suite, and went to the Great Hall, which served many functions. At the moment, it was serving breakfast. There were several dozen people in the room, with small numbers leaving and arriving in a well-established routine. Breakfast was what looked like porridge, but surely wasn't – where would the oats come from? Kala and Kira ate it with the enjoyment of people who are well and truly used to it, and have come to like it due to constant exposure. Sheena ate it without much thought, she had eaten far worse for decades at a time, and her modified metabolism would handle it without a problem, whatever it was. But, she asked what it was, and where it came from out of curiosity. Kala said, it was seaweed. Sheena looked at it, amazed. "Seaweed? It isn't anything like any seaweed I have ever seen!" Kala nodded. "Our transformation magic has grown and matured over the centuries. It had to. We're used to it of course, but my reading of the records shows that we have both forgotten many skills and learned many others. We have broken the seaweed down to its basics, and put the bits back together differently."

"It tastes very much like oats!" Sheena marveled. "We have done well, then? I am glad you like it."

"And this, which you use with it – surely it is not milk?"

Kala said, "We call it milk, though it is not true milk. We know milk, of course, and sometimes obtain seal's milk. But no, this is also made from seaweed." "And the honey?" "Seaweed also. We have no shortage of seaweed, which is a good thing because we have little else. Occasional driftwood – we scour the coastline for anything that washes up. A few useable minerals. Whale and seal meat, and the important oil from them, and fish, and a tiny amount of metal. We have no iron other than what we brought with us eight hundred years ago and that which washes up on our shores, a tiny amount of copper and a bit of zinc. By need, we have learned to extract a new metal, light and quite strong, from clay – but it's hard work. Only the best of us can make it, and not very much in a day. We have a hothouse, where we grow a few precious fruits and vegetables with great labor."

People passed Kala's table, and said good morning in the quiet and dignified way of Ice Witches, genuinely present but not intrusive. They greeted Kira too, and also Sheena. Some had heard of her arrival, but none knew who she was. Despite no stranger having come to their shore in their lifetime or that of any of their ancestors, their natural reserve, poise and politeness stopped them from intruding, even if their greeting was somewhat formal. Sheena didn't mind, and they responded well to her. Perhaps they could read that despite her polite exterior, she was thrilling to see Ice Witches walking all around her, and feeling the soft wash of their power.

The Great Hall was big enough to hold perhaps a hundred people, but always seemed empty during the time they were there. There was no crush. Sheena asked how many people lived on the island, and was taken aback when Kala said there were only ninety-two. "You have survived ... but not flourished" she remarked. Kala nodded. "Indeed. That is why it is essential we leave this place, as I have charged you. It's hard living here, there are not enough resources, and not enough room."

186

While they were eating and talking, Bronn and Kara came in for some breakfast too. Kara looked a little smug, and Bronn perhaps a bit dazed, but as Kala said, they looked about as happy as it was possible for two people to be. "Oh, we are" Kara smiled. "And, I'm hoping you will make us even happier, and marry us sometime soon."

Kala thought for a moment. "Well, if you don't mind a simple ceremony with nothing but the basics in front of everyone, I have called a meeting at noon. If you want everything, announcement, ceremony and feast, it will take longer. If ... you don't mind me suggesting it, I would take the simple ceremony, that is, if you want it to be me. I'm no longer sure from day to day if I will still be here on the morrow."

Kala shrugged. "A simple ceremony is all I need. I'd be perfectly happy with none at all, but I know my people, things will be much easier when Bronn has to leave on this pesky quest if we are properly married."

"Good, well you have several hours. Kira and I are going to show Sheena around the Hold. Would you like to see it too, Bronn?"

Kara laughed. "No, he would not. I hope you don't mind me answering for you there, darling. He will have to go away all too soon, and I am planning to make the most of the time when he is here. We're just here for a bit of sustenance, and then we will see you again at noon."

Kala smiled, and said "We will leave you to your own devices, then. Come, Sheena and Kira, let us wander." They took Kala back to her rooms, one of her Avatars taking her arm, and seated her in her favorite chair. As an experienced and powerful Ice Witch, she had mastered the ability to take a nap, yet have her Avatar active. Sheena ruefully said it was an ability she had often wished she had. The best she could manage was to have her Avatars sleep at the same time, yet not dissolve, and that was a great skill for a Fire Witch. Fire Magic couldn't keep them active if she was asleep, and she had not learned Ice Magic well enough. So, Kala's Avatar went with them, talking about the Hold as she did. She spoke of a nicety new to Sheena: in this Hold, where *everyone* could project an Avatar, it was common to use the letters "Av" in a name to distinguish Physical from Avatar: and so, she said, call me Kalava.

The Hold was built in the shelter of a natural change in level of the island, almost a cliff, slanting away to the north. This was convenient as the wind skipped up and over providing shelter, while snow did not bank up and fall on the Hold much at all. It was built in a diamond shape that allowed most of the sleeping quarters to face south-east and get as much sun as possible in winter, with the great hall and other rooms to the north-west. The side to the north-east was flush up against the rock of the cliff, and Kalava told them that the earliest records said that the very first Hold was little more than some tents built as close to the cliff as possible. That was soon expanded by disassembling the ship they had arrived in and using the wood for walls. And so it had stayed, at least partially, for a long time.

The south beach faced into the winds and the currents, and a great deal of seaweed washed up on it. They had learned how to preserve it and bind it together using Ice Magic, and they could make tough sheets of building material, but it was hard work. The Hold gradually grew from a tiny, crowded makeshift arrangement to something bigger and more spacious. However, for several generations tiny and crowded was good. They were forced to huddle together for mutual warmth, the Witches keeping themselves warm, and their bodies then warming the Ungifted. In most of autumn and spring most of the work had to be done by the Witches, only they could stay warm enough to do any useful work outside.

They ate whale, seal and a lot of raw fish, as otherwise essential things in the meat would be broken down by cooking. A few Witches had preserved the art of producing some vital supplements by Ice Magic, from things such as sugar, producing a white sour acid that prevented scurvy, normally found in fruit but which they could not grow in any quantity, another that aided night vision, and a few more. They survived, but it was hard. Fortunately they had crammed the ship with as much as it could hold of useful things.

Over the generations, people changed. Many who had little Ice Magic died, while those with more, lived. Some, who had no useful talent at all chose to leave and live elsewhere, usually Peace Island or further south. They voluntarily underwent mind magic so they forgot where they came from and forgot Ice Witches existed. A very hard choice to leave family behind, but they would have lived a miserable, cold life, mostly inside. Sheena mused that that was probably why there was a slightly higher incidence of spontaneous Ice Magic on Peace Island; while Ungifted themselves it would have been in their heredity. So that now, though there were only a few more people on the island than when they came, there were no Ungifted. Kara was currently the least powerful one, and that only because her Gift lay in her abilities as a Seer.

After a hundred years, they made real progress with the seaweed. They could now radically change its basic structure, making solid, opaque walls, mostly transparent windows – Kalava explained that they could make a very transparent window, but it was

189

dangerously flammable – beams, and as they had seen at breakfast, food and drink. And also clothing, furniture, firewood and a very passable beer. Everyone who could do so took their turn hauling great quantities of it from the beach in carts in summer and early autumn when the sea was not frozen. Sheena asked Kira if she worked with seaweed, and if so, what she made. "No" she said proudly. "I can, of course, but I'm one of the very few who can work with metals. I transform our poor copper ore to the metal, and separate out the tiny amount of silver and the even tinier amount of gold. And I train others in how to get the light-metal out of clay."

She took them through the workshops, to the hothouse in the middle of the Hold where fruit trees grew, apples, oranges and lemons, and a few peach trees that looked as if they were only kept alive by personal dedication and love. A team of specialists worked constantly, treating the soil, and for most months of the year the ingenious heating system where the chimney went all around the room was used to stop the trees from freezing. Kalava explained that the greatest problem was that the trees often did not get enough light. Still, they had adjusted over the centuries too, and were now far hardier than their southern ancestors. Kalava also explained that the seeds that had taken with them had all died because there just had not been the facilities to keep them alive, and that the tale of the Ice Witch who had travelled south to get seedlings and remained incognito, and brought them home would make a saga in its own right.

Despite their innovations and adaptions, Sheena could see it was a subsistence economy. Everything depended on everything else. The only reason why so much knowledge and so many skills had survived was they were all absolutely essential. Still, it would make it that much easier for them when they returned to Iceland.

All too soon noon was approaching, and they returned to Kala's chambers for a rest and final talk. "Kira, you must be careful" Kala said. "While sleeping, I had a dream. I am more than ever convinced that Marko will challenge, and I see a danger to you. As for me, it could go either way. Please, be careful."

Kira said she would be as careful as she could.

Kala nodded. "I am no Seer. In some ways, I wish Kara was a part of this, but she is totally ... otherwise occupied at the moment, any Vision she might have would be suspect. Ah, well. Sheena, what did you think of our little Hold?"

Sheena spoke truly of her thoughts and fears. The Hold was barely sufficient. It was a miracle that no disaster had occurred in eight hundred years, but a single problem could put the whole Hold at risk. The sooner they all returned to Iceland, the better. Kala agreed. She knew everything Sheena had said to her Avatar. The number of people on the island had dropped below seventy-five seven times, but risen over a hundred only three.

"And now, the time has come. Sheena, you must re-energize me."

The spell, or rather the concentration, meditation and alteration of the mind necessary was normally a complex one. But Sheena, though limited in what she could do was un-surpassingly skilled, and placed herself in the right state easily. Then, she simply held both of Kala's hands, released a pent-up sigh of breath, and it was done. Kala seemed to expand, as her old bones straightened. She rose easily from her chair, keeping one cane for appearances, and wonderingly exclaimed – "oh, oh, oh ... I had forgotten!"

She laughed, and projected three Material Avatars. They danced around her in perfect time, smiling. They looked even younger than the Avatar she had sent to guide them around the Hold.

"Oh, how wonderful!" she exclaimed again. "Sheena, this is marvelous. If the worst comes to the worst, and today is the day I die, it is worth it, to feel like this again. Thank you, thank you." She merged the Avatars again, and with one taking an arm and the other arm holding her cane, she left her rooms and they all followed to the great hall.

They were on time. Most of the Hold had already arrived and were waiting; a few latecomers trickled in as Kala slowly walked up to the podium that had been prepared. Standing there as the last stragglers came in, she smiled at and talked quietly to a few people in the front row, with the calm control of the true leader.

Finally, the time having come and gone, she spoke. "My people! We have a difficult thing to face and a difficult time ahead. But what better way to begin such a meeting than with something joyous? You all know my beloved niece, Kara. You all know she is not greatly gifted as an Ice Witch, but makes up for it with her abilities as a Seer. So many of us have benefitted from her Visions. And one of them concerned herself, and has been ongoing for nearly four years: that she would have a husband, and he would come from over the sea. Many laughed. Yet, here he is, vindicating her ability. I welcome him in full gladness, for he is a Seer too, and though the first outsider to come to our shores in recorded history, we remember the Seers were our friends. More than that, he has made her happy. There is little more to do than to speak the marriage vows – unless anyone here has any reason why they should not be wed?"

A pause for a few tens of seconds heard no nays. Most people there looked happy for Kara. Marko stood with crossed arms, but even he, the most obviously dissentious had nothing to say.

Kala called Bronn and Kara forward. She asked them both the time-immemorial words, little changed despite nine hundred years isolation, and Bronn and Kara both clearly and happily forsook all others and declared their absolute devotion to each other. A happy calm descended over the company: the side-effects of the Gifts are many and subtle, and when two people in such a situation speak the simple truth with enough experience to back it up, the lack of any doubt is clear and delightful. Everyone there knew those two were bonded for life.

They were declared wedded, and Bronn was told he could kiss the bride. A wag in the crowd called out "Oh good, they've been waiting for that" and there was general laughter – but Bronn took advantage of the permission, anyway. And then they were allowed to leave once more.

Kala called for silence. "Yes, once more the Seers of our tribe have shown the truth and accuracy of their Visions. Kara is the greatest to have blessed us for some generations. But let us not forget our sainted Sitrata, who saw the need for us to leave Iceland and come here, hidden from the entire world for these nearly nine hundred years."

She paused for effect.

"It has been hard. Few of you here have not lost a family member to this harsh land, and many more than one. And yet. Our guests tell us that there have been no Ice Witches in the rest of the world in all that time. It was come here, or let the Gift die."

She paused again.

"And now, to the reason for this convocation. I would like to read to you from the writings of Saint Sitrata."

She lifted a large volume, and put it on the lectern of the podium. Opening the book to a marked page, she read in a clear voice: "And when we had come to Far Ice Island, we were dismayed, for the land was harsh and cruel, and bitterly cold, Ice Witches though we were. And the people said to me: can we survive here? And I was troubled. But that night another Vision came to me, and I was able to reassure them: we will survive. We will hold on. It will be hard, but we will bend this land to our need, and the land will bend us. And we will live on this island for ever, unless the one whose evil has caused us to flee relents and leads us back home again."

She looked up, and closed the book with a snap. "And so it was, and so it has been, and so it is today. And once again we are humbled by the power of her Vision. For here before you, by my side, stands the one who caused us to flee our homeland, and has relented. Sha'Lin'Tra the Great."

Ice Witches are cool headed, and hard to disturb. But that news would stir a stone statue, and there were many reactions, from indrawn breath to cries of horror, and fear. Kala let it build for half a minute and then cried out in a great voice that rose above the din, augmented by magic: "I have not finished speaking!"

She addressed the crowd, riding the wave of their uncertainty and concern. "Firstly, let there be no doubt. This is her, Sha'Lin'Tra the sorceress. Master Fire Witch and Warrior, she also knows some Ice Magic, though she has no great gifts there. Secondly, she has truly relented. She has spent nearly eight hundred years trying to atone for her sins. Thirdly, she and Seer Bronn need our help to defeat another sorcerer, Narn, another who would rule the world."

There were questions from the crowd. However, they were asked in a typically Ice Witch way. There was little jostling and dissention, each person was prepared to let others speak, and wait their turn. Sheena ruefully thought to herself that if Fire Witches had been involved, two dozen firebolts would have been thrown by about now.

"How do you know this is truly Sha'Lin'Tra?"

"I have questioned her. She knows Ice Magic which we have forgotten, learned in the time when she studied on Iceland. She does not have the skill to perform that magic, but she knows it. And my granddaughter Kira has put a truth spell on her, and questioned her under it."

"How do you know she has relented?"

"If Sha'Lin'Tra the Great was on our island and had not changed, we would even now be lost. We could not stand against her. She has shown me the edges of the magic she used, and I am horrified, amazed and most glad I do not need to know more, either by learning it or by trying to fight it. She has bound herself to our service. And again, Kira confirms it by her truth spell."

"Why does she not face this Narn herself?"

"As a part of her atonement, she has self-limited the degree of magic she can perform, until certain conditions are met."

There were many other questions. But the last one came from Marko: "Even if this is all true, we do not have to return to Iceland. Why should we do so? Why should we not demand revenge on this Fire Witch, since she appears so conveniently limited in her magic before us? What if all the conditions are met, and she seeks to enslave us once more?"

"As tribe elder, I have considered these things. Ice Island is harsh. There is no opportunity for growth. We would be far better off on our natural homeland. Kira's truth spell tells us she has changed permanently; you may cast your own if you wish. And we cannot demand revenge, for she is our guest for one, and in recognition of hundreds of years of atonement I have forgiven her in the name of the tribe."

Marko was speechless for a count of ten. Then, he shouted, "No! You are mad! Or worse, senile! Our ancient enemy, the reason why we live in this barren wasteland is delivered into our hands, and you *forgive* her? Hundreds of our people enslaved and then dead by her magic! I will not permit it!"

Kala shook her head. "Nine hundred years ago, Marko. Eight hundred years of repentance and sorrow. What do you *want*? Her death? It would be easier, I think than what she is trying to do. And you will not permit it? I remind you, I am tribe elder here, not you. I have spoken, it is my right and it is *done*."

Marko held his clenched fists by his side, in barely controlled anger. "I have waited, Kala. Yes, I was prepared to let you live out your days as tribe elder. What did it matter, with one day much like the other?

But no longer. I say you are no longer fit to be elder, and I challenge!"

There was a stirring in the crowd, who had been looking from one strong person to the other as the debate went on. "You challenge? My kin, you challenge me? No elder has been challenged for over four hundred years. I beg you not to do this. You cannot release the guilt you feel by blaming this woman. I know what you are thinking. If not for her, we would not be here, and then those in your party that were dear to us would not have died. But you cannot avoid things in that way."

Stubbornly, Marko shook his head, and spoke the ritual formula. "I challenge you, here and now, as you stand, with no other help to be given to either of us. We stand in the great hall, the pattern is on the floor. The people are here, we only need two judges. Or, you can admit you were wrong and retract your forgiveness. You know you cannot win, I in my turn say to you, I have no desire to harm kin."

Kala shook her head. "A leader must stand by her decisions. I will fight, as I stand now, and with no further help. Knives and Avatars, and at least I agree on one thing, we shall do it now."

For the first time, Marko looked unsure. Was the old lady truly senile? He knew that she could barely summon two Avatars these days. He could also summon two, and they would engage hers, leaving him free with his knife. No contest against an ancient woman who could not walk without a cane.

Ice Witches are nothing if not bound by tradition. And tradition is a great help when unusual circumstances arise, it tells you what to do, short circuiting the need to think difficult thoughts. The other elders were unsure in the face of these extraordinary events, and so fell back on the tribe law. The ritual challenge had been given and accepted according to required protocol and using the formal words. There was nothing anyone could do, or needed to.

Two knives were speedily brought. Sheena knew the knives would be – or should be – largely symbolic. Ice Witches were nearly as pacific as Seers, who didn't fight at all, and the ritual contests almost never ended in anyone hurt, less so than in the Seers Hold Tribe. The Warriors fought all the time, of course – but there it was for training and evaluation – or work, not the settlement of issues, which was done by arbitration. No, the real fights with injury and bloodshed happened between the hot-headed Fire Witches.

The crowd drew back from the traditional square marked on the floor, and the leader and the would-be leader opposed each other.

Marko projected his two material Avatars. And to the great surprise of all present, Kala projected her three, and let her cane fall to the ground.

"What? How?" Marko exclaimed, stunned.

Kala replied in a loud, clear voice. "I knew you would challenge, Marko. A leader must know her people, and I knew you would. It is your nature. I can project my full three Avatars, because Sha'Lin'Tra is lending me her energies. Fire Witches are better at it than we are, and she is best of all, and can hold this spell for long enough."

"This is trickery! It is not allowed!" and indeed, there were murmurs from the crowd.

Even in this extremity, the nature of Ice Witches came through. Marko allowed Kala the right of reply. "It is trickery indeed, but it is allowed" she said, in her ringing voice. "She was lending me her strength before you challenged, as I commanded her to. And you challenged me, according to the old formula, as I knew you would. Here and now, as I stood, with no other help to be given. Well, no other help has been given since your challenge – just the help I was already being given, as I stood there. And so now, you must fight me, in my full strength."

To give Marko credit, he did not just concede. Hoping to shatter an Avatar, he lunged with his knife. But, energized, Kala was a match for him, her reactions swift and sure. Balancing Avatars and one's Physical is an art form, and Kala had over a hundred years more practice than Marko. While he concentrated attention on one Avatar or the other, hers moved independently and simultaneously. Two of her Avatars engaged Marko's two, and the third easily avoided the knife, ducked around his back and grabbed his arms in a lock. And then, stasis achieved, all that remained was for her to slowly walk across the floor, and put her knife to his neck. "I say the fight is won" she called, "and I ask the judges to award me the victory. I have no desire to harm kin." And the judges concurred.

Kala remounted the podium and spoke again, while Marko fumed to one side, angry and defeated. "My people, I am done. My decisions are vindicated. What needs to be done for us and our future is now set in motion, and as your leader I am happy it has been done well. This fight, where Sha'Lin'Tra, or Sheena, to give her preferred name, gave me her support according to my specific command and against her will, is over. But there is a price to pay, which I pay gladly. Sheena will continue to support me up to the limit of her powers, though it gets harder each minute that passes for her. But when she withdraws it, as she must, it may be that the strain will prove too much and I will pass on."

There was a stirring, and many a shocked exclamation. "No matter, I would not have lived many months more in any case, and I am happy to have been of service to the end. And, it may not be so – I may yet linger on, if Sheena can support me for long enough and slowly withdraw. But while I am still full of strength I would like to thank you all. It has been a privilege to lead you. I have loved you all, you are a worthy people. When Kira returns from her great quest, I hope she and Sha'Lin'Tra, as foreseen, will lead you back to Iceland and you will once again become a *great* people. And now, I must go to my bed, if there is any chance that I might survive the day, and there are yet tasks to be done by all of us. I bid you, depart to your various tasks – though any who would say farewell, I suggest you hasten to my chambers as soon as you might. That is all."

Disciplined and ordered to the end, the Ice Witches dispersed from the hall. Kala and her Avatars were almost the last to leave, though Sheena and Kira remained to help. A few people stayed to move chairs and clean up, but largely the convocation was over. But Marko stayed. He moved towards Sheena, and said, with passion and fury in his voice: "you may think you have won, that you have beaten me, but ..."

Sheena replied in an even voice "I have not won, because I have not fought. I have no right to do so. I serve only, here, I must ..."

But she got no further, because Marko lunged towards her with his knife. All of her strength was going towards supporting Kala, and she could not project her one Avatar. She was in no danger, of course – a

200

man with a knife against a Red Warrior. But Kira was there, with her Avatar, and did not think or know of that. She flung herself between Marko and Sheena, and cried out, "Stop!" But Marko would not be stayed. "Stupid girl, get your Avatar out of my face!" He snarled, and thrust with his knife high up into her chest before Sheena could do anything.

But the Avatar did not dissolve, fractured and dissipated. Instead, Kira cried out in pain and fear, and sank to the floor. Her Avatar, off to the side, did shatter then. And there was blood everywhere.

Kala span around in the doorway, and two voices cried out as one, with the same thought: "God in Heaven, what have you done?" and "Oh, God, what have I done?"

And the third major player turned to Marko, no longer Sheena, but in some way Sha'Lin'Tra the Great. Though still committed to supporting Kala and still limited by the spell constraining her magic, in the extremity of emotion something still boiled over, and dangerous magic crackled about her. A wild red and green aura swirled about her. There was a sense that something terrible was about to happen. But quickly, quickly she brought it under control. With a sharp voice of command, she snapped: "Marko. You and your Avatars, pick her up and take us to your infirmary, sick room or hospital, whatever you have." And she sank to her knees, waiting for everyone else to gather their wits, herself feeling with experienced fingers into the wound on Kira's chest, seeking ruptured veins and arteries that might be at least temporarily blocked. "Move!" she screamed in passion, as everyone seemed to be frozen in horror.

Kala spoke. "Sha'Lin'Tra. I command you as is my right. Release your strength from me, use your Avatar.

Kira must be saved. Marko, this might be my final command. Do whatever is required of you to fix this madness."

Sheena looked at Kala in agony. Gritting her teeth, she forced her will away from the ancient woman. In an astonishing display of recovery, she projected her Material Avatar and caught Kala as she collapsed, and lowered her gently to the floor. Then, she changed the Avatar to an Ethereal one and made her diagnosis. Ethereal Avatars have some advantages: they can penetrate solid matter without affecting it, like a ghost. She quickly investigated the deep wound in Kira's chest, and finding those severed vessels at most risk of ending her life, re-materialized the Avatar to hold the two major ones closed. In itself an amazing display of a virtuoso of magic: most Witches would have needed to reabsorb and re-project their Avatars to switch between their natures, wasting precious seconds if not minutes.

She screamed at Marko: "Come on, man, pull yourself together! Pick her up, and Kala too!"

And commanded from two sides, without thinking, Marko and one Avatar bent to their tasks. Weeping, he carried Kira's slight frame while his Avatar carried Kala's somewhat heavier one at a run through the halls, past passage after passage, window after window showing an ever-changing view onto the snow like a surreal nightmare.

Finally, after what seemed like an eternity they came to the sick-rooms. Fortunately, not much used at that time – there were beds available, and healers came at the run. Sheena explained what she had found with her Ethereal Avatar. The healer nodded, and using Ice Magic did what he could. He shook his head dubiously: "I have her stable. I have closed the vessels with constrictions, and can hold it. When I weaken, others can take over. But it is a stopgap measure at best. The wound is severe, fatal unless we treat it, and disabling if we do. It would take all three of our best healers, and there will be much scarring. She may lose the use of her arm. She could die, if infection sets in." He seemed uncertain. "What would you have me do?"

From the next bed, Kala seemed to be nearing her last. It was a miracle of will that she had held together for as long as she had. "Attend me" she gasped. "Sheena, you must lend me your strength again."

"Kala, if I do, when I release it, you will die, for sure!"

"I am dying right now. I command you!"

And once again, Sheena acknowledged her burden and debt, agreeing to Kala's command and recognizing her right. Kala's breathing eased. She drew a shuddering breath, and another. And then, she sat up in bed, to the healer's astonishment. "No time for that" she said, waving him away.

"Marko, come here." And Marko went, tears streaming down his face. "You have done an unbelievably stupid thing. And you must pay the price. For though Kira's life is in great danger, it may yet be saved."

"I will do anything, grandmother. Anything!" he said.

"I have forgiven Sha'Lin'Tra. She works in our cause. And you must work with her. The oldest records we have say that the greatest Fire Witches and the greatest Ice Witches working in close harmony could perform wonders of healing. Do you know the techniques, Sheena?"

Sheena nodded. "I do, Kala. But they are hard. I will be limited, because of my class one status, though my strength will be an asset. But Marko knows nothing of them. The only way it can work, and it will be a poor compromise at first, will be if he totally surrenders his will to mine and I show him. I do not know if he can do this."

Kala looked at Marko. "You must. I cannot, I am only alive because of Sheena's strength, we can't work together on this anymore than you can lift yourself up by your belt. You're only third-best healer, but you are the strongest Ice Witch we have."

Marko looked at the two of them in horror. He shook his head. "I cannot! I cannot! How can I forgive her? How can I trust her? How can I subjugate my will to hers? What if she takes over my mind and does not release it?"

Kala exclaimed in frustration. "Tschaaa! What if? What if? This is not a time for what-ifs. You said, you would do *anything*. Would you not give your *life* now, if your sister's daughter could be saved? This is your *responsibility*. If she takes over your mind, who *cares*? What value is your mind? I know what you did. I know what you *thought*. You thought that Kira had put her Avatar between you and Sha'Lin'Tra. Because you thought, she would not be so foolish as to put her body at risk. But she is only fourteen! She is less used to her Avatar than I am, or even you are. It was *natural* for her to use her body, in that extremity. Surely she would not expect that her uncle would use a knife on her, even on her Avatar. But you did. What *use* is your mind, if it thinks like that? What use is your *life*?"

Marko sank his head, the tears flowing freely.

"And you cannot forgive, and you cannot trust. I have forgiven Sha'Lin'Tra. I trust her. And I have forgiven you for the death of Kira's mother and father. Yes, I

204

know, it was an accident and not your fault. But still, your responsibility, you were the lead hunter. But I have forgiven you. And Kira has forgiven you. And you have killed me, for though I breathe yet, I am but a dead woman on borrowed time. And I forgive you for *that*, too. And you have all but killed Kira. But I will forgive even that, if you will do what you said. You said you would do *anything*. Do it! Have the courage of your word!"

Marko sat on the edge of the bed. In total abject surrender, he said, "I will do it. I will do whatever it takes."

Kala nodded, in regal dismissal. She turned to the healer, and asked: "Kira. Is she truly stable?"

The healer replied, "Yes, as I said. If there is really anything this Fire Witch can do, it would be better done soon, but it won't matter for a few more minutes."

Kala again nodded, "Good. Then, if you have some wine in this place, I would like you to bring me a glass of it."

A glass of medicinal wine was speedily brought, and Kala raised it. "I drink to you, Sha'Lin'Tra. Do as I have commanded and my people will be well served." She turned to Marko. "I drink to you Marko, for all your stubborn ways I love you still, great grandson. You will be a fine leader of our people when I am gone and until Kira returns. I hope you find peace, and what path in life best suits you." Lastly, she turned to Kira. "I drink to you, Kira. You will be an extraordinary woman and a great leader. I am sorry I cannot say goodbye to you, for I love you. But perhaps you will farewell me in your dreams."

And she drained the glass, and with a sigh of satisfaction laid her head back on the pillow and closed her eyes. After a second, she opened one, and said to Sheena, "Well, what are you waiting for? Get on with it, girl. Woman. Whatever you are. And may God bless you too. May God bless you all."

And she shut her eyes, and as Sheena withdrew here energizing support, breathed her last. The healer reverently felt her pulse, and shook his head in amazement.

Sheena turned to Marko calmly. "I hope you are truly committed to this. It cannot be done if you are not." And Marko replied, in a dead voice, "I am. Let it be done."

Sheena led him to Kira's bed, and directed him to one side, his arms to be over her pale, barely breathing body. She went to the other side, and also kneeling, put her arms over in the same way, clasping his hands.

"What do I have to do?" he said calmly. "Do nothing. Close your eyes. When I begin my spell, it will feel a bit like a truth spell, but firmer. Perhaps, unpleasant. Some people say it feels slimy, other rough, other smooth. I can't tell you what to expect, only that it will be hard if you resist."

"I will not resist" Marko said flatly.

Marko had experienced a truth spell. As with so many of the forms of magic, there is nothing like having it done to one to help make one understand the principle. He felt a slight intrusion, a numbing of the will, that suddenly there were things he could no longer do, though the things that remained to him were still under his conscious control.

All Ice Witches are taught healing, if only to discover their potential. A good healer is valuable beyond all price. He felt Sheena's will sliding over the fibers of his mind, towards (if parts of the mind can have a direction) where he would have said his healing ability was located. He understood how different people would feel it in different ways: it felt to him like someone running their hand lightly over his forearm, and that can feel anything from sensuous to frightening. To him, it felt intrusive and ticklish, the feeling that would make one withdraw that forearm and hold it close to one's body. He forced himself to stay unresisting as the feeling crept over him.

And suddenly, her power was in his mind. With the gasping shock one might feel when, having tried to jump and only achieved a foot or so, one is propelled to the height of a champion pole-vaulter, he felt that healing part of his mind suddenly focused and lifted. While they were far above his own levels, he could see how it was done. Marveling, he felt his perception being extruded towards Kira, in a very similar way to how Avatar sense perception operated. Like a net, his and Sheena's meshed consciousness met Kira's exposed flesh, and radar-like images came back to him.

He saw the severed ends of major vessels, and watched as Sheena clumsily forced two of them together, and drew deep of his strength. The edges were made to fray, like tiny tendrils of cloth, and the tendrils divided further, almost down to the cellular level. And then the two ends were held in place, and a command given. Individual cells changed the nature of their membranes, and they stuck. Over and over Sheena projected a wave of healing to them, and he felt his strength waning.

Finally, Sheena sighed, "It is done. One large vessel is mended. Poorly, and not the largest, but I am not good at this. Marko, do you see how it is done?"

"I do", he said, unbelievingly.

"There are at least three more that must be done today. Tomorrow will be another story, but you cannot be the source of strength. You must do the work and I will direct the strength. It will not be easy, this is not the proper way of doing it. The Ice Witch should be the director. But that's how it must be today."

Hesitantly, Marko did a role-reversal, letting his mind wake up. Sheena groaned and the mind-mesh shifted. He moved the net slightly, and focused on another, smaller vessel. Remembering what Sheena had done, he tried to do the same. It was hard, but somehow his control was finer. He could never have done it by himself the first time, he felt Sheena driving the strength into him, buoying up the intensity of perception. But he felt a wash of pain from the side. He opened his eyes, and saw Sheena grimacing.

"Am I doing it right?" he asked. "You are hurting!"

Sheena snarled: "It *will* hurt. It *must* hurt, doing it this way. Teaching it *always* hurts. Don't worry, I can take it. Do what must be done."

He divided the vessel walls and the tendrils as he had been taught, meshed them and fed the joining command. It seemed easier than what Sheena had done, somehow. He could see that despite it being his first attempt, he had done a better job of it, the ends were better aligned and straighter. But she had to direct both his and her energy, to push it, and it hurt her as he learned. In pain, the first one was done, more on the second, and the third was agony. He could feel the distress coming in waves across Kira's body.

Finally, Sheena told him to stop, and to do his best to direct. He must do the largest vessel, and both direct and draw the strength from Sheena. And it was easy, far easier than when she was showing him how the energy should flow. But still exhausting.

"The major vessels are healed. There are others, but they can wait, or heal themselves if need be" the healer marveled, his Avatar having observed the process. "But there is still damage to the top of the lung, tendons and ligaments, muscle and nerves. Still, she may live. Certainly, she is out of immediate danger."

"That is good" Sheena said in aching relief. "I'd forgotten how hard this is. But now, Marko, I must take control again, and show you how to heal those things. We can't possibly do it all today, but you will need to know for next time."

Once again, he felt the intrusion along magical pathways, easier to take this time. She showed him the techniques for joining ligaments and tendons – similar to the blood vessels, except the tendrils had to be far longer but could be coarser, much like interweaving two pieces of rope. And muscle, which required something in between, and nerves, which were hardest of all – tiny little strings that had to be aligned perfectly, cell to cell, and then joined with the smallest of stitching. Sheena knew how, but she was clumsy, unbelievably clumsy it seemed to Marko. And though he was near-exhausted, she made him role-reverse again, and do one example of each type. He stopped when he could no longer do it, and Sheena's whimpers of pain through clenched teeth were more than he could bear.

"Done for the day, thanks be to God" Sheena groaned, and done they were. They sat, exhausted, while the healers salved and bound Kira's wound, all they could do. At least they had the technique for keeping her asleep mastered, so she did not need to suffer.

But others suffered that day. The news travelled fast that Marko had caused Kala's death, and nearly Kira's as well. Perhaps surprisingly, Sheena was his greatest ally, repeating patiently and calmly that Kala had forgiven him at the end, and it was her life, so if she could do so, they should do so too. And she told them that Kira was out of danger for the moment, and that over the next few days she was going to make sure Marko healed her, but it was going to be hard work, so could everyone please leave him alone?

Bronn and Kara came out again later in the afternoon to eat again, and Sheena brought them up to date. Kara was shocked that Kala had gone so suddenly, but not devastated. She too had known that Kala had only a little time left, and shook her head admiringly at how the old leader had managed her last few hours: in full strength, and looking to her people's future. As one of the elders and also kin, it would be Kara's responsibility to organize, or at least initiate funeral arrangements. Bronn, of course offered to help where he could, and they went off to seek the other elders.

Marko had in the meantime discreetly made himself scarce. Sheena tracked him down, and finally found out that he had gone to his own room. She knocked on the door, and when an ambiguous grunt came out, opened it and went in. She saw, as she somewhat expected, a tired looking man, about as despondent and bitter as it is possible to get.

"Sheena" he said, turning his head slightly. "Have you come to make my misery complete." He paused a second, then gave a bitter laugh. "Even that sounds pathetic. What use am I?"

Sheena shook her head. "I have sworn to harm no Ice Witch, if I can avoid it. No, I have come for other reasons. Firstly, I have a request, that two or more of your hunters and a sled be dispatched due west, to look for a red pennant on a stick, which marks the position of my balloon, about two miles away. We will have no great need for it for the moment, but it should not be lost, if possible. Too late for it today of course, but tomorrow should be soon enough, not much snow is predicted."

Marko nodded, without much interest. "It shall be done. I will send two good men at first light tomorrow. Is that all? I would rather be alone for a while."

"Not quite. You have had a hard day. Many evils have befallen you. I would like to help you, if you will let me."

"Many evils have befallen me? Say, rather, I have done many evil things."

Sheena agreed. "Indeed. And the worst evils that can befall one are those that one does oneself."

Marko slapped his thighs in self-anger. "How could you know what I feel? I have killed kin, my great-several-times grandmother, and half-killed my sister's daughter. And for what? Cold revenge against you, for something done to people I never knew, against the will of my tribe's leader. I know now, as Kala pointed out to me in her dying breath, it was all for guilt, the guilt I have felt for so many years over Kira's father and mother."

Sheena looked at him soberly. "I assure you, I know very well what it is to do terrible things, and then to suffer for them when the realization of the evil of what one has done becomes plain. Very well indeed. I say it with no pride that few know it better than I do."

Marko raised his head, and looked at her. "Hmm. Perhaps you do. Yes, perhaps. I can see that. And what do you advise me to do?"

Sheena half-smiled. "It is mostly done. Seek forgiveness. Kala has already given it to you, and Kira will, no doubt, when she is recovered, she is full of kindness. Seek to heal the harm you have done. You have already made a good start there, and we will do more tomorrow and in the days to come. Vow to never do it again. Do a penance. And then, you will have done all you can, and should be able to forgive yourself."

Marko breathed in shakily and deeply, and sighed it out. "You give me hope. I thank you, I do feel better. What penance should I do? Go and fetch your balloon myself?"

Sheena shook her head. "That's no penance. It is simply an act. Acts of contrition are good, but a penance must be something you would not ordinarily do. An act of trust, selflessness. I will give you one, if you wish."

"Well, you had me in the palm of your ... mind this afternoon, and no harm came to me. What would you have me do?"

"You cannot know beforehand. You must simply agree that you will allow me to command you, and will do as I ask, no matter what it may be. That is penance."

Marko thought for a while. Finally, he sighed again, and replied: "Very well, Sha'Lin'Tra, I place myself in your hands. Give me a hard penance, and I will perform it as well as I can, without argument or complaint."

"Very well, then, Marko. Rise off your bed. Now, firstly, don't call me Sha'Lin'Tra again. Sheena is my name. Secondly ..." - she approached him and stood only inches away – "kiss me."

Marko looked at her completely dumbfounded.

"Kiss me. That is my command."

Though commanded and committed to obey, Marko was hesitant, and Sheena had to do most of the work. "Not very good. Now, put this arm around me, and that hand *here*, and do it again, with some feeling this time."

"Well, I didn't expect that" Marko marveled some time later, looking at the incredible woman lying next to him, in the circle of his arm. What ... why? What have I done to deserve this, to deserve your favor?"

Sheena looked at him. "Can you not just accept it? Do you have to know?"

Marko looked troubled. "You mean there *is* a reason. Yes ... I ... yes, I need to know."

Sheena sighed. "Very well. But, there is more than one reason. You must agree to hear them all."

Marko agreed. By mutual consent, they moved a little apart, and Sheena lent on her side, supporting her head with one arm. Although covered by the sheet and blanket, this exposed quite a lot of her body to Marko's view, and he momentarily forgot what they had been talking about. As Sheena began to talk, he forced his gaze upwards.

"Well, firstly I could see that you were strongly affected by today's events and disasters, that you were carrying a burden of guilt and sorrow. Quite rightly, of course, you did terrible things. But I felt sorry for you. I know all too well what that burden feels like."

"Ah. Pity." Marko looked despondent once more.

Sheena reached out and touched his nose with her finger. "Hey. You said you would hear all the reasons."

"Sorry" Marko muttered.

"Secondly, I have sworn to hurt no Ice Witch, and more, to actively help them wherever I can. When Bronn and Kira and I are gone, the tribe will need a strong leader, to do what must be done, and prepare for evacuation and the move when we return. They will need you. And you couldn't do the job if you were off in a mess of self-loathing. I have lived a long, long time, and I know what a strong man needs to get him out of that state."

Marko went to speak again, but restrained himself.

Sheena nodded approvingly. "Thirdly, tomorrow and most likely some days after, we will need to continue to work together to heal Kira. You will need to lead, to direct, and draw the strength from me rather than having me force it. That sort of thing works best if there is a bond between the two people. It doesn't have to be *this* kind of bond of course, but it works well. So, if you have to, think of it as sacrificing yourself for Kira."

214

Marko threw back his head and laughed at that. He didn't speak, but looked at Sheena in a happier way.

"And fourthly ... I have been inside your mind. It's a strong one, full of passion and conviction. More like mine than any Ice Witch I've ever met, they are generally a cool headed and restrained bunch. Placid. It was full of the wrong ideas of course, but I'm the last one to hold that against you. Frankly, though we were working on healing and it was hard and painful, I found you interesting and exciting. Yes, to be sure there is certainly duty and need involved. But the most pleasant duties are those you want to do."

Marko lay back with his hands behind his head. His vanity had been stroked, and he was well pleased. Being an intelligent man, he knew that Sheena had probably intended that to be the case, but he was content, he would ask no more.

"And besides, it will be something to tell your grandchildren ... when the old stories come up in Iceland, and people mention Sha'Lin'Tra the Great ... you will be able to say, 'Oh, Sha'Lin'Tra. I knew her well, of course ... I used to call her Sheena. We were lovers for a time, I still remember the first day she came to my bed ... we made love so many times!'"

Marko turned his head to her. "But we've only done it once!"

Sheena smiled, and drew herself closer to him. "Ah, but the night is still young."

Chapter 8. Awakenings and healings

It's a long, long road
From which there is no return
While we're on the way to there
Why not share
And the load
Doesn't weigh me down at all
He ain't heavy, he's my brother.

The Hollies

"Well, I didn't expect that" Bronn marveled, as he lay in bed, Kara snuggled up delightfully to him. The firebox had burned low overnight, the cold had seeped into the room, and though the bedcovers were warm, they were only just comfortable in their little nest. One of them would have to get up soon and put more seaweed-wood on the fire, but at the moment they were both too comfortable and drowsy, having just woken up.

Bronn was speaking about his dream, which Kara had shared with him. Synchronized dreaming was amongst the rarest of Seer phenomena. Apart from Seeing what would happen if Kara accompanied Bronn and Sheena on the trip back to Iceland and the quest (unpleasant death), they had Seen a Vision of a possible complex move of the Ice Witches back to Iceland and how it might be done, with ships and sleds. And then, they had dreamed they were walking along a quiet beach somewhere, and talking. But they did not dream of what they would say sometime in the future: they dreamed they were together in the present, and talked as if they were awake, lucid dreaming, and both remembered it clearly.

Kara had been saying how much she disliked the cold of Ice Island, and hoped Iceland would be warmer. Bronn had told her that it was, marginally, but still bleak and icy in the winter, and much of the other seasons too. Kara had thoughtfully replied: "I love my people. But I don't suppose there is any chance you could take me away from all of that? I could still come and visit them ... in the summer. Couldn't we go away and live somewhere warmer?"

In joy, Bronn had told her about Seer's Hold. He would have lived with her anywhere she wanted, of course, but to return home and live with her there would be paradise doubled. He spoke feelingly about the warm seas, the pleasant climate, and the thermal springs and the natural spa baths of all temperatures, mineralized water or pure, sulfur if you wanted it. He said that of course, as a gifted Seer she would be welcomed and there would be important and satisfying work for her to do. Her Ice Magic skills would be well regarded too, she could be assured of a prominent place. She agreed that it would be paradise to her, as well. And so they hugged each other in an ecstasy of anticipation. They both knew the quest still had to be completed, and there was no assurance of its success, or even Bronn's survival, but somehow it was impossible to think that way in that moment. Time enough for fear, worry and doubt in the loneliness coming all too soon.

Sheena and Marko woke somewhat late too, and made use of the Ice Witch habit of communal bathing: a large tub, big enough for twelve people to sit comfortably and holding a goodly amount of heated water was available. Quite apart from the pleasure of the bath itself, there was a need to have such a resource available in case the very young, old or sick got hypothermia or a Witch over-extended his or herself and needed warming up. It was a rare day when the tubs were used only for soaking and not for need. Of course, people cleaned themselves before getting in, with oil, soap and a wash in a minimal amount of water. Perhaps strangely amongst a people who were by necessity clothed most of the time, there was little in the way of a nudity taboo amongst the Ice Witches, and men and women soaked together without a second's thought. A rotating shift of two dozen Witches, six on duty, whose abilities lay in that direction, heated the water. It was done in much the same way as Fire Witches used heat, though rather than the powerful linking to a volcano they used the temperature difference between the surface of the world and the deep sea to do work. Very capable themselves, they were interested in the difference between their magic and that of a Fire Witch, and were delighted when Sheena heated the bath a good ten degrees in a few minutes. They could see how it was done, though it wasn't their kind of magic.

Perhaps implicit in the ability of a group of people to be naked in the same tub without concern was that pairs or groups of people could have conversations that anyone *could* overhear, but were essentially private. Sheena was talking to Marko about what would have to be done today. He had already dispatched two hunters to fetch the balloon, but Kira would need to have the bulk of the healing done that day. Otherwise, the severed ends would tend to scar over naturally and everything would be much harder. After today would come more subtle work: integrating the healing and retraining muscles and nerves. But today would be hard. Marko would have to direct and guide, and draw on Sheena to provide the energy. Today would be the opposite of yesterday, Sheena's mind would be wide open and defenseless. She warned Marko not to take too much advantage of that: if he explored her mind and went down memory chains, he would most likely encounter things that would be hard

218

to face, and would detract from the healing process. Despite eight hundred years and the best of intent, hers was still not a normal mind, in some ways not a sane mind. Best not to look too closely.

After a cool rinse and breakfast, Sheena returned to her room and changed. Someone had volunteered to clean her outfit and rework it with warmer furs and materials; they knew more and could make much better and warmer clothing than Bronn had been able to buy at Carm. This left her very little, but she made do with some warm leggings, the housboots, a halter top and the warm cloak, it would be enough for a few hours.

They walked slowly down to the sickrooms. Kira was still in forced sleep, but had had basic needs of food and toileting seen to in one way or another. Sheena explained to the healer what they were intending to do. Opening her mind, she showed them the techniques of Ice Magic she had used so clumsily the day before. They were simple and elegant, obviously an order of magnitude or more than what an Ice Witch could do alone – but equally obviously they needed the opposite polarity of a Fire Witch to work. And the Fire Witch had to be in the submissive role, not a natural state for them. Sadly, this simple necessity had been the cause of a lot of resentment a millennium ago. A pair of level one Witches working together could handle simple ailments and problems effectively. Two level twos could work wonders, and two level threes perform miracles. While there might be a level three Fire Witch on Fireland, with the death of Kala there was no-one above level two in Ice Island, and the only Fire Witch they had was Sheena, level one – but with an extraordinary level of skill and internal energy. They would do what they could.

They set to work. Better organized this morning, they had suitable chairs either side of Kira. Sitting with arms crossed over her body, Sheena calmed her mind and opened it, and Marko did his best to do what she had done, engaging her mind without penetrating it. Something like a truth spell, and something not quite the same. He used the healing concentration mantras, and as yesterday felt his perception going out to Kira. As before, it was like seeing with an Ethereal Avatar, though this time while he could feel the steady flow of energy he was taking from Sheena that boosted him and allowed him to focus so finely, down to the individual muscle, tendon and nerve fibers, there was no accompanying sense of pain. They were working well together, their bond from last night making it easier.

He worked without sense of time. Painstakingly, dozens of muscle bundles were re-tied together. Tendons and sheets of ligaments were located, matched and joined. He did not know what to do with the lung tissue, and left it for later. And there were simply too many tiny nerves to fix them all. He chose an arbitrary size and stopped when he could find no more above that. He knew from his past healing experience that small nerves would regenerate with time.

He decided to stop, and ask Sheena about the lung. Slowly withdrawing his control, he allowed his consciousness to return to normal. Suddenly, a bone-deep weariness came over him, and he struggled his eyes open. Sheena was slumped over Kira, exhausted. The healer said, "Marko, thank God you have awoken! We didn't know what to do – you have been at it for four hours!"

Marko looked around him blearily. Four hours? It had seemed like only minutes! Was Sheena alright? He shook her, and her eyes slowly unglazed. "Marko ... Marko, you can't do it like that! You have to do small amounts of work at a time! If you work like that, you'll kill your co-worker Fire Witch!"

"I'm sorry, I didn't know – you didn't tell me!"

Sheena sighed. "My fault, I suppose. I haven't done that for hundreds of years. Well, let's see how we are going. Healer Matrolo, how is Kira now?"

Once again, the healer was amazed. "Nearly completely healed! At least, everything I can see, apart from the skin, and we can stitch that. Wait a minute, the lung itself is still damaged."

Marko nodded. "Yes, I didn't know what to do about the lung"

"There's not much you can do, Marko. Lung tissue is too hard to fix. You can't heal it, we would have to rebuild it from scratch. Just close off any exposed veins to stop the bleeding, and if the damage isn't too great the lung will heal itself quite quickly, it has good regenerative powers."

The healer said, "If you don't mind, we should not wake her up just yet. She has been asleep for a long time, but the injury is not fully healed. There would be pain, especially if she moved."

Sheena agreed. "Yes, that will be fine. When we have had a bit of a rest, Marko can seal off the lung vessels, I'll show him what to do about the skin, and he can go over the whole area again and fix up anything we've missed."

Sheena said that she was going to take Marko to the great hall, get some food, and leave the healer to clean up the wound in preparation for the skin healing, and

221

give her a general check-up. Kira began to cough in her sleep, and brought up quite a bit of blood. But Sheena reassured the healer that most of it was left-over, and the little bit of bleeding that was still happening would be sorted out very soon.

They went to the hall, where a late lunch was still served, and ate. Puzzlingly, the Witch who put food on their plates looked at Sheena with simmering resentment. Marko didn't notice, and Sheena had other more pressing concerns. But she filed it away for another day.

Once again, Sheena ate ravenously; Marko had drawn deeply on her reserves. She said that he had done good work, fine healing – and by that she meant fine as in detailed. She said that they should be finished in a couple of hours, and that with frequent interruptions to catch their breath, not two hours straight.

"And then what will we do?" Marko said suggestively. Sheena laughed. "Not what you think" she replied. "For one thing, you've totally worn me out with the healing, I'll sleep like a log tonight. For another, Kira will need someone to be near her tonight. And also, if I am with you every night, you will become dependent on me, perhaps even fall in love. That wouldn't be good for you, for I have to go away soon, and may not return. And if I do return, I will have many responsibilities for many years ... and when they are done, I don't know what will happen."

Marko looked down at the table. "I see. You've done your duty, and now want to move on. You could never love me. Well, I suppose I should be happy with what I have had, but somehow ..."

Sheena reached out and touched his arm. "There are many days – and nights - before I must leave. I'm not saying we will not be together again. Just not every night. It wouldn't be good for you. I know what you're going to say – you've never met anyone like me. Well, that is true enough. But unusual or different is not necessarily good. And you've never felt as intensely. Yes, I know – I can see these things, long experience helps in these matters. My take is, you've been carrying guilt about with you over Kira's parents' death for a long time, and that has gotten in the way of intimacy for you. But I believe that Kala's formal forgiveness will make a difference for you, and you will find things easier. As for the last … let me tell you a part of my story."

She told him of how she had loved, and burned the capability for love out of her mind, to her bitter regret over the centuries. He did not understand, he had thought they had had joy together, but she explained that though she could still have pleasure, and the time with him had been a happy one, while pleasure and happiness are often involved with love, they are not the same thing.

"So, Marko" she said, looking at him bleakly, "please understand. If I thought that by staying with you I could rediscover the capacity to love, nothing would keep me away. I would give up everything, do anything. But I have tried it before, and I would not expose you to the result."

Marko didn't really understand. Who could? But like most Ice Witches, he was a realist and practical, and nodded, and said "So, we'll see each other again? Well, that's something"

Sheena nodded. "Yes. It's something. Not enough, not by a long way. But it is something."

By mutual agreement, they returned to the sickrooms in silence. The healer removed the bandage and exposed the last bit of the stab wound, a hole in the skin, now with sound muscle underneath. Well attuned now, Sheena led and showed Marko how to use one's fingers to pull the skin together till the edges just touched, and then mesh the edges. The tendrils had to be small, though not as small as for nerve fibers, but most important was the alignment. The slightest misalignment would lead to healing, but with a scar. And then, the loose skin had to be reattached to the lower layers. Not too tightly otherwise there would be wrinkles, nor too loosely or it would be vulnerable.

Then Sheena relinquished control, Marko took over and did the work, and as before Sheena supplied the energy. He stopped after the skin was rejoined; amazed again that it had taken twenty minutes. They rested, and he did the subcutaneous linkages. Then, they looked at the result. It was perfect, except for one small scar less than half an inch long. Marko frowned. "I don't understand why that is there" he said. Sheena replied, that was the little bit of skin she had done. "It will disappear with time" she apologized. And then, some more work to seal the last bleeding capillaries in the lung, tidy up a few loose ends inside and it would be done. Pretty much right on the two hours.

As Marko was finishing for the last time, instead of simply withdrawing, he hesitated at the last minute. With the feeling that he was doing something wrong, he sent his attention off in another direction. With Sheena's mind quiescent he could see an overview. He had only seen a couple of minds in this state when learning about and practicing truth spells. He could perceive the great stores of energy, and a finer structure and greater complexity than any other mind he had seen. He could feel the limiting spell, lying like a great brooding dragon over it all, and watching him in case he tried to make her do high magic. But appallingly, he could see the great slash across her mind, worse than darkness. He could not bear it. Against his will, he felt his own energy sucked down to it, desperately trying to heal it. No chance. He couldn't have done it with a level three Witch to help him, and without Sheena supporting him it was futile, like a leaf trying to fight the wind. He felt his consciousness fading into that awful absence of anything.

That was what saved him. As he slipped away, he released his hold on Sheena, and she became aware. Quick as a flash, she screamed "You fool of a man! What are you doing?" She pushed him away and out of her mind, dragging him out of the void, like a limp swimmer from a current.

Slowly, he recovered. "Don't *do* that!" Sheena said, angrily. "I *told* you not to! Can you not *listen*? Don't touch things you don't understand and haven't been trained for! Don't you know you can't possibly do *anything* with a mind you are linked to? And certainly not against an internal spell like that! Don't you think that if it *could* be fixed like that, that I would have done it long ago, when I had the best of the best at my beck and call?"

"I'm sorry" he replied miserably. "It seems I'm doomed to failure. Kira's parents, Kala, nearly Kira herself, and now this."

Sheena calmed. She reached out and touched his face. "Don't worry. You wanted to help, and that is a good thing, a kind thing. We all make mistakes, the key is to learn, and not make them again. But now, now we must wake Kira up. And … I think, all in all, it's best if you are not here for that. I'll tell you how it goes." And Marko left, to go his own way for the evening.

225

She waited while the healer relaxed the hold he had on Kira that kept her asleep. Soon she was stirring, and slowly she woke. Seeing Sheena, she smiled, and weakly said, "Oh Sheena, I had the most terrible dream ... I dreamed ..." and then she sat up, gasped, and clutched her chest. She looked down, and saw the tiny scar. She looked up at them in shock, and stammered – "was it real? What happened? I remember ..."

"Easy, Kira, easy. All is well. You were hurt, and badly, but you are nearly healed. Marko made a terrible mistake. He thought your Avatar stood between me and him, and in his anger tried to shatter it. He was at wit's end when he saw it was you, Physical, and is deeply sorry for what he did. He has been working for hours – days - with me to try to set it right."

It is somehow easier to accept harm done by others when it has been fixed, and Kira lay down on her bed, though winced a little as she did, and put her hand up to her chest again.

"Yes, it is healed, but there is still some internal adjustment and retraining to be done. Exercise, stretching and massage will see it as good as new in a week or so. Marko may be an impulsive fool, but he is a very good healer."

She paused. "Kira, I must tell you sometime. Kala ... Kala did not make it when I released my supporting energy, as we feared. She might have lived if I hadn't had to release it so soon, but she might not. It was her choice, she ordered me to release so that I could tend to you. Her last words were forgiveness to Marko, and love for you."

Trembling Kira asked for a detailed account of what had happened. Sheena judged it was better to give it now, after her long rest, rather than let it go on. And Sheena got a chance to repay Kira, and held her while she cried.

"I must ask you to do a hard thing, Kira" she finally said, as the young girl's tears finally subsided.

"Marko did a bad thing. A terrible thing, with many consequences for you, your grandmother ... and himself. Though prone to passion, he has an Ice Witch's sense of duty and responsibility. He was near to emotional collapse when I found him, and though I have spoken with him and consoled him, if you don't forgive him for what he did, it will be the end of him as a man, and more importantly for your tribe, as a leader. You must go away with Bronn and me, but the tribe will need a strong leader while you are gone, and he is the best choice. He will do a good job preparing them for the move home, yet hand over control to you when you are ready."

"I ... I don't know if I can ... if I am ready to forgive him ... "

"You must. It will be hard, but a leader must often do things against her personal inclination, but for the good of the tribe."

"I don't know if I even *want* to be a leader."

"Don't be silly. Your grandmother knew you were the best one for the job. And so do I, and I am sworn to help you. It's obvious you will be the most powerful Ice Witch of your generation, and it's usual that the most powerful is at least offered the job."

"Do you really think so? Do you really think I will ever project two Material Avatars, or even three, as grandmother could?"

227

"You will definitely achieve three. You have the capacity for more."

"More than three? But no Ice Witch has done more than three for hundreds of years!"

"More. I won't say how many more, in my opinion, because if I give you a number, you will take it as a limit. Accept no limits other than what your mind tells you is enough." She grimaced. "Excellent advice. I wish I had heeded it myself."

"Will I maybe be able to project as many as you could?"

"Probably not, because Fire Witches are generally better at pure numbers than Ice. But Ice Witches generally have much better control. And, I was a freak."

"I'd like to learn how to project more. It's so useful! And fun. But the best I've been able to do so far is one Material, and a very tenuous Ethereal one, but only when both are right by me, close."

"It's a skill, a bit like juggling. I'll be happy to teach you as we travel together, and you'll be amazed how easy it is to make progress. Don't be discouraged now, how old are you? Fifteen?"

"Fourteen. I'll be fifteen in five days."

"Well, your progress is very exceptional. I bet there aren't many Witches your age in the tribe who can project one Avatar, let alone send her out of sight and across the ice!"

"There aren't many Witches my age at all. But you're nearly right. All of them can project an Ethereal Avatar, but only one other can send one out of sight, and that not far, and almost none can do a Material one yet."

Sheena nodded. "There you are, then. And already starting on your second! And now ... you should get a good massage from the healers, and a good night's rest. And I must go and speak to Marko again, for he's feeling down again, he did a stupid thing and tried to heal me. Fools rush in ...." She shook her head. "Please think about what I have said, and have an answer ready for him, next time you see him. He will blurt it out, I am sure. That's the way of men." She deliberately smiled at Kira, implicitly including her in the world of grown-up women. Kira took to it at once, and nodded thoughtfully.

Sheena left the infirmary well pleased. She thought she had got the point across to Kira that they had to move forward. The healing had gone well – very well, better than she could have expected. If Marko wanted to, he could have a fine career as a healer, if and when other Fire Witches became available. She navigated the turns to the private quarters, intent on having a word to Marko, and then to a well-deserved early bedtime. But she must have taken a wrong turn, for it became darker and there were fewer lights. Looking ahead, she saw the glimmer of a light not too far off, and went towards it, hoping for a way out rather than having to retrace her footsteps – she hadn't really been paying attention. She found herself, as she turned a corner and went to the light, not in a passage but instead in a storeroom. The heavy smell of seaweed permeated the air, and there was a woman packing dried powder into containers. Sheena said, "Oh, I'm sorry – I've taken a wrong turn. Can you tell me the way to the private quarters from here?"

The woman turned and glowered at her. "You go back and turn right instead of left, then along and left, left again." Simple words. But uttered with concealed venom, a barely subdued bitterness and hatred that amazed Sheena. "Pardon me ... I've seen you before. At lunch, today. Why do you hate me so?"

"You wouldn't understand." The woman turned, and resumed ladling the dried seaweed from the big container to the smaller ones.

"I might, if you explained. And I am sworn to help Ice Witches, and do no harm, so I need to know if I have done something wrong."

"Alright, then!" she said through clenched teeth, and turned to face Sheena. "For two years, I tried to make Marko my man. Two years! And for all he noticed, I might as well not exist. And you're here two days, *two days*, two cursed *days* and in his *bed*. Two *days*! And going there again, I've no doubt, miss lost-because-you-are-a-stranger. Well, you know the way now, so go, go and leave me here. But you've failed, if you've sworn to harm no Ice Witch. You have stabbed me to the heart, and Marko will be no better when you drop him like a soiled rag and leave us. Go!"

Sheena stayed. "I am sorry. I went to Marko's bed, because he was in desperate emotional need. I didn't know anyone else was interested in him, and he certainly didn't tell me. I would not deliberately take another's man, especially as what you say is true, I must leave, and soon. And I have told him this, and he understands. If he's your man, why didn't he tell me?"

"I *told* you, he doesn't notice me. I *love* him, but he just smiles at me and is polite. It takes something more than I have, apparently. It seems he wants what you have, so why don't you go and give it to him? Go, *go* and leave me."

Sheena snorted. She may have sworn to hurt no Ice Witch, to help, but the lack of plain, common get-up-and-go, of the want of a bit of spirit in some of them was hard for a Fire Witch to put up with. The best of them were fine, but some … perhaps a few hard words would stir her out of her self-sacrificing anger.

"Do you *really* call that loving a man? You'll just *let* someone else have him, if that seems to be what he wants? What are you, a woman, or a bit of wet seaweed waiting to be recycled as a doormat? For heaven's sake! I've told you I'm sorry. I've told you I wouldn't dream of being involved with him if he's yours. Why don't you go out and *make* him yours, if you love him? He's in his room right now!"

It raised some reaction. She angrily replied, "What do *you* know of love? Sha'Lin'Tra the Great. Hah! I bet you aren't capable of loving anything or anyone, and you never will!"

Sheena went white with shock. The woman had somehow hit at the core of her fears. She might have fallen, if she had not steadied herself on the wall. And then, exhaustion gave way to rage. "Get out" she said in her turn, between clenched teeth. "Get out! Or oath or no, I will blast you where you stand!" Trembling as she held her white fury under uncertain control, her aura began to flare, a half-inch of danger red, and small crackles of electricity ran down her arms. To an Ice Witch who had never seen a Fire Witch angered it was a terrifying display, for only Fire Witches show an aura, of the four Gifted people. She fled. Sheena waited as long as she could, no more than a few seconds, and ran out of the room. She caught her housecloak on the door latch, ripping it open. With it flapping about her, she ran along the corridors, heedlessly banging into the very few people who didn't get out of her way, and then through the triple doors that kept the cold out, out into the frozen wilderness.

Screaming a primal scream of rage and pain and anguish, she shot bolt after bolt of fire and lightning up into the unyielding sky, using her own internal, depleted energy rather than sourcing the power from elsewhere, until it was exhausted and her aura flickered out and she slumped unconscious and barely alive into the soft, yielding snow.

Two Ice Witches came out to see what the pulsing light was, and two more that were already outside came to help. No stranger to people needing assistance, they lifted her body out of the ice she was not dressed to lie in, took her inside and to the infirmary. They were directed to a bed next to Kira, who sat up, and as the healer rushed over the rescuers told what they had seen as clearly and carefully as they could. The healer nodded, and did a quick diagnosis, checking all the vital signs.

"She's still alive" he said, "but very weak. It's as if she tried to kill herself by using up all her energy. I'm not sure what to do … ordinarily, I would say nothing, she will either recover or not, our healing skills are not up to transferring enough energy to her without killing ourselves and making no difference. But perhaps Marko has learned other techniques from her that could be used here. Someone please run and get him."

The healer did what he could, but his own energy was soon so lowered that he had to sit down. Sheena looked perhaps a fraction less dead, but there was not much in it.

After perhaps three minutes, Marko came at a run. When he was told what needed to be done, he shook his head. "I could maybe do something" he said, "but we would need another Fire Witch."

Kira said, "Can I help? Can you use me instead?"

The healer protested weakly from his chair. "No, you must not. You have had shock and trauma, and need all your energy for yourself. Someone else must do it."

The three remaining rescuers all said they were ready to do whatever was needed, and Marko tried. But it simply didn't work. It was like trying to rub a grater with his brain.

While he was trying the second man, a woman ran in. "I heard ... I heard ... is she alright? I'm sorry, I'm sorry ..."

Marko looked at her, and said, "Shira, what? What are you sorry about? Have you done this to her?"

Shira said, "I ... I don't know. She came to me by accident in a storeroom, and we ..." - she blushed red – "we argued, and said words, and something angered her greatly, and I fled ... and they said she ran outside and collapsed."

Marko looked at her, and asked, puzzled, "What could you say to her that would make her do something like this?"

Shira flushed again. "It ... doesn't matter right now. Is there anything I can do?"

Kira said, gently for the woman was obviously upset, "Shira, what you said may matter and be the key to helping her. Please understand, she is a very old and unusual woman, with very old and unusual problems."

Shira looked at the floor. "Well … I said many angry things. But the last words I said, that seemed to set her off, were that I didn't think she could ever really love anyone or anything."

Kira covered her mouth, with a startled "Oh!" Then she nodded, and replied: "I can see how that would do it. You couldn't know, Shira. But we must do something quickly if we are to help her. Can you work with Marko to try this new form of healing?"

Shira looked at Marko for a moment, but then quickly looked away. "I … would be happy to work with Marko. I'm always happy to work with him, and healing is good work. I'd be happy to learn."

Not having anything else to try, Marko told her how she should relax her mind. She seemed to manage easily enough, considering the situation, and he tentatively let his mind flow to the channel he had learned of so recently. And what a difference! Instead of the grating sensation of the men, it was a cool sensation, almost pleasant. No, not almost – it *was* pleasant, easier than it had been even with Sheena. But he knew he would have to be careful. There was far, far less energy to call on from her than in his previous sessions with the Fire Witch, and though the meshing was exceptional even though it should not have worked, Shira was simply not a very powerful Witch.

Tentatively, he reached forward, and sensed the dearth of energy in Sheena's mind, a flickering net of barely alive parts. Carefully, he tried to funnel energy to the key nodes and channels, stopping after only a few seconds to check if Shira was coping. Three tiny attempts he made before he judged she should give no more. It was barely enough.

"Do you see what I did, and how?" he asked Shira. When she said yes, he said, "Do you think you could do it, and use me as the energy source?" Shira a bit doubtfully said she thought so. "Please try. But please understand, time seems to flow differently. Do no more than a second or two's work, or you may save her but kill me."

Shira's mind slid over his relaxed one, and it was just as pleasant. He relaxed in the pleasant cocoon of control by someone else, letting her guide and supplying energy. It was like when Sheena had led, it didn't work nearly so well with the roles reversed, but at least Shira could draw on his energy instead, and although it made only a fraction of difference that way, every little bit helped. Soon, she was done, and he was exhausted again. But Sheena looked better. She still looked like she was at death's door, but as though she might recover rather than about to go through it.

The healer asked the rescuers to go and get some food, and wine. They all needed sustenance. When they returned some time later, all three were feeling a little stronger, and were able to eat and drink. The healer said all was under control, and the rescuers went their way.

As they rested, Marko said, "Shira, we worked well together. If you like, we could do more healing if the need arises." Shira replied that she would like that, it was good and useful work. Marko nodded, and looked away, the conversation ended, and Shira sighed, and looked at her hands. Marko and Matrolo didn't notice anything, but Kira did, though she kept it to herself.

While they were resting a little, their energy returning, Sheena began to moan in her sleep and toss, as her regenerative systems slowly came alive, and was soon blearily awake. "What … where …" she looked around the room and saw who was there, and memory returned. "Oh." She slumped back on her bed and closed her eyes. "Did you have to call me back? Couldn't you just let me go in peace?"

Kira looked at the others. "This will be a job for me" she said. All of you, please leave the room for five minutes and then come back." The words of command and the tone came easily, and they all obeyed without thinking for a moment that they were being ordered about by a fourteen year old girl.

Kira looked at Sheena for a while. After nearly a minute of silence, Sheena opened her eyes. And Kira wasted no time on sympathy. "You *fool*."

Sheena's mouth opened in shock, but Kira gave her no chance for reply. "Eight hundred years, and finally things are happening, and you want to give it all up because some random Ice Witch says something in the heat of the moment that hurts you."

Sheena flushed, sat up, and angrily began, "How dare you!" but Kira cut her off. "How dare *you*? You are sworn to help me! To help us! Your life is not your own, to do with as you please, any more than mine is! Less! You are sworn to help Bronn in his quest against Narn, and then you are sworn to come back and guide us back to Iceland. We can't go unless you do! And then you are sworn to teach me what I need to know! How dare I? You have sworn this to Kala, and so to *me*! I dare, because I have the *right*!"

And she stared Sheena in the eyes, it was clear that despite still being a young girl, she had the makings of a leader. Sheena dropped her eyes first. "You are right, Kira. I'm a fool to the end. Of course, I am so sworn. I'm sorry ... I'm sorry to have let you down."

236

Kira got out of her bed, and came over, and sat down on Sheena's. "I forgive you ... again" she said, and held her once more. As Sheena sighed and dropped her head once more onto Kira's shoulder, Kira added "And don't forget." She released Sheena, and looked into her eyes. "Things all go together. Things you have been seeking for a very long time are suddenly happening. There is still hope."

Marko and Shira came back into the room. Kira said, "Ah ... Marko, I am sorry, but I think there are still some things we three need to talk about, girl to girl. Would you mind ... ?" and Marko obediently left again.

Sheena looked at Shira, stirred, and then said in a bleak, flat voice: "I formally apologize, Shira. I am afraid you may be right, it may be impossible for me to love anyone or anything. But that is no excuse for me to have flown into a rage when you said it. And I will leave Marko alone, as I said. He would be far better off with you, anyway." She remembered the rituals, anyway.

Shira acknowledged the ritual, essential for life in a close community where for many months of the year it was hard or impossible to go outside or get away from people, and gave the expected reply. "I formally apologize, Sheena. I had no call to so insult you, a guest in our tribe, doing no wrong you knew of."

But then she had a surprising personal addition, not required by ritual. "Sheena, I said what I said, to hurt you. I didn't know that what I said would strike so near to the mark. But, I spoke out of the depths of my fears. I did not foresee anything, I lied. My intuition said ... otherwise. It said that you *were* capable of loving, and I was afraid. I was afraid that whether or not you leave, I would lose Marko forever. But I have spoken to him, and he agrees he knows whatever you

237

have will not last. And ... I now have hope again. This stirring up has at least made Marko notice me. I don't know what I will do now, or what I should do, but I hope ... I hope I will do something. But I lied when I said I thought you were incapable of love. I'm glad Marko and I were able to heal you."

Sheena sighed. Perhaps, easily angered and upset as she had been by Shira's original words, she was now too easily swayed the other way, with the typical emotional swings of a Fire Witch, but a great weight was taken off her heart once again.

She looked at Shira soberly. "Thank you, Shira. I hope you are right, otherwise I've wasted a lot of time looking. I ... I will try to learn from this, too. And perhaps ... perhaps I can give you some advice?"

Shira nodded, and with grace said, "I will at least listen."

"Marko is ... a man. At the best of times, they may miss what's going on around them, and Marko has had his problems. For years, he carried a burden of guilt, which was I think lifted from him by Kala at the end. And he is an important, busy man, leader of the hunters, and also a man very full of a sense of the rightness of his opinions, though he is somewhat capable of change and learning, painful though it may be. And he's had a lot to think about lately. Don't be too diffident. Smiling at him and batting your eyelids won't do it. If you were to go to his room and jump naked into his bed, he might catch a gentle hint that you find him interesting, if you use a few well-chosen words as well, but anything less subtle could well be missed with his mind preoccupied as it is. Well, perhaps I exaggerate. But not by very much."

Shira nodded, with perhaps the tiniest of smiles. "I will … give some thought to what you have said." And she slowly rose, and left the room.

Sheena sagged, and reached out for a bottle of wine, half-empty. She poured some into a glass and drank it. And then she sighed. "Has it come to this, after all these years? Am I still so easily mastered by my passions? For decades, centuries, I felt I was getting somewhere. I lived at Nun's Hold, serene, calm and liked. Never had an argument. I went out into the world, and did what I could, learning compassion. And here I am, and a simple statement triggers off behaviors as bad and foolish as if I was still Sha'Lin'Tra the Great." She poured and drained another glass.

"I don't know, Sheena, maybe it's different. Although you were very angry, you didn't hurt her, though I'm sure you could have. It was all inwards, at yourself. Remember, one of your next steps is to forgive yourself. Maybe the reason you were so easily upset, and the reason why you hurt yourself so much, was that something is beginning in there. No-one said it would be easy."

Sheena sighed again. "Perhaps you're right, Kira. Thank you. You're wise beyond your years, probably wise beyond mine. I hope you are right. Oh, I hope so." And she poured the last glass, and drank that too. She looked at the bottle, and noticed it was empty. "Oh, I'm sorry, did you want some of this? It's not bad, how is it made?"

"A bit late now" Kira replied, tartly. "Never mind, I had a little one with some water, and I'm probably too young to have any more anyway. As for how it's made, we make it from fermented seaweed."

239

Sheena rolled her head and her eyes. "Silly question, I suppose. I should have known."

The next week passed relatively quickly. Bronn and Kara came out of their nest and helped plan and prepare, which was just as well as Marko and Shira were unavailable. Marko had, the next day, found Sheena and apologetically told her that he really appreciated what she had done for him, and could now see that he might not have survived if she hadn't, but that Shira had told him in no uncertain terms that she was interested in him. He admitted it had come as a bit of a shock, but thinking back, the signs had been there, and he had always enjoyed her company, so given that Sheena was going to leave soon, and had said their arrangement was only temporary, he hoped that she wouldn't mind, if ...

Sheena had hugged him fiercely and kissed him on the cheek, and said she couldn't be happier for him. And to make it fair, she had sought out Shira and done the same.

But before they disappeared, Sheena had a technical talk with Shira. She was fascinated that Shira and Marko had worked together as a viable healing pair using the new techniques (or rather the re-discovery of the old ones) that she had taught. They were really only possible with an Ice Witch and a Fire Witch. Otherwise, they would have had to use Ice Witch healing techniques, which, while effective in their own limited way, were completely unsuitable for energy replenishment. Healer Matrolo, one of the most talented in the tribe, had shown this: his best effort was not enough to make the difference between life and death.

Sheena mused that there was really only one explanation. With their minds somewhat attuned because of Shira's work with Marko, and Sheena's own talents, she showed Shira basic Fire Magic. And wonder of wonders, Shira could do it. Not much and not well, but she had had no training and there was no large heat source available. Shira wasn't a great Ice Witch. Like Kara, she was often cold, she could not really effectively balance her inner temperature except in relatively mild conditions. She had about two-thirds the skill of a normal level one Ice Witch. She could just project a Material Avatar, but only animate it if she kept her Physical still. Sheena said, she had the potential to also be two-thirds of a level one Fire Witch, and when she mastered the skills that would make her a pretty good Witch overall. She showed Shira the drills, the practice techniques, the concentration enhancers, and told her to go for it. When the quest was over, Sheena would arrange for her to go over to Fireland and bond a volcano. The combination was really rare; Sheena herself had never mastered as much Ice Magic as Shira had the potential for with Fire.

Kira spent many hours stretching, exercising and being massaged, to get the muscles, ligaments and nerves all working properly again.

And that left Sheena, with increasing help from Bronn and Kara, and several Ice Witches assigned to help her, to get ready for their trip back. It would not be an easy trip floating in a balloon, it would be muscle power. Nor could they just use a sled over the ice, spring meant that it would be too thin near Iceland. They would have to use a compromise between a sled and a boat. The sled they would have to pull themselves, but as for the boat, Sheena spent hours tinkering with bits and pieces from the balloon, new metal made by Kira, and strange substances made by the Ice Witches. Many things had been forgotten, and the Ice Witches were delighted when Sheena showed

241

them useful, flexible materials they did not know how to make anymore. She could only haltingly show them the general direction and principles, not do it herself, but they were quick to learn.

The hull of the sled-boat was made of seaweed, of course – the same transformed seaweed used for the walls of the Hold. The thwarts, rudder, seats and so on were made of the same stuff. Oar runnels had to be of metal, and the Witches delightedly wove sheet after sheet of thin, flexible material like the balloon cloth to serve as covers in case of rain or snow, and tents, after Sheena showed them the material and described how it was done.

But there were compromises to be made. They would have to propel their vessel fifty miles, so it couldn't be too heavy – they could only take limited supplies. While much of the weight would be food, and it would grow lighter as they went along, even with what hunting they could do in the spring with three people and two Avatars they would likely arrive hungry at the end of Iceland. Fortunately, if they had to wait for the ship that Satro and the others on Nun's Hold would have sent there would be fish, the waters off south Iceland were rich, and not much fished these days. They could take more supplies, but they would need more people, which meant a bigger vessel, which would be harder to build.

There was no great hurry. The later they left, the warmer it would be and the easier the going across Iceland. And the more likely that Satro and Intira would have managed to charter a ship to cross to Iceland and wait for them. Of course, the initial journey would be easier on ice than in the water.

After they had been on Ice Island for ten days, Kira had had a subdued birthday party with her friends.

Aware that a mighty responsibility rested on her shoulders, she clung to the last vestiges of childhood, and had a private party, girls only, where they did all the little-girl things she was going to have to leave behind. They played hide-and-seek, an interesting game when there are Avatars involved. They did truth-or-dare, who-will-I-marry (again, rather interesting given the prevalence of Seer talent), how-many-children-will-I-have. They had pillow fights – again, Avatars added another level. They ate party food, transformed on the spot.

The only adult Kira invited was Sheena. When she asked what birthday parties had been like in Sheena's day, Kira was amazed and saddened when Sheena said that she didn't know, she had never had one of her own, nor been invited to another's, and invited her on the spot. She was a great success. The other girls were shy at first, but thought she was amazing once they became confident. She told them stories of long ago, carefully edited to be interesting but not frightening. She showed them tidbits of Ice Magic that had long ago been forgotten, and how Fire Magic worked. She spoke to them about boys, in ways that their parents would probably not entirely have approved of. She told them about the quest and Narn, as much as she could safely share.

She told them in simple terms what she had done to herself, and why she was limited to level one magic. She glossed over it a lot – they were only fifteen or less, after all – making it appear a lot less like a disaster and a lot more like an adventure and a mistake that was just going to take a long time to fix. And she implied that Kira was more of a friend and equal than was strictly true, and it was obvious that the girls were thinking something along the lines of "wow, Kira is friends with Sha'Lin'Tra the Great!"

And she was overwhelmed when, at the end of the party, all of them included her in the group hug-and-kiss farewell. With a slightly hollow feeling, she realized that her hundreds of years of experience had dealt almost exclusively with great powers, desperate decisions, world changing events, aching regret. She had missed out on all of this. She was too young at Fire Hold, and Fire Witches are less gregariously social, more independent anyway. And she was too sullen and angry to have had such friends at Ice Hold when she was the right age. The closest she had come was as Sister in charge of Novices at Nun's Hold, but the girls there were already grown up. The feeling was different. And no matter what happened over the next few years, even if she rebuilt her capacity for love, she would never have a daughter like one of these girls. It left a bitter-sweet ache.

Kala had been buried with solemn ceremony and ritual, and her name entered into the journal of the colony, together with many stories and reminiscences of her long, long life. There were dozens of large, thick journals, logs, diaries and stores of wisdom and Ice Magic techniques, written on snow-white fine paper made from seaweed. Sheena thought how delighted Intira would be to get copies for the Nun's Hold libraries if their quest was successful. Marko had been sworn in as tribe's leader. He had taken the job on willingly, but had posed the question, what if the tribe wanted him to continue on when they returned, or he came to enjoy the job?

"By the time she's twenty-one, Marko, I think you will have had enough of it. And she will be – and please don't tell her this, or anyone else – at least a four Avatar woman by then. It'll be obvious to everyone she is the best choice for leader. And also, Marko ... you're too much like me. You are too easily ruled by your passions, too sure you're right. People like us don't make good rulers. Facilitators, yes, if we have someone to follow. She will be better than either of us, I believe. Far better than I am or was, certainly."

"But you ruled the world!"

"Not well, Marko. Not well. The world wasn't better off because I was the strongest. Nor was I better off, or wiser for that matter, but there it is. She will be powerful, and strong, yes, but also good and kind. And, if that isn't enough and you still wanted to keep power, I would have to challenge you myself, and I wouldn't like or enjoy that."

"You would?" Marko frowned. "After all ..."

"Yes. Not by choice, but because I am so sworn, to Kala. And to Kira, as she reminded me."

They set a target of another two weeks, to be ready to start their journey.

Chapter 9. Back on the trail

Back on the track
Back on the trail
On the way through the snow
With no wind at our back
No wind for our sail
On foot we slowly go

Anon

Feel like Scott of the Antarctic
Base camp too far away

Australian Crawl

At ground level, the wind was just about bearable, but still harsh and in their faces. It picked up snow, now really more like ice, and threw it at them, abrading their skins. The Avatars could feel it, of course, but it did them no permanent harm – Sheena and Kira could dissolve them and reform them at need. So, they set up a team – the Avatars in front, Sheena and Kira behind them, their faces completely covered, and Bronn behind them, when he was able. The three Physicals just walked, blind. Sheena and Kira could see what was ahead through their Avatars, and it was enough.

The Avatars felt the cold, but it made no real difference. Kira was completely comfortable, under her thin layers of clothing, enough to keep the wind-driven snow and ice from her skin. Sheena managed, dressed more warmly and exercising hard, she and her Avatar did far more than their share of the pulling. But Bronn switched between feeling miserable and cold and struggling under five layers of clothing while trying to pull the sled, and feeling miserable and cold in the sled while the girls and their Avatars pulled. Of course, one of the reasons he was feeling miserable was that he had finally had to part from Kara, and his heart was aching to have left her behind. He'd been married for just under a month, and it seemed very unfair to have to go away without her.

With the wind in their faces, a heavy load on the sled and ridges of ice and drifts of snow to go around, they made very slow progress. The first day, Sheena was doubtful they had gone ten miles towards Iceland. They had travelled more than ten miles in distance, but by circuitous route, round obstacles. They couldn't start from the South Beach, even at this time of the year there was no navigable ice there – the surf and the tides kept the ice broken, a good thing as the island depended on the seaweed washed up. They had started well back, at the pier where they had first landed.

The second day, they did better. It worked more efficiently to have Kira rest when Bronn pulled, and send her Ethereal Avatar out in front to scout the best and easiest path. Sheena worked with her, trying to get her to also control her Material Avatar. She could just do it, for a few minutes at a time. Her Physical stayed still, her Ethereal roved out of sight, and her Material Avatar did not have to do anything other than pull on the traces. Sheena said she was doing very well.

Halfway through the second day, they were attacked. As they went around a field of broken ice, an ice bear roared to the attack. Running faster than anyone would have believed, it rocketed out of the shadow of a giant slab of ice, and fell on them. With one sweep of a paw the size of a man's head with claws six inches long, it slashed at Kira. It happened too fast for even Sheena to react, and the claws sliced Kira in half, or

247

would have, if the bear hadn't hit Kira's Avatar rather than her Physical. The Avatar fractured and shattered, and Kira screamed and staggered with the shock. Sheena's Avatar sprang to the attack, and the bear swiped at it as well. More agile and quite a bit more robust, it stood up well under the attack, but finally it too shattered. But by then, Sheena was turned around, oriented and in control, having dropped the scarf shielding her eyes. Although less than a second had passed she was ready, and drilled a firebolt straight through its head. The bear fell, dead on the instant. It fell forward, collapsing on the ice only inches from where Bronn was pulling.

They decided to stop there for the day. The ice there, a jumble of sheets and floes thrown up into tiny mountains by currents in the sea mimicking the effects of continental drift on a much smaller and quicker scale, would shelter them from the wind if they dragged the sled around a bit. And Sheena and Kira needed time to rest, and reform their Avatars. And the ice jumble, though capable of sheltering them from the wind, was really quite a small one. There was virtually no chance of another bear in there, they were very territorial.

With some looking around, they found a clear channel that allowed them to take the sled-boat into the sheltering ice hills. Everyone found the relative calm a welcome relief. It was still freezing cold, of course, and they could not set a fire. While it was certainly possible to have one on the ice, they had no fuel. Sheena could have heated a rock, which would have remained warm a long time, but there were no rocks. She could project pure heat as a warm air stream, as she had done to fill the balloon, but that would be an exercise in futility – the warmth would dissipate as soon as she stopped. But Kira, with her finer control, could heat water in their containers without damaging them, and so Bronn

248

and Sheena could sit in reasonable comfort, with the equivalent of a large hot water bottle in their laps.

Sheena mentioned there might be good eating on the bear. Kira volunteered to go out and cut a few steaks, but Sheena said it would be good practice to let the Avatars do it. Besides, they needed to reform them. They sat and meditated, forming an image of themselves in their minds, and slowly moving it outwards, separate from themselves, investing energy into it, making it an Ethereal Avatar, and then reabsorbing it, and finally projecting it as Material. And then, when they were ready, both Avatars walked out into the wind, Kira's carrying a sharp knife, and Sheena's projecting light. Sheena got Kira to hold a small metal ball which she had had made specially, and pass it slowly from one hand to the other, just an inch or two. Her Avatar wavered a bit, but she held it in the end, and got the knack fairly quickly. It would take a long time of progressively more intense and complicated movement, but eventually Kira would be able to hold her Material Avatar out of sight and active, while her Physical did other independent tasks.

Then, when the Avatars returned, Sheena did a fine job searing the steaks, and let Kira handle the more delicate cooking. Between the two of them, they came out just right, quite rare. Kira liked them, she was used to eating seal and that was what the bear tasted like, as seal was the main part of its diet. Sheena ate it without any problem but not much enjoyment, but Bronn didn't like it at all. Still, they had enough of other foods with them so no-one needed to go hungry.

Sheena and Kira talked about Avatar control and balancing with the Physical. Bronn basically just sat there, half listening, staring into the darkness. When they asked him why he was so quiet, he replied he was missing Kara dreadfully, already. Still, he said, it was just as well she had not come. Together, they had dreamed exactly what would have happened – Kara would have been pulling the sled at the exact time the bear attacked, and it would have killed her. They had seen the event, but not the place or the time.

They settled down for the night. They had good insulating mattresses, light because it was made of a flexible material full of bubbles (made out of seaweed like everything else), and able to keep the cold out fairly well. They had warm blankets. Kira could keep a protective shield over them to keep the wind out but allow some air in, even while asleep, but it was still going to be a cold night; they were sleeping on the ice. Bronn went to bed pretty well rugged up, but had Sheena to keep him warm on one side, and Kira on the other. That kept him just about right, and Sheena too. Kira just slept under a light blanket in order to give the other two more covers. Bronn was careful to not drink much water at supper, and relieve himself before going to bed – the thought of having to get up during the night was too much to bear.

The next morning was bitterly cold, although it was now well into spring and the sun was rising earlier each day. Bronn stayed in the sled, rugged up for as long as he could, but the going was rougher. They had left the flat ice, and were now almost in pack ice. Although Sheena and Kira sent Ethereal Avatars far and wide, they were hard put to it to find a navigable way. Many times, Bronn had to get out and the combined efforts of all of them were barely enough to keep the sled moving. Twice, they had to unload as much as they could and carry it in packs to get the sled past a rough area. It became clear they were not going to make it like that, and Sheena was glad to find a passage of clear water some ten miles to the east. They struggled over to it, the first few miles very hard going, the last few much easier as the ice was flat and smooth. This was just as well as they had no easy way of telling how thick the ice was, and at some point it was going to get too thin to bear their weight. At that point, they only wanted Avatars pulling the sled.

There was a slight chance that they would get to a point where the sled would go through the ice and become a boat, but the ice would still be too thick for them to pass through. They avoided this by careful use of Ethereal Avatars; they found a shelf of reasonably thick ice leading straight to the water. The best they could find was a drop of about a foot – still too large to drive the sled over – but Sheena was able to melt a ramp down into the water, and so they launched their boat.

Sheena and Kira estimated they still had nearly forty miles to go to Iceland, so they set about paddling. Although the boat had been designed to be as streamlined as possible – more like a canoe than a boat – and the sled runners were designed to be a kind of keel and they had a rudder and sail, the channel was not very wide. They could tack across the wind, but progress was slow. And there were places where all they could do was paddle, and it was hard work despite having three people and two Avatars to wield the paddles, and Sheena's nearly inexhaustible energy. They probably made fifteen miles that day, and were lucky to do that, with the wind in their teeth. They were also lucky that the weather was holding fair. The days were much longer now, and that was not luck, just a simple matter of the winter equinox being long over. And finding a usable exit at the southernmost end of the channel was part luck and part good management: Avatar searching again.

It was still a hard exit. The sled had to be nearly emptied, and it would not have been possible to get it out of the water without the two Avatars, Kira who didn't mind the cold at all for extended periods, and Sheena who could stand it for long enough to help haul it out of the water. Bronn didn't even try to help. He gratefully accepted Sheena's Avatar's help out of the boat – Sheena frankly carried him out in a simple lift and deposited him on the ice. He watched the whole operation with morbid fascination, doing his bit in moving their supplies out of the way. He shuddered when Sheena and Kira went behind a convenient ridge of ice to change into dry clothing, and Sheena told him that Kira, instead of wetting a towel, had simply rolled naked in the snow, letting the freezing flakes take the water off her body. She reappeared, dressed in another of her simple dresses – they were so light she could afford to pack several, their weight was negligible. As they were setting up camp, she hadn't bothered to put shoes back on, and wandered about barefoot as they moved everything well away from the channel, in case it widened during the night – though it was more likely to freeze up.

And so they settled down for the night again. Bronn was mightily glad for Sheena's protective shield, and the warm bodies either side of him, for there was no convenient ice jumble to take the edge of the wind. Sheena got Kira to practice leaving her Avatar to keep watch as she went to sleep. It was a difficult task, somewhat similar to the lucid dreaming of the Seers, and Sheena did not expect too much success at first. She was very pleased when, the next morning, she was able to tell Kira that Kirava had stayed awake for over an hour, and that Sheenava had been able to talk to her for much of that time.

The next day, they could see that they were both further south, and spring was advancing. They woke well into twilight, and Sheena estimated they would have as much as seven hours of sunlight, albeit low on the horizon – it was nearly the end of the second

252

month. And the ice looked smooth. They were unlikely to make it all the way to Iceland, and in fact would be well advised to stop short of where the ice ended – spending the night on the open sea in the boat would not be pleasant. They made an easy fifteen miles that day, leaving only ten more – only! Bronn went to sleep uneasily, despite having dreamed no vision of disaster, and knowing Sheenava would be on watch during the night, and Kirava for at least an hour. The thought of falling through the ice in the middle of the night laid heavy on his mind.

But no such thing occurred. The next day they woke to twilight again, ate well – the Ice Hold porridge, well heated by Kira – and got into the sled. The ice was smooth, and the wind somewhat lower, so they let the Avatars do the work of pulling them along. Sheena got Kira to pace her Ethereal Avatar alongside her Material one, in step, as the first stage of separating them. She did so well, Sheena got her to practice with the metal ball, and she even managed that, though she was now coordinating three entities. To be sure, she lost focus on the Ethereal one occasionally, and had to start over, but it was fine progress.

To keep warm, they occasionally got out and pulled with their bodies for a change. But they did that only a few times, for Sheena said soon enough the ice would become too thin to support the sled, and they would break through, and it would probably be better if it was the Avatars who went through the ice, though they would dissolve. Bronn was surprised. "Can't Avatars go into water?" he asked. Sheena replied that it would dissolve them, but that it was different from shattering them; they could be re-projected with no difficulty. But salt water would short out even an Ethereal Avatar, that was why projecting over the sea was so difficult. One had to observe and anticipate every ripple, every wave, and keep the Avatar above it.

Doing it with a Material Avatar was impossible, they had true weight and had to walk with their feet. Sheena said that she had been able to do it, but it was nearly as hard as physically flying. It took very advanced techniques, a lot of energy and strength and wasn't very reliable. That was why she had been concerned that Narn's Material Avatar had been on Seer's Island. Yes, a level three Witch could send an Avatar far, far further than a level two could – there was virtually no limit - but how had it got there? Still, it could be done by simply sending the Avatar on a ship, though even there for a Fire Witch to keep it alive while he was sleeping showed remarkable skill. It had to be Material, switching an Ethereal Avatar to Material couldn't be done at a distance, and usually only by level threes. Sheena could still do it, despite being limited to level one – as long as the Avatar was close by.

By scouting ahead, they once again found a place where the ice ended and clear water began, and where there was a convenient ledge where they could unload the sled, float it as a boat, and gingerly load everything in again. Sheena and Kira twice lost their Avatars when a wave surged up the ledge and dissolved them. That was not too bad, the Avatars were helping lower the sled into the water, and the three Physicals were up to the task of at least holding it while the Avatars were reformed. Far more serious was when Sheenava picked up a heavy sack of provisions and took it close to the edge. Against all expectations, a large piece of the ledge broke off, pitching Sheenava and the sack into the water. Again, the Avatar was no problem – but the provisions were lost, along with two pans, rolled under the slab that had broken off and turned over, and then slowly sinking.

Sheena watched the last little bit of color disappearing from view, and thoughtfully said "That's going to be a problem. We would have needed all of that food, it's a long haul across Iceland. We'd best be very careful with whatever remains."

As before, Bronn was the first into the sled – now boat – and Sheena second. For some reason, the waves had been rising steadily, and it was only just possible with both Avatars and Kira holding the boat steady for Sheena to get in. After that, with two bodies in it, it was too heavy. Kira got both Avatars to push it away as hard as they could, and Sheena and Bronn paddled to keep the fragile craft clear of the ice. Bronn was told to turn his head, and Kira stripped off, wadded her dress, underclothing and shoes into a ball with her belt, and tossed it to the boat. It was not an easy shot, and was some few feet short. Sheena cleverly got her Avatar to jump out towards the falling bundle, catching it in mid-air and quickly throwing it the rest of the way, before falling into the water and dissolving again. Kira calmly waited for the right opportunity, and dove into the freezing sea, swimming over to the boat. Sheena pulled her in, handed her a towel, and then she and Bronn and the two Avatars paddled hard to get as far away from the ice as possible while Kira dried herself and dressed.

Bronn shook his head and marveled. "I don't know how you do it. I think my heart would stop if I fell in there. Surely you can't generate enough heat to stay warm in the sea?"

Kira shook her head. "No, not for ever. I can keep myself warmer than you would be for a while. You'd probably die after two or three minutes in there. I could manage a few hours, but heat loss would get me in the end. But it's not so bad for a minute or two, and I'm nice and warm again now. We train for it, of course. This is nothing, really, and it's quite nice and warm out, now. You should see it in winter!" Bronn shuddered.

Land was clearly visible now, no more than ten miles away. It was still hard going, even with four or five paddling at the same time, with the wind still in their faces. Still, every mile brought them marginally more shelter from the wind and a lessening of the waves. When they got very close to land they could hope for flat sea, or at least a bay they could land in.

And so it was, a mere four hours later they dragged the boat up well over the high water mark. They would have no further use for it, but it seemed a shame to simply abandon it after it had served them so well. They turned it over and settled it down into the sand as best they could. Who knew, some day it might be of use to somebody, unlikely though it seemed.

With what they had eaten crossing the ice and the sea, what they had lost, and what they no longer needed, they could carry the remainder of their possessions, as long as the Avatars helped. It was not far to Ice Hold, no more than a hundred yards. To be sure, it was mostly uphill, and quite slippery. A recent fall of snow, probably the last for spring, had left drifts here and there that had to be negotiated, but warmer weather was on its way. The first eager growths were pushing through the soil, for they only had a few months before the winter freeze would start again. It had been so long since any of them had seen anything green outside of the hothouses and conservatorium of Ice Island that they all felt a little guilty when they were forced to tread on the new shoots.

They found out how lucky they were to have landed when they did, as not far from the Hold it began to rain. Gently at first, but by the time they got under the big shelter in front of the Hold, they were just beginning to get seriously wet. But once there, no problem of course – the covering was wide and long. Sheena suggested they shelter for as long as necessary in the Hold itself, rather than simply under the covering. She remembered where a small side entrance was, that would let them in to an area near the front, basically a series of self-contained guest apartments that would be easiest to clean out and keep warm.

One or two of the apartments were not useable without considerable work, the shutters on the windows having failed. One more was barely livable, the windows were still sealed but the door seal was leaky and there was a bit of dust and traces of insect life – not much, as for most of the year it was simply too cold unless heated. But several of them were still properly sealed and dust free, though everything had an old, stale smell at first. Much of that was fixed by circulating fresh air through, and some more by wiping down the surfaces. The bed mattresses were unused, and they, like the linen, were sealed inside airtight wraps that had kept everything at least usable over more than a hundred years. Sheena had seen to it that everything was left as well prepared for yet another attempt at repopulation as possible, after the last had failed.

Each apartment had a good fireplace and a chimney well-sealed at the top. Sheena and Kira sent their Avatars up through the dubiously safe stairways to the roof, to unseal them, and fires were soon crackling merrily in the grates. There was nothing like the heating pipes on Ice Island; the people there had advanced considerably in heating technology. While many things took time and were difficult enough, two Witches with complementary talents at least made it viable. Kira sanitized the mattresses, experimenting till she found the main sources of some smells accumulated over the decades, and breaking down or transforming the causes. Sheena washed the linen – they had soap from the stores, one of the things there that would last virtually forever. Sheena and Kira dried it, using a combination of their talents. Bronn did the best he could with the ingredients they had – he was a talented cook – and since he had a bit of room to work with, they had a very decent dinner, on real plates and using real cutlery.

The next morning, they all met for a group discussion, what was to be done. The rain had set in, and Sheena said that a few thousand feet up, where the navigable ridges and paths were, it would be snowing again. With the steep walls of the valleys, it was virtually impossible to keep to the lowlands. You could walk through a valley well enough, but the hills soon rose to a slope that only a mountain goat could navigate before you got to the next one.

Bronn came in to the meeting and breakfast, looking as happy as anyone could be. He was well rested and smiling, relaxed and looking like the world was his oyster. On questioning, he said that he had slept very well indeed on the soft mattress and in the warm quilt, and that he had been blessed with another synchronized dream with Kara. He had lucid-dreamed four hours with her, and it was almost as good as being with her physically. He was able to tell them that Ice Island was running well, Marko was doing a fine job of leadership, balancing the immediate needs of the settlement with the long-term needs of returning to Iceland. He and Shira were going to marry. Shira had managed to convince him in three weeks flat that he could not live without her, which pleased Sheena immensely, and Kira was happy for him as well of course.

On Sheena's advice, they stayed two more days while the rain petered out. That, she said, would give them enough time to climb up to the ridges with some hope that the snow would have begun to melt. But they had to move soon, because there was the ever-present worry of food.

The land and the seas on the northern end of Iceland were all poor. There were rich valleys with good grass in the summer only a day south, but the hills near the Hold were rocky and bare. The seas were underwater deserts, a few patches of algae and some subsistence fish, but nothing compared to the southern end where the winds and the currents brought rich, nutrient filled water up to the surface and powered a dynamic biocycle. Seabirds and seals preyed on the fish, and there was nothing to prey on them except a few weasels that might take a gull. You could throw a fishing line in the water there, and the fish would practically nip their way up the line until you hit them over the head with a stick. But that was a long, weary way away, two weeks and more if all went well, and they didn't have anything like two weeks worth of provisions.

Kira said, she could do something with seaweed if there was any. It would not be what could be done on Ice Island, where there was an industry involving boiling coppers, chemical processes and lengthy magical transformations to convert the seaweed into whatever was wanted. But still, she could transform seaweed to something edible that would sustain life, although it would still taste like seaweed, which could become disheartening after a few weeks. Or days, in fact. But there simply wasn't much seaweed to be had, the winds blew it all north. They would have to walk the ridges, and descend into the valleys to find something to hunt, or at least to work with. Kira could make even grass edible, though it would still taste like grass, and it was a toss-up whether that was better or worse than seaweed. It wouldn't have much nutrition in it, anyway. There were rabbits, of course, though they would be lean after the winter. There were herds of sheep, but they were the property of the Hold tribe, and the shepherds were never far from the sheep, though there were a few wild ones. At this time, they would be driving the nearly-starved sheep from one valley to the next as the new shoots of grass sprouted, and Sheena said that all in all, it would be best if they could make do and avoid the Tribe. After nine hundred years, their proper relationship with the Ice Witches was a matter of legend, corrupted and fantasized, and not to be relied on.

They used the two days they were rained in to make improvements to the Hold, without overworking themselves. They repaired broken shutters as best they could, and cleaned out rooms where those shutters had let the dust and snow of the last century in. Their Avatars patched up areas where it was unsafe to walk. And, they rested, they would need their strength. Bronn did not have another synchronized dream the next night, but he did the night after, and a happier man could probably not be found on the known side of the world.

On the third day, they rose and bid the Hold farewell. They followed the remnants of the old road up to the mountains, until it faded away and became a path, and then a mere trail. Soon, it became even less than that and they had to rely on Ethereal Avatars to scout forwards and pick the way to go. They walked that way, their supplies steadily getting lower despite a rabbit or two, choosing a valley to spend the night purely on the basis of which way the wind was blowing, for three days.

Finally, they had to make a decision. Continue on hoping to find enough to eat, try a descent into a large valley and see what could be found there, or walk right down to the water's edge and try to fish. Sheena said that to the best of her memory, the fishing at that point was somewhat better than near the Hold, but still marginal at best. Of course, things could have changed in the last hundred years, and it might be better now. Or, of course, worse. In any case, it was practically impossible to walk along the shoreline or near to it. High cliffs separated the sea from the land, and the bottom of the cliffs was boulder strewn and usually completely underwater at high tide. The top of the cliffs was no better than any other part of the island, being separated periodically by virtually un-climbable ridges, boulder fields and fast running streams.

The decision was almost made for them when they came to the next major valley. Broader than most, it descended quite steeply at first though there was a clear path, which meant more area in the lower altitude. Perhaps they had passed a line where the season was more advanced, or the winds were kinder, but the grass was considerably more grown than any previous valley. And there was a hardy wood of conifers low down, which meant shelter for rabbits, and probably stores of nuts that had kept them a bit fatter through the winter, maybe berries or edible fungi. There was a way down to the water's edge that looked easier than most as well, so they could try their hand at fishing.

They scouted the valley a bit, with Ethereal Avatars, but it seemed deserted. They made their way slowly down the steep path, Sheena looking back reasonably frequently to make sure of the way out. After an hour of descent, on one of those checks, she stopped, and made an exclamation of dismay. "This is not good" she remarked.

The other two turned and looked back. There were a few sheep coming down the path, and higher up and lower down shepherds. It was really too far away, but Bronn was almost convinced he could see a look of sardonic appreciation on their faces – there was no escape, there was only the one way out. They hurried down the path – if at least they could make it to the little wood, they would have something at their backs, but even that was not possible. The Hold tribe had far more experience on the steep slopes of the valley, and easily outstripped them. Sheena could have made it by herself, but a couple of slips by Bronn and Kira showed that it would be folly to rush down the slope.

"Keep your Avatars in reserve" Sheena murmured to Kira. "We'll see what words can do first."

They were able at least to get to lower ground before the sheep and the men and women of the tribe caught them. There were about forty of them in all.

"Well, well, what have we here" a large, stocky man asked rhetorically. They were mostly tall and well built, a survival mechanism for the cold land, of course. Only the Ice Witches could afford to be slender.

"We are travelers, passing through. We ask for nothing, though any help you can give will be welcome. We will be away from this land in a few weeks" offered Bronn, taking the lead as it was obvious from the way people stood and deferred to one another that this was a male-dominated society, as were the Hold tribes of Seer's Island.

"That is not our way" replied the spokesman. "This is a harsh land. We are opportunists, we take fish, seals and whatever flotsam the sea throws up to us as our natural right. If you are of use to the tribe and will swear service to us and our truthsayer says you mean it, you will live. If you are of no use, you will die. So, speak openly and tell me what you are, what skills you have, and how you may be of use to us."

Sheena was about to speak, but Kira stepped forward. "It is not for you to say where we will go or what we will do. You are Hold tribe. You are bound to serve me, I am an Ice Witch."

The man threw back his head and laughed. "Nice try, girl. The Ice Witches all died out hundreds of years ago. We have legends that sometimes people come back here and try to live in Ice Hold. They all fail. We don't go near that cursed place, and neither does anyone else." A man standing close by him leaned over and murmured something in his ear. He looked askance, frowned, paused, and said with a little wonder in his voice "However, our truthsayer says you at least believe what you say. So. I will reserve judgment for now. And you," he added, casting an admiring look at Sheena, "do you also claim to be an Ice Witch?"

Sheena smiled slightly, nodded, and carefully said, "I have received training in Ice Magic, yes, and can do a few simple spells. But I am nowhere near as powerful an Ice Witch as Kira here."

The truthsayer again whispered to the man, and he frowned deeper. "And you" he said to Bronn, "what are your skills? Are you an Ice Witch too?"

Bronn shook his head. "No indeed, I am a Seer. A Master Seer." Again, the truthsayer spoke quietly.

"So, a Seer. We also have legends of Seers, and a few lucky people who have washed onto our shores with useful skills have told us of the world. A great skill.

Unfortunately for you, we have no need of it. Our lives are constrained by the seasons, and we have little change that we need to worry about. Your life hangs in the balance."

He turned his attention to Kira and Sheena again. "So, Ice Witches, or people who call themselves Ice Witches and believe it, or madwomen. Let us find out which. Do you live in Ice Hold?"

Sheena spoke for both of them. "Not right now" she said. "We have recently left Ice Hold, to travel south."

He nodded. "I can see you are going to use words carefully. But it will not help you in the end. During the winter, there is little else for us to do but use words, and we are past masters. Let me ask you again. Have you lived in Ice Hold for any real length of time?"

Sheena nodded. "I lived there for years as a girl, and on several occasions after that" she offered.

"Really" he offered. "Fascinating. I'm sure the truthsayer will tell me what you say is true. So, I will at least tell you my name, which is Johnno, and by that you may understand I am at least interested in the pair of you. Tell me your name, and also tell me, young Kira, have *you* lived for any real length of time in Ice Hold?"

Sheena spoke her name, and Kira replied that she had not.

Johnno mused for a half minute. "I am half inclined to believe you. Certainly, none of our people would walk near-uncovered as your Kira does, at this time of the year. Our tales say that Ice Witches could send ghosts of themselves out, to walk freely where people cannot go, a useful skill if you have it?"

Sheena and Kira looked at each other briefly, and projected their Ethereal Avatars and sent them off on a quick run away and back. The tribe murmured among themselves.

Johnno nodded to himself. "The skill is not entirely unknown among us" he said. "But in my lifetime I havc ncvcr bcforc sccn a ghost scnt morc than a fcw dozen yards away. Do you have other Ice Witch skills? We have heard of healers, people who could fly, turn themselves into animals and many other tales."

Sheen replied that they had some little healing skill, but could not do any of the other things. But Kira froze a section of the hillside, turning the grass white with frost. The truthsayer leaned in close once more, and spoke again.

Johnno said, "The truthsayer says that you are at least not lying. But he is convinced that you, at least, Sheena are holding something back."

Sheena replied: "I am something of a Witch, but I have another skill. I am a trained Warrior."

The truthsayer nodded, and Johnno spoke again in his measured voice. "We have little need for that skill here. We live in relative peace. We are expert shots with bow and arrow, for hunting rabbits and birds, and we have some ability in hand-to-hand fighting which we do for entertainment. But there are forty of us, and no matter what your skills you surely know you cannot protect all three of your party, so I advise you not to try anything. So. Good."

He paused again.

"I am leader, and I am used to making quick decisions. So, here is my judgment. You are not Ice Witches, or not true Ice Witches despite your skills, at least not here, because you do not live at Ice Hold, and there are only two of you. Our stories of Ice Witches say they were also a tribe, and two people – or even three – do not make a tribe. If there are more of you elsewhere, it does not matter, because you are here and not there. Still, you have skills our legends speak of, and our legends also say that we lived in harmony with the Ice Witches, and had obligations to them. So, the two of you may go your way without hindrance. But the life of the man Bronn is forfeit if you do, or at least ours to do with as we will. On the other hand, we have need of healing skills. For instance, one of our tribe is near birthing, and the child is too large. We could open her and take out the child, but she will most likely die, and there are the other usual ills that befall man and woman aplenty. If you will join the tribe, a place will be made for the man, whatever his other skills. This much I can offer you, but no more."

Sheena replied for them. "Leader Johnno, we will not make a decision now. Either way, we are willing to do what healing we can, and we will see your tribe and make our decision. It cannot be made lightly, for we are all oath bound on a quest. But we will give you our word of honor not to try to escape or do violence for two days until we make our decision."

After a word with the Truthsayer, Johnno nodded. "I accept, We will postpone the final decision for two days. You are clearly a clever woman." He stroked his chin thoughtfully.

With few words, they all wended their way down the valley. Johnno strode on ahead, assigning tasks and sending others ahead. It fell to the truthsayer to guide the three strangers and speak to them. He explained that this valley was the main home base for the tribe because of the caves, but the grass was richer further south, and also it didn't make sense to leave the bulk of the sheep in the home valley, destroying the grass and possibly the trees and getting in the way. They moved the sheep from valley to valley regularly, and had brought only a few back with them today, those that were to be kept in the valley for milk and one or two to become mutton.

The truthsayer was quite garrulous, and there was little to hide, so Sheena and Kira and Bronn learned that besides the sheep and the caves and the wood, the tribe was blessed with a good supply of coal from a mine, and a beautiful green stone with light and dark layers, very easy to carve, but which they also smelted copper from with the coal, and fine clay which was used for casting, making crockery and the like, and a large reliable stream flowing down the valley which served for water, washing and waste disposal, and quite reasonable fishing to the south of the stream's outfall.

There was a little way to go, and Sheena, Kira and Bronn managed to get a few words together. Bronn asked if Sheena could not get them away safely, despite the numbers. Surely, as a trained Warrior and Fire Witch besides, she would overwhelm them. They would have no experience with such a combination. And Bronn had his firestaff, and could no doubt account for a few of them himself.

Sheena caught her lip in her teeth, and mused. "Yes, probably. If it finally comes to that, well ... yes, most likely. There would be danger, I can at the end only handle three or four at a time, and however fast I move one of the ones carrying bows could shoot you, or Kira. I know you can both shield, but the danger is there. And they might well scatter, and Warrior or no I can only go in two directions at once. We might be dogged at a distance and run risks all the way to the southern end of the island – we might make it by moving as quickly as we could, possible if we had enough food, which we don't. And also ... I am oath-sworn to not harm Ice Witches, and though they're Hold Tribe, there is as you know – or should be – a close relationship. They are not quite Ice Witches, but they are part-way. I would feel like I am compromising the spirit of my oath if I were to deliberately harm them greatly. It would be better to see how things develop over the next two days. There is always the chance we can sneak away in the night, if need be."

The truthsayer saw them talking as they walked of course, and approached them to ask what they were saying. Sheena replied cautiously that they were taking counsel amongst themselves, and that it was a weighty matter to consider, lives and oaths were at stake. She was careful to word it in such a manner that no falsehood was spoken.

The truthsayer was clearly good at his job. "You are not telling me everything" he remarked. "Still, it's clear you will keep your oath, and that's good enough. We cannot tell you everything either in this short trip to the caves, but we have few secrets, and you will see much of what you need to know for yourselves. But, I will tell you something more."

He paused, gathering his words. "Johnno is our leader, that much you know. He is a good leader ... but the burden lies heavy on his shoulders. He had a wife, but she died of a wasting sickness some three years ago, and despite there being others willing, I have never seen him look seriously at another woman since, not until today. I know, Sheena, there is a place for you and Kira in this tribe as healers, but I think there is also another place that you could have with not too much asking, if you follow me. Just a thought. We do not force men or women together, that is not our way.

Even outsiders are not forced. Killed, yes, perhaps – ours is a harsh courtesy, but harsh by necessity. Just a thought, just a thought."

The caves were extensive, opening into large limestone caverns past the relatively small openings, and so well sheltered from the winds. There were some natural daylight holes and some manmade, some of which had been carefully fitted with copper pipes and sealed with clay to be chimneys, and some which could be covered with woven shutters or opened up as the weather dictated.

The caves were not very well heated, because while the coal seam was extensive it was a resource to be conserved. The use by the Hold Tribe had already burrowed a hundred feet into the hills with carefully shored up mineshafts, and the Tribe lived with the uneasy thought that one day they might come to the end of it. The wood was also quite large – a mile long and perhaps half as wide, but the hardy pines were very slow growing. The Tribe made do with deadfalls and trees that died, and put quite a bit of work into keeping the little forest healthy. Only very rarely was a living tree cut down, the aim was to grow the little forest, not to use it up. Conditions were optimal in this relatively well sheltered valley; attempts to start other woods in other places by planting seeds and transplanting seedlings had been met with limited success – a few sister groves had been established in five other valleys, but progress was slow, even by Hold measurement of time, which worked in generations rather than years or even decades.

Instead, the Tribe used insulation, warm clothes and general hardiness to manage the cold. They had plenty of materials to work with – dried grass as filler, and pelts from rabbits, fur seals and sheep. Highly prized were the pelts of weasels which preyed on the rabbits, but which were hard to trap as they were very clever and cautious.

Fire was reserved for smelting, kilns, cooking (though a lot was eaten raw), and heating water for washing children, women and the elderly. Most of the time that was kept to a minimum, with no more than a sponge bath, and that far from every day, though everyone enjoyed the river in summer and early autumn. Adult men vied with each other as a sort of local sport, as to who could bathe in the river the latest into winter and enjoy it, or at least pretend to.

The Tribe led a simple life. They tended their flocks, their forest and the groves, cast pottery, worked the copper, and carved wood with the loving attention to detail only achievable by a people who spend whole months at a time in caves during the winter. In spring and summer they planted crops suited to the climate - potatoes, turnips, carrots, cabbage, kale, and cauliflower, and a few grains – rye and barley. The limitations of the short growing season were offset by the virtual lack of insect pests – none of them could survive through the winter. The grains and the potatoes, and sometimes beets, were used to brew a beer that was virtually undrinkable by anyone not inured to it from childhood, but which could be distilled to an approachable if strong spirit. This they flavored with herbs, caraway and anise.

One of their greatest treasures was sixty large barrels, forty medium and ten smaller ones, rescued from a ship that had been wrecked in a storm and had somehow drifted empty and washed up on the rocks several hundred years ago. Too old now to impart any flavor from the oak, some were still used for storing the distilled spirit to age it and take the edge off. Through careful imitation, the Tribe had started to make barrels out of pine, the resin of which imparted a unique flavor. And the barrels were immensely useful for storing dried or salted provisions for the winter. Damaging a barrel was practically a capital offense. Good use had been made, of course, of every other component and content of the ship, and others that had come the Tribe's way every few hundred years, not to mention flotsam and jetsam – as of course Ice Island did, further north. Nothing was wasted.

Life in cold climates is usually full but simple. The three of them had really seen everything there was to see in a few short hours, and Bronn remarked in a low voice that all in all, if it came to a choice between staying with this tribe away from Kara in a cold climate and devoting the remainder of his life to basic survival, or death, he'd prefer the latter, so there was no need for the two of them to decide to stay to spare his feelings. Sheena laughed, and said she hoped it wouldn't come to that.

The few hours they got to look around and ask questions they got as breaks between looking over the sick and the elderly of the tribe. There were not so many of the latter – there were few infectious diseases as there was little contact with the outside world, and people tended to stay in fairly robust health until late old age, when something went wrong inside their bodies or they had a bad fall, after which they tended to fade away pretty quickly. The very few who became incapacitated but were likely to live a long time usually chose to sit outside one cold night with some company while they were awake, and a flask of the fierce distilled spirit to help them to sleep.

For most of the sick or the temporarily incapacitated, Sheena and Kira could not do very much. Kira, despite her burgeoning magical strength was just not cut out to be a healer, her mind did not work in that way. And having Sheena as the healer was a poor way of working, worse than it had been with Marko. There were a couple of broken bones, most of which Sheena said were quite well set, and might as well be left to heal by themselves rather than wasting their limited talents and energy. Infections and sores were very hard to treat with magical healing, basically every single bacterium had to be dealt with one by one. A more gifted pair of healers could stimulate the body's own defenses, but that was beyond their capabilities. Still, Sheena had centuries of experience, and knew herbs, natural remedies and combinations far better than the Tribe, and was able to offer some suggestions that would in time help some of the harder cases.

She was also able to show them how to brew a painkiller out of a particular kind of lichen stewed with ground seashells, which eased the suffering of several people. A couple of nasty-looking but relatively minor and fresh cuts, Sheena and Kira were able to knit back together with combined Witch healing, but it was a poor effort compared to what Sheena and Marko had been able to do, there would definitely be scarring. Apart from doing it quicker and painlessly, there was not much difference in the result over what could have been achieved with needle and thread, and time. It was barely better than what Sheena could do all by herself.

About the only person they were truly able to help was the mother with the large child. A combination of the new painkiller, some pressure on nerve points and a bit of judicious compression of the carotid arteries by Sheena put her out. Then, with freshly washed and sterilized hands (as best they could, using a variety of things altered by Kira, including freshly distilled spirit) they carefully opened her belly using a combination of as little knife cutting as possible and as much cutting with healing techniques as they could they took the child out. Then, with Sheena's intimate knowledge of the structures of the muscle layers they put her back together again.

It was not well done. They had barely enough energy between the two of them to get her half back together, and sewed the outer layers and skin up temporarily with fresh sinew. It would have to do till the next day, and she would wake up very sore. But wake up she did, while Sheena and Kira went to sleep. The next day they removed the sinew stiches and finished off. Again, it was not done anywhere as neatly as Marko had, there would be extensive scarring and quite a long recovery. But, she would live. Sheena said there was minimal infection visible, nothing a strong body couldn't take care of by itself. And so they ate and rested till the early afternoon.

The leader Johnno came to talk to them after the midday meal. "As I suspected, you've placed me in a difficult position" he began. "I probably should have insisted on your decision two days ago, but to see the ways of the tribe first was not an unreasonable request. Still, what I feared has largely come to pass. You've shown us many new things, done a little healing, and saved the life of Mortha and her child. Even if your magic did not go a long way to supporting your claim to be Ice Witches, I'd now have a hard time enforcing my word against your man Bronn. Even though he has only helped a little with a few items of knowledge, still he is known now, and has charmed the children with his stories. And yet ... I must do something. We could use your skills in the Tribe, and there will be some grumbling if I just let you go. To be sure, I myself ... well, I think I will pay you back, by asking your advice – what should we do with you?"

Kira deferred to Sheena's experience on this question. As so often happened, Sheena had her own ideas, and they were somewhat unexpected.

273

"Are you a gambling man, Leader Johnno?" she asked.

"We are all great gamblers, Sheena. We make entertainment for the winter months, and stories, challenges and betting on one thing or another help to pass the time."

Sheena nodded. "I thought it must still be so. Legends of the Ice Witches, you know. You must also know, we are on a quest. A quest to bring the Ice Witches home, to Ice Hold. But to do that, we must be clever, skillful and lucky. And so, I will pit my skill and luck against you. Do you still run the Courses, as the history of the Ice Witches remembers?"

Johnno frowned. "You know of the Courses? More and more I come to believe you and your claims. Yes. Yes, we do. You want to challenge me to running the Course? That is usually a matter for the men. Not exclusively, mind you, but usually the women compete amongst themselves if they have a mind. And you should know I am not often beaten, I don't know how you think you could win, particularly the drinking part – you're not half my weight. And it is really too early in the season, the river is swift and there's still a lot of ice in it. You should choose something else, in all fairness."

Sheena smiled. "You are a fair man. And if it's really too cold for a man of your age, I suppose ..."

Johnno bristled. "It's not a matter of being too cold for me! It's too cold for you!"

"Hmm." Sheena paused a second. "I tell you what, I will up the stakes. If I win, we go free, all of us ... but if you win, we will stay – and I will willingly come to your bed."

Kira gasped. "Sheena!" she said, in shock. "How ..." but Sheena interrupted her. "Kira, you delegated this to me. Once done, you can't interrupt the process. I'm sorry if this is not what you expected, but I have gone down this path now. For good or ill, the challenge is issued, and Johnno must accept, or forfeit." Kira subsided, but was still clearly stunned.

Johnno smiled. "Well, there's an unexpected wager. I'll not deny that you interest me, and I've not been interested for ... a long time. I'll accept your challenge. There are enough witnesses" he said, indicating two of the Tribe who had been listening nearby. "I suspect you have some trick up your sleeve ... but it's a fair challenge, and we will see. One hour will be enough to prepare."

Bronn was not so shocked, or worried. He had seen Sheena sparring against Satro, working vastly beyond Bronn's endurance in the snow, and knew of her other skills. Kira, of course, had only seen Sheena in the Hold and paddling a canoe or pulling a sled, and working as a healer. She suspected, and was told she was quite right, that Sheena could not use overt magic or her Avatar. Sheena explained that the Courses were an endurance test. There was a short run to the river, a crossing in the chest-deep, icy, fast-running water, a run up a hill and down, re-cross the river, run back, and then sit and down a good sized cup of wine – she supposed they would use their spirits – and then do it again. The loser was the one who had to drop out.

Bronn laughed. It really wasn't fair, Johnno could not possibly know what he was up against. But, they had work to do, and fairness could not come into it.

Those not unavoidably busy with the ongoing work of the Tribe stopped to watch as a matter of course. The challenge was issued, accepted, and the terms agreed

275

as usual. The first to drop out would be the loser, or one could win by lapping the other.

Johnno had the choice of who would open, and chose to go first. He stripped down to a well secured loincloth. He was a fine figure of a man, and like many who live in a cold climate almost hairless on his body. He carried some fat, as everyone of the Tribe did – a survival matter – but underneath it Bronn, Sheena and Kira could see there was solid muscle in good shape, rippling like the powerful muscles of a seal. He turned to the crowd, gave an almost boyish grin and ran down to the river. Plunging in, his dive carried him almost a fifth across. He rose with a roar for the cold, and determinedly forged his way across, going deeper and deeper. It was not easy going. The current was strong, and a straight-across crossing was not possible. He grudgingly gave as little ground as possible, fighting his way across, and in a few minutes was on the other side. Jogging at just the right pace to generate some warmth but not tire himself, he ran to the agreed point, back to the river, and repeated the crossing, coming out perhaps twenty or thirty yards downstream. He jogged back to the starting point, scraped as much water off as he could, accepted a fur seal wrap and sat down at the table set up for the purpose and downed his measure of drink.

Sheena in the meantime had stripped down to similar, minimal clothing. Johnno even had enough energy for an admiring glance. He was breathing only moderately heavily, and seemed only slightly affected by the cold.

Sheena ran for the river, and executed just as fine a dive. With her narrower profile it carried her further into the river, and she swam a good distance as well. It was clear she was a much better swimmer than Johnno. Soon, she had to stop, or be washed downstream too far, but again it was clear that her slimmer form made it a bit easier going through the current, though of course, everyone expected her to tire sooner.

She didn't seem to, and the crowd murmured. She ran up the hill and back far faster than he had, and plunged into the river, swam and fought her way across, and back to the starting point. Johnno was almost completely recovered, but Sheena didn't seem the slightest bit out of breath as she knocked back her glass of spirit in one go. It was obvious that her round trip time was less than Johnno's.

By the time she had done this, Johnno was already well on his way. It was Sheena's option, how long she would choose to rest. Go too soon, and a runner could overtire themselves, too late and there was the risk of being lapped.

The crowd susurrated again, as Sheena chose no rest at all. Thumping down her glass, she turned and ran, not even bothering to shake the water off (in the cooling afternoon air it was already starting to freeze) or to warm herself up.

By the time Johnno got back, puffing and blowing a bit and downed his measure of spirits, Sheena was already determinedly fording the river. Johnno had the choice, rest a minute or go straight away? The onlookers told him, of course, that Sheena had not rested, but would she rest this time around? He decided he could not risk it, and set off again, without rest.

It was as well for him that he did, for once again Sheena ran up and downed her drink as if she was only just getting started. She turned and dashed off again.

And so it went. She lapped him on the fifth crossing, and stood smiling, pleased with her performance but not crowing as Johnno came running up, tired and shivering but not done in.

"God in Heaven, it's been a long while since I've been lapped" he panted. "The race is well won."

Sheena replied as courteously, "I'm lucky that my slight body allows me some extra speed. If we had to cross and re-cross and win or lose on endurance alone and drink each time, the result might have been different."

Johnno nodded, and replied "I thank you for your gracious words, and I cede the race." Under his voice, he muttered so that no-one but Sheena heard, "I suspect it bloody well would *not* have been different ... five glasses you've put away, and I know of no woman of the tribe who could do that and still be standing, yet you're not even swaying ... ah well, the problem is solved, at least."

He moodily went his way, after instructing that the three of them could depart any time they liked. Sheena and Kira said they would stay another full day to finalize the healing and gather what food they might, by fishing or hunting.

That night, after the communal meal, Johnno retired to his private alcove, really a cave-within-the-caves. As leader, he rated his own space and privacy. Morosely, he readied himself for bed. As he went to douse the oil lamp, there was technically a knock at the door. Actually, as his space had only a leather curtain for privacy, there was a knock at the wooden panel specifically mounted for that purpose.

He called "enter", with little interest. He was surprised to see Sheena, when she entered. "Oh, good evening, Sheena. What can I do for you?"

Sheena smiled a friendly smile. "Johnno, we are on a serious quest, the end of which is to bring the Ice Witches back to Ice Hold. My life is largely not my own to do with as I will, I am oath-bound to do many things. My skills and talents are many, and yes, when I issued my challenge saying that if you won, I would come to your bed, I knew that I could and must win. But, still ... you're an attractive man, and a part of me would wish that perhaps things might have been different. And the race is run and won, but now, for a few short hours my time is my own to do with as I will, and so ... I am here."

Kira was appalled, and unforgiving. She did not speak to Sheena the whole of the next day, except out of sheer necessity. And when they were to set off on the day after, after farewells to the Tribe, she was still silent, mulishly silent with firmly pressed lips. A few minutes after they crested the valley ridge and were truly on their own again, Bronn gently asked Sheena to scout the way ahead, and knowing what he was going to try to do, agreed, though with a sigh.

Kira had a good idea what Bronn was going to try to do too, and as soon as Sheena was out of sight, got in first with an angry outburst. "How could she. How *could* she! With that man! Refusing to acknowledge us as Ice Witches, despite what we can do! Practically kidnapping us into the tribe! And you, now you're going to defend her, against *that man*, who would have cut your throat without a second's thought!"

"Kira, there is no harm done. And she is sworn to aid and help us, yes, and obey your commands. But she is still a grown woman, and may cast her favors where she will. And look at the result. Once she had won her race, the Tribe would have let us go, yes, on their honor. But now, we leave as friends. Look, we have food in our packs for a long time, fresh footwear, bowstrings, everything we need."

"That's even worse! You're saying, she has sold herself!"

"Well, I wouldn't put it quite like that. In any case, she is sworn to you. If you want to punish her by withholding your regard and judging her, I suppose I can't stop you. But it will make it hard for us to work together; we won't be a real team. And perhaps, you might consider this. As a future leader, it is unfair to judge and condemn someone, without hearing what they have to say. You are young, but that would be a lesson well learnt."

Kira flushed, and walked on for a good while, but eventually became calmer, and said in a faintly apologetic tone, "You're right, of course, Seer Bronn. I owe it to us and to her to at least hear her side of the story. I will speak to her at our next rest break."

The rest break came after a few good hours walking. They found another ridge leading down to a valley and followed it down far enough to encounter the inevitable spring and stream, out of the wind, and rested, ate and drank. Bronn made an excuse to answer the call of nature, and left the two alone.

Kira, with the formality of the Ice Witches, both a natural tendency and a social rule, apologized for pre-judging Sheena, but said that she did have strong feelings and would like to hear her side of the story.

280

"That's the formal part of my feelings" she added. "For me, I just can't understand it. But I will listen."

Sheena sighed. "Well, Kira, for a start, he *is* an attractive man. Given the nature of his upbringing and where he lives, and how, he is about as fine a man as he could be. A natural leader, a strong personality. You must understand, we Fire Witches are attracted to such types. He is harsh, yes, but he lives in a harsh environment, his harshness is out of necessity, not nature. And while we're on serious business, still, we have to eat, and drink, and sleep. There is no rule that we cannot enjoy these things, nor other natural functions as chance offers."

"All things being equal, perhaps I might not have chosen him as my bedmate. But all things are not equal. He had, in fairness, gone against his natural inclination to keep us captives for the tribe, respecting some half-remembered alliance with the Ice Witches, after hundreds of years. He treated us well. And, there would be some loss to his prestige as leader since he was beaten at the Courses by me. Partly because of my training as a Warrior, but partly by unfair magic because of my altered body. It had to be done, but a great deal of that loss would be wiped out by my choice to go to him. The Tribe knew, of course. And, his personal loss of self-esteem too."

"And also, don't forget, while they are not Ice Witches, they are related. In the days when Ice Witches lived at the Hold, as we hope they will do again, there was a relationship like that at Seer's Hold. People could and did leave one society and join the other. Everyone lived under the Hold roof in winter; the caves are a new living place since my time. There is a connection, perhaps tenuous, and I'm sworn to not harm Ice Witches. There is a carry-over, I am reluctant to harm the Ice Tribe."

"But still …" Kira began, but her words trailed off.

"Also remember, Kira, that though I look young, I'm not. The days of my first love are long gone, and what I can do now has little love in it, from my side at least. Not because I don't want to, but because I can't due to my own folly. Pleasure, yes, of course. But most of the normal considerations don't apply. I will not catch a disease, even if the Tribes had one. I cannot become pregnant. To ease his being beaten, the loss of our skills to the tribe, it's not such a big thing. And also, I eased his heart. He has been grieving the loss of his wife for too long, unable to break free because every other woman there he knows too well, that I could do, also, and I was glad to do it."

"I think I see" Kira said thoughtfully. "You mean, it was good for the Tribe, him personally, and for us. So, you faked desire and went to him."

Sheena shook her head. "No, not faked desire. He is a sensitive and intuitive man. He would have known at once, the desire had to be real. But that in itself was not hard. As I said, if you look at him the right way, he is an attractive man."

Kira shook her head. "I hear the words, Sheena, but I just don't understand. I couldn't do it. And I don't understand how you could."

Sheena nodded. "Of course you couldn't Kira. And you shouldn't. Your first should be chosen for love. And your second and others afterwards for quite a while, if there are any, that is, if your first love is not your last. But eventually with time and experience, you might become confident enough that you could help someone else without hurting yourself. And that can be a good thing."

Kira shook her head again, but much less emphatically. "But how could you fake enjoying it, or rather, force yourself to?"

Sheena smiled. "The body tells you how. And as to forcing oneself – have you ever done something because it was your duty, or you felt it should be done, or to help someone? How about the times that you helped your grandmother? Would you naturally want to cook, clean and otherwise be helpful to the elderly?"

"Well, maybe not just anyone, unless there was no-one else. But I loved Kala, so it was no burden."

"Just so. And no doubt, when you helped her, you did not do it grudgingly? You did it unstintingly, as well as you could, and took pleasure in her appreciation and in doing it as well and as lovingly as you could?"

"Yes, of course."

"And so it was with me, and Johnno. It was something I felt needed to be done. And because I have been trying to rekindle the flame of love in my soul, I did it as well as I could, and took pleasure in it, and with as many of the actions and feelings of love as I could muster. I did it for him, and for the Tribe, and for us, and I did it as lovingly as I could, for me."

"So ... do you mean, you loved him?"

Sheena hung her head. A sad, and hollow look came about her face. "No ..." she said in a small voice. "As always, I tried ... and as always, I failed."

Impulsively, Kira opened her arms and hugged her, and said in a gentle voice, "I think I understand a bit better now. Kala always said, there is no shame in something that is done with the best of motives, and I can see you had them. And never forget, you have

283

been told your goal is not impossible." And it was all right between them again.

Chapter 10. Warrior's Hold

WHO is the happy Warrior? Who is he
That every man in arms should wish to be?
--It is the generous Spirit, who, when brought
Among the tasks of real life, hath wrought
Upon the plan that pleased his boyish thought:
Whose high endeavors are an inward light
That makes the path before him always bright:
Who, with a natural instinct to discern
What knowledge can perform, is diligent to learn;
Abides by this resolve, and stops not there,
But makes his moral being his prime care;
...
This is the happy Warrior; this is He
That every Man in arms should wish to be.

William Wordsworth

The rest of the journey to the southern end of Iceland was relatively straightforward. They had enough food, with careful management and good hunting of the rabbits, and some forays down to the water for fishing, which got better as they went along. Water was no problem. They took it easy, there was no hurry. With the time on Ice Island, and the crossing and the time on Iceland itself, they would still have several weeks wait before they could expect Satro and his ship, assuming it was on time.

Shelter would have been the main problem. While getting out of the wind at night was always easy – just a matter of going to one side or the other of the ridges, and to the southern or northern end of the valleys as the wind direction dictated, they did not often find anything like the caves that now lay well to the north. Sometimes they were lucky and found a bit of a rock overhang, but that was all. If they had not all been Gifted, it would have been a wet and uncomfortable journey. It didn't rain every day, but it was often enough. Still, the three of them *were* Gifted, and could raise a shield to keep the rain off. It meant they had to take watches, and Bronn's shield was a bit patchy at times.

Sheena, through long years of practice could keep her shield mostly together even while asleep, although stretching it to three people and their packs was not easy even for her – she was still a Fire Witch after all - and she preferred to shield while remaining awake. Kira, better at that sort of thing as most Ice Witches were, was quite as good at it while asleep as when she was awake.

But she, too, tended to keep her watch awake, because Sheena gave her constant exercises to develop her Avatar skills. It wasn't easy, Bronn and Kira were generally a bit tired at the end of the day. Sheena said Kira would find it easier to learn when they reached the southern end, and could set up camp. But still, she made steady progress. By the time they neared the end of the island, Kira was quite comfortable with her Material Avatar walking at the same time as her body, and could manage it being out of sight quite nicely. If it was within sight, she was making good progress with having the Ethereal one active as well, although she had a bad habit of 'stuttering' – making one Avatar move, then the other, then back to the first. Sheena said she just had to get over that, and got her to work with her body still and just the two Avatars, and then the passing of the ball from one hand to the other, but it was slow progress. Sheena didn't let Kira get depressed over how hard it was – she reassured her that everyone had to go through these stages, and not only was she doing it much earlier than most, in fact most Witches never made it to two Avatars at all.

And so, the miles and the days passed, some sunny and relatively mild, some rainy and freezing cold. Some over hard trails that were up and down over uninspiring rock hills, some with breathtaking views over green valleys – for the brief spring was now well and truly under way – down to colored rocks and into fjords as beautiful as one could want. They didn't hurry as they were nearly at the southern end now, and it was still too early to expect Satro and a ship. It was good exercise for Kira to send a material Avatar down into the valleys to the water's edge and see if the conditions looked right for fishing. It was really quite a pleasant time, although there was one lack – firewood; they had not seen another decent stand of trees. In a few valleys there was evidence that the Tribe had tried to establish trees, but they were not thriving. It seemed just too cruel to cut the barely living wood, and there was little in the way of deadfall. Presumably the Tribe visited each valley to see how the trees were doing and graze sheep, and wood being so scarce took any fallen branches.

Finally, they came to the southern end of the island, or near it. The season was still advancing, and they were moving towards the warmer end – it became almost pleasant during the day, or so Bronn said. Sheena preferred it warmer still, but her unnaturally high metabolic rate and the amount of exercise she did to keep her Warrior training up compensated, and of course she had a tiny degree of Ice Witch talent. Kira didn't care if the weather was pleasant as it was now, or ten degrees below freezing, it was all the same to her.

Satro and the ship were not there yet, of course. They waited in an enhanced natural bay, with a good, sheltered promontory out to the right where one could look out to sea with a nearly two hundred and seventy degree view from the top, or fish in comfort from one side or the other depending on the wind and waves. The water either side was deep, and the fish sheltered in the abundant seaweed. A rich soup of nutrients brought up by the current hitting the land, the shelter and the fact that practically no-one had cast a line there for a hundred years meant that large fish would snap up any bait in an instant. Seals and seabirds took their share, but the water was really too deep for diving birds, and there weren't too many seals. None of them really felt like trying to catch a seal, the fish were so plentiful and delicious.

There was even some shelter. Sheena's last visit, a hundred years ago, had seen the stone storage huts refurbished and repaired, that had been easy – ship's crew had been happy to earn extra silver doing a bit of work on land, though they would not march across the whole island to help at the Hold itself – the summer was indeed short, and to be sure of getting back before the seas froze or got too rough with oncoming winter meant it would scarcely have been worthwhile, let alone the risk of encountering the Hold Tribe.

It didn't take much to make the huts at least habitable again. Against a cliff and mostly sheltered, the wood of the doors and the metal of the hinges, well painted, had stood up fairly well to a hundred years of neglect. Before leaving, Sheena and the latest group of failed Ice Witches had sealed all gaps with clay. It took only a few days to clear the debris and clean out the interior. There was nothing like well-preserved mattresses and linen as there had been at the Hold, but there was crockery and cutlery, a few cooking utensils and aids, and a convenient stream nearby. There was even a useful deep hollow in the stones of the stream, a clear pool some six feet deep, which with the aid of a few rocks and a bit of work could be blocked off from the flow. Sheena could heat it up quite easily, and they all

288

enjoyed a nice warm spa. Or at least, Sheena and Kira did, and then Bronn did. Kira thought Bronn's reluctance to undress and get into the pool with them completely bizarre, though Sheena did her best to explain other people being uncomfortable with nudity. Kira loved the pool and the water, having been raised with such things, and Sheena enjoyed it, but Bronn practically wept in ecstasy, really warm for the first time in weeks and remembering the pools and spas of Seer's Island. Sheena was happy to indulge him every day, or twice if he wanted, and he wallowed in the hot water till he wrinkled like a prune.

Waiting for the ship was really quite a pleasant time. They had shelter, and even some firewood. An old, lost ship's boat had washed ashore broken up and battered. Though the Hold Tribe had obviously been there several times over the hundred years, Sheena supposed they didn't go there often, or they would have salvaged every plank and beam. The sign of the Witches – crossed lightning and an icicle – was above every hut, otherwise the doors would be long gone too.

They had leisure; they could exercise as much or as little as they chose. Sheena would usually start the day with a little 10 mile run up and down the hills, and a variety of exercises to keep her arms in shape, and a good session of stretching. Kira delighted in swimming, the calm waters of the bay were warm compared to what she was used to, and she could stay in for ages. Sheena, with the inbuilt dislike of Fire Witches for large bodies of water, especially cold ones, rarely joined her, and it was just too cold for Bronn as well, he preferred the hot pool in the stream. Sheena taught Bronn and Kira what she could, putting them through their paces with quarterstaff, knife, wooden swords and unarmed combat. You never knew when it might come in handy, she said. They were never going to be Warriors, but they improved. On the right day,

Bronn could even make Sheena have to take him seriously with the sword – Seer prescience, knowing what move Sheena was going to make a second before she made it could somewhat compensate for her overwhelmingly superior speed and strength.

Kira came ahead with her skills too. Having time to practice made all the difference. As the days passed, she ironed out her 'stutter', and the day came when she could manage her two Avatars and her body reasonably smoothly together, as long as they were all in sight. She still wasn't nearly as good as Kala had been with her three Material Avatars, but Kala had had over a hundred years of practice. And she could mostly manage her Material Avatar and body, even when well separated.

Bronn, with leisure time and meditation time found he was synchronized-dreaming with his beloved Kara more and more. Not every night, but two or three times a week. It took him a little while to work out there was a time difference, but that was soon compensated for. He told them that Marko and Shira had married, which pleased Kira and delighted Sheena. Not having too many responsibilities, he could, waking from such a dream, lie in bed remembering it, then rise leisurely and bumble his way through breakfast with a contented smile on his face. Kira and Sheena were happy for him, too, of course, but it did get a bit irritating after a while.

Bronn also had plenty of Seeing dreams too. It seemed inevitable that they were going to have to go to Warriors Hold, though it was still not clear exactly why. Satro should have been able to pass the message on, but perhaps the young Warrior they needed simply didn't believe the message, and would need convincing by Bronn. It was also not quite clear to Bronn exactly what they needed him for, but the feeling of need was definite.

Having kept track of the date, Sheena thought it was still a week short of the date that Satro had agreed to try to be there with the ship, though there was some hope he could be early. In the meantime, they kept to their training schedule, keeping themselves fit and Kira honing her skills.

Sheena also worked with Kira, teaching her how to pass herself off as a Fire Witch. It wouldn't do to let the world know there was an Ice Witch at large, that incredible word would get back to Narn very quickly. The training was mostly about choosing her spells and actions carefully. Avatar projection was fine, of course, and so was anything to do with heat. Offensive work she had to avoid, there was no getting around the fact that she did not project an aura as all Fire Witches did when in fighting mode. Heating things up was fine, but she had to pretend to be a lot more clumsy than she was, and she had to learn how to have more of a temper – or at least fake it.

The thing that had to be covered was her inability to project fire. The price for their much more delicate control over temperature and their precise focus was that Ice Witches could not do it. They could boil water, but getting something so hot it would burst into flame was beyond them. They could throw a concentrated force similar to lightning, though not quite the same – anyone who had seen a Fire Witch do it wouldn't be fooled for a minute, so best not to try. They could freeze water, or an unshielded opponent, but again that was very different from Fire Magic. Sheena tried to teach her, hoping for perhaps some talent in Fire Magic as she had found in Shira, but there was nothing usable.

In the end, Sheena reluctantly decided that Kira's use of magic would have to be severely curtailed; there was just too much chance of things not looking right. They would have to pretend Kira was Blocked. This was a reasonably uncommon but by no means unknown problem that young Fire Witches sometimes had, where they had a mental block about using their Gift. Most got over it in a few years, a very few never did. Sometimes the Block only affected one small part of the Gift, or was erratic. Sheena said Kira would have to pretend that she simply couldn't do anything with fire, though she could shield, project an Avatar and do some heating. And while she didn't need it, Kira would have to get used to wearing a lot more clothes and complaining about the cold. No problem there of course, she could cool herself down under warm clothes just as easily as she could keep herself warm with almost nothing on.

They would pass Kira off as Sheena's daughter. The difference in their skin colors would be no problem, Fire Witches were anything from very dark to very pale, and seemed not to inherit their skin color directly from their parents. More remarkable would be Kira's hair color. Her very fair blonde hair would be unusual for a Fire Witch, and the lack of any red highlights almost unheard of – but fortunately not quite unique. The lack of any known credible alternative to her being a Fire Witch would be the saving factor.

Satro and the ship came early, a good three days before the nominal meeting date, towards the end of the day. Sheena sent Kira away as soon as they saw the ship, and after the initial meeting and reunion with Satro, found a pretext to take him aside and fill him in on the news. Because of Bronn's prediction he had told the captain that they would be picking three people up, but had not given very much more information. Satro quite understood the need for secrecy, the fewer people who knew there was an Ice Witch about the better. He understood they would be pretending Kira was Sheena's daughter. They called her over to meet the captain and crew, and Kira (introduced as Kir'Ana'Va, , after the Fire Witch naming conventions, and Sheena as Shi'Ana'Va). Satro, falling in with the plan, said in a voice just loud enough for the captain to hear if he was listening carefully out of curiosity (which he was), "so, not much luck, eh?"

Sheena shook her head. "No, we got to the Hold easily enough, but there has been no-one there for a hundred years. And though we searched, no magic texts where we could find something of use against Narn." "Shhhh" cautioned Bronn. "The walls have ears. Well, I know there are no walls, but you know what I mean. So, we found nothing. That's still knowledge in itself, best kept to ourselves."

Kira fell in with the whole ploy like someone born to it. "Easily enough?" she scoffed. "Weeks slogging through the snow, freezing our tails off, not enough to eat, a cold deserted rockpile with nearly nothing in it at the end, and another long slog back. At least it was warmer. I still don't understand why I couldn't have stayed at home." She finished the last sentence with a creditable teenage whine in her voice.

"I told you, Kira, things are none too safe at Fire Hold at the moment, and anyway you're far too advanced for your age. I wanted to keep an eye on you. Crossing Iceland was far safer than leaving you at home, especially with the way you were looking at Ton'Ra'Lo, young lady. Yes, I know, it's hard when more than half your friends are doing it, but you know – or should know, anyway, that getting involved with someone while Blocked is dangerous."

Kira sighed. "Well at least we're off this frozen lump of uselessness in a few days, even if we do have to go in a boat" and she stomped off back to their camp.

Sheena sighed also. "I'm sorry, captain, young Fire Witches tend to be a bit ... mercurial. I though a good long trek through the wasteland might settle her down, and I could work on her Fire Block, but much as I love her it's been a bit of a trial. Don't worry, I'll keep her under control."

The captain laughed. "Not a problem, ma'm, and please call me Sim'Bo'Lo – Sim for short. I've seen many a young Fire Witch in my time, and she's really not too bad, from what I've seen so far – especially for someone with a Block, that usually gets them very bad tempered."

"Thank you, Captain" she replied, and Bronn added "I suppose you'll want a couple of days here for rest, repairs and to get water?"

The captain nodded. "A couple of days will do it. We could go today, we didn't know for sure if we would find any good source of water here so were prepared, but fresh is always best if you can get it. And it's always good to let the men stretch their legs. I see you've built us a fire, ready to go – thanks for that. We'll let the men have a wander and a bit of grog, but don't worry, I'll let them all know your daughter is off limits of course."

Sheena nodded. "Thank you again, captain ... she is a Fire Witch of course, so your men would find her a bit hot to handle if she wasn't interested – she'd probably blow her Block and scorch their tails if pressed ..." Sheena casually flamed the woodpile they had built from the remnants of the boat, setting it alight in half a minute – " ... but the thing I'm afraid of is, she might be … wouldn't matter normally, of course, but it could leave her Blocked for life."

The captain nodded sagely at this, and all was well. The next two days went smoothly, a continuous stream of barrels were brought over, patched, filled at the stream and taken back. The main form of relaxation for the men turned out to be the stream; they were mostly from Fir'Caram, the capital of Fireland (or the Witch controlled county, at least) or nearby coastal cities. The Witches were somewhat fastidious and liked themselves and their servants well-washed and groomed, and the habit stayed with the men if they left for a more independent lifestyle. Though Fireland had no hot springs like Seer's Hold except near the central volcanoes, there was plenty of water, and being on the equator there was little need to heat it. Sheena cheerfully heated the little spa-pool as often as was required, though she let Kira do it often enough to underline her pretense of being a Fire Witch despite a Block. The men adored her, for she was very attractive, and even with her best efforts and Sheena's coaching about having a temper, she still came across as a particularly nice young Fire Witch.

Soon enough the ship was ready to go, and they all boarded. It was Kira's first trip on a vessel of any size, and she really didn't have to feign nervousness too much. As they passed beyond the promontory, the waves started to rise, and one large one sent a fine spray over the front starboard side. Sheena and Kira both shuddered convincingly, and Kira said, "Oh, I hate it when it does that … I really hate it!"

The captain, nearby, chuckled and said, "Oh, there you go … no-one quivers quite like a Fire Witch when the seas get up. Well, I'm sorry, this won't be like your trip from Fir'Caram, with the wind at your back most of the way. We'll have to tack across to Warrior's Hold,

295

and the spray will be coming over the side pretty regular, and if we have a storm or two, which is likely, waves as well. Then, it'll be batten down the hatches and all landlubbers in their cabins or be washed overboard." Kira bit her lip and whimpered convincingly at that, and the captain laughed out loud. "Aye, a Fire Witch for sure. But don't you worry young miss, I've sailed these seas for twenty five years, and never lost a ship yet. Or a Witch for that matter." And he patted her cheerfully on the head, and went his way. Sheena pretended to comfort her, but really just hugged her and said with a laugh, "You were brilliant, Kira."

Once under way, with everyone having sated their desire for a view of the waves and the fresh air, Sheena, Bronn and Kira met with Satro to learn what he had found out. As a registered Warrior, he had of course gone to the Hold, and spent most of the time training and re-training. The Masters had said he was capable of attaining Silver rank if he would only stay and study and train for a few more years – probably not much more than four, certainly no more than ten (shielding was a weakness) – but he said that was not to be his way, while he would of course return at intervals, he was ensconced at Nun's Hold for the foreseeable future. The Masters respected his decision, of course.

Satro had, however an ulterior motive as well, and had kept an eye out for a suitable candidate to meet Bronn's Vision of a young Gold Warrior. As he had suspected, there was no-one like that. One of the five Masters was young enough to be possibly considered, but he was a Prince of the Hold, which is to say his time was mostly caught up in the politics and running of the place. He would not be enthusiastic about leaving.

Bronn shrugged. "We got over that sort of problem just fine at Nun's Hold" he said. "We found Sheena, hidden though she was. We will see what we will see, when we get there."

Satro hesitated. Finally, he pulled himself over the brink of uncertainty, and said, "There is one remote possibility ... a young man, no more than nineteen, and not long in training. He was the son of a farmer on Peace Island, and had little need to fight. But one day, shortly after he attained his majority and was allowed to go to the tavern as a man, a fight broke out between the locals, and some drovers who were bringing cattle in for shipment. He waded in and laid all five of them all out cold, without a mark on him. The Warriors heard, of course, and came over to evaluate him, accepted him and took him away. Everyone agrees he has great potential. He learns his lessons quickly, and his skills are far greater than any other in his year. But he's really only just getting started, it will be more than two years before he's allowed to even try for Orange grade. And, there are issues ... despite his skills, he lacks discipline. His position, despite talent, is dubious. Everyone agrees he has potential, but it remains to be seen if it can be developed. He's the only one I could find who could be considered Gold class material, but as he is now, Sheena far outranks him, both technically and in actual skills. I can't see how he can be a help."

Bronn nodded. "Well, thanks Satro, we will of course look him over. But it's not necessarily all about fighting skills. Sheena's the best of us all, of course, both physically and magically, but we need Kira, and me, even though all I can really do is See the way forward. We know everyone is needed, but not necessarily why – it might be something quite unexpected, subtle or small."

They were hoping for an uneventful passage, but if was not to be. A few days after rounding Peace Island and their first stop, perhaps midway between it and Nun's Hold, the captain came to see them, frowning. He came straight to the point. "We have a ship following us" he noted. "It must have come from Nun's Hold, but it's flying Narn's flag. Yes, his following is great enough that he can command ships of his own. Fir'Caram is secure, as is Fire Hold and all of the Witch lands, but there is talk that he has completely taken over Fir'Alan'Atrah, and managed to suborn a good dozen Witches to his cause before the Queens at Fir'Caram caught on and put a stop to it. No level two Witches so far, thank God. But as Lord of Fir'Alan'Atrah he is a legitimate ruler in his own right, and can command ships. I've heard tell of his ships, privateers essentially. With a couple of Witches aboard, they stop other ships. Not for true piracy you understand, but they're hoping to find other Witches, who they will take. With you two aboard, I'm worried. I think we're a bit faster than they are, but we can't sail these waters in the dark. During the night, if they can find us – and there's a nearly full moon at the moment – they could easily sneak up as we anchor to whatever reef or islet we find. We could outrun them, but we'd have to go almost due north, well away from where you want to go. If we have to take our chances then so be it, but I thought I'd better ask you if there is anything you want us to do? Can they find us in the dark if we show no lights?"

Sheena nodded. "Probably, if they have some general idea of where we are. Like calls to like, you know, and one Witch generally knows if there's another around. If they have the knowledge, there are various seeker spells that can be of use. Let me see, let me see ... no level two Witches, you say? We might do something, then ... you've worked with Witches before, captain, do

298

you have a good understanding of how far a level one Witch can throw a firebolt?"

The captain nodded. "Aye, about a decent arrow's flight, according to my understanding, some a bit more, some a bit less."

Sheena nodded again. "That's right. There is not so very much variation … level two Witches use a different technique and can go further, and level three a different one again. So … do you think you can, without making it look deliberate, let them catch up to us about that far, and a quarter again for safety, so they cannot fire our sails? You have to be sure, now – I don't want them to unexpectedly get closer and have both of our ships on fire."

The captain thought for no more than a few seconds and nodded. "I can do that, easy. They're comin' downwind, and we're tackin' upwind. I can do a clumsy tack or two, to bring them closer, and drop the spanker. With care – and I'm a careful man – it will look no more than poor seamanship. And aye, I can hold them there. You clearly have something in mind." He scratched his chin thoughtfully. "Ah – I hope you don't mind me mentioning this. Your friend Satro has hired us, and we're your ship and crew. But he hired us for normal work only. He didn't hire us for danger work, and it's too late to pay us more and up the contract, so to speak – I'm not afraid for myself you understand, but for danger work I'd leave some of my crew ashore what have wife and kids, and take on some younger men or those with the need or desire for better money. So, I'll do my best to help you – but I can't endanger the ship and crew. You'll have to tell me what you've in mind."

Sheena again nodded her understanding. "Don't worry, captain. I'm planning to have them just outside range of their Witches, but hope to be within mine. I'm pretty sure of what I can do there. If I fail, well, then you can heave to and hand us over, and we will have to take our chances. I doubt they'd blame you, you can always say we forced your hand."

The captain pursed his mouth, nodded once more, and finally said, "Aye, well, so let it be."

He was an artist. He swung the ship about twice, each time a fair bit more slowly than he had done it so many times on the days before. Each time, the other ship followed a fair bit more smartly and gained, and now the captain held a straight line as if trying to outrun it. Difficult to tell at a distance, the ship did not have every bit of sail it could hold out. The other ship was gaining very, very slightly but there was not much in it.

Sheena and Kira stood at the stern, looking back at the other ship perhaps a one and a quarter thousand yards away. They could see two others standing in the bow, facing them, long hair streaming sideways in the wind. One of them raised her arm and cast forward. A substantial firebolt shot out but burned out well short, though not as short as Sheena would have preferred. Having prepared Kira for what she wanted to do, she held an arm out, and Kira clasped it. Letting her mind go blank, Kira calmed her thoughts and opened her natural shields. Sheena's mind came into hers, on a different 'channel' to the healing one they had used before, closer to the one used by Kira when she had used her truth spell. A more direct and intimate channel, better for energy transfer. It required very high level of trust, because once open the dominant partner could hold it open, effectively taking over the other's mind. And sudden panicked resistance could harm or even destroy both minds. Ice Witches were better at trusting; the last time Sheena had done this was when she had the Fire Witches under firm command of her mind control spells.

Sheena gathered her own considerable force of will and strength, and mustered the best firebolt she could. It would have been just about enough to do the job, but they would have had to risk getting a bit closer. Then, holding it ready to go, she drew sharply on Kira's own mind and energy, to give it an extra boost.

She threw the firebolt out towards the other ship. A superb shot, as it had to be to compensate for wind, it flew straight and true straight through the other ship's foresail, which began to burn with some enthusiasm. Sailor scurried over the rigging like ants in the distance, and with heroic efforts cut the ropes and dumped it over the side before it could set the rest of the ship or the other sails alight, though it took them some time. They surged ahead, and the other ship turned away, no doubt the captain resuming his original course. Sheena could imagine what was going on. The Witches would be furious, perhaps even to the extent of agreeing to a concerted effort of their own- Narn's control and mind magic might even be enough to let them take that difficult step. Or perhaps not, that being more likely. But they would have threatened the captain, and he would have said that he wasn't going to risk having his ship burned out from under him, they would have replied that they could do that too, and he would have said they could if they liked, but they would go down with the ship as well, and Sheena doubted Narn's control was tight enough for a Fire Witch to risk that.

Their captain was impressed. "Your pardon, my lady, I had no idea you were nobility. Only a level two Witch could do that." Fire Witch rank was purely on the basis of ability, and they did give themselves airs. Level twos were 'Nobles' and level threes 'Queens'.

Sim'Bo'Lo didn't display the normal complete deference of an Ungifted Fireland person to any Witch, after all he was the master in his own domain, but a Noble would be different matter.

Sheena smiled and shook her head. "No, captain, I'm only level one. That was the two of us working together, our minds merged and as one. That got us up to about a one-and-a-half level, enough to do the job."

The captain was surprised. "Never heard of it before. How come it isn't used all the time?"

Sheena explained that it left the one supplying the extra power very vulnerable to the dominant partner, and both minds at risk. Fire Witches were notoriously paranoid, and for good reason. Intrigue and jockeying for position were the normal state of affairs, and each Witch looked out for her own interests. Not that they were incapable of cooperation, far from it, but it was always an uneasy alliance. She said that they could do it in this case as Kira was her daughter, and an exceptionally well behaved and trustworthy one at that, for a Fire Witch. She could trust Sheena, as her mother, not to do anything wrong.

And so the problem was avoided. But the news that Narn had taken over an entire county was worrying. Fireland was a vast continent compared to the other island Holds, with a population in the tens of millions, perhaps even a hundred. The Witches, in their own county of Fir'Alan'Cara had little to do with the others, and no-one had united the continent since the days of Sha'Lin'Tra, but if Narn was putting his mind to it and succeeding then the chance of him building an unconquerable power base was there. A few hundred (or possibly a thousand if they were all gathered together) Fire Witches, as many Seers and Warriors and the newly discovered Ice Witches could not stand against a properly coordinated onslaught from Fireland, assuming the army could be transported. They would have the support of all the Ungifted on the various other lands of course, but in sheer numbers they could not begin to compete there either.

Having rounded Peace Island, they kept to the middle of the passage between Happiness Island and Nun's Hold, avoiding the reefs. Then, they tacked west again, quicker with the wind aiding them rather than hindering them, and began the climb back south to the narrow navigable passage to Warrior's Island (named Strength) itself. Because of an extensive trailing reef, there was no approach to Warrior's Hold from the sea, except perhaps at high tide in a very shallow draught canoe. But the chance of storms, holing on the rocks and other mishaps meant that was hardly ever done. As Bronn grumbled, as usual they would have to walk across the island. In this case, just a few days, a matter of a mere hundred and twenty miles, with the chance of hiring horses or a cart if they wished.

Satro made it easy to get onto the island, at the main port, called somewhat unimaginatively, Entry. The Warriors, more aware than most of the trouble brewing on Fireland and the dangers of Narn's uprising, simply because of their Gift, had clamped down on border control. No-one got in anymore without being vouched for, or under questioning by a truth spell from a half dozen Witches kept on the payroll to do just that, or both. Satro knew all the protocols, who to ask to see, what to say, and he was known himself having been on the island only a few weeks before. He was able to say quite truthfully, as were they all, that they were on the island seeking a young highly qualified Warrior, with the intent of attempting Narn's downfall. The port guards pursed their lips at that, but didn't laugh, though they were surprised at the presumption. Sheena answered easily that she was a level one Fire Witch, Bronn that he was a Master Seer (which lent credence to the idea of a quest) and Kira said she was a young Witch but could not cast fire, and was being looked after by Bronn and Sheena, also all true.

Satro had brought ample funds from Nun's Hold, provided by Intira, so they booked themselves into a quiet, comfortable, well-appointed inn. Then, with a list of things they wanted or needed each, they set off around the city. Bronn went with Sheena, and Satro took Kira. Not that it would have mattered in the slightest if Kira wandered off on her own, Entry was just about the safest city-town in the world. Any pickpocket or thief would be only too aware that the place had the highest ratio of Warriors to civilians in the world, and they kept the place safe just as the Seers kept Carm safe. Any form of violence was a chancy idea, the likelihood of passers-by being too afraid to step in and help was not great, and the most agile thief in the world would have a hard time of it running away from one Warrior, let alone the others who would naturally join in. And the Warriors themselves were honest by nature, training and sworn oath. However, the chances of Kira getting lost were high, and the whole island was patriarchal in the extreme, though not misogynistic. They liked their womenfolk very much and were not afraid of them, but both Sheena and Kira would attract far less attention if they were properly in the care of men.

Satro, like most Warriors, knew little about the hiring of horses or the like. When he had to cover the hundred or so miles to the Hold, he jogged most of the way, stopping for two nights, or more if he was feeling lazy or the weather was bad. He carried little more than water, money and a bit of food, and a change of clothes. He said it would be interesting to mostly walk the whole way for a change. There was no problem about food and shelter along the way, Warrior's Island was very different to Seer's Island. While just as lush around the coast and at the same latitude, a cold current made it cooler, and the soil was richer and the rains more reliable. Without central mountains – not much over a hill – there were no swamps, but also no bare grasslands. It was rich farming land, and there were many villages and even small towns at major road junctions or river crossings.

Sheena and Bronn looked over what was for hire, and finally Sheena recommended against mounts. Kira had never ridden, Satro and Sheena didn't need to, and Bronn had not ridden since Seer's Island. For the few days they would be on the road, it was not worth making Bronn and Kira miserable with sore riding muscles. They did, however hire a couple of sturdy ponies so they could easily carry their possessions, mostly changes of clothes, a bit of food and so on. All of their winter stuff they left in storage at Entry, well mothballed as they would not need it for some time – if ever. Satro left his sword – he would have no need of it on the island except possibly at the Hold, and there were plenty there. They even left their bows. The high likelihood of rain meant they could easily get ruined, and the chances of there being anything to shoot was low, they might as well buy their food. They did buy new footwear. The walking would be easy, so large heavy boots were not needed, but something more or less waterproof was advisable, and they also bought hoods and umbrellas.

As the island was essentially a network of roads connecting towns, there were many ways from one end to the other. The shortest way had naturally evolved over time to be the preferred one, with the best accommodation along the way. Still, there was nothing unusual about people choosing a slightly different

305

way, perhaps to save money, visit friends or relatives, or simply for a change. Satro and Bronn decided to take a route just a little bit longer, a little bit out of the way, a simple precaution to keep their presence hidden. Not that there was any reason for it other than plain paranoia, but they had already run into Narn or his agents several times. Of course, they didn't choose a way so far out of the ordinary that it would be remarkable in itself.

Satro suggested a simple form of disguise, using much the same identities they had presented at Entry; best after all to keep their story straight. He said with some hesitation that while he could pass Bronn off easily enough, the simplest thing for Sheena and Kira would be to present themselves as not too bright.

And that all worked quite well. The first night they stopped, the inn's regulars asked why the party was passing through, and Satro said when asked that he had taken a commission to guide Bronn through Warrior's Island to the Hold. When he was asked why Bronn wanted to go there, he shrugged and replied "Never thought to ask. Not my business. All I needed to know is he has no ill intent, and that was established by the border control at Entry." Bronn replied that he was quite happy to talk about it. He'd had a Vision that he needed to go to the Hold and meet someone there. When asked who, he also shrugged. "No idea. Visions are like that. It's the same with the girls, here. I know I'll need them too, but it's not clear whether it's because of something they did, or something they're going to do. I've learned to trust my Visions and just go along with the flow."

The locals then turned their attention to the girls. They asked Sheena if she had done anything unusual. With a remarkably well done vacuous expression, she nodded and replied, "Oh yes indeed, sir, I have left my home, where I lived all my life, and travelled with Seer Bronn here!" That didn't quite satisfy them, so they probed a bit more, and Sheena told them that on Nun's Hold she had done a bit of looking after the novices, and a bit of work in the kitchens, and generally anything that needed doing. She subtly put across the idea that they were generally the things that others didn't like to do because they were too boring, but she didn't mind. As a last attempt, they asked if she knew of anything unusual she was going to do. Again, she nodded cheerfully, and said she was going to Warrior's Hold. They didn't get any further with Kira. Asking her why she was on the journey, she looked at them blankly for a pause, and then in a sort of dull, uncomprehending way replied "'cause they said I had to go with Seer Bronn." The locals gave up, and one of them remarked that he hoped Seer Bronn's Vision wasn't going to be relying on the girl's wits, causing general laughter, the more so when both Sheena and Kira joined in, with that particular kind of laugh that everyone knew meant that they didn't really understand the joke, but were afraid to admit it.

And so they travelled in easy stages across the island. There were no issues. Travelers and strangers would have been well advised to watch out for unexpected costs at the inns, but people took one look at Satro's Bronze belt medallion and the party had respect. The rooms were universally clean, safe, small and quite costly, and the food always good and always expensive. Sheena had always liked the island, and Bronn approved of it – it was all very orderly. Kira was in awe of the place, it was so different from her home. Iceland had been different enough, with things growing without human help, but all cold climate ecosystems are fairly simple. The sheer variety of living things she now saw, particularly as they went through the frequent woods and occasional forests amazed and delighted her, in particular the songbirds. And, of course, the trees. She had seen the fruit tress so lovingly cared for at home, and the small wood of not much larger trees on Iceland. But the Warriors loved their island, and kept the people in balance with it. Large areas were designated preserves, and trees and animals lived there in a state that while not really wild was mature. She saw truly big trees for the first time, towering high above and too wide for all of them to put their arms around together. At the farms, she saw animals living out in the open, and plants growing in well ordered rows, but without intensive care. Seeing a cat for the first time, and her soft cries of enchantment at holding a kitten were almost worth the troubles that they had encountered. She was delighted when Sheena told her that Iceland was big enough and sufficiently warmer than Ice Island that such pets were possible.

Finally, they came to the Hold itself. There was a massive stone wall around it, perhaps three times the height of a man and nearly as thick, and well-built so as to be virtually unclimbable. It had been built over the centuries, and was one of the many things about the Hold that was maintained through hard labor, the Masters always being on the lookout for difficult but worthwhile things for the students to do to build up muscle. Another task used in training was that of courier – students would regularly run between Entry and the Hold, and to other parts of the island for that matter, and so their papers had arrived days before they did, and they were all checked off.

Bronn, as Master Seer commanded respect, and so was able to request an audience with one of the Masters, where even Satro would have had to wait. Again because of Bronn but also Satro, they were assigned good sleeping quarters and use of the dining facilities free of charge. They settled in, and Satro showed them around the Hold. Sheena was still familiar with the general layout, though much had changed. Bronn had never been there before, but found it interesting how very different it was to Seer's Hold. There was a quiet silence about it. Not brooding or menacing, but everywhere there was the projection of confident strength held perfectly under control. There was elegance and beauty, but little to put the visitor at ease. To be fair, visitors were not all that common, mostly the residents were students, teachers and support staff, and they decorated the place in accordance with their needs, nature and training. Unlike Seer's Hold, where people regularly came for readings, those who wanted a Warrior sent a request by message, spoke to a local agent, or, rarely, came to Entry, but there was no real need for them to come to the Hold.

The Hold was big enough to house and meet the needs of the five hundred students (most of who would be weeded out – only about fifteen made it to Orange each year), the fifty trainers and the five Masters – and a greater number of workers, and as many again spouses and children, or almost four thousand people all in all (with more than twenty times as many not directly working for the Hold), and had gardens where vegetables and greens were grown, ten good wells and an aqueduct bringing water from the outside, and a well-designed sewer system. Meat animals were grazed outside, though they could be housed in the Hold in case of a siege – which had not happened since the time of Sha'Lin'Tra. Still, those who train in the art of war do these things as a matter of course. As well, there was housing, foundries, baths, shops and all the supporting trades and needs. A bustling, busy little microcosm of a metropolis, but all ordered around the over-arching needs of the students, the dojos and the Masters – as was the whole island, to a lesser extent.

After they had had a few hours to settle in and freshen up, they were summoned to the office of the Master who had agreed to see them. Neither the oldest nor the youngest of them, he was a man in his late forties or early fifties – allowing for the Warrior lifestyle. He looked about thirty-five. If Bronn had thought Satro a stable, confident man, Master Thirro was a rock. Imagine a normal leader or noble, confident in their power base and abilities, with a career full of achievement behind them. Then imagine that in addition, they have been trained so that they are mentally stable and without any significant vice, and that any emotional issues or conflicts are long resolved. Then, further, that they are at the very pinnacle of physical fitness, and able to defend themselves against any reasonable physical assault, and you have a man who is centered, not easily impressed, but not arrogant, dismissive or confrontational. Those things come from the need to prove oneself to others; he would have already proved everything he needed to, to the most important and critical audience of all – himself.

His office and workroom reflected his position. Large enough and airy, with a view over three training grounds, it was pleasant but not ostentatious. Bronn was reminded of his abbot's rooms. It was simple but not Spartan, there were pleasant wall hangings, two very fine swords on the wall, a portrait of a woman and two good-looking children, most likely family, and a semi-organized clutter of papers and scrolls on various tables. There were comfortable chairs for the visitors, water and fruit juices, and a small tray of delicate little cakes, which were offered and accepted.

After examining his credentials, he took Bronn's statement of his Vision and the quest at face value, as a stated and agreed Truth. Seers didn't lie, no more did Warriors, and they both knew it. He well knew about Narn's ambitions and achievements, and though by no means worried – yet – he was naturally concerned. Relations with Nun's Hold were good, and he had received their opinion on the inevitability of conflict at some time, and he was naturally in favor of any group looking to avoid that. Warriors did not go looking for fights.

He welcomed Satro back to the Hold as well, and gave passing consideration to Sheena and Kira, but they clearly did not rank highly in his concerns, though he obviously took them a bit more seriously when he learned they were both Witches. But a man of his position would normally deal with Nobles or Queens.

When Bronn stated his Vision had seen them taking away a young Gold Warrior, or one with Gold potential though, he was surprised. "Really. Well, we have a handful of candidates amongst the Silvers, and perhaps half as many amongst the Bronzes. Most, if not all won't make it of course – I can't remember the last time we promoted anyone to Gold below the age of forty. But as to taking them away … I doubt if they would want to go, or that we would release them. Either they are totally focused on their training, or we think they should be." He smiled briefly, in an open and friendly way. "Still, it's easy to take a look, if as you say you have seen their face in a dream. They are all, of course, in advanced classes, and we can find them in short order."

And so it was. A few brief questions and a bit of walking took them to dojos where very intensive, personal training was happening. Focused but relaxed students slashed, whirled and exercised their way fraction by fraction closer to the pinnacle of human capacity and capability. All of them were courteous and pleasant, and obviously a step or two above Satro's level, and none of them had the face Bronn was looking for.

311

Returning to Thirro's office, they sat again. Thirro steepled his fingers, and nodded. "So, as I thought, not one of the high rankers. They all aspire, and some of them might well make it to Gold later in life, if they are of service to the Hold. There is actually one student there who truly has the potential, a skills master if I've ever seen one. But I know him well of course, and I doubt he's your man. He will most likely only leave the Hold once, for his mandatory tour of duty, and return to teach. One day, he will be one of the Masters. I wonder, Seer Bronn, if you spotted which one he is?"

Bronn shook his head, and said, "No, Master Thirro. I can't, any more than you would be likely to pick out a Seer with a particular talent if you visited our Hold. They are all so far beyond any skills I have in that area, I am not qualified to judge. Of course," he smiled "I might dream it tonight, in which case I'll tell you tomorrow. What about you, Satro?"

Satro mused a moment, and then hesitantly said, "The slightly older Silver in the third class we visited, with the black hair and the green tunic?"

Thirro shook his head. "I know why you chose him. Good guess, but while he's fantastic with the sword as you saw, he has a limitation in anything involving two hands. You wouldn't have seen that, of course. And ... ladies, would you like to have a guess?" he smiled pleasantly in their direction. Kira shook her head, but Sheena spoke up with a definite voice: "That young man in the second class, with the short, sandy hair and green eyes, who was doing the fifth rank quarterstaff work."

Thirro raised his eyebrows in surprise, and replied, "Quiet correct. And, you're quite definite about it too, I hear. There's obviously more to you than meets the eye, young lady. I look forward to talking with you more." He adjusted his position slightly, conveying in one simple movement that interesting as the subject and Sheena's perception was, they had to return to the matter at hand, which was the concern of men. "Well, Seer Bronn, you are of course free to wander our halls and training fields and rooms as you will, for as long as you like. And of course there will be men out on courier duty and in the fields coming and going. But I really can't think of who you might be seeking."

Satro stirred in his seat. "Your pardon, Master Thirro, but when I was here a few weeks ago, I heard of young trainee, who showed extraordinary promise. Shilo, his name was, as I recall, a discovery from Peace Island."

Thirro's face darkened. "Him! A disgrace. We bungled on him, I'm afraid. Not suitable for a Warrior, despite his talent. No self-discipline. He's in the cells, awaiting trial, and it is virtually certain we will vote for expulsion. After we do, you are welcome to him of course, but he will not be a Warrior, let alone an aspirant to Gold."

Bronn leant forward. "A young man, then ... tall, dark haired? For so I have Seen him. Well-favored, with an almost foxy, triangular face?"

Thirro sat back. "Yes, that describes him well enough. But almost untrained, he has only been here six months. True he's picked up over a year's worth of skills in that time, but again, as I said, undisciplined."

Sheena coughed gently, and said, diffidently, "If I may ask, Master Thirro, what is he in the cells for? What lack of discipline has he shown?"

Thirro looked at Bronn, who managed to convey with a shrug that while the question was asked by a woman, who would have very little understanding of the ways

313

of Warrior's Hold and should probably just be decorative and quiet, he would like to hear the answer too, if it wasn't too much trouble, please.

"Well, since you are concerned, Seer Bronn, I will answer. I hope this doesn't shock the ladies, however. You must understand our students are all men, mostly young men, and vitally alive young men at that. We do not impose chastity on them beyond the need to ensure that they can and will control themselves. This we do in the first year, where they are all young and indeed most of them under the age of consent, eighteen. After their maturity and the first year, they can make their own arrangements. Periodically, we ask them to be celibate for a week, a month or as long as we need to satisfy ourselves that they don't have uncontrollable urges in that area. Or any other area, of course. They must encounter and resist the temptations of drink as well, gambling and all the other evils. But Shilo ... Shilo has a problem with women. He can't resist them. Twice we caught him out of bounds, for we are not stupidly trusting, we have a network of informants for such matters, and all others. We warned him, and he promised he would conform. But a week ago, we caught him out again, out in the town. He thought he would fool us by choosing a young girl of a good family and meet her in secret."

He shook his head. "Well, he begged us for yet another chance. But we have a principle at stake here, three violations for the same offence and you're out. A pity, but despite his talents, we will not turn out a flawed Warrior. It's not fair to the others who have worked so hard, not fair to our clients, and frankly not fair on the young man himself. If he's not cut out to be a Warrior, best to find out while he's still young."

Sheena nodded in understanding. "Your pardon again, Master Thirro, but my understanding is, notwithstanding three violations, it is still possible for a reprieve – if a Warrior of standing will vouch for him and take him under personal training."

Thirro creased his brows. "You are right, ... Sheena I think you said your name is? There aren't many women who know our ways so well, though I suppose travelling with Satro here ... that's the reason for the trial. If any trained Warrior with seniority will step forward and take him on, he could get a reprieve. His chances are not good, it really doesn't happen often. It hasn't happened in *my* lifetime. Your friend Satro here can't do it, his skills are sufficient of course, but he has not yet been granted seniority, which happens after fifteen years of qualification."

Sheena nodded again. "I understand, Master Thirro. Still, since we need him, I will do it. I will take him as my personal trainee."

Thirro sat back in his chair in shock, and his mouth fell open. Something that had probably not happened to him since he was a boy. He laughed. "You? A woman? Did I not just say, only a Warrior, and an experienced one can do it? This is madness, Seer Bronn, I am ..."

His voice trailed off. Sheena had taken something out of a small bag she was carrying, and placed it on his desk. It was a large, heavyish gilded medallion, broken, or rather, cut in half.

Thirro picked it up. "Where ... where did you get this?" he asked weakly.

Sheena replied calmly. "I have been carrying it for a long time. You know what it means, Master Thirro. It means, assuming it matches, and I assure you it will, that you must at least listen to me and consider my request, if it is possible."

Thirro was still dumbfounded. "Yes, of course ... but only the five Masters know of this, and none of them would tell anyone. Seer Bronn, did you see this in a Vision, duplicate it and give it to this woman?"

Bronn shook his head. "No, Master Thirro. I have never seen it before. Still, I must ask you with all the weight that my rank carries, to treat this matter seriously. Sheena is more than she seems."

Thirro pulled himself together. "Yes ... in any case, the medallion carries its own weight, no matter who brings it. Still, this cannot be answered by one Master alone." He rose, went to the door, and called out to his personal assistant who waited in the anteroom. "Shado ... find me another Master, straight away. Priority ... priority one." Shado looked shocked. Priority one was 'drop everything'.

In a very short time, another Master was found. He was very similar to Thirro. Not physically – Thirro was tall and athletic, the new arrival shorter and stocky, with an aura of great physical strength. But the feel of both people was similar, the centered competence, the effortless confidence without a need of outward show. He nodded towards the visitors, and introduced himself as Master Cordubo. But immediately, he asked, "What is it, Thirro, that warrants a priority one?"

Master Thirro passed over the half-medallion, and Cordubo went through much the same series of expressions of amazement and incredulity. He looked to Bronn, and held out the medallion, and began, "what ...?" But Thirro shook his head, and said, "It

316

was brought by this woman, a Fire Witch, who is called Sheena."

The event of the medallion being dealt with by two Masters, both of them relaxed a little and regained some of their poise. "We are obliged, as you say, to listen to your request, Witch Sheena and grant it if possible" Thirro stated. "I frankly do not know what to say. We can of course release the man Shilo to you. It may even be that we are obliged to do so … but I can't see what good it will do. You cannot train him. I suppose Satro here could do it if you requested that, the medallion would allow us to make an exception. But you didn't ask that. You said you will train him yourself."

Sheena nodded, and said, "The medallion is, or as far as I know, should be, only known to the Masters. The rule is, one Master will pass the knowledge on to another as he is elevated. But there is something else besides the obligation to listen and aid. If I remember … it is something like … 'the one who comes to you with the medallion will tell you something about it that no Master will know'."

Thirro sighed, and turned to Cordubo, and said, "It appears she knows everything … still, if she tells us something new, that will at least show she hasn't learned it from one of us, incredible though that would be in its own right." Cordubo nodded, and added, "I agree. I don't know what else to do, to be honest."

Sheena sat back in her chair, and folded her hands. "When Sha'Lin'Tra the sorceress broke up her empire, she did so slowly, granting each Hold its autonomy. In the case of Warrior's Hold, knowing their love of procedure and formality, she did so by decree, and the issuing of three scrolls detailing firstly the authority, secondly the duties and thirdly the rights of the Hold itself over the island. But at the same time, she caused this medallion to be made from silver, broken and gilded, giving to the Masters of that time the obligation to respect and aid anyone who brought the other half to them, and to pass that obligation down the generations."

Both Thirro and Cordubo nodded, and Cordubo said, "This is the known part. Go on."

Sheena smiled, and added, "If you read the second scroll, and take the second letter of the second word of each line and put them all together, you will find a hidden message in it. You will need an exact copy of the scroll, however, for if it is merely transcribed, the word spacing may have changed."

Thirro stood up from his desk, restored by the possibility of simple action. He strode again to the door, opened it, and spoke to Shado once again. "Shado, do you think you can find us an exact copy of the original decrees of Warrior's Hold? Not a transcript, I have one of those, but a copy of the original, word for word, line for line, with nothing altered?" Shado nodded, and replied, "Yes, Master Thirro, we have one in the Master's library. It has been re-copied every generation, and verified against the original every few hundred years. I'll just step next door and fetch it at once."

While they were waiting, Thirro remarked, "Well, this has been a remarkable afternoon, without doubt. But still, when all is said and done, medallion or no, you cannot train him. It just can't be done. If you want to change your request so that Satro here can do it, well and good."

Sheena rose from her chair. She walked closer to the desk, and held out her hand. She said, "Shall we at least shake hands on this matter and agree to look at it further?"

Thirro nodded, and held out his hand also. "We are, of course, obligated to do so by the medallion." His larger hand engulfed hers, and they shook – but Sheena did not release it. Slowly, to allow Thirro time to get used to it, she gripped tighter. Thirro frowned, and looked at her, and then at their clasped hands. In puzzlement, he gripped more firmly, and more firmly still as Sheena did the same. Finally, he looked up at her, released her hand, and went to open his mouth. But Satro spoke, for only the second time in the meeting, with a little humor in his voice, saying "Comes as a bit of a shock, I know, Master Thirro, it certainly did to me. Yes, she is Hold trained, impossible as it seems. I have sparred with her, and she can train him, no doubt about it."

Cordubo, who had not been a part of the physical contact, looked at Thirro and Satro, but anything he might have said was interrupted by Shado's return. He came in, handed over the scrolls with a simple word, and left the room again. Thirro sat down at his desk, saying under his breath, "Second scroll, here it is, the duties ..." - he rolled it out and weighed it down at the top – "Second word, second letter ... here we go ... 'Theonewhoco' ... that would be "The one who co ... comes toy .. to you with themed ... that would be, the medallion ... oh, God in Heaven, this says what the obligation is, doesn't it? How? How could you know this thing that even the Masters don't? And be Hold Trained? Did you pretend to be a man, or something?"

Sheena laughed, and said, "No, no, Master Thirro, nothing like that ... I'm a bit surprised, Satro guessed it almost at once. No, the reason I know the words are there is, I wrote them there myself, on purpose, and the reason I am Hold trained is, I trained at a time when you were still accepting female students."

Thirro and Cordubo looked at her, once more in amazement. "Sha'Lin'Tra. You are saying, you are Sha'Lin'Tra. It is the only thing that can explain your words."

Sheena nodded soberly. "I was. Yes, I once was Sha'Lin'Tra. No more, I am no longer a great sorceress, only a level one Fire Witch, by my own choice, limited by a spell. And I use the name Sheena. And I seek only to keep the world safe, which is why I am now, with Seer Bronn, opposing Narn."

Cordubo showed the degree to which he had been affected – he walked over to a chair, and sat, in obvious need of doing so. Sheena gave them a brief rundown of her life, ascendency and decision to abandon rulership of the world, because they deserved to know more. Perhaps the thing that convinced them the most was the clear evidence that she was Hold trained. There was just no explanation for that in any other way.

After she had finished and the Masters had asked a few questions and digested the information, Cordubo said, still with wonderment in his voice, "The first Masters accepted the decrees. Well, they had to; they were under Sha'Lin'Tra's rule. And, I suppose, they were glad to. It changed the nature of the Hold, the decrees laid down the principles of absolute discipline and trustworthiness which go to make the Warriors what they are today. But in reaction to her rule – to yours, I suppose I should say, they excluded women from training. It will cause great comment if we release him into your care, something neither we nor you would want."

Sheena nodded towards him. "A good point, Master Cordubo. Yes, the need for secrecy is paramount. Obviously, what you have learned here today can and should be shared with the other Masters, but it should go no further. I thought it a pity they made the decision about women, but I had other concerns – and of course, a decree of autonomy wouldn't have been worth the parchment it was written on, if I had attempted to change their first decision. But now ... if I may make a suggestion, a long time has passed. And we have another sorcerer wanting to take over the world, a man this time ... clearly, not training women as Warriors doesn't stop that kind of problem. You might consider a change. If we are unsuccessful in our quest, you'll have to face Narn yourselves, not today, nor tomorrow, but in a few years. Perhaps long enough to train women as Warriors too; you will need every one you can get, and all the ones who don't fully qualify but gain serious fighting ability, to form the core of an army."

She paused a second or two. "As for the other, that is simple enough – conduct the trial, and say that Shilo is to be released into training under a Warrior whose name is to be kept secret, by request of Seer Bronn, and we will be on our way."

There was further talk, of course. But Warriors are focused people, and despite the staggering news they had been presented with, Thirro and Cordubo acknowledged that the initiator and driver of the whole process was the medallion, and they were obliged to aid and respect Sheena's requests. Satro brought up the point that even though Shilo was under threat of expulsion, he had to agree to come with them, they could not force him. He had to understand what was going on to some degree, as little as possible as if he chose simple expulsion and a life outside the Warriors; he should not be able to give the information away.

321

Taking charge, Cordubo organized the mechanics of that himself, and straight away. He checked the schedules and found a small, private dojo. He called for Shilo, from the cells, and he was brought. He was a tallish, good looking young man with the somewhat foxy face Bronn had seen, not long adult and with the leanness of someone who is athletic, active and has not yet finished growing. He would need to put on a fair bit of muscle yet before he could be considered a Warrior. Cordubo spoke to Shilo himself.

"Student Shilo, you stand in disgrace. You stand in danger of expulsion – in certainty, unless someone agrees to vouch for you and take you under their personal supervision. Yet, the Masters have agreed you may have this chance, for you are talented, if undisciplined, and if you can be turned around you may be needed – these are difficult times. You will have a fair trial, but sometimes the outcomes of trials are known beforehand, and this is one of them. Someone has come forward, and will take you. We, the Masters, are inclined to release you to them. But in fairness, you will be allowed to make the decision yourself."

Shilo looked at the group of people. The Masters he dismissed, obviously if it was one of them, there would be no need for the group. Kira and Sheena he barely glanced at, and one look showed him that Bronn was untrained. That left only Satro, and he pointed. "Him, I assume." He had a pleasant, baritone voice, and the few words spoken suggested he would be quite a good singer. "I have seen him before. Yes, of course, if he will take me, I will be glad to be his student. I really have changed, and will not disappoint him." He bowed to Satro. But then, he added, "Your pardon, though, Masters ... isn't he too young?"

Cordubo nodded. "Yes, by our traditions. But as I said, these are difficult and interesting times, and changes will have to be made. But no, although your assumption is reasonable. Not him. If you agree, the one who will be your new Master and trainer will be ... this woman here, who is named Sheena."

Thirro and Cordubo smiled somewhat at Shilo's reaction. Having been surprised themselves, they knew he would be astonished, and he did not disappoint. His mouth fell open, and he looked from person to person, with random words coming out of his mouth for a while. "I ... you ... she ... no, ..." he pulled himself together with some effort. Anger wasn't called for, no-one in their right mind would get angry with a Warrior Master without great cause. "Is this ... is this some joke, or a further punishment? Are you wanting me to voluntarily withdraw?"

Cordubo continued to direct the conversation. "You confusion is understandable, student Shilo. But no, we are serious men. Not to say we never relax, but this is Hold business. You may take it as read that there is more to this situation than meets the eye, and you will be informed in good time if you make this choice. But choose carefully, it is this or nothing."

Shilo looked uncertainly at the masters, and at Sheena. A kind of sadness came over his face, but before he could speak, and possibly irrevocably reject the situation, Sheena spoke.

"Perhaps I can help in this difficult situation, masters. Shilo, the student must of course have confidence in the teacher, and I am not a conventional choice. I propose this: we are in a dojo, and various weapons are to hand. We will have a training session, you may choose any weapons you like, and I will defeat you three times. If I do not, one of the Masters here will be your trainer, saving you from expulsion. At least," she turned to them, "I hope they will agree to this, as my request."

Cordubo hesitated, but Thirro nodded, he having been presented with the medallion first. "Very well, I accept. You are a lucky man, Shilo. Three hours ago, I would have said you would be leaving this place very soon, for the last time. I warn you, though. If you do defeat Sheena here, your time under me will not be an easy one. Put one foot wrong, and you'll be out the door."

Shilo smiled, a pleasant smile. "So, all I have to do is defeat this woman, and I am re-instated? I accept." He turned to Sheena. "And, I am grateful. I will do my very best not to injure you." Sheena merely nodded. "You must understand" she said seriously, "I am not without abilities. I am a level one Fire Witch. But I will not be using fire or lightning, our relationship is not to be about whether or not you can shield. Now, student, what is your first choice of weapon?"

Shilo chose the quarterstaff, the staves were brought, and the observers retired behind the lines of the sparring ring. It was a very quick match. No more than three touches of the staves, barely enough to evaluate any presence of skill, and Sheena projected her Ethereal Avatar. Taken by surprise, as the Avatar threw her hands into his face (causing no damage of course, it being insubstantial), he completely dropped his guard, and Sheena's staff whistled through the air, stopping just short of his head.

"You are defeated, student" she stated calmly. "But .. but, that's not fair!" Shilo said angrily.

"Your judgment, Master?" Sheena said to Cordubo, who had agreed to act as referee.

"It is fair" Cordubo stated. "Student, you were told Sheena is a Fire Witch. You know Witches have the ability project an Avatar. You should have been expecting it, you have trained with such Avatars. What is rule one, Student?"

Shilo looked like he was going to argue further. Certainly, very few Witches indeed would have been able to muster the concentration need to project an Avatar in the middle of a fight. But clearly he remembered there were two more bouts, and he only had to win one. He bowed, and said "Rule one is, never underestimate your opponent. I concede. Thank you for the lesson."

He faced Cordubo again, and said, "For the second match, I choose double training daggers, level one." Level one daggers were little more than dagger shaped pieces of wood. They could give a severe bruise if the rounded point was used harshly, but were most unlikely to cause any permanent injury.

The two fighters faced off again, and once more Sheena projected her Avatar. Shilo paid no attention this time, and jumped through it to the attack. Sheena jumped back just as quickly, keeping a body's length between them, and quick as a flash threw one of her daggers. Even quicker, Shilo leant to the left, and it flew harmlessly by, two handspans from his throat. "Do you concede?" he asked, for Sheena now only had one dagger to his two. But again, that was the end of the match. Sheena had 'switched' her Avatar, it was now her Material one. It had caught the dagger, come up behind him, and had it at Shilo's throat.

"You are defeated, student" Sheena said again. "Your judgment, Master?"

"The student is defeated" Cordubo calmly judged. "The skill to change an Ethereal Avatar to a Material one without re-projection is rare, but not unknown. If a Warrior is fighting a woman by her choice, he must consider that she is likely to have unusual skills. What is rule one, student?"

Shilo stood, breathing heavily, not because of physical exertion of course, but out of emotion. "Master, rule one is, never underestimate your opponent. I concede again." He paused for thought. "However, while I accept Sheena can teach me how to fight a skilled Fire Witch, a Warrior has to learn much, much more. For the third bout, I choose single swords, level one. And I request that no special Fire Witch skills be employed."

Sheena seemed uncertain, and looked to Cordubo. He nodded. "The request has merit. You will have to fight him with your physical skills alone. You may concede now, if you wish."

Sheena muttered to herself, looking worried but determined. The swords were brought – again, without edges – and she swished it to and fro, to get the feel of the balance. Shilo looked at her closely, as she warmed up, and as she finally she took a fighter's stance. He could see from the way she stood that she was trained, possibly well trained, but not to Warrior level. Of course, he had only six months training, but he was confident in his skills, as Thirro had remarked he was as far advanced as they would normally expect after a full year.

Shilo moved like a ballet dancer, smoothly flowing. Sheena seemed almost clumsy by comparison. Shilo moved in quickly, and Sheena seemed barely to counter. A quick thrust, parry, and thrust again, and Sheena was out of position. Shilo brought his arm back – too far. Against a normal opponent, one whose skill level was as he had judged her, it was a valid move. He would never have done it against a Hold trained Warrior. Sheena recovered instantly. Her blade-staff flashed out at just the right angle, knocking Shilo's away, then back and down again, giving him a fair rap across the forearm, away again and the 'point' was at his throat.

"You are defeated, student" Sheena said for the third time. "Your judgment, Master?"

"The student is defeated" Cordubo calmly judged again. "Your skill is remarkable, Sheena. Your feigning of low skills with the sword was artistically done. Even I, who was looking for it, could not easily see it was a pretense. No trained Warrior would have made the mistake of allowing you that opening, however, because ... what is rule one, Student?"

Dejectedly, Shilo said, "I concede again. Rule one is, of course, never underestimate your opponent." He raised his head. "I will abide by our agreement, of course. But ... it is trickery! Three times, she has tricked me! I admit I fell for it every time, but it is still all just tricks!"

Sheena spoke, saying "What is maxim three, student?"

Shilo replied, "I ... have not memorized the maxims. I ... am not sure."

Cordubo answered: "A deficiency, student. The rules are there for a reason. The maxims are there for a reason. Learn them. Maxim three is this: 'there is no fairness in fighting. All fighters use their abilities, training, experience, determination and luck to obtain an advantage over their opponent. That is their purpose.' What you call 'tricks' allowed Sheena to defeat you, and they are as valid as any other technique."

Shilo hung his head. "I hear you, Master Cordubo. Still, if it had been a real fight, I would have fought differently."

Cordubo nodded, and replied: "Yes, very probably. *That* is why you are still a student. You still have much to learn. If you finally obtain a ranking, you will never do so, you will *always* fight and train to the maximum of your ability."

Sheena said, "The afternoon is still young, Masters, and student training can never begin too soon. My suggestion is, I will conduct my first training session here and now, and we will leave discussion of further plans to this evening. I suggest this, because while student Shilo has agreed to our plan, it's clear that he still harbors some doubt about my usefulness as a trainer. Satro, may I suggest you show Kira and Bronn around the Hold? There are many things worth seeing, and training can be tedious."

Thirro said, "I think that's a good idea. I would like to watch, if I may." Sheena bowed, and said, "You are welcome, of course, Master Thirro." Cordubo said he had other calls on his time, but would likely see them later in the evening.

Satro showed them around the Hold, with enthusiasm. There were of course many grounds and dojos, gyms and everything to do with training. But Warriors were trained in the mind as well as the body and in the shielding arts, and there were classrooms, and quiet places for mediation aplenty. In order to mix thought and mediation with physical activity, there were sculptured gardens, extensive fish ponds, gazebos, and running tracks through beautiful woods, smithies and

328

foundries, creative art displays of all kinds. Students were encouraged in any activity requiring skill and striving for excellence. And, with nearly a hundred thousand people, there were flourishing shops and markets of all kinds. Kira was overwhelmed and dazzled, and Bronn impressed. The whole environment was more vital, more alive than Carm, more varied, yet happier and calmer. Centered was the word.

Kira said that when their quest was over, she would love to return and buy a large number of small, beautiful things as presents for all her friends and family, and there were many exquisite creations available for very reasonable prices – with all those students creating and studying for excellence in one area or another there was a surplus of fine goods, which kept the prices down. Occasionally, merchants would come and buy wagonloads of things and take them around the world. Bronn bought a couple of durable small items for Kara – a stunning necklace of turquoise and lapis lazuli and a ring to match, which he thought would be safe enough in a small padded pouch. Kira bought herself a pair of amber earrings and then, greatly daring, got her ears pierced so she could wear them (Sheena healed the minute holes later), and bought a pair of small gold keepers. Satro recommended they both buy a good knife for everyday use – they wouldn't get a better one anywhere else in the world, especially for the money. Bronn bought himself two sets of very light cotton shirts and short pants. He knew they would be going to Fireland, and it would be hot, hot, hot. Kira did much the same, though she chose her outfits for durability and good looks – the heat was not going to bother her. Satro did a bit of careful shopping himself, as he by now had some experience with Nun's Hold and knew what was available, and what was in short supply. He, too, made a good selection from jewelry, obviously having some recipients in mind.

All in all, they had a very pleasant afternoon, with Bronn making only a small inroad into the gold forwarded by Intira. They didn't have to pay for food or drink when they stopped to refresh themselves, that was charged to the courtesy account they had been granted by the Hold. Like most Holds, it was a center of wealth: all Warriors paid a guild tax on their earnings and faithfully remitted it to the Hold, wherever they were in the world.

Early in the evening, they all met again. The other Masters had been notified of the extraordinary events of the day. All had wanted to meet Sheena and talk a while out of interest, see the medallion, and had then held their own private meeting, agreeing to secrecy, the desirability of opposing Narn in this way, and the releasing of Shilo to Bronn at a trial to be held the following day. Thirro was delegated to pass on the news, as he had been the first point of contact. Shilo was also present, and Thirro asked him in the formal way of Warriors if he was now prepared to accept Sheena as trainer. Shilo rose, and bowed. "Yes. It has been an ... interesting afternoon. I have learned much, but I can see quite clearly now I have a long way to go, and that Sheena can teach me. I do not know how this can be, but it's clearly so."

Thirro nodded. "Indeed. She is skilled. You do deserve to know the reason, though you must swear to secrecy."

Shilo did so, awed by the Great Oath Thirro demanded, and was once more stunned on learning that he had the legendary Sha'Lin'Tra as a teacher, and why she was Hold trained. Sheena revealed the Red badge on her belt. "Do you mean, she obtained her ranking hundreds of years ago?" he marveled.

Thirro, who had recovered himself to the point where the dry wit of his personality was becoming manifest, replied: "Yes, that is the case – in the distant past, when we still trained women. So, conveniently, we have to compromise very little - the requirement that the Warrior who vouches for you must be over thirty five years in age and have fifteen years qualification is also met."

"However," he added, "I have consulted the records and find that her certificate of seniority was never issued, and I am pleased to remedy that lack now" and he passed over a signed and witnessed sheet of parchment. "Also ... I sparred with her myself, after she had run Shilo here ragged and beaten him soundly with every weapon in the dojo, and is now fully convinced that she can help him in training" he added with a smile, but did not wait for an answer – "and can also say that the defects that were noted in her file as to endurance and strength have been addressed, and I am also pleased to award her full Bronze status."

He bowed and passed her a Bronze medallion to replace the Red one. Sheena also bowed as she received it, but said, "You do understand, Master Thirro, they were not remedied naturally, but through research and magic?"

Thirro replied, "We do understand that, and it does you credit to raise the point. There is nothing in the rules as to how the attributes should be attained, however. As it seems unlikely that there will be many others doing it that way, we feel we can pass over that technicality this once. Besides," he smiled his wry smile again, "we like to see our students bettering themselves. Though I think I can safely say, without detailed examination of the records, that no other student has taken so long to reach Bronze – nine hundred and seventeen years after reaching Orange!"

There was general laughter at that, but Thirro had not finished. "And it is my duty as Master to say that you have the capability to attain Silver. After your quest is over, we would be pleased to re-admit you, for I must tell you the Masters have begun to consider your idea of admitting women for training. We are not there yet, but it is my opinion this change will come."

Sheena was delighted, and bowed again. "You do me great honor, Master. Assuming our quest is successful I will seriously consider your offer – after I have discharged my other obligations of course."

They then sat down to a small, private supper. Satro and Sheena sat with Master Thirro, and spoke Hold business. Bronn was fascinated to hear that they had records of every Warrior back for thousands of years. With a bit over a dozen Orange graduates a year, a few less Bronze and a Silver or two it was feasible, though the older records did get abbreviated after the third copying or so. But key elements were kept, which was why Sheena's records were still known. Students who did not make it past the first year, whether for lack of ability, motivation or moral questions were also recorded, but those records discarded after fifty years. Others who dropped out later had their records kept for a hundred. And Thirro was of course fascinated with the details Sheena could remember from times long, long past.

Bronn switched his attention from the Warrior group to the remaining two, Kira and Shilo, trying to get to know Shilo a bit better. But it was hard going to break in to the conversation. Kira and he were getting along very well. Kira was wearing a very fine light grey dress with some muted blue embroidery, bought for the evening, which showed off her best features very nicely. Of course, though only fifteen she looked much older, in the way of Ice Witches. She was also wearing her new earrings, and they looked very fetching. Shilo had dressed in simple grey trousers, soft black boots with a wide cuff, and a pale blue shirt which contrasted his dark brown hair very nicely, and being in excellent physical shape after the initial training, the combination of his grey-blue eyes and musical voice was obviously having an effect. Sheena frowned to herself once or twice, looking their way, but made no comment.

The next day was full of formality. Shilo was tried in front of a drum-head court, and pleaded guilty. There was a small crowd of interested people, three of the five Masters, Shilo's instructors and some of his friends. Master Thirro spoke his judgment, that as this was Shilo's third offence expulsion would normally be automatic. However, he explained that Master Seer Bronn had seen a Vision, and had found a Bronze Warrior who would sponsor him, and continue to train him off-Hold. There was quite some stirring in the crowd at that.

Thirro raised his voice sternly. "Do not think, the rest of you, that this is a privilege, it is a last-hope attempt to redeem this student. Only his skills record allows it to be possible, that and Seer Bronn's need. We grant this request to our Ley brother in acknowledgement of his Gift, and ask no questions he cannot answer yet, his Vision being incomplete. But you would all be well advised to learn from this and mind your own lessons and discipline – it would be unwise to hope that this unusual event might be repeated. Any who wish to do so may have a limited time to wish student Shilo farewell – but there will be no celebrations, no farewell parties – he is still in a state of disgrace."

Shilo was allowed his farewells, but they were monitored. The rest of them worked with staff from the Hold, getting ready for their departure the following day. When everyone who wanted to had said goodbye to Shilo, he came and asked what he could do to help, and also what he should be taking with him – all useful questions, but both Bronn and Sheena noticed that he seemed to be asking a lot of those questions of Kira.

After a while, she called Shilo apart. "Student! A word with you, please." She led him away, to stand near a pond, filled with slowly moving golden and red fish. She looked him in the eye, and said: "I am sorry that one of my first orders to you must be one of denial. I'd rather be positive, teach you things, but so it must be. Kira is a very lovely girl – but there cannot be any romance happening between the two of you while this quest is going on."

Shilo, as so often happens when an accusation is made that isn't quite accurate but in which there is at least some truth, replied hotly that there was nothing of that sort between them.

"I am sure of it" Sheena replied. "But now, if you will, look me in the eye and say there is no such thought in your mind. And remember I am an old, experienced Fire Witch. I can cast a truthspell if needed. There is no romance yet ... but you have both made a beginning, I think."

Shilo blushed and led his head drop a fraction, which told Sheena all she needed to know. "As I said, I can't blame you, Shilo. It's a normal thing. But there are three things you need to know and understand. Firstly, a romance just isn't practical while people are travelling together. You get very little privacy and it makes the others in the team edgy. We need to *work* as a team, not as a pair and two outsiders. Secondly, it affects our safety. We need to be alert at all times, and consider the needs of the group. That gets compromised, if two people are mooning over each other and not watching what is going on around them. There may need to be decisions made by quick thinking, which can also be compromised if there is love in the air."

Shilo appeared to be listening, and no doubt was doing so, but Sheena could see by the set of his jaw that she had his intellectual understanding only.

"Thirdly ... well, Shilo, she is physically advanced, but she looks and acts more mature than she is. In fact, she's only fifteen, and at that only by a month or so. She is under-age, forbidden to you by law as well as by morality and my command."

Shilo's mouth fell slightly open. "Fifteen?" he said, in a slightly weak and incredulous voice. "*Fifteen*? I ... I thought she was about *my* age! She ..."

He gathered his thoughts. Sheena was relying on the fundamental morality of the Warriors, and all of the inhabitants of the island group. They were the most conservative of the four Gifted people, and had the age of consent set high, at eighteen years of age, adulthood. Full weight of judgment could be expected against any proved breaking of the law, though in practice exceptions were made for youngsters differing in age by a year or less and where there was no coercion.

Shilo bowed, and said, "Of course, Sheena. I understand, that makes a huge difference. I will keep well away from her, naturally."

Sheena rolled her eyes skywards. "Typical Warrior, it's always all or nothing, isn't it? Look, Shilo, I'm not saying never speak to her. We're a team, on a quest. We will depend on one another intimately, for our everyday needs. Who knows how our interdependence will affect our ultimate success or failure. There is absolutely *no* reason why you shouldn't be companions and good friends. And never forget, young though she is, she's a Witch, and a powerful one at that. Not as powerful as she will be, but enough that her skills and abilities will be a key part of our resources – don't think of her as a child, for she most definitely is not. She can't be a potential lover, but things will be hard enough for her, for she's not an adult yet either. Having a friend near her own age will be a great help and source of comfort."

That all being settled, she then took Kira aside, and put forward much the same argument. "Kira, I've seen you and Shilo getting on very well. That's good, but you must understand he can't be a romantic interest for you. At least, not while our quest is on. There is too much conflict of interest." She spoke the arguments she had used with Shilo, including the one that it was illegal for him. Kira was, not unsurprisingly, a little put out by the whole thing, but the age problem was a telling point. "It's unfair!" she protested. "You have had a couple of dalliances along the way. As far as we know, we're marching to our deaths! I know my duty, but can't I have a bit of enjoyment of life too?"

Sheena sighed. "Yes, Kira, I understand it seems unfair. And unfair that I should say, this is one of the prices of leadership. But there are many differences. You know, for one, my – ah – dalliances, as you put it, were not for me, or not just for me. There were good reasons. And, those people are not coming with us, and I can't get with child, and also I can't – much though I might wish it otherwise – fall in love with them. I'm not saying, don't speak with him, nor even don't become friends with him. While he's older than you, in many ways he is inexperienced. Almost untrained, he is vulnerable. He will need a friend. Be a friend. A good friend, even – but no more. Don't flirt with him, or at least not too much – remember, he has three times failed in his responsibilities with self-discipline where girls are concerned. I'm not saying he would force you – he is a good man, and knows the law – but it's not fair to tempt him and put him through frustration."

Kira sighed in her turn. "Yes, I suppose all that makes sense … but it's still not fair. I like him a lot, though we've only just met, and he's a very good looking young man."

Sheena laughed, and said "Oh, yes, he is that … he is that, indeed."

Chapter 11. Tropical Fire

We sweat and get wet and we never forget
'Cause the heat just won't let us be
It's hot in the sun, it fries everyone
And it's hot in the shade of a tree
The heat's like a pyre, it kills all desire
Except to jump into the sea
When it rains, you get wetter but the heat's not any better
You just have a longing to be free
Free from the strain and the drain and the pain
Of the tropics that are killing you and me.

Anon.

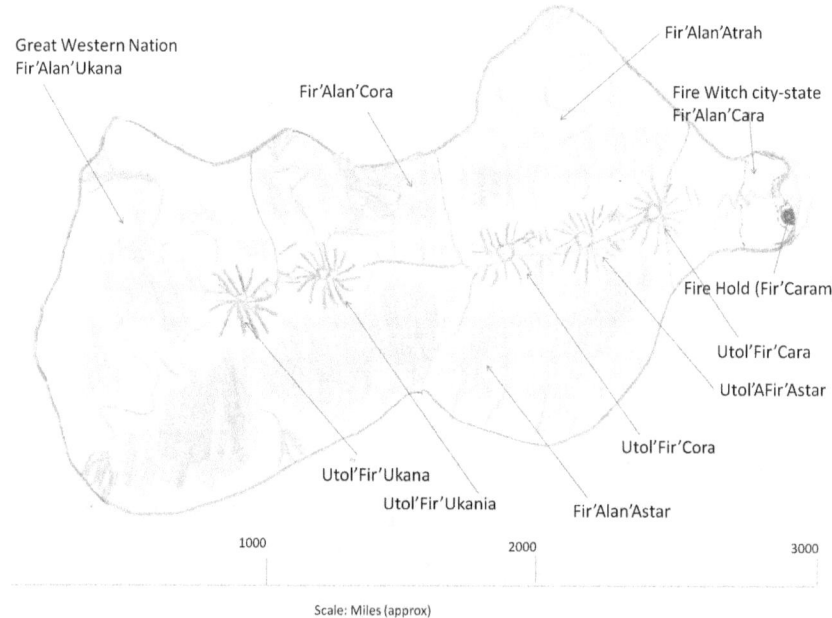

Scale: Miles (approx)

Their leaving was as unremarked as their arrival. Even if anyone had been interested in watching under normal circumstances, everyone was far too busy talking about the announcement that the Masters of the Hold had decided the ages-old tradition that only men could train as Warriors was likely to change, and five people and two ponies leaving the Hold and going back to Entry were not noticed, after all visitors were merely uncommon, not unheard-of.

Their path back through the island was similar to the way they came, though for variety Satro chose towns along the south coast. Spring was over now, and summer well started, and once again Kira was delighted with how different the land was. No frozen shores, sea birds everywhere and trees, endless varieties of trees and plants. In some of the coastal towns there were houses with well laid out and cared for gardens with beds of colorful flowers that she would look at for ages. Shilo found or bought her flowers with a heady, sweet scent which sent her into raptures. She had, of course, seen flowers before, but the small wildflowers that grew in Iceland and for a few short weeks on Ice Island, pretty though they were, were nothing like these florid blooms.

And welcoming people everywhere. Though they often stayed in inns and hostels, it was not uncommon that some well-to-do local would see Satro's Bronze belt medallion and offer them food and lodging for the night. Several times, Bronn more than paid for the value of that with a Vision seen in the night. Shilo spoke little, saying only that yes, he was a student, but he had been sent away to study overseas for a while, which satisfied inquiries as it was by no means unusual. Sheena and Kira kept to their previous plan of pretending to be nice, pleasant, well-mannered and not too bright girls, which worked admirably. A few uncomprehending looks and an "oh, I don't think that would be right for *me*" when told about the news from the Hold about the possibility of women training as Warriors was received with some approval, for the country and town folk were far more conservative than those in the Hold. A few times there were some disapproving looks at Shilo and Kira, followed by embarrassed confusion when they found out she was well under the age of consent – no-one believed for one minute there was any relationship after that.

And so they made their easy way back to Entry, for the way around the coast was a little longer than the shortest route. Arriving back in Entry a fortnight after leaving, they went to the agents looking for a ship, and were delighted to find Sim'Bo'Lo was back in port, having taken a cargo of furniture to Joy, and brought one of wine back, with a day's stopover at Prosperity Isle. The captain was quite happy to take on another charter and drop them anywhere they liked on Fire Island on his way to the Hold – there were plenty of cargos available, and paying passengers were pure profit. He told them with a twinkle in his eye that the trip would not be rough till they rounded Prosperity again – but after that, he could make no promises. Sheena rolled her eyes, and Kira shuddered convincingly. Satro would continue on with the ship to Nun's Hold, or wait for another if no suitable cargo was available.

Sheena and Bronn discussed where on Fireland they would land. Sheena said that Alana's Wand was guarded in a small cave on Utol'Afir'Astar, one of the five volcanoes on Fireland, and the only dormant one. She said that apart from flying, the usual way was up the relatively gentle slope from Utol'Fir'Cara, the active volcano in the Witches' land and the one most Witches bonded to as a source of their power.

While that was the easiest approach, it did mean landing in the Witch lands. Sheena was most reluctant to do that. With Narn holding Fir'Alan'Atrah the whole country would be on the alert and mobilized. Witches would be scanning the land with Avatars all over, and the chance of detection was very high. If detected, the

Nobles would want to know all about this unscheduled party, especially as they would detect Sheena as an unregistered Witch, and Kira as something needing investigation. And the leaders, the Nobles and the Queens might have their own opinions about what they should be allowed to do and where they should be allowed to go.

Fir'Alan'Atrah was also out of the question. What Narn was doing in there as far as surveillance was unknown, and best not to try to find out. Fir'Alan'Astar was right around the other side of Fireland, and it would take far too long to sail there; besides it was mostly a vast swampland, with a few cities on the coast. The Great Western Nation (Fir'Alan'Ukana) would be safe. Although heavily populated, they had no native Witches of their own (though quite a few chose to emigrate there), but the country had its own huge reaches of tropical forest. The only known path, along the ridges of the volcanoes, would be an enormously long way, and hard going. Up on the high ridges there was little in the way of food or water.

The only reasonable course would be through Fir'Alan'Cora, landing just east of the great river. That would mean crossing a fair stretch of jungle too, but less impenetrable than the other options. There were frequent villages, and sort-of-paths between them. It would still be hard, wet going but hopefully they would be far enough away from Narn and the Witches to avoid problems.

And so, they made their way from Warrior's Hold, past Happiness and Prosperity with little trouble. They stopped at Prosperity to discharge a small cargo of metal work and raw iron. Prosperity was well and truly large enough to have blacksmiths of various ability in the villages there, but they did most of the large work, forging hoes, horseshoes, and nails and the like. They good coking coal, and Joy, fortuitously close, excellent iron ore – good dense hematite, some of it gem quality. A large town at the north end produced iron, the prevailing wind usually blowing the smokes out into the uninhabited northern sea. The town itself and numerous villages made use of the iron. Some of the things they made were exported all the way across the world, to Seer's Island, and of course to Fireland. But the best work was done in the Hold itself, where there was no shortage of students prepared to pound hot iron for endless hours to build up strength, and where excellence was expected, and also little need to make a profit.

They also took on fresh water, a cargo of Prosperity's excellent apples, some salted beef and mutton, and a little fresh for a few days eating, and of course some of Prosperity's unequalled smoked fish, both as cargo and for personal use. Kira loved the fish. They produced only a little on Ice Island, for fuel was scarce enough that there was little to spare for such endeavors. Despite their best efforts, seaweed didn't make good smoking fuel – and for most of the year, preservation was simple, just leave it outside.

The days passed pleasantly in fair weather. As Sheena was unwilling to reveal her Warrior status to the crew, Shilo's training was mostly done on deck by Satro. He was in fact a poor teacher. His skills were excellent, but he did not have what was needed to adapt what he knew for the particular needs of a student. Shilo was taller and faster than he was, and the ideal stances and movements were quite different for him. Satro would tell him to stand and move in a certain way, but Sheena would subtly tell them no, and they would have to leave that part of the exercise until they were alone and Sheena could tell Shilo the right way. Satro could see the difference once it was pointed out, but

342

he could not change his nature and become a better teacher. Mostly, she got Satro to schedule physical conditioning.

She continued to train Kira as well. That could be done in the open, for much of the work looked the same to the untrained eye. They focused on Avatar work, but after a few days Sheena reluctantly concluded Kira was not ready yet to try for a third Avatar, she would be better off working with the two she could manage, most likely work towards making the second one a Material Avatar. Sheena also worked on Kira's shielding work, making it more stable and stronger. She said the jungle would provide them excellent opportunities for working on second-level shielding, far better than on the ship where the rolling motion made concentration hard.

Sheena told them about the task they had a head of them. With the careful use of scouting Avatars to find navigable paths, they might hope to achieve as much as ten miles on a good day towards their goal – slow progress. It would take them at least two months and probably longer to get to Utol'Afir'Astar. Sheena would not tell them much about what they could expect there. "Everyone's experience is different, so they say. I can't tell you much, it may have changed or be different from what I know. No, I can't tell you about my experiences. I'm not even going to say I have been there, or had any – or deny it. You will see why yourselves, hopefully."

She did tell them a lot about the other countries on Fireland – the simple people to the south, who were in awe and fear of the Witches, the relatively sophisticated and numerous people of Fir'Alan'Atrah – now controlled by Narn – the strange ways of Fire Hold itself, and the people of the Great Western Nation, incredibly numerous and with ways equally strange of their own. One that stunned them was that Sheena said, that they did not follow the convention that all women's names should end in 'a'. Privately, Kira and Shilo thought it weird enough that the Seers had men's names ending other than 'o', but *that* ...

She also spoke about the unknown rest of the world, where in her day there had been rumors of vast lands and enormous populations of primitive inhabitants. No-one ever went to explore. Once a ship went too far from the Ley continent, magic didn't work anymore. With no Seers to predict success, Witches to heal, shield and fight, and Warriors limited in skill to the purely physical, no-one went.

They were hoping for an uneventful trip, but once again they were disappointed. They had no intention of going anywhere near Fir'Alan'Atrah with Witches on board, but they were seen by a ship patrolling far to the west. Sim'Bo'Lo told them once again the ship had come out of nowhere, but he thought he could out-run it. It was not to be. While they were still a long way off, a brilliant warning firebolt flamed overhead. Sheena immediately said, "You may as well heave to, Captain. That's no level one Witch, nor level two. That's level three work, a Queen. She could blow us out of the water, and there's nothing anyone on this ship can do about it. On the plus side at least, it won't be one of Narn's ships. Unless it's Narn himself I suppose, but that seems unlikely."

Any fears of that were soon put to rest. Once again, two Witches were on deck. One of them peremptorily beckoned their ship closer, and the captain maneuvered so that they were as close as possible on a downwind run with few sails up, just enough to keep way. When they were as close as reasonably possible, she projected an Avatar. Being level three, she did not need to have it project from her body, she could make

344

it appear some distance away. In her case, she had enough skill to bridge the gap between the two ships with ease.

She strode confidently – arrogantly – across the deck, and stopped a few paces from the group. Without asking a word of permission or offering excuse, she stretched out her arm and cast a truthspell. No simple, low level intrusion – Kira gasped as her mind was seized, and even Sheena winced a little. "I am Queen Shi'Mal'Tara" she stated. "What are your names, and are you under Narn's control."

Forced to answer, Kira replied, "My name is Kira. And no, I am not under Narn's control nor do I serve him."

Sheena chose to answer next. "I am called Sheena. I am a Fire Witch, level one. I am not under Narn's control, nor do I serve him, nor am I any friend of his."

Proving she was quick of wit as well as powerful, the Queen frowned and asked again: "I did not ask what you are called. I asked what your name is. Do not try me, I can feel your resistance, level one though you may be. Your name, please. Stated clearly."

Sheena answered reluctantly: "My name is Sha'Lin'Tra."

The Queen raised her eyebrows. "Is it, indeed. I hear and feel you speak the truth. I am surprised. I had thought no Witch had been given that name in known history. If I search the rolls at Fire Hold, will I find you there?"

Sheena shook her head. "You will not, I am fairly sure."

The Queen nodded. "A renegade, then, or more likely the daughter of a renegade. Good enough. These are

345

difficult times, you will be useful in our ranks, we will take you. Gather your possessions. Captain," she said, turning to Sim'Bo'Lo, "ready a boat and have these two ferried to my ship. That is all."

She turned to go. Bronn spoke up, saying, "A moment, if you will, Queen Shi'Mal'Tara. These two are with me. I need them. You cannot take them."

The Queen turned, and looked him up and down. "Cannot? I think you will find I can. What are *you*, that I should take any notice of your wishes?"

Bronn inclined his head a fraction. "My name is Bronn, Master Seer Bronn. I travel on a quest, against the cause of our common enemy, Narn, with these two Witches and a Warrior in training."

The Queen nodded. "I have not cast a truthspell on you, Seer Bronn, but you were close enough to be caught in the backwash. I can tell you are at least sincere. The two of you can come as well, I suppose, though I must tell you, times are hard, our need great, and I may well decide against you. I will expect you on my ship within half an hour. Do not tarry."

With these incisive words of command, she turned to her ship, and disappeared from sight, re-absorbed by her Physical.

Sheena blew her breath out between pursed lips. "Oh dear, oh dear. This isn't going to be easy. A level three, and I can tell you, there is at least one other Witch on that ship, also strong though I can't say what level, but more than level one. We are outclassed, and in danger here."

346

Bronn said, with some worry in his voice: "What can we do? Would she really override a Master Seer's request?"

Sheena nodded glumly. "A Queen would. Look, all Fire Witches are temperamental, prone to snap judgment and caprice. Combined with power, that leads to great confidence and arrogance, and the female ones are the most powerful. There is a ratio of ten to one, one Gifted man for ten women. Fir'Alan'Cara is as much a woman oriented land as Warrior's Hold is a patriarchy. Men are second class citizens, protected playthings, and among the women only power commands respect. While you *are* a Seer, you're a man. She will do what she feels is right, and within her rights, and it will not be easy to sway her with argument. As to what we can do ... nothing at the moment. I suggest we gather our belongings, say farewell to Satro, and get in the boat."

And so it was. Kira was sorry to part from Satro, she had grown very fond of him, he had treated her with courtesy and good humor, and she had responded well to it, they were fast friends. But they had known this moment was coming, anyway.

The trip over to the other ships was uneventful. The swell was quite large, but there was little chop, they didn't even get wet with spray. Trust a Fire Witch ship to have a solid landing platform where there was no real chance of anyone going overboard in a transfer. Still, the crew solicitously gave them ropes and harnesses to secure themselves with for the climb up the ladder.

It appeared there were more than two Witches on board, for they were met on deck by another one, and not the other powerful Witch Sheena had sensed – no more than an average level one. She nodded to the group, and said: "Welcome onboard. Your possessions will be taken to your quarters. I believe your names are Sheena and Kira. The Queen has said you are to go straight to her cabin. I will take you there." She inclined her head slightly to Bronn. "You are welcome on board too, of course, Master Seer Bronn." Shilo, as a mere trainee and a man besides, clearly did not rate a mention.

Sheena replied, "Thank you. May we know your name? I am guessing you are a part of the Queens' personal staff?"

The Witch nodded. "My name is El'Lan'Tra, and you are right. I am an assistant to the Queen. Not highly ranked. Her personal assistant is her daughter, the Noble Shi'Kal'Tara. Come, if you please. It is never well to keep the Queen waiting."

Sheena replied, "Certainly, El'Lan'Tra. May Seer Bronn come too? He has information that is relevant."

El'Lan'Tra frowned. "Well, the Queen hasn't requested it, but neither has she forbidden it. What to do, what to do … As Master Seer, if you ask it, we're bound by agreement and courtesy to at least give your request consideration … I suppose it can be done. The Queen will certainly turn you out if she doesn't want you there; I can do no more than that. I can't extend that courtesy to your young Warrior here, Shilo. Perhaps someone will show him to your quarters, and for now at least he may freely walk about the ship."

Sheena replied, "Many thanks for that. Shilo, I'm sorry but we will have to go, just the three of us. Stay out of trouble." she managed to make it more of a request than a command.

They were guided across the ship, up to the poop deck and the captain's cabins. El'Lan'Tra knocked at the door, and opened it immediately the commanding "Enter!" was heard. "If it pleases you, my Queen, the two Witches are here as you commanded. Also here is Seer Bronn, who requested an audience. As you had not said anything about his presence and he is a Master Seer, I felt he should at least be granted the right to ask you himself. I hope I have done no wrong."

The Queen spoke, with a little annoyance in her voice. "No, I suppose he may as well come in too."

The three of them entered the well-lit cabin, roomy by ship's standards, which was to say that the five people could actually sit and move their arms and legs without serious danger of hitting one of the others. There was a table, screwed to the floor of course, with hooks where chairs could be secured. A comfortable bed covered and with cushions served double duty for two or three to be seated. There was little on the table, for they were at sea and the swell was up. The cabin was a long way from being strictly utilitarian, but well short of luxurious and elegant. There was a feeling that the Queen regarded it as a rightful prerogative, but did not actually spend much time in there other than for sleeping.

Anyone entering the cabin would probably not notice much about it, their eyes would be attracted to the Queen. She was even more impressive in her Physical than in her Avatar; she fairly crackled with restless energy, and when she became intense (which was often), her aura hovered on the edge of visibility. Enraged, or in offensive mode, she would have glowed like a beacon. She was tallish, though not extraordinarily so, and well built. She had a strong face, long and with a firm jaw, not what one would call beautiful despite her straight red hair, but her vitality would make her handsome by anyone's measure. In contrast, her daughter was very pretty, with lighter, ginger hair with a bit of a curl in it and conventional Fire Witch red highlights, a petite, triangular face and large, pale eyes.

"Enter. Sit!" she commanded, somehow managing to imply that Bronn was excluded from that direct command, which was confirmed when she added "And you too, Seer Bronn, be seated if you will." She spoke brusquely and in short sentences, a habit common in Fir'Caram.

"Now" she began when they had all complied, "let us begin. We are here, patrolling these waters, because we have decided to take the fight into Narn's territories. To fight fire with fire. He has suborned many Witches. Perhaps a dozen, with his mind magic. Very well. We can play that game too. When we catch a ship of his that is searching for other Witches, we can use the same spells. We will reclaim our sisters. And so we hope to go on. Even if we were to face Narn himself, we hope that we have enough strength to stand him off at a distance. But that is another matter, for today we have found you. So, tell me, Seer Bronn, why I should respect your quest. What you hope to achieve and who are you."

Bronn spoke about his vision, how he had found Sha'Lin'Tra and the Ice Witch, how they intended to travel across Fireland and claim Alana's wand and face Narn. Shi'Mal'Tara listened without comment right to the very end.

Then, she spoke. "Hah. A pretty story. And full of holes as a fish net. No!" she held up her hand as Bronn made to speak. "I have listened to your tale, and understand it fully. But still, Master Seer though you may be, Seer's visions are not always reliable, that is known. But from the end, backwards. Alana's Wand? A myth, I fear. Witches have pursued it now and then, and got nowhere. A few claim to have found a guardian tribe, but none have come back and said anything meaningful. And even if you did find it – so what? Legend says, it could only operate at the level of the Witch wielding it. It would perfect the magic of that level, strengthen it, sublimate it. But these two, even with the Wand, to face Narn? I think not. This one" (she indicated Sheena) "has some strength, but is clearly no more than a level one. And the other, this girl, is not much greater, if any. For them to face Narn and his five Avatars is laughable. I could not do it. I and my two co-Queens together cannot do it. Otherwise we would have done it!"

"And Sheena. Named Sha'Lin'Tra. You say, the great sorceress from legend, supposedly self-limited to level one. Absurd. Why would the ruler of the world do that? How could she live to this day? I have heard her sincerity – but just because someone believes something, it does not mean it's true. A far more plausible reason is, she is mad. Mentally unbalanced. That is the most likely explanation. But even if it were all true – how could she face Narn? What do you say to that, do you have an answer?"

Sheena shook her head. "I do not know. But I have faith in Seer Bronn's vision."

"Well, I don't. I'm sorry, Seer Bronn, but I reject your vision. You may go your way freely, but these are Witches in my domain, and I will use them as I see fit. The best course is to treat them as if they *were* Narn's subject. Tara, are you ready?" she asked her daughter.

It had gone too fast. Kira looked alarmed, but Sheena rose from her seat, and angrily said, "No! I will not permit it!" she projected her Avatar, but almost casually Shi'Mal'Tara shattered it with a gesture.

351

Sheena staggered, and the Queen said, "Don't be ridiculous, girl. You, a level one, oppose *me*?"

Surprisingly, Sheena projected her Avatar again, and this time the Queen set up a shield, encasing it and holding it immobile, and another immobilizing Sheena herself. Kira projected her two Avatars, which were also shattered, and she sank back into her chair, stunned. She could not re-project so soon.

The Queen nodded. "Impressive" she allowed. "Sheena, level one though you be, to have another Avatar prepared, even if you can't project two at once. And you, Kira – two Avatars, and under twenty by my guess. You will be valuable assets to our cause." She looked at Bronn, who had also risen. "I wouldn't advise it" she cautioned. "You have our respect and hospitality, but offer me violence and I will fry you on the spot." Bronn sank down.

"Tara, your turn" she added, as her daughter approached. Sheena shrank back in her chair. "No" she finally pleaded. "No, please don't. I *beg* of you. This magic is dangerous; you will harm your daughter! Please, no!"

But neither Witch listened. Shi'Kal'Tara frowned in concentration. Finally, she admitted defeat. "I can't do it, mother. Her will is too strong, you know how it is. We will have to use the poppy, unless you want to do it yourself?"

The Queen shook her head, keeping all four of them subdued – Sheena, her Avatar, Bronn and Kira. Kira was obviously struggling to rebuild her Avatars, but it would be some time before she was able, not that it would do much good. Shi'Kal'Tara crossed the cabin and opened a small case, and took out a little metal cylinder. She fitted a needle to it, which seemed to be

352

hollow for she used it to suck up some liquid from a flask. Sheena looked at her in horror, powerless to resist as she calmly walked over, pushed the needle into a vein in an obviously practiced way, and pushed a small handle.

Then, she sat and waited patiently. After a few moments, she began to talk in a low, crooning voice. "There we are, Sheena, more relaxed now, aren't we? That's better." And indeed, Sheena slumped into the chair, with eyes still open but pupils dilated. "There now, my love, everything will soon seem better. We all have our little fears and past pains. I will share them with you, and you will feel better. You will love me, you will do anything I say." She smiled, and said, "And so I will have Sha'Lin'Tra the Great under my command. Or, someone, anyway. We will find out. And an Ice Witch. Hah, I'd like to see some evidence of that!"

Without saying anything, Kira stretched out her hand towards a glass, resting in a secure holder on the table, and containing water. In an instant, the water froze solid. Shi'Kal'Tara stuck out her lower lip, and said, "Well, I'm impressed. Certainly no Fire Witch could do that, you clearly have the Ice talent."

The Queen said, "But wait! I thought that was impossible. This changes things. We may need to go a bit more carefully here, daughter. Let me ..."

But Shi'Kal'Tara interrupted; "Oh mother, don't be so cautious. Such people do crop up from time to time." And as the Queen raised her arm and voice in protest, she smiled, closed her eyes, and extended her mind and will.

And then, she gasped. Her eyes opened, wide and staring. She drew in her breath and screamed, a wail of shock and horror, on an increasingly shrill tone.

But before her breath was finished, her eyes closed again and she slumped forwards, unconscious.

The Queen looked at her, in horror herself. "What ... what have you done?" she gasped. "What? What magic is this? Release her. Release her, this instant!"

But even in her shock and distress, it was clear that there was no point in threatening Sheena. She was out like a light, drugged into unconsciousness.

She turned to Kira and Bronn, and in a fury demanded to know what had happened. Bronn, more mature and less easily intimidated, answered: "I do not know, Queen Shi'Mal'Tara. Certainly, I have no such magic. Nor, I am sure does Kira. You can of course question us under truthspell."

Still in a fury, but a little more under control the Queen did so, and she was not gentle. Bronn and Kira winced under the mental onslaught, but there was no denying they spoke the simple truth: they had no idea what had gone on.

The Queen tried to wake her daughter, but she was out. Hunched forward over the table, knees up, she would have been in a fetal position if she was lying down. There was no feeling of power about her. The Queen attempted a healing mind touch, but was thrown back, clutching her head in pain. "Ice Witch! Ice Witch! You have healing powers, bring my daughter back!" She was clearly approaching desperation; her aura flamed wildly with red anger, but also grey with fear.

Kira tried, extending her mind as Sheena had taught her, but after an instance stammered, "I am sorry! I'm sorry, Queen, but I am not much of a healer. I can't do anything alone! Her mind is like a bright, shrunken

354

ball of pain! I don't know what to do! Even if you were to make a healing team with me, with all your strength, *I don't know what to do*! The ... the only thing I can say is, wait until Sheena wakes up. Maybe *she* can do something?"

The Queen pounded the table hard with her fist. "No! She won't wake till tomorrow! My daughter could be dead by then!"

But Sheena was already stirring. "Whrrrr ..." she said blearily as her eyes opened vaguely. "What ... where am I ... what was that?"

Even in her state of desperation, The Queen was astounded. "What? How are you even awake? That dose of poppy would have stunned an ox!"

Sheena, obviously waking up fairly fast, shrugged and said, "Poisons affect me but little." She looked at the Queen's daughter. "Oh, no – she didn't." She frowned, and opened her mind. "She did. Oh, no, no, no. How tragic." She looked up at the Queen. Anger began to stir in her eyes. "You. You arrogant bitch. You disregarded everything we said. I asked you not to. I *begged* you! When have you *ever* heard a Fire Witch beg? Didn't that, even for a *moment* give you pause?"

The Queen screamed in outrage, her aura flaring, outshining Sheena's pale by comparison flame. "Free her! Free her from your spell! Free her, or I will burn you alive where you stand, I swear it!"

Sheena stood too, and faced her. In just as towering a fury, no mean feat given she had been unconscious a minute or two earlier, she shouted back. "Oh, the great Queen acts without thinking, and threatens now, because she cannot act! Well, I have done nothing. She is as she is now, because of her own spell. She did

355

it to herself. I have done nothing. *Nothing!* If I could have done this to her, while drugged unconscious, I would have been able to fight you both! Well, blast me where I stand, then. Go ahead! I don't care! But if you do, your daughter's life will be short and her death long and horrible. Go ahead!"

The Queen made to lift her hand, but Kira screamed, "No! Sheena! You cannot do this, you cannot throw your life away! I *command* it! Queen Shi'Mal'Tara, hold your fire! There must be another way!"

The two Fire Witches faced each other, breathing heavily, neither giving an inch. But after a pause, the Queen turned to Kira. "*You* command it? What right have *you* to command this Witch, old enough to be your mother? And *what* other way? Tell me, tell me if you know something. *Tell me!*"

Kira calmly replied: "Sheena is sworn to my and Bronn's service. But as to another way, I know nothing. *Nothing!* But Sheena is old, and wise, and she may know something, if you ask. Ask! You have nothing to lose."

The Queen's shoulders slumped. She sat, heavily. She looked at Sheena, still in a black angry mood, but with the beginnings of despair about her eyes. "Well." She finally said. "I will ask. Do you know what has happened to her. Can you fix it."

Sheena slowly calmed herself. She sat, too. "Yes." She sighed. "Yes, I know what has happened to her. Can I fix it? Perhaps ... perhaps not. It would be dangerous, painful and hard. She is a level two Witch, and nearing her prime. She would be aspiring to level three, soon enough, her mind is strong and hard to change. And what will you offer, if I – we – make this effort? Why should we do so, when it's not our fault?"

The Queen relaxed a fraction, as some hope dawned. "You can go your own way, of course. We will aid you as best we can. And why should you do it ... to save a life. To save my daughter. Willful Fire Witch as she is, and hard to control, still I love her. And so, I ask it. I ... I will beg in my turn, if you want."

Sheena looked at the Queen, and the anger slowly drained out of her. "You love her. You will beg. Well. Well. I ... I will try, if Kira will permit me to. There is no certainty of success."

Kira replied, "Yes, of course, Sheena, why do you even need to ask?"

Sheena said, quietly, "I will need you to be in a healing circuit, Kira. With the Queen – and she will need to be in the submissive role, supplying power. But not to heal her daughter, mainly to heal me. The effort could be too much, you must understand. It could kill me. And you must promise not to go to your full limit, because that could take you too. You must let me go, if it comes to that. And if it comes to that, I will not be there to lead your people home."

The Queen stirred, anger surfacing again "I don't *understand*! What is it? What has *happened* to her? Tell me! What are these risks you speak of? *Tell* me!"

Sheena sighed. "Very well, Queen Shi'Mal'Tara. I will be as brief as possible, though there is no immediate danger for your daughter. We must act soon, but a few minutes won't make any difference. Firstly, when I said I am Sha'Lin'Tra, I spoke no more than the simple truth. I am her, from over eight hundred years ago. I gave up power after having harmed myself and others, having suffered in love and made other suffer, and placed a limiting spell on my mind. On advice, good

357

advice. You can't understand this right now and I don't have time to explain, but please, just accept it as-is."

The Queen looked at her, emotions and thought warring in her mind, but finally nodded. "All right. For now. Because, I don't have any better idea."

Sheena nodded herself, once. "Good. Now this mind magic you've copied from Narn. It's powerful stuff. Not as powerful and dangerous as what I used in my time, but you can't use that with a normal and sane mind, God be thanked. You can only deal with people one by one. And, at the end of the day, what you are using is a love spell. A modified love spell, but that's what it is. You make your subject love you."

Sheena continued. "Now, the way this spell works is that every person has issues, pains, regrets, sorrows. The Witch casting the spell shares them, lets the other know to the depth of her mind that she *understands*. She has experienced these things herself. She understands how the other feels, and empathizes. Everyone is looking for someone who can do this, and love follows naturally, and then the submission."

"Now the reason this is even possible is, of course everyone feels things differently. The spell caster can feel what the other felt and not be devastated by it. "

The Queen nodded. "You show great understanding. I ... begin to believe you. No level one could know so much, and understand how the spell works."

"Yes, normally. It's level two work, though a level one could do it, if someone had done it to them. And usually, the spell works fine. But I ... I have lived for over nine hundred years. I have done terrible things, many of them half-forgotten, and my mind is different ... scarred. For eight hundred years I have been

358

seeking forgiveness and atonement. My feelings are intense and have happened over a long, long time. But your daughter ... she tried to experience all that I have experienced and felt, in a few seconds. It can't be done. Even if my mind were fully sane, it couldn't be done."

"She ... she is catatonic. She is slowly going mad, though her mind is fighting it. But unless she gets our help, she will succumb. But, the effort may be too much for her, and for us."

The Queen bit her lip. "What do we have to do?"

Sheena replied, "Basically, what is happening is her mind has walled the memories off into a small part of her brain, which is on fire, and the rest of her mind is trying to fight it. But they will slowly leak out. Two things have to be done: first, I will essentially have to cast the same spell on her, and relive the memory of those memories, drain the poison. All of them. I am used to them, and I am tough ... but to re-face them all in a few moments, well ... it may be too much. Hopefully not, but the two of you will have to be in a healing circuit to support me if parts of my mind start to fail."

"The second thing is, if I am successful there, the pressure will be off. But the memories will remain. They are only short-term memories, normally they would be processed as dreams and her mind would decide if they should be kept, or not. We cannot allow them to be kept, nor allow her to dream – that would finish her. You will have to wall off that memory sphere, with something like a shield. Over days, they will slowly fade. But you can't wall off all of it – otherwise she will just do it again when she wakes. You must leave enough to warn her off, but not so much that it blights her life."

"And that is why, Kira, I say you have to decide, if you will take the risk – the risk to the quest, and all of your people."

Kira looked at her. "Sheena, I don't know ... I just don't know. How risky is it? What would you do, if it was entirely up to you?"

Sheena said, soberly: "If it was up to me, I would do it, despite the risk. Because if we don't, she will die of it, and her last thoughts and experience would be trying to face and reconcile all the things I have done. I know what that's like, and I would not wish it on anyone. As to the risk ... there is risk, but I think it might be done. Yes, I do."

Kira, given her trials with the Ice Hold Tribe, had enough experience to put herself in the right healing mode easily enough. She was still clumsy at it, and would never be very good, but what she could do, she was reasonably familiar with. It was much harder to get the Queen to submit, to put her mind under the control of another. Time after time they thought they were getting there, only to have her mind flare up in rebellion, and once in plain panic. Finally, Sheena told her in a firm voice, either she had to pull herself together, or abandon the attempt. Kira was getting a headache from the backlash. She added, sympathy filling her voice, she knew what it was like. In the end, she had to show the Queen. She put herself into the submissive mode and let Kira take control, while the Queen watched. Then, Kira released her, and she came back with a sigh. "There, that's how it goes. And all there is to it, do you see?"

The Queen muttered that it was all very well for Sheena, but she hadn't had anyone controlling her or questioning her lightest word for years. Still, she sighed, set her mind to the task, and slowly sank down into the correct trance state, not without a few mental hiccups.

Sheena said to Kira calmly, "Well, there she is. I was afraid it might be beyond her. God knows, I know how she felt. And now, you need to decide, Kira ... do we go ahead, or simply leave her there and take command of the ship. She's at your mercy, now."

Kira nearly let the Queen's mind go, in astonishment. "What?"

Sheena explained. "At the moment, we are in control. We can kill the two of them, and there is no risk. We can continue the quest. If we go through with it, there is risk – quite a bit. Your people might be marooned on Ice Island forever. It's not my preferred choice, to go back on my implied word, but there it is."

Kira bit her lip. Agonizedly, she looked at Bronn and Sheena. "I ... I don't know if I can! Bronn, what should I do?" Troubled, Bronn shook his head. "I've not seen this ... I just don't know. It's not the Seer's way to do such a thing. I ... would say no."

Kira looked at Sheena. "Is this really what *you* advise?"

Sheena shook her head. "No, I am merely pointing out the possibility. You are by right the leader in this position, Bronn can do nothing either way, and I am under your command."

Kira replied, "Well, what *is* your advice? If you were in command, would you do it?"

Without hesitation, Sheena answered, "Absolutely not. For the reasons I said before, I would risk it, I would risk all rather than let Shi'Kal'Tara die that horrible death. Eight hundred and fifty years ago, I would almost certainly have made a different decision, but now ... no. Not even to save my own life. And I'm sorry, Kira, but not even to save your people – they can still live on Ice Island, if not as well as on their homeland."

Kira nodded, slowly. "Well, I can't bring myself to it, either. It would haunt me to the end of my days. So, we will go ahead."

Sheena nodded, and without further words set about the spell. Putting her mind into a trance of a different type than Kira had ever seen, she slid past, not through the girl's barriers and shields. Muttering words about love and support, much as Shi'Kal'Tara had, she opened her mind, and wrapped it around the glowing core of pain, like a hand around an apple.

In her turn, she cried, letting out a hopeless, horrible groan that went on and on. Her breath came in ever increasing pants, and she screamed in agony. Finally, she began to cry out – "No, no, no, oh God, no, I'm sorry ... *I'm sorry*! I didn't know, I didn't know any better, oh forgive me, please, *please* ..." It went on for long, agonizing minutes, and slowly her will dropped till she could not talk any more, and could only cry weakly and helplessly. Kira could see the glowing sphere of memories was dimmer by far, but Sheena' mind was going under, areas flickering black, as Marko had described back on Ice Island. She even saw the great limiting spell, stirring restlessly. She fed energy into the areas needing support, poorly and wastefully but buoyed up by the tremendous power of the Queen's mind. Kira noted, even under the stress of the process, that Sheena's mind had had far more power when they had done the healing on Iceland. But the channels the Queen could use, level three channels, were far, far more effective than the level one channels available to Sheena. She noted the difference, for her own training.

It seemed to go on forever. Even the Queen's great resources and abilities began to waver. But Kira finally saw that the memory sphere was dim now, no more active than other areas of Shi'Kal'Tara's mind. Perversely, the pressure being off, the memories started to leak out. "Oh no you don't" Kira thought firmly, and drew mercilessly on the Queen's energy to set up a barrier as Sheena had described. That at least was easy for her, it was more like shielding than healing. She left a fraction and a few tendrils out, to serve as reminders, as she had been told. And then it was just a matter of balancing Sheena's need for support with the Queen's energy. In the end, rather than risking any further drain, she used her own energy, as much as she could.

It still wasn't enough. But just before she gave up and let it all go, she had a sudden thought: what about Shi'Kal'Tara's energy? There was plenty there, her problem was the memories, not energy lack. Quickly, she set up a diverting shunt, and drained energy out. She shored up Sheena's mind. She put some back into the Queen, noting guiltily that she had really overdone it a bit there, the Queen desperately needed it. And finally, she took a bit for herself – just enough to get back above exhaustion level. And then, she released the Queen, and they rested.

They sat there, slumped, for the best part of a quarter of an hour. The Queen groaned. Sheena had clenched teeth, and made little whimpering noises. And Shi'Kal'Tara sat, glassy-eyed, struggling to deal with the remnants of the memories. Kira was really the best off of them all, and put her arms around Sheena. Sheena finally came back to the verbal level, but for a while, all she could say was, "forgive me ...." Kira murmured to her: "Yes, Sheena. We forgive you. Kala forgave you. Intira forgave you. I forgive you. We love you." And Sheena sighed, and the achingly tense muscles eased a bit, and she slowly came back to the bearable level of simple tears.

Finally, all four Witches came back to the point where they could talk. Bronn, of course was energetically fine, he had had no involvement. But empathic as he was by nature, he had to some degree shared in the suffering, and was profoundly emotionally affected. Shi'Kal'Tara slowly came back into mental focus, but Sheena was quicker, being vastly more experienced and having greater depths of resources, both natural and enhanced. As the young Witch became aware, she gazed at Sheena in horror. The small remnants Kira had left were more than enough to give her some memory of what she had been through.

Sheena smiled painfully, and said, "Well, Shi'Kal'Tara, I hope you will be more careful next time … that's dangerous magic. We've pulled you together again this time, but …" she shook her head. "Next time …"

Shi'Kal'Tara shook her head. "No next time. Nothing in the world could bring me to risk …. *that* … again. And I know full well I remember only part of it. How can you live? How can you survive, sane, with all that in your head?"

Sheena sighed, leaned back and put her hands on the table. "Much of it came to me slowly, over the centuries. I didn't start out knowing or even thinking I had done so much wrong, really. To be sure, there were … things. I'll not talk about them right now, if you don't mind. But I have had time, long leisurely time to realize my sins and deal with them one by one. It's re-confronting the whole parcel and package at once that is hard, having it all thrown up in the harsh light. And given the way the spell works, un-ameliorated by the things I have done over the centuries, seeking forgiveness, making reparations,

364

coming to terms with it all. And, again, I don't, really – not sanely, anyway. It's certainly a worry – one thing I hope for and work towards constantly is to repair my mind. What will happen if I achieve that is, to be sure, a concern."

The Queen now stirred. "I felt only the edges of all that. I think I was the lucky one, all I had to deal with was Kira's energy drain. I thought I was going to die there, at one point, but … I think I can use the spell if I have to, but I will be more circumspect about whom I use it on."

She shook herself, her magnificent energy was already rising again. "Well. I think we have to take your point as made, Seer Bronn. Certainly, there is little of the ordinary here. We will release you. I'd like to know how your Quest goes. If you are successful, I will do my best to have the other Queens support you with what forces we can muster. I begin to see now we are at best fighting a holding pattern against Narn." She leaned on the table, resting her hand on her chin, and gazed thoughtfully at Kira. "So, the Ice Witches are a force in the world again. Interesting. I am guessing there are not many of you, to have escaped notice. I guess also you would prefer this not to be common knowledge?"

Kira, Bronn and Sheena all agreed, practically at the same moment. "Very well, we shall keep our lips sealed, do you agree, KalTara?" Shi'Kal'Tara nodded. "And in return, I ask that you *do* let us know how the Quest proceeds. And help us, if you are successful." Sheena and Kira nodded again. "Done, then. I'd also like to hear the story when it's all over, but that's just what I'd like. It's not necessary, it is outside of our agreement and bargain. Still."

They exited the cabin, and the Queen spoke with various crew and the captain. There were a good three day's sailing till they would come to the great river, Fir'Acual'Cora, in Fir'Alan'Cora. People were delegated to work with the team to put together the best set of gear they could for the travelers. As the crew knew their business, the four of them were largely free for other activities. Sheena made good use of the time, getting the Queen and Shi'Kal'Tara to show Kira examples of level two and three work. While not quite the same as how an Ice Witch would do it, and while Sheena could describe the techniques, focal points and theory, there was nothing like seeing it done to aid understanding. Also, every Witch would use slightly different techniques and approach things from a different viewpoint, and seeing those was also very useful.

In her turn, Sheena could help the Queen. While KalMara was a level three, Sheena had mastered level four, and had an unparalleled understanding of subtleties and techniques of level three work. Often, it is only after one has moved on that the fine detail of lower levels can be fully seen and appreciated. Finally, she accepted Sheena as being who she said she was, emotionally as well as intellectually, because no-one else living could have given her that instruction. The Queen said she hoped Sheena would achieve her goals and return to help further with instruction by example, which Sheena said she would, if it was possible.

Shilo's training was not neglected either, and Sheena kept him hard at work. She regularly bested him in every form of combat and physical exertion, though she encouraged him that he was making rapid progress. He was nearing the end of his last growth spurt, and was, as Sheena said, eating like a bird – one and a half times his own weight every day – an exaggeration, perhaps, but not by very much. He was putting on muscle at a rapid rate, and Sheena privately admitted to Bronn that she expected him to be stronger than she was before too many more weeks had passed, and his skills were coming along at a very fast rate. If he had stayed at the Hold, he would have completed Orange in about half the normal time, extraordinary progress.

Bronn was already a Master, and his skills were not in demand very much. So he spent most of the time in light training, resting, going over the travel gear, and dreaming of – and with – Kara.

Finally, they came to the great river. Going further east for several tens of miles to avoid the bogs and swamps of the delta, they made landing at a suitable looking place. After a farewell and a good breakfast, they shouldered their packs – the idea of taking a pony or any other beast of burden into the jungle was ludicrous – they began their journey.

The jungle was almost impenetrable. They had left their swords behind and chosen well-tempered machetes that would not go blunt too quickly, but even so they were cutting a hole in almost solid vegetation. The heat hit them as soon as they entered, and after the first few yards it and the humidity soon mounted to a physical oppression. It made no difference to Kira, of course, and Sheena was a Fire Witch, born on Fireland and by nature bred to the heat, and by physical alteration well and truly capable of handling it. Bronn was not too badly off, Seer's Island being semi-tropical, though he quickly stripped down to the minimum clothing. But Shilo suffered from the start. Peace Island, his home, was the most northerly of the Warrior group, and he was used to cold weather, and the high metabolism of a growing youth didn't help. He was tough of course, and did not complain at first, merely stripping down as Bronn had done.

After a half hour of hacking, the group asked Sheena if this was possible. How could they make it through hundreds of miles of this? It would be a lifetime's work. But Sheena explained that jungle really only occurred at boundaries: the river, the shore, or where large trees had fallen. Most of the time, the forest floor was dark – too dark to support much growth – and relatively easy to walk through. And so, it was. With just a little more time, the way became easier, and soon they were walking on a soft mulch floor with giant tree trunks around them, enormous ferns, and not too much else. However, the heat was still oppressive and there was little in the way of a breeze.

In addition, the insects were frankly ferocious. Mosquitos from the river and various biting flies swarmed around the travelers in such clouds as to partially block their vision. Kira had a strong shield as would be expected of someone looking to start level two training, and Sheena's was like a rock. Bronn's shield, after the training of going through the fens on Seer's Island was steady and solid, and besides he had the maturity of long experience to hold it well. But Shilo was young, and while his shield was very strong, he had difficulty maintaining concentration to keep it up all the time. The insects provided him with a good incentive to learn quickly, and he didn't complain too much. Sheena helpfully shored his shield up when he had had enough and needed a rest, but he still got bitten occasionally. She said that she and Kira would have to do some healing at night to prevent Shilo coming down with one of the many varieties of fever that could be caught from the bites. Fortunately, preventative healing of that type would be very easy, aided by a bitter infusion of the bark of a tree Sheena knew. Curing the fever if it got a hold would have been a very different matter.

And so, Shilo struggled on. It was clear very quickly that he was beginning to hate the place, but Sheena was not worried about that. A Warrior did what he had to do. But surprisingly, phobias started to emerge. Walking bctwccn two fcrn branches, he nearly walked into a large spider web. There was a beautiful spider in the middle of it, black with yellow patterns, and large, golden joints on its legs. Shilo had, of course, seen spiders before. But this one was larger than his not inconsiderable hand, and having it only a few inches from his face completely overwhelmed him. He screamed like a girl, and raised his hand to his face, springing back on the path. "What … what is that?" he asked in a high-pitched, horrified tone, pointing at the offending arachnid.

"A spider, of course. Golden Ball. Nice specimen" Sheena calmly replied. Bronn had seen them before, though not nearly as large, and Kira had almost never seen insects of any kind, and so had no learned prejudice. But Shilo had only seen small ones, and disliked even them. This monster got past his guard and past his training and discipline, and spoke to his innermost fears.

"I … I hope there aren't too many like them?" he asked in a hopeful, pleading voice. "No," Sheena replied laconically, "it's pretty rare. But there are plenty of other types, just as large. There's one so big, it catches small birds rather than insects, as big as a mouse, but with very long legs." Shilo moaned as Sheena continued. "If one of them fangs you, it stings a bit, of course. But they aren't so much of a problem. The ones you have to watch out for are much smaller black ones, with a red hourglass on their backs. They are deadly, as are the larger pure black ones. But they

369

mostly come out at night. Good incentive to learn to keep your shield up while you're sleeping, if you can." She laughed a bit at Shilo's expression. "I'm sorry, Shilo. You do realize that as a Warrior in training, you're going to have to get over this fear. Don't worry, one of us will be on watch at all times during the night, and will keep the shields up."

Shilo kept on going, but was wilting as the day progressed. They stopped in the middle of the day in the coolest spot they could find – no sunlight penetrated the canopy far overhead, but the warmth sat on top of them like a blanket. Sheena didn't make him exercise in that heat, but did get him to do stretches, and meditate, and concentrate on shielding. She worked with him slowly and patiently to try to get him over his issue with large insects, but she could see it was going to be a long piece of work. It seemed to be innate in him, a deep rooted phobia.

The next day was worse. Even hotter and more humid, they slogged their way through a patch of dense undergrowth. Ethereal Avatars helped a bit, allowing them to scout out the easiest paths, but there wasn't much in it. Thorns would have ripped them to pieces if not for the Witch's shields, but the constant pressure on the shields sapped energy, leaving them weary. Bronn and Shilo did what they could, but Bronn's shield was not strong enough for more than half an hour of that kind of strain. Shilo did a little better, and Sheena told him that he was improving well in that area too, but he was not much help really. They had to stop for longer and longer rests. The heat was getting to Bronn too now, and even Sheena was beginning to be affected. Kira, of course, was as comfortable as ever. Bronn and Shilo began to see that while the Fire Witches might have more impressive, obvious skills, Ice Witches had some very useful ones.

They did little more than four miles that day, if that many. Sheena gave them some hope, saying that eventually they would start to rise into the foothills, and the temperature would drop and the going be easier. She admitted that that was many weeks away, however. They set up their camp, with low-slung hammocks to keep them off the ground and away from creeping things as much as possible. Metal supporting wires allowed them to put up a shield around the hammocks – string ones would have been cut. They did not have a fire – the heat would have been unhelpful, even if it was possible to find something that would burn, but Sheena's light spell was easy for her to do. In frustration, she sometimes projected a ball of fire into the clouds of insects following them. There were so many that they burned in their own right, becoming a cloud of flame. But there was an almost unlimited supply.

Water was also easy, Kira used her transformation magic to squeeze it directly out of the foliage around them. She was so good at it that there was only the very faintest tang of vegetation in it, more intriguing than intrusive. And it didn't hurt that she could cool it so that it was refreshing.

Kira, while unaffected by the heat, was tired from the shielding and pushing through the undergrowth. Bronn was tired from both, and Sheena was a little tired herself, but felt more need for stretching. But Shilo was exhausted. He fell into a deep sleep. Kira and Sheena had to take turns shielding him otherwise he would have been eaten alive. But he tossed and turned during the night, the oppressive heat preventing him from getting the rest he needed. The next morning, he looked terrible. Making a self-evaluation, he had to tell Sheena and Bronn. "I'm sorry, I just don't know how much longer I can go on.

Today, certainly, and also tomorrow. But this heat, and the lack of sleep will catch up with me soon."

Sheena looked at him thoughtfully. It was clear to her that he spoke no more than the simple truth. "I can't do anything, I'm sorry, Shilo. But maybe, Kira?"

Kira said she could, yes, up to a point. She frowned, pointed, and Shilo felt blessed relief as the heat drained out of his body. With fine control, she cooled the layers of his body everywhere, but less in the core than at the surface. Tension he did not know he was holding left his muscles. He was truly comfortable for the first time in days. "That's wonderful!" he sighed.

Kira replied that she was glad, but the problem was that he would start to heat up again soon, especially when he was moving and his muscles generated energy. Controlling her own temperature was quite easy, controlling that of someone else – or two someones, as Bronn was looking hopeful, too – much harder. She could do it for a while, but not if she had to shield as well, and force her way through the bushes. It was far easier to freeze something, the fine control needed to cool a body without killing it was very hard, and draining. Heating or cooling a pool of water was easy by comparison. Sheena bit her lip, and said they would just have to go as slowly as necessary to keep everyone cool, sane and not exhausted.

The going was easier again. The undergrowth patch was over, but the ground was becoming more marshy. Their waterproof boots were essential. But still, the need for Kira to do less shield work slowed them down further. Sheena doubted they had equaled the previous day's four miles. A major concern was that at this pace, food would become a problem.

The night started out poorly. Though they were well sheltered, a thunderous rainstorm meant shields had to be up, firm and in close, which minimized the amount of airflow. The purity of rainwater made it possible; salt spray would have been a different matter. The others managed alright, but Shilo was both kept awake by the noise and stifled by the heat. Finally, Kira suggested that they set up hammocks as close as possible, and she held his hand while she worked to keep his temperature down. Without movement, and with physical contact, it was easier. She was able to set up a rhythm, doing cooling work only every hour or so, subliminally, in the same way as she could keep her Avatar awake while she slept, much as a mother Ice Witch would with her child. It worked surprisingly well, part of it being that Shilo sank, exhausted, into a low metabolic rate sleep.

The next day started off much better. When they arose, Shilo was far better rested. The going was easier. But things deteriorated as they day wore on again. Kira became tired again, and even Sheena's previously inexhaustible energy was showing some limits. Towards the middle of the afternoon, they came to a small hill with a rare fresh stream - surely there was a spring not too far away. They were too weary to try to find the source, but set up camp. Kira said that the cool water nearby would make her temperature control work with Shilo much easier.

The two women made their way off a discreet distance into the trees and downstream for toiletry and preparation for a mid-day nap, and there was the sound of splashing in the distance. Bronn busied himself on the other side of a large tree, unpacking their backpacks and getting out everything they would need for the evening. Sheena had said there was a good chance of fish in the stream, and he was locating their lines. Shilo was far too hot again, and stripped off his boots and socks. He walked over to the stream, and waded into it, nearly up to his waist. He was just standing there, letting the cool water lower his temperature, and wondering if he should strip off entirely and submerge himself, when Sheena returned.

"I wouldn't stay long in that stream if I were you" Sheena advised.

"What? Why not?" Shilo asked, a little uneasily.

"Leeches" she answered succinctly.

Shilo gasped, and surged out of the water. Sure enough there were nearly a dozen attached on each leg, and not little ones such as he knew from Peace Island – large, thick, black creatures, as long as his finger. He looked at them in horror, his mind and will dissolving. "Get them off! Get them off me!" he wailed. "Oh please, help me, get them off!"

At least he kept enough control to not try to pull them off with his fingers. He had been warned that would tear a hole in his skin, dangerous in these hot climes.

"Easy, student. There is no danger" Sheena reassured him, as Bronn came over.

"I know! I know" Shilo cried. "I just can't stand them! Oh please!" he repeated, shuddering.

Sheena said, "We could use salt, but we have little to spare. And fire is not the answer, although I suppose I could heat up a knife and that would do it. But best is to wait for Kira. With her fine control, she can simply freeze them and they will let go and drop off. She'll only be a minute or two."

Shilo stood there, shivering in a mental fugue. For want of anything else, and in his revulsion, he pointed a finger at the one closest to the top of his leg, and in a shaking voice, cried "Freeze!"

And almost unbelievably, it did. The few inches of its lower body turned white with ice, and the head let go. It slithered wetly down his leg and landed on the ground, the unfrozen part of its body writhing and twisting obscenely.

Sheena was flabbergasted. "Ice Magic!" she exclaimed. "You ... you did Ice Magic!" She looked at him in wonder. "Can you do it again?"

Shilo looked at his legs, trying to remember how it had felt, what he had done. The remaining leeches hanging there gave him impetus. Hesitantly, he reached out and touched the next one, and after a few seconds of reaching for the right feeling, he was successful again. He pointed at the next half dozen, and shouted in wonder, "Yes!" as they dropped off, one by one. No longer powerless, he felt all fear of them leave his mind, and almost casually he froze the rest off one at a time, doing the last three as Kira came running up, worried about the shout.

She too stopped in wonder, and asked in an unbelieving voice: "You – Shilo, you are an Ice Witch? Why didn't you say anything?"

Shilo laughed, a laugh of mingled joy and hysteria, oblivious to the blood streaming down his legs from the many bites of the leeches. "I didn't know, Kira. I didn't know until a minute ago!"

Sheena shook her head. "Well, I am more surprised than I have been in a very, very long time" she said. "However, there it is ... it looks like you'll be having two sets of lessons from now on, Shilo, that should keep you busy. We will have to stay here, close to this stream. Kira, the first and most important thing you'll have to teach him is temperature control. If he can learn how to cool himself, there is still a chance we can make it to the mountains before another year passes and without you being exhausted every day."

His first lesson, however, was observing Kira and Sheena healing his wounds. Although tiny, it was important not to leave them open. It wasn't too hard – Kira was no better as a healer despite practice, but the wounds were very small, and didn't need too much work or energy. Shilo observed, as best he could. With no prior practice or experience, his mind was not yet open to understanding the flow of power and magic between Kira and Sheena in detail as the healing was done – but he did feel something, at least.

They rested, and while the light lasted Kira sat and went over the basics, the first easy lessons of Ice Magic. Sheena could do little to help, her own mastery of the subject was extremely limited, and the little she could do learned centuries ago. While she had a very good grasp of theory, learning to do it was best done by observation and copying. Shilo was at first a poor student, because he was learning it far beyond the usual age – Ice Witches learned it from their mothers and fathers, about the same time as they learned to talk. Some of the things that related to personal comfort, such as temperature control, they often learned even earlier. But Kira was patient, and unlike her healing skills her teaching skills were excellent, and Shilo took the first few hesitant steps.

Sheena and Bronn sat a little apart. Sheena watched the two young ones talking, completely absorbed in each other, and gloomily remarked that this development was a two edged sword. "I was getting really worried about Shilo and the heat, of course. If she can teach him temperature control, that will be a wonderful thing. But remember the obvious attraction they had for each other at Warrior's Hold? This is going to throw them together again, and make for distractions."

Bronn said that surely Shilo's cultural ethos, the strong moral code forbidding relationships between those over and those under the age of consent would hold?

Sheena came as close to calling Bronn simplistic as she ever had. "Bronn. You're a Seer. You're a professional empath, for Heaven's sake. A relationship isn't forbidden, they can spend time together, talk together, train together – as indeed they will have to, if he's to learn the Ice Magic he needs. That will lead to them liking each other, inevitably, because they are both as fine a pair of young people as one could hope to meet. And because the chances of meeting anyone else their age in the next few months are somewhat low, they will likely fall in love. None of that is forbidden! Only the physical expression of that love is disallowed. And that will cause tensions, and we'll have the distractions and the problems as surely as if they were hopping off into the bushes every couple of hours. Perhaps more so."

Bronn had to agree. More, he added: "I can see that. And also, Sheena, don't completely discount the sex side. They will be, as you say, thrown together constantly, with no other alternatives around. We're a long way from Warrior's Hold, and though she may still only be fifteen, as you said on Iceland – Ice Witches grow up fast, and she *looks* nineteen or older. Warriors are good at keeping to the law in general, but remember he has a weakness there, and there will be constant temptation."

Sheena frowned further at that, and agreed. They would both have to keep an eye out, and provide occasional reinforcements of the words they had had at the Hold.

The next two days were rainy, on and off, and Sheena decided to stay where they were. Kira gave Shilo intensive training in temperature control, patiently going over and over the techniques again and again. Feel the river, the cool river nearby. Feel the heat in your body. Extend the mind, like ... so. Move the heat to the water, against a gradient so you don't lose your core temperature. Leave the connection open, and throttle down the flow so you don't get too cold. Let it all go to the back of your mind so it becomes automatic. Release. Start again.

Shilo had naturally managed the freezing of the leeches, under stress. But that was a technique that used energy from within. Using the cool river was harder to master, easier in energy demands, but it took him a long time to begin to get the hang of it. It wasn't till the second day that he finally began to get some real energy flow and actually cool himself, and it was clear that it would be many more days, if not weeks, before he could keep the connection open and let in run in the background. But it was enough. There would almost always be something nearby, maybe underground, that was cooler than his body, and which could be used to drive the energy flow. It would still tire him out, particularly if they were moving – Kira could keep a connection usably open over a distance of ten miles or more, but Shilo would have to make and break new ones all the time. Fire Witches kept their connection open across hundreds or thousands of miles – but it was a less efficient process. Of course, the volcanoes they usually used also had a much greater temperature difference.

At the end of each day, for a change of pace, Sheena renewed Shilo's Warrior training. He surprised himself by making far greater progress than before, but not her. A phobia was always a barrier to progress, she explained, even if it was unknown or the problems did not come up during training. Shilo's newfound ability to freeze the insects and other slithery things had conquered his fear of them, and he was much more of a whole man.

She also worked with Kira, beginning the work on second-level shielding. There was an optimal distance from one's body to set up a shield. Too close, and it wasn't possible – a shield had to be a sphere, and the mind wouldn't let one make it so small that it cut off a foot or a hand that was sticking out. On the other hand, making it too big was hard – the energy required went up very quickly – and it became impossible to walk. In a crisis, one could sit down and fold one's legs, making a smaller, stronger shield possible, but mobility was nearly always the key. Within the two limits, one set up a shield. It had physical dimension, a level one shield was generally about half an inch thick. But with level two techniques, one could compress it, and set up a second, third or even fourth shield next to it, forming layers.

The way it was learned was to work with Avatars. The first step was to get to the point where one could shield oneself and one's Avatar. Then, keeping the Avatar unexpressed, one put up both shields. Then, with that mastered, one did the same thing with the Avatar. There was no real limit, but the number of people who could project three Material Avatars was very small, and anyone who could manage it would be moving on to level three techniques anyway.

"What is level three shielding?" Kira asked, and Bronn and Shilo were interested too. Sheena answered them as best she could, though she said a demonstration would be better: "There are two things you learn in level three: one, to weave those shields together, so instead of being layers they are an integrated whole. They can't be peeled away and broken, layer by layer, and are much stronger. The other, you saw Queen Shi'Mal'Tara do it. To separate the shield from the body, so you can protect – or restrain, as she did to us – others. It's linked to the skill of projecting an Avatar at a distance from one's body."

"And level four?"

"Ah, that's hard to explain. Not many have done it, it's a different order of magnitude. The shield becomes changed in nature, stronger, more integrated. Different techniques are used, not directly related to one's own internal energies. You can build it quicker, and use it as a weapon – for you don't have to make it a sphere anymore."

"And could you do it? Can Narn?"

"Oh yes, in my days as Sha'Lin'Tra, I could do a level four shield. Several at the same time, in fact. Narn ... with five Avatars, it's just about possible, I suppose, but pretty unlikely. In fact, my guess is, no, he can't. He wouldn't be working in secret so much, he'd be taking more of a direct approach. He would have a very strong level three shield, though."

"And are there other levels? How high does it go? Could you do them?"

"Oh yes, there are other levels, no doubt. As to how high they go, you would have to ask the Angels and Archangels. And I ... well, I did a level five shield. Once. Once, only. In extreme rage and anger, to my bitter regret. I shouldn't have. Please don't ask me any more about that." She shivered

The others sensed uneasily that there were parts of Sheena's story they had not heard yet, and moved on to other subjects. Kira began working with creating a shield around her Avatar, with some slight success. She also worked on making her second Avatar a viable Material one, and was now able to do it, as long as her body was still and it was close by. She was a little subdued by how hard it was, but Sheena just laughed at her. "Fifteen, and well on the way to your second Material Avatar!" she chuckled. "It's all too hard – don't make me laugh. You're doing fine. I doubt if there's another Witch in the world who was able to equal your progress at your age."

Kira smiled too, in spite of herself, and replied, "Apart from you, of course."

Sheena lowered her head a fraction. "Apart from me. Yes, perhaps. But don't take me for your model, Kira. Be yourself. I'm proud of your progress"

Kira smiled again, more softly. She reached out and touched Sheena's arm. "I think you're doing fine, too, Sheena. I'm proud of your progress, too." And Sheena hugged her, thanked her and blessed her.

At the start of the third day, they moved to break camp. Bronn had spent most of the time fishing, and after a few false starts had got the hang of the stream and the local fish. A few weren't worth eating, but Sheena had been a help in identifying the ones that were. Sheena and Kira together had cooked them very nicely, and they had stuffed themselves, Shilo in particular having a few days where he had been really too tired and hot to eat much to make up for. And Sheena had been able to set up a smoking station, finding the right sort of wood and leaves, drying them out and setting them alight, and containing the smoke with enormous leaves from a nearby fern. It worked surprisingly well, despite a tendency for the leaves to dry out eventually and catch fire. They ended up with a good stock of smoked fish, which would last a fair bit longer than fresh.

Shilo really didn't do very well at first. It was very hard for him to get into the right state of mind to perform a temperature balance, and he could only do it if they stopped moving. The heat wasn't too bad, there was still a bit of rain about, but the humidity was oppressive, it was a full 100%, and so he did have to stop, regularly. He tried to make do with an hourly stop, but Sheena saw very quickly that he was overdoing the cooling when he did - he was lowering his core temperature to the danger point, so that he was actually shivering before they set off again, and she told him to stop it, he would just make himself sick doing that. So, instead they stopped every twenty minutes. As it took him at least five to settle himself down and manage the magic, it meant constant stopping, but it was at least something. They got to the end of the day without issue, though Shilo was still tired. It took a lot of effort for him to do temperature control, but at least he was not exhausted, and he was able to do a good bit of Warrior training as well.

On the next day they found the great river again. Much too large to cross, what with the dangers of crocodiles, they were forced nearly due east for most of the day by the wall of vegetation. It swung away to the west on the following one. But being so close to the water gave Shilo a close-by cooling sink, and for the first time he was able, a couple of times, to regulate his temperature while still walking along. It was easier for Kira too, and she was able to help Bronn keep cool if she walked along holding his hand, which he greatly appreciated.

Two more days of winding to and fro, and the river mercifully straightened out. It was impossible to walk too close to it, but there was the occasional trail that made walking almost a pleasure.

They began to find small villages, where tributaries joined the river. The country, particularly the interior, was fairly primitive in many ways, yet surprisingly sophisticated in others. This was due to the presence of Witches, sometimes men. Sheena explained that male Fire Witches were sometimes annoyed or angered about their status as second class citizens (though some quite liked being pampered; as there were few of them they were in demand) and would leave Fir'Alan'Cara. Female ones sometimes travelled abroad, as Bronn had found out, but the men preferred to remain on Fireland. In general, they were not as good at keeping their bonding to their volcano open across distance, and would often prefer to migrate to one of the other countries on the continent. Every village wanted a Witch, for protection and the limited healing they could offer, and status. Not every village could have one of course, there were far too few to go around. But where a Witch chose to settle, life was easier, the village prospered and so grew. Mostly, they were poor level ones, able to light a fire, heal trivial wounds and project an Ethereal Avatar or maybe a Material one for few dozen yards, but it was better than nothing.

Husband and wife pairs that didn't like the female dominance of the capital or the dangers typically went to the Great Western Nation, where they were well received. But by and large, any Witch of real ability stayed in the capital, or went to one of the other lands on assignment. Still, Witches were well known and respected, and the four of them were received with hospitality and often awe by the villagers. There was always something to do, usually healing, and Kira perforce became better at it. It was still too early for Shilo to even try.

A great benefit was being able to buy or barter for insect repellent berries. A few eaten every day, and use of the oil on the skin gave a sharpish lemony aroma that kept the insects off. They were not so easy to find, and required preparation to extract the oil, so it was better to buy than try to make their own.

At one of them, they were able to buy a canoe large enough for all of them to fit in, though the villagers said it would be hard going for them to paddle upstream. Still, the wind varied here, and it might be possible for them to use a small sail sometimes (they had a tent that could do double duty there), and the villagers did acknowledge that while paddling would be hard, it was going to be easier and cooler than the forest, which was thicker than ever, and they were going to run into many smaller rivers and tributaries as they were in a hilly area. Not as big as on the other side of the island, where the clouds hitting the mountains unleashed a positive torrent of rain, but big enough – and each surrounded by almost impenetrable jungle, and needing to be crossed.

The paddling was hard. But still, they had two Warriors, and quite often they could use the sail. Sheena said it would be excellent conditioning for Shilo, and let him paddle pretty much all day, as she and her Avatar did also. Sometimes, Kira and one of her two Avatars paddled, and sometimes both of them while her Physical rested. She struggled to get all three of them paddling at the same time, with some limited success that improved day by day. They couldn't *all* paddle at the same time of course; while Avatars have less need for comfort than physical bodies the boat would have been just too crowded with four bodies and three Avatars. Bronn also took his turn paddling, to avoid boredom and to stretch his muscles.

Crocodiles were a problem, at first. They were somewhat used to canoes, and often came up to investigate. Who knows, sometimes the occupants might be asleep, or dead. They were used to disappointment, and the occasional bump on the nose with a paddle. With constant discouragement as young crocs, when older they didn't attack the canoes anymore, there was generally enough to eat in the river anyway. But Sheena didn't like them, not at all. Water was bad enough for a Fire Witch, but the thought of being dragged under by a crocodile was just horrible. When she remarked on that, Bronn assured her he wasn't too keen on the idea either. Shilo cheekily remarked that perhaps it was a phobia she needed to work on. Sheena laughed, and said perhaps it was, but it was more a dislike than a fear for her. As nearly everything could be a lesson, she added that an opponent could possibly learn of Shilo's fear of insects and throw a jarful of spiders at him to throw him off balance, but she would take her chances on someone trying to sneak up on her carrying a river, a large crocodile, or both!

Still, when they came too close, she zapped their noses with a good bit of lightning or a small firebolt. And amazingly, word seemed to get around as they continued on, crocodiles seemed to stop attacking them. Sheena shook her head in wonderment, she had never heard in all her centuries that crocodiles could communicate at all, let alone over long distances in the river.

Fish were plentiful and good. The only real problem they had was landing spots, to get out and stop for the night. More than once over the three weeks they paddled upstream, they spent a horribly uncomfortable night in the canoe, although eventually they came to some accommodation. Sheena was quite alright staying up all night and the next day, even two days, but needed a rest on the third, so she kept watch, and a shield over part of the boat to keep insects out. Kira shielded the other part, while asleep, as usual, the two shields merged in the middle to make a double bubble, and ending at the waterline. Bronn would stretch out as best he could. Shilo would keep watch for long periods too, but was able to sleep sitting up on the floor against the side of the canoe due to rock hard muscles and flexible joints, and Kira found she could make a reasonable bed in what remained of the room, provided she used Shilo's lap for a pillow. Sheena saw Shilo sitting there for many long hours, a troubled but tender look on his face as he rested his hand on her shoulder. She could see their constant closeness had had the inevitable result.

She did her best to keep them aware of the dangers. She told them, increasing closeness will cause troubles in the future. But when they asked her when and why, she could not answer.

And so the days, and the weeks passed. The river ran straight, and they could see the mountains gradually getting closer and closer. Paddling, and their small sail, was getting them there by as much as thirty miles a day. By now, Kira could paddle competently with both of her Avatars, and walk – slowly – with them in sight. Sheena kept her at it, but in many ways it was Shilo's admiration for her skill that boosted her efforts most – as hers did for him, although the constant pressure of the heat did a lot there as well. Shilo was quite comfortable; he could keep his temperature regular despite paddling. He had by no means mastered doing it without thinking, and woke several times during the night hot and uncomfortable. Bronn was getting grumpy, his bones were not appreciating the time in the canoe, and the heat was getting to him a bit too despite regular help from Kira. It didn't help when Sheena remarked he might well have to do without it when they started to climb up the slopes of the mountain.

Finally, the river took a sudden turn to the west, and ran on that way as far as the eye could see. As they wanted to climb up and go east, they reluctantly decided to leave the river – reluctantly, because the forest didn't look any easier, and after they had forced their way through it for a while, they would then have to do it uphill.

At least they had the option to go on for a bit, and choose a likely looking trail of reasonable size, and eventually they did find one. They landed, and with their hearts in their mouths set the canoe free, to drift back downstream, for so they had told the village they had bought it from they would do. If it got caught up in vegetation, sank, or drifted past in the night, too bad – they had paid for it outright and at a fair price, but if someone could recover it, well, that was a bonus.

The trail made its way to a fair sized village where they received the usual awed welcome. They were glad to be back on their feet, and stretching their legs, for a while. There was also a network of trails out the other way, where the villagers went to find fruit, useful timber and a limited amount of game – mostly they relied on fish for meat, and the occasional crocodile. But the trails didn't go very far towards the mountains – villagers who had travelled that way had found nothing useful enough to justify keeping a trail cleared. They knew of no other villages in that direction, which worried Sheena – she had hoped to find somewhere where they could pick up some cold weather gear.

"Cold weather? Here?" Bronn asked.

"Yes, Bronn. It may not feel like it here, but it's winter, just as it's now summer on Iceland. Remember how much cooler it was by the beach? It's the forest that keeps the heat in, if we climbed to the top of the trees it would be much cooler, and as we go up the slopes it will get colder fairly fast. By the time we get to the ridge I want to walk on, it will be cold, especially at night. And the thinner air won't help."

"Great" muttered Bronn to himself. "Come to sunny Fireland, you can be broiled and frozen on the same continent. I should never have left Seer's Hold." In a louder voice, he asked Sheena why they hadn't brought some warmer clothing, then.

"Do you honestly think we could have carried it through the jungle so far? And it's going to get harder for a bit, too." Bronn supposed not.

After a rest for a few days and a little Healing (Shilo was now at the stage where he could observe that and see vaguely how it was done), they gratefully took food the villagers gave them, and went on their way. Three days of relatively easy going were a blessing, and they had been told where to look for fruit along the way and help themselves. It allowed Shilo time to become accustomed to the difference between the river and land, and search for cooling sinks to keep his temperature down. He was really doing quite well, Kira had said he was about as good as a five year old on Ice Island, which discouraged him a bit, but Sheena said *she* had not made it that far, and he was a two-Gift man, extremely talented in one of the Gifts, and shouldn't be complaining. With practice, he would easily become a good level one Ice Witch, maybe higher, but it took time.

And then, the trails ran out, and it got harder. With three Avatars, it should have been easy to scout out the easiest paths, but the environment was so very wet that it wasn't easy. The leaves were dripping with water usually, and succulent inside, which tended to 'short' out the Avatars. Kira, who could drive hers fifty miles across the ice with ease, was hard put to send it out two hundred yards in the jungle. Marshy patches didn't help, either. If the Avatar wasn't completely shorted out by some wet patch, it was only because there was a dry cover on top – but that didn't mean people could walk on it. Many times after a promising stretch had been found, Sheena would send her Avatar out, switch it to Material and lose it as it dropped through the crust. And even though they would eventually find the best way, that didn't mean it was then easy.

One of the greatest problems was food. There was plenty of it up in the trees, if you didn't mind monkey, but they had no way of getting to it. They seemed to instinctively dodge Sheena's firebolts. There were birds, though again most of them were a long way up. Sheena said there were anteaters, and they heard wild pigs off in the distance, but those were very wary also. Close to the clearings there were smaller, fruit-bearing trees but they were hard to get to. They were very lucky to come across a large snake, with a neck as thick as Shilo's leg. It rustled off into the distance at their approach, but Sheena sent her Ethereal Avatar after it, switched it to Material when she got close and got it through the skull with a firebolt. They had fruit, which Kira had squeezed all the water out of with transformation magic, and close to patches of jungle they found immense areas of vines, one of which sprouted from tubers in the ground that looked a little like huge, orange potatoes, but sweet in taste. It had to do.

Kira experimented with her talent, and found she could do something like the transformation she was used to doing on seaweed with some of the plants. She could extrude a sugary, honey-like liquid from plants with the right kind of sap. It didn't always taste good, and Kira said that it was not a good long-term diet, but it helped to eke out their supplies.

They forged ahead for two more weeks, the going not too bad. Once they were fortunate enough to find a massive, recently fallen tree that had crashed over, flattening a patch of jungle and protruding into a small river. They were able to walk on it and fish, which they did for days, until they had enough fresh, dried and smoked to keep them going. Sheena continued Shilo's training. Paddling the canoe, hard training and the need to hack and slash their way every now and then had hardened his muscles – and he was filling out into full maturity. The day came and went where he was now clearly stronger than Sheena, and also the day where he won his first bout with the practice sword. Soon he was winning more than half, and Sheena said he was well and truly a Bronze level swordsman. She told him not to get too cocky; there were many other weapons he had to master, and his unarmed combat skills needed work.

Eventually, they had a real sense that the ground was rising. The trees became more sparse, but thankfully the jungle didn't take over; the ground was much rockier, and grass competed with the other plants trying to take hold. The going wasn't much easier in an absolute sense, but it was easier to use Avatars, and they had better luck choosing the best path. They began laboriously to climb, ascending perhaps a third of a mile per day, and ten times as many along and up-and-down. As far as Bronn was concerned, while it was hard work, he was happier as there was some breeze to be had.

Food became easier. Hardy goats climbed the rocky slopes with ease, eating the tough grass, and tried to avoid the leopards that preyed on them. Sheena could usually manage to shoot one with a firebolt, and fortunately Kira was able to do some transformation magic that tenderized the flesh most wonderfully, because otherwise it would have been hard to distinguish the meat from the leather of their boots. The only other thing they could have done would have been to stew the meat, which they didn't have the utensils or the time for.

As they rose, they could occasionally see the way ahead, and where they were going. They aimed for the best point on the connecting ridge that joined Utol'Fir'Cora to Utol'Afir'Astar, climbing up, and where they could, moving east as well. They could see the peak of the active volcano far above them and to the west, snow capped yet giving off smoke. There were runs of solidified lava that were weathered to a greater or lesser extent, and a couple of times they were able to shelter in lava tubes.

It became pleasantly cool despite now being out in the sun (though it was often cloudy), and eventually actually cold. They took to finding shelter, and gathering firewood. Sometimes this meant going back downhill some distance, for the ridge they were approaching was mostly bare. Kira (and now Shilo) was unaffected by the cold, and Sheena also to a lesser extent, but Bronn needed the fire, and also a bit heavier clothing. Kira was able to help, after goat hides were well scraped she was able to tan the hides nicely

- tanning is a simple chemical change, and the transformation needed was well known to all Ice Witches, they used it on seal skin.

One evening, they sat in the twilight, resting after the day's walk. Sheena said, she hoped to reach the ridge on the next day, and really start to make some time up. Sheenava and Kira's two Material Avatars were away, gathering firewood. As they returned, carrying armfuls of wood, Shilo remarked, "Having an Avatar or two about is really wonderfully helpful. I hope that I can manage to project one, someday."

Sheena nodded, and replied "Yes, indeed, they are. And the Ice Witches' fine control over them made them very much desired as husbands and wives. Of course, very often they would intermarry."

Shilo nodded. "I can see that. Having a set, or even two sets of extra hands around the house would make life a lot easier, especially as they'd know what needed doing and when."

Sheena looked at him, head tilted to the side. "Housework? Is that all you can think of?"

Shilo looked at her puzzledly. "How do you mean? I suppose they would be a great help in the nursery, too."

She laughed. "And can you think of no other area in the house where it might be nice, or interesting, to have ... ah ... two sets of hands? What about the bedroom?"

Shilo looked at her, his mouth falling open. "You mean, Avatars can ... ?" He looked at Kira momentarily, and looked away again. Although the light was fading, and the fire cast a ruddy glow, it was clear that he was coloring.

Kira and Sheena fell about laughing. Cruelly, Sheena, gasped, "Oh, look at him blush! That's as fine a red as I've ever seen!" Even Bronn chuckled a bit.

Finally, when Sheena decided he'd had enough, she sobered up. "Yes, Shilo, Ice Witch Avatars *can*. Some of them. Fire Witches also, though much more rarely."

She paused for thought.

"It's probably time I told you a bit more about Avatars, seeing as the next step Kira will be teaching you is probably going to be projection." She told them a little of the theory of Avatars, how they were related to lightning (as were shields), and what they could do and what they couldn't. She spoke about how important it was that the image of the Avatar looked and acted as much like the mental image one had of oneself. "Trying to project an Avatar different to oneself is the major cause of lack of progress, and burnout in wild talent, especially boys. Young people in the Holds are guided carefully in these matters, of course, so it doesn't happen so often."

She explained further, when Shilo asked what she meant. "Boys, if they manage to project a Material Avatar, often wonder if it might be possible to change the form and appearance to that of a girl. And yes, it is, just, although it sets up tremendous stresses in the mind. The next inevitable step is, they wonder if things can go further. And the mind baulks. Essentially, the strain of trying to be oneself and one's complement at the same time becomes too much, and in self-protection the mind shuts down the ability to project, usually permanently. And yes, it happens to girls too, though a bit less often."

She lifted her head a fraction, and looked at Shilo and Kira in turn. She spoke very deliberately and slowly. "The lesson here is, sex and young Avatars don't mix well, either. Kira should know this already, but you need to understand it too, Shilo. The process of skills development is a slow, tricky one that can easily be disrupted. And we *need* Kira to keep on advancing. For herself, for the Ice Witch Hold, and for this quest we are on."

She waited until Shilo nodded, and said, "I understand."

Chapter 12. Guardians

How fares it with the happy dead?
For here the man is more and more;
But he forgets the days before
God shut the doorways of his head.

The days have vanish'd, tone and tint,
And yet perhaps the hoarding sense
Gives out at times (he knows not whence)
A little flash, a mystic hint;

And in the long harmonious years
(If Death so taste Lethean springs),
May some dim touch of earthly things
Surprise thee ranging with thy peers.

If such a dreamy touch should fall,
O turn thee round, resolve the doubt;
My Guardian Angel will speak out
In that high place, and tell thee all.

Alfred, Lord Tennyson

Finally, they made it to the ridge. The way was very easy for several days, despite the high altitude. They were on a slightly downhill slope, and there was firm soil or rock underfoot. With Sheena, Shilo and the Avatars to help carry what little they had, they could walk quickly, and for five days they managed at least twenty-five miles per day. On the fifth day they saw a mountain stream far below, and Bronn rebelled, wanting a wash. Kira was not averse, either. It took some time to get down; they lost almost a mile in altitude, but they found a goat path that helped a lot. They decided that they would be coming back up that way, so only took down with them what they would need.

The stream, perhaps four feet wide at the point where they stopped, had the potential to be much larger. They found a pebble bottomed depression that would only normally get water when the stream was in full flow, and remembering the pool they had had on Iceland, Bronn and Shilo enthusiastically worked on diverting the stream's flow to fill it. After watching them for a bit, Sheena, Kira and the Avatars pitched in and helped, and eventually it was done. They let the water fill the pool and wash away the dust and dirt for a good hour before re-diverting the flow, and Kira and Sheena heated the water good and hot – too hot, but it would cool fairly quickly as the stones needed warming too – and then it was ladies first. Sheena and Kira bathed and washed their clothes – Sheena had brought soap, which was running low.

Sometime later, the men returned with the news that they had found an edible palm, some high mountain chilies shaped like bells, and against all expectations some early raspberries in a little microclimate spot the goats had not found. There were goats about, they said, but they would leave that to Sheena. They opened the barrier to the stream and freshened the water, and Kira heated it again. It was easy for her this close to the active volcano, she was still able to keep a strong connection to the underground lava. They left the soap, and the men made their way to the pool. Kira called to them to pass over their boots. They did so, not understanding, and she bent down and filled them with water. "Hey!" expostulated Bronn and Shilo, for both of them knew that water would be hard to dry out, and would make the leather tough. But Kira upended them, and then passed her hand over them, frowning in concentration. Then she turned them upside down again and did it again. Fresh streams of water ran out. Then, she did it again, right side up. "Feel them, inside. And then smell them" she instructed.

Shilo did so. "They're dry! And softer than ... well, softer than any boot I've had before!" He sniffed. "They smell ... new?" This was a good thing. Their boots, after a month's hard use in the heat had become a bit ripe. Shilo's in particular almost had a life of their own.

Kira nodded. Sheena remarked, "Removing water, transforming smells and softening leather ... all useful Ice Witch skills. Better than mine – I could get rid of the smell of boots, but only by burning them to ashes ..." And so they left the men to their ablutions.

There were sighs of contentment as they lowered themselves into the water. Bronn called out, "Oh, my God, this is fantastic" and Shilo sighed "I love you, Kira." Kira glanced at Sheena and blushed bright red. Sheena laughed, but not unkindly. They went to set up camp, and Sheena hunted up a goat without too much trouble. The palm heart was a welcome change; their diet had been a bit too rich in protein for a while since they ate the last of the potatoes. When the men finally joined them, Sheena said that this would most likely be their last stop before Utol'Afir'Astar. As long as they didn't run out of water, it wouldn't matter if they got there a bit hungry, she said, they would be assured of decent food at least. The others were a bit taken aback as she was so sure: it implied that she knew more about the Guardians than she was letting on. But when they asked further, Sheena simply shook her head, and replied: "I cannot say."

Kira looked at her thoughtfully. "'Cannot say' can mean I can't say because I don't know, or can't say because I'm not allowed to" she remarked. Sheena nodded. "You're right, Kira, it can mean either of those two things" but would not say any more.

They nearly did make it all the way, but were forced to descend again twice in order to let Kira squeeze water out of the vegetation. But they did not have to go so far, as the ridge itself was descending to the low point between the volcanoes, and there were enough trees about to provide the firewood they needed to keep Bronn warm, and be a comfort during the night. After they had passed the lowest point and started to climb again, Sheena said that she expected them to arrive at the Guardian's village, Utol'Afir'Caram, on the next day.

And so it was. The village clearly had lookout sentries, because they were expected. A tall man, obviously a senior person, and two young helpers – a boy and a girl – were waiting for them, and a few others could be seen round about, going about their business but looking over at the group in curiosity. Quite different from any village they had yet encountered, the people were tall, very dark-skinned, and had black, somewhat wavy hair. They tended to be a bit long in the face, in an unusual way. He was dressed quite differently too, in a green robe of some weight, for it was cool at this height, but a rich cloth with a chatoyance to it that saw a ripple of yellow-green when he moved, and intricately embroidered. His sandals were of fine leather, and he had a slightly conical cylindrical hat, a formal piece decorated with gold thread. He was calmly confident, with no concern in his eyes, and his words were friendly.

"Greetings, travelers! My name is Kal'Ton. We get few visitors here, you are the first we have seen for some years. We travel ourselves, sometimes, for trade, but few know we are here, and fewer come to seek us out. You are welcome, of course, whatever the reason you are here, but may I ask what that reason is?"

Bronn stepped forward. They had the agreement that if a place appeared to be male oriented he would do the talking, and if female, Sheena. As a man had come forward, he made the assumption that it should be him, and anyway this was his moment. He had had the vision, brought the quest together.

"Greetings, Kal'Ton. My name is Bronn, I am a Master Seer from Seer's Hold, and we have come on a quest, to seek Alanna's Wand, and hope to use it to stop Narn the sorcerer in his plans to rule the world."

Kal'Ton pursed his lips. "Welcome Seer Bronn. We receive the occasional explorer, or the even more occasional lost wanderer, but it has been many decades since anyone has come seeking the Wand. And we have never received a Seer in my lifetime, which has been longer than you might think."

He paused for a second, and spoke again. "I must begin by saying that any who come here seeking the Wand must agree as the first step that they will never speak about what happens here once they leave, and that this agreement is enforced as an oath. Are you all in agreement with this condition? If not, you will still be our guests, but you must go aside and will be met by someone else who will care for you in your time here. I must ask each of you to agree in turn, if you will."

Bronn readily agreed, as did the other three. He found the way of speaking Kal'Ton had fascinating and in some ways quaint. Friendly, but formal; there were few contractions. It was like they were a people apart and had evolved their own language.

Kal'Ton nodded. "Very well. I must also tell you that no great swearing of oaths is needed, your simple agreement is enough. But you will find it is enforced by magic, you will be quite unable to talk about what happens here, except amongst yourselves. The magic is strong, and subtle: if you go to talk to each other but find you cannot, you will know that someone else is listening in."

He paused again.

"Some people do not like the thought of such magic, and again if you wish you may bow out at this point, and only silence about what has been said so far will be enforced. But let me reassure you, this is not our magic, but it comes from the Angel guarding the Wand, so while it is powerful, there can be no thought of evil intent."

They all agreed again, and Kal'Ton smiled. "Good, good! Well, may I know the names of your two young companions? Sha'Lin'Tra, or Sheena as she prefers now we know, of course, for she has been here before."

Bronn introduced Kira and Shilo. Kal'Ton opened his arms in greeting, and said, "But I am most impressed! Representatives of all four Gifts – a Seer, a Fire Witch, a Nun of Knowledge, two Ice Witches and two Warriors wrapped up in only four people! This will be a meeting to go down in our history. And for a good cause! The Angel tells us that it would be better if Narn the Sorcerer was stopped in his attempt to rule the world."

Bronn thoughtfully asked, "Sheena has been here before?"

"Oh yes, indeed, we have records going back a long way, and many other resources that are not immediately apparent, we remember her well. She would not have told you of course, because even she is forbidden by the oath."

400

"And now, I must tell you the third thing. Each member of your party that wishes to make the ascent to the Cave of the Wand and ask for its use must agree to be tested, and the testing is not easy, and may even seem harsh. Many people have failed. However, you do not have to take the test – you can choose to remain behind and not make the ascent."

Bronn replied that his Vision saw all of them in the cave. Sheena said that she would take the test, although she had some idea of what was involved, having been there before. Kira and Shilo, full of the confidence of youth, agreed readily. But surprisingly, Bronn was the one who was not fully committed.

"You can test me as you will – within certain limitations. If you give me a test that requires me to give up my wife Kara, or has a high probability of that happening, or us not being happy, then I will refuse the test or fail it. If you can't guarantee that, then I will stay behind."

Kal'Ton frowned at that. He tilted his head to the side, as if listening, but finally smiled, and said, "Agreed! The Guardian Angel is impressed, and also amused. Apparently, no-one has ever agreed to being tested but with conditions! Still, as I said, the Angels do approve of your quest, so all is well."

"But please! Follow me, you must be tired and hungry. While the tests can come at any time and there may be more than one, you will not be tested this afternoon. This afternoon, you can relax and get to know us, rest and look around."

And he took them in to the village, which consisted of quite large huts and houses, well-constructed using stone and good wood that had been carefully fitted, and airy, open dwellings carved into the stone of the quiescent volcano itself. He handed them over to a plump, middle-aged woman who was very friendly, less formal, and competently organized everything. Grinning youths were told off to take, unpack and clean their belongings. They were asked if they preferred to sleep outside in the huts, or inside the mountain and they chose to stay in one hut with four bedrooms and the usual facilities.

The Guest Housekeeper, Sha'La was happy to answer questions, and Sheena knew quite a few of the answers already. Still, much had changed in the hundreds of years since she was last there. The Guardians had been there for a very long time. It could be seen in their physiognomy, quite different from any of the other distinct types on the continent. A pressing concern was washing, they were uncomfortably aware that they were more than a little rank in comparison to their hosts. Sha'La giggled – she seemed to giggle at nearly everything – and said, "Oh, yes! Of course! Our facilities are free for your use any time. We will give you some new, suitable clothes as well! Ah, Bronn! We have a treat for you! We, too have baths heated by thermal springs, from the volcano. Not as extensive as yours!" She giggled again. "But a little home away from home, we hope. And Sheena and Kira, some of our people are talented barbers. By the time the evening meal comes, you will be quite refreshed."

"But, Oh!" she said. "Perhaps you are hungry now?"

It was past midday and they had recently eaten pretty much the last of their supplies, but Shilo said he could eat a little something. After a few inquiries, they all found the idea of some fruit, bread and some fruit juice to be wonderful. They had been eating too much meat. Sha'La dithered a bit, but eventually decided that the best thing would be to go to the bathing areas and they would be brought something there.

It turned out there were bathing areas both inside and outside. The inside ones were hotter and more specialized, and sex-segregated, the outside ones were communal, but people wore clothing. There were private cubicles for washing, with warm water brought in pipes, which rose over head height and ended in a large cup with holes in it, giving a spray of water much like a heavy rain. Bronn and Kira had never seen anything like it before, and Bronn though it a very good innovation. He stored it away in his mind for later, on Seer's Island. Kira thought it worked well here, but would not suit Iceland. Shilo had seen something like it before, but more like a large bucket with holes in it, that had to be manually filled. Sheena had seen it before, of course.

The outdoor pools were warm and inviting, but after their much needed wash, they sat down at nearby tables rather than staying in. They had been provided with bathing garments, and large wraparound coats of toweling material, as well as slippers. Kira was ecstatic that not only had there been a special soap for washing her hair, there was also a creamy after-wash that made the hair very much easier to comb. And Shilo was delighted that not only was there fruit, fruit juice and bread, someone had also thoughtfully provided butter and a variety of cheeses and nuts.

Sheena allowed that the place was very civilized, and there were many far worse places to live. She added, it had not been uncommon for those seeking the Wand to ask to stay after their quest had been unsuccessful. She explained that the village was nurtured and supported by the Angel.

"How many people have been successful in obtaining the Wand?" Bronn asked. "None that I know of" replied Sheena. "Many have tried, over the centuries. Mostly Fire Witches, and some very powerful ones amongst them. I can tell you this much: selfish requests cannot succeed, and you need the right words. Words of command, or magic."

"Did you succeed?" Kira asked. Sheena shook her head. "No, they wouldn't give it to me. They said it would be of no use for what I wanted to do, anyway."

"What did you want if for?"

Sheena lowered her head. "I ... can't bring myself to say. Perhaps another time."

Bronn said, perhaps a bit smugly, that he had Seen the words to say. Sheena nodded, and said she hoped it would work, their cause was a good one and would benefit the whole world.

And then, they soaked in the pools. Sha'La joined them, to answer any questions. They looked at the people around them, there were many coming and going all the time. She explained in answer to their questions that there were about a hundred people in the village, and their numbers were naturally limited. People only had children occasionally, just enough to keep the population stable. They lived a long time, longer even than the Ice Witches, and theirs was a rich and rewarding culture to live in. They provided a service to the Guardian Angel, winnowing out the travelers who might otherwise flock to the cave, and to some extent keeping him company. In return, he protected them, gave them knowledge, purpose. Sha'La giggled again. "In some ways, we are pets! Still, we know what we are, we do it of our own free will, and we like it."

Shilo said that it seemed like a very happy life and a wonderful place to be. Sheena said, a little darkly, he should wait till he had been tested. Sha'La said, "Well, yes, the tests are hard. Very hard, sometimes. But they are all for your own good! You will see that in the end. Though of course, they do not seem so at the time."

After a pleasant hour in the baths, Sha'La advised them to go visit the barbers, then go back to their hut and get dressed for dinner. They had plenty of time, hours yet. They first visited the hut, where casual clothes had been laid out, and then made their way to the barbers, where people shaved Bronn and Shilo, cut their hair and then pretty much sent them on their way - and descended in a cloud on Sheena and Kira, intent on trying to brush, file, massage and pamper two months of hard trail walking away and turn them into proper looking women. Sheena took it in good part and let them have their way with her, but Kira was overwhelmed, never having had anything of the kind done to her. Sheena smiled at her, a little wanly, and said: "Enjoy it to the full. The tests will begin soon enough."

And indeed, once she had been washed, oiled, creamed, plucked, steamed and coiffured, Kal'Ton himself came to her. Somberly, he said to her, "I am sorry, Kira, that the first test should fall on you, the youngest, and that it will be a hard one."

Kira was jolted out of her relaxed state with apprehension. Sheena had been hinting that things would be so.

"This is your test. Tonight, at dinner, we will be seating you next to people we judge you will like, of a similar nature to each of you, to be entertained. A very fine young girl, a remarkable fighter in her own right, will be seated next to the young man, Shilo, and she will be doing her best to seduce him. Not, I hasten to add, something against her nature, for she has already seen him and is taken with him. And your test will be, you must allow it, allow him to be taken away without sign of distress, to encourage him if needed. You cannot tell either Shilo or Bronn about it."

Kira's heart beat as though it would burst out of her chest. "What?" she stammered. "How is this a fair test? What good does it do? How can anyone want to *do* this to me?"

Kal'Ton spoke in a low voice, sadly but firmly. "Kira, you must understand that right now he loves you. But our opinion is, and we have guidance from the Angel, that if he is too close to you, your quest may fail. You might not obtain the Wand, there is a chance Sheena will die, and your people will never return home to their native land. You must do this, it is your duty."

Kira looked at him, trembling. But she could see that he truly believed what he was saying. And after a while, a long while, she bowed her head. "I will do it" she whispered. "I don't know if I can do it with a smile on my face."

Finally, they left the area and walked back together. Kira told Sheena what her task was, and she put her arm around the girl's shoulder. "Ah, Kira, I am so sorry. I was afraid of something like this. I'm sorry, you will have a hard time of it. But there is no certainty this girl will be successful. And if it is, it won't be a long term thing, for she can't leave here and I don't think Shilo will want to stay. When the quest is over and won, it may well be that the two of you will be able to pick things up where you have left off."

"But if he is so easily led astray, what hope is there for us? And anyway, the age difference is still there." And Sheena could give no answer for that.

They came to their hut, where they found that clothes had been laid out for them. In a demonstration of their own skill, and possibly assistance from the Angel, the clothes both fit them and suited them.

Sheena had been given a dark red skirt with matching sandals, a lighter and paler red blouse embroidered with gold thread, and a light gold necklace to go with it. The Fire Witch colors matched her personality and looked splendid against her brown skin.

Kira had been given a dark blue dress, strikingly similar to the one she had bought at Warrior's hold, quite low cut, and a necklace of blue stone with gold patterns in it, and she wore her amber earrings. Shilo said she looked magnificent, and she smiled as best she could, but it was a bit of a sad grimace.

Shilo himself had been given a simple outfit in black, with a studded leather belt, quite snug trousers and a loose, short sleeved shirt which showed off his impressive musculature. And Bronn had been given looser trousers in brown and a cream shirt with full sleeves.

Impressively, they had all been given symbols of their rank, though they had not discussed it. Sheena had a replica of a Warrior's Bronze medallion on her belt, and a golden flame indicating her level one status on her right shoulder. On her left, there were four smaller flames, which Sheena explained with a catch in her voice was private Fire Witch symbology, not often see outside the Hold: it meant that she had demonstrated the capacity to use those levels, but could not reliably do it at the moment. Bronn wore a Master Seer's talisman. Kira had two white icicles high up on the right hand side of her dress, and Shilo had a trainee's badge and one bronze sword on the left.

Sheena noticed that Shilo was subdued, and asked about it, but he only said that he had been given a task, and it was going to be a hard one, but he could not talk about it. Kira nodded, and said she had been given one too.

Unexpectedly, Bronn said he had already been tested. He had fallen asleep in the hut, waiting for the girls to return. Kal'Ton had come to him in a dream, a Vision where he had been told that he had a choice: although he had Seen the quest, formed it, gone from one Hold to another and brought the players together, there were two paths at this point. One led to fame and fortune for him as the continued leader, the other was for him to retire more into the background and be a support for the other three – but there was a slightly better chance for success if he did. No more than five percent, and no-one outside the group would ever know. He shrugged. "Of course, I chose the latter one; it took me no more than two seconds to decide."

Kira commented, "That doesn't seem like much of a test, then."

Bronn nodded. "Kal'Ton was somewhat put out, and asked me if I really didn't care about the personal glory? I laughed, and said, no, one of the qualities of a good Seer is they know themselves well. Give me a five percent better chance of success, and what's fame to me? I'm quite happy to live on Seer's Hold with no-one knowing what I did, as long as Kara is there with me. He was quite puzzled. In the end, however, he simply acknowledged that they had never tested a Seer before, and hadn't quite expected to be so easy. He added that the tests were hardest on those who were not centered, who had matters they needed to resolve."

Sheena nodded. "I have not been tested yet, nor told what my test will be. Frankly, I am afraid – more than afraid. But best to hold our heads up high and march to our fate. At least we will get a good dinner."

And that they did. The Guardians had done their very best to make them feel at home. There was no opulence to over-awe them, the dining area set aside for them was private and cozy. There were fires burning in well-chimneyed fireplaces, low tables and comfortable cushions to recline on. There were a limited number of people there, in order to not overwhelm them with new faces and names. Each of them had two companions, who acted as servers, conversationalists, question answerers and anything else needed. They had obviously been chosen because they liked that role, nothing seemed forced.

The food came in variety, nothing too elaborate and small portions. They clearly knew their guests would be looking forward to something different from what they could get on the trail, and there was a lot of fruit, fresh well seasoned meats, good water and wine. In particular, they were plied with the wine, or at least Bronn, Sheena and Shilo were. Kira was counted too young, though she was allowed a glass or two of wine and water. Sheena drank glass after glass with great enjoyment, her modified metabolism preventing her from becoming more than momentarily tipsy to the bemusement of their hosts. Bronn was far too old a hand to be led astray, and kept his imbibing modest, but Shilo was pressed to drink more than he should by the two very attractive young women assigned to him. The somewhat protruding jawline of the people was less pronounced in the women, and they were intriguing and exotic with their midnight black skin. Sheena warned him, and as her student he paid attention, but there was no doubt that his inhibitions became a bit relaxed as the evening wore on.

409

They learned many new things, even Sheena. She explained that her visit had been quite short. The Guardians had been there for a long, long time. Theirs was the tradition of two part names, which had become modified into three part names in the Queendom of the Fire Witches. They were by far the most knowledgeable and civilized of all the kingdoms, their knowledge rivaled that of Nun's Hold. But they did not study so much, they lived in a kind of group collective where they knew what they needed to know, grace of the Angel. And so they learned many fascinating things that evening, even Sheena, whose experience was lengthy and broad.

But there was a tension in the air, a subtle undercurrent. Shilo became more and more absorbed in conversation with one of his companions, Kal'Tia, and when the evening came to an end – not too late, because they were still tired despite their relaxation during the afternoon – and they left to return to their hut, Shilo and she went a different way. Sheena thought she saw him turn a guilty look to Kira, but only for a moment. And so, they went to their separate beds. Kira was sad and downcast, but not crying. Sheena was sad for Kira. Only Bronn slept happily, lost in another dream with Kara, who had taken to having a nap in the middle of the day, half a world away.

The next day, they rose late. Kira gave a half hopeful glance over to Shilo's bedroom, but it was clear that he had not returned. They made their way over to the communal areas, and were served breakfast. Shilo was already there, and by the look of them had no idea what to do. Sheena beckoned him over peremptorily, and motioned for him to sit down. Drawing a breath, and clearly calling on the iron will implicit in all Warriors, he began, "Kira, about last night ..." but she cut him off. Not angrily, no more than the tiniest bit of regret in her voice, she said, "There is no problem, Shilo. I have no call on you, no right to say what you should or shouldn't do. As long as it doesn't affect the quest, and my people's chance to return home, your time and how you spend it is your own. Shilo bowed his head, and said, "I will do my very best to see to it that these, our joint goals, are reached." And the group was one again. In some ways the focus was clearer, though the people were not happier.

After breakfast, Kal'Ton came to see them. They were keen to know when they might begin their ascent to the Guardian's cave. He replied, "You may possibly go up today. Your testing is nearly complete. But you, Shilo, must face another one this morning. You must face one of our people, and defeat them. It will be a serious fight, and if you lose, your group will not be allowed to go on."

Shilo was perturbed. "You've all been my hosts, friendly and welcoming. How can I face one of you in a serious fight? That is, if you mean by 'serious' what we mean at Warrior's Hold, that one must be clearly victorious, even if it means the other is badly hurt, or even killed!"

Kal'Ton nodded. "That is exactly what we mean. And, how can you? You must, as it is your duty. Duty can be hard, at times, for certain. The one you face will have a duty of their own, which is the price we pay for being Guardians. We have a great privilege to serve, we are provided with many benefits and a way of life available perhaps no-where else in the world. But we all know there may be a price to pay someday. Your challenger would obviously prefer it if you can win without great injury, and we know that you are a well-trained Warrior. Sheena has said, you may one day aspire to Gold, and you are even now very good indeed.

But one of you must win, that is the test the Angel has decreed."

Sheena interjected. "Shilo, my student. There is no point arguing against this test. The Angel will not be moved. I know that all too well. I have confidence in you."

Shilo protested once again, however. "But I have already been tested! It was hard, harsh!"

Kal'Ton agreed. "So you have. But there is no rule that each person will only be tested once. And sometimes what appears to be a test is not the true test. Come, the test cannot be avoided. You must either take it, or withdraw – and in this case, it will be counted as a fail, and as I said, your group cannot go on."

Shilo bowed his head. "I will fight. It is, after all, what a Warrior is for. Where will this test take place? When? With what weapons, and what rules?"

Kal'Ton replied, "We have a chamber set aside, with a square marked out. You may not step outside of the square. You may fight when you are ready, and with what weapon you choose and all of your skill – but only the skill of a Warrior. You cannot use any of the Ice Magic you have learned."

Shilo replied, "I've only had a light breakfast, and I am rested. I'm not one who cannot fight just after eating, so we may as well begin as soon as possible."

And so it was. They all walked towards the cliff, where the volcano had been carved into chambers and caves. Sheena said to Shilo that his only real choice of weapon was the sword, it was by far his greatest area of proficiency, and he so advised Kal'Ton. They were taken to a large room, with a square perhaps a dozen paces on a side had been marked off. The room was well lit, with artificial lights, something no-one of their group had seen, other than Sheena. There were few spectators, just the three from their group, Kal'Ton himself, two people who had volunteered to be judges, and a handful of senior people from the Guardians. And one other, Kal'Tia, the girl from the previous night. Kira cast her a look of dislike, but well-guarded. No-one saw it other than Sheena.

Kal'Ton called her forward, and simply said, "This is our champion, Kal'Tia, who you will fight today." And they saw that she was ready, dressed in sturdy pants, a close fitting blouse, boots, and with a leather armguard. Shilo's jaw dropped. He said, in a shocked voice, "I can't fight *her*! She and I, why we ..." his voice trailed off. Kal'Ton spoke again. "What happened yesterday is yesterday's business. Today, we must turn our mind to other matters. You must decide. You do not have to fight. But as I said before, that will count as a loss."

Even Kira protested. But Kal'Ton was adamant. "Yes, I understand. You would prefer not to fight, and not to fight her. She would also prefer not to fight you. I would prefer you not to fight her, if it comes to that, but that is the price. We know our duty as Guardians. You must learn yours, hard though the path is."

Sheena, as teacher, took Shilo aside, and spoke to him in a low voice. She told him, he was good, very good with the sword. Perhaps he could win without injuring the girl. She said that it was indeed not fair that they had pushed her towards him last night, and he must face her today. But he must take that feeling and wrap it up, and fight like a true Warrior, not in anger, but balanced and neutral, with no focus other than the win. Otherwise, all could be lost.

Shilo looked at Kal'Tia. He looked at Kira. He looked at the ground. And then, something hardened in him, and he raised his head. With a steady voice – not devoid of emotion, for determination is an emotion – he said, simply, "I will fight."

And so they began. Cautiously at first, Shilo using every opportunity to become used to his sword, which he had chosen from the ones on offer. They crossed blades, and carefully turned each other's strokes away with the small oval shields. Gathering confidence, they moved more quickly, tried different styles and sallies. Sheena pursed her lips in surprise. The girl was good, very good. In a quiet voice, she said as much to Kal'Ton. "I didn't think it was possible to develop such talent outside of Warrior's Hold." Kal'Ton replied that it probably wasn't, and no doubt the Angel was lending a hand.

"And that is counted as fair?" Sheena protested. "An Angel could grant as much ability as it wanted. Superhuman ability!"

"Do not worry, Sheena. The task is never set to be impossible. Your Shilo will be able to win, if he is determined enough."

And the battle continued, in earnest now. Every attack Shilo made was turned away, but every riposte Kal'Tia made Shilo was able to deal with. It seemed to go on for ever, but a tiny mistake by both fighters led to the first blood – a small nick on Shilo's leg, and a slightly larger one on the girl's side. They both separated, breathing deeply, but not heavily, and according to the rules agreed to a time out.

Both wounds were tended to. Assistants used a sticky tape to bind them up, and a stinging liquid to stop the bleeding. Shilo's cut was perhaps the more debilitating as it was on his leg, but he said it would be no problem. He conferred with Sheena.

"She is skilled. Perhaps as skilled as I am. And fast. But, she's smaller, and I should be able to tire her out."

"I wouldn't rely on that, Shilo. I think the Angel is involved here. She may tire no faster than you."

"Well then ... I don't know what to do."

"Yes, Shilo. You do. You must *win*. And there is a way. You are, after all, bigger and stronger. I think you are much stronger than she realizes."

"Yes ... I know what you mean. I can force her out of position, if I give it everything I've got. But, defense is easier than attack. I might only get the one chance, she will be more wary next time, and it will leave me exposed. Whatever opening I force, I will have to take it. And ..."

Sheena nodded, soberly. "Yes, Shilo. You will have to take that opening, when it comes. And do what you have to do. Can you do it? For your duty, for your code, for Kira, the world and for me?"

Shilo did not answer, but turned and walked slowly back to the combat zone.

Kal'Tia entered too, and raised her sword. Both of them knew it was going to be serious now. And Shilo strode forward, and threw his shield. Kal'Tia had to block it, and as she did, he brought his sword down with all his strength and smashed hers out of the way. Quick as a flash, he did the same on the other side to her shield, numbing her arm. She brought her sword back up, but not strongly – though strongly enough to cut a deep gash in his side. But she was wide open,

415

and knew it. Without thinking, he twirled his sword around with his wrist in a quick circle, and plunged it into her chest, just a little to her left.

It was a killing blow, and she knew it. Despite the pain, she managed a brief half smile, and a gasped "Well fought" before collapsing, the blood pooling around her.

Shilo sank to his knees, and half lifted her body, but it was obvious there was no hope. Oblivious to the pain in his side, and with tears streaming down his cheeks, he lifted his eyes to Kal'Ton. "Well, I have won. But is this what you wanted? Is this what your Angel wants? To have one of yours killed? How does that *help*? What does it prove?"

Kal'Ton nodded. "One of ours, indeed. My daughter, in fact."

Shilo gaped at him.

Kal'Ton continued. "You have done well, and passed the test, in all aspects. But it is not as bad as you think. We are not monsters." He raised his hand and pointed. From the doorway came a young woman. Kal'Tia.

Shilo looked at her in amazement, and down at the girl still in his arms. She walked over, bent down and stroked the dead girl's hair. "Well fought, indeed" she murmured. And the girl melted away, in a soft shimmer of light. Including most of the blood, the only part of that remaining was what Shilo had contributed.

The live Kal'Tia stood, and reached to hold Shilo's arm. "Stand, if you can" she asked. He struggled to his feet, and Sheena could tell there was a cracked rib or two in there. She ran her hand lightly along his side, and Shilo sucked in his breath. He lifted his shirt, and though there was still a lot of blood about it was clear he had been healed. While he was looking, she bent down and touched his leg. Then, she stood back a pace, bowed, and said, "Shilo. Warrior. Ice Witch. I am proud to have known you, and been the instrument of your testing." And she turned and walked out of the room.

Sheena shook her head, and said, wonderingly: "Well. An Avatar. Even I didn't guess. And how, how was it done, to not shatter? And all that blood! Oh ... the Angel, of course."

Shilo looked around, and at Kal'Ton. "An Avatar? But *why*? What purpose does it all serve?"

Kal'Ton looked him in the eyes. "It is deep, but simple, Warrior Shilo. You now know that you have it in you, to do your duty as every Warrior must. You will see it through, you will support this quest you are on, no matter the personal cost or what you may feel about the people involved. You have been tested, and not found wanting. You will kill, if you have to. This should, this *will* give you a confidence in your own abilities and resolve that you may well need before it is all over."

Shilo looked at Sheena, who nodded. He looked at Bronn, and then at Kira, and a fleeting sad look came over his face, but he quickly looked at Kal'Ton. In the way of the Warriors, he bowed. "I am indebted for this lesson, Guardian Kal'Ton. I am stronger for it. Not happier, but that is not needed at this time."

Kal'Ton bowed in his turn. "Well spoken. And true, though happiness may well be allowed to us when our duties are done."

He turned, and addressed them as a group. "This part of the testing is complete. You are permitted to ascend to the Angel's cave, and may go at any time. I suggest you change your clothing, however, Shilo" he said, referring to the fact that though Shilo might be healed, he was still covered in blood.

It was a quiet and thoughtful trio that headed back to the hut, while Shilo went to clean up and receive fresh clothing. Kira hesitatingly said, "I suppose that test was the hardest of them all, and the most complex. A part of the test must have been ... last night?" Sheena nodded, and said, "Hard. Harder than yours? I don't know. Perhaps. Yes, perhaps, especially after last night. Certainly harder than Bronn's."

Bronn agreed that his had been easy, very easy by comparison. He said, all in all, he was very glad he had asked for his exclusions, and hoped the Guardians didn't feel they had to test him again.

Kira persisted. "But, last night? Do you think that she .. that Kal'Tia, wants, you know ..."

Sheena was more straightforward. "Does she have any long-term designs on Shilo? No, I would say not. She would have found him attractive, of course. Neither the Guardians nor the Angel would have forced her to spend the night with him – as you've said in the past, he is a very attractive man. But she's not going to leave here, nor is he going to come here to live, I think. But still, it will stand between you. I think you will find Shilo will be more distant, more focused on his duties. And you won't be able to stop thinking that he was quite easy to seduce. I think the tests will have had the desired effect, however painful it may seem to you personally."

"Yes, but still ..." Kira mused. "Yes. Still." Sheena agreed. There was more unsaid than said, she thought to herself.

"It occurs to me" Bronn said as they neared the hut, "that you haven't been tested yet, Sheena."

Sheena nodded. "Yes. It may be that I don't get tested this time, because I've been here before. But I have a feeling of uncertainty that they may be saving the best for last. Apprehension. Well, alright, outright fear. I don't know what they could ask of me that's worse than what I have been through these last eight hundred years, or these last few months for that matter. However, as Kira said ... 'but still'."

While they sat waiting for Shilo, Bronn asked Sheena what they would need to take with them up to the cave of the Angel. "Not much" she replied. "The way is easy, and not long – an hour's walk at most. Some water. We could easily stay here for lunch, take a little snack with us, or leave it till we get back. It's a sunny day, perhaps a hat. Strange to think we are so close now, after all these months."

They changed into their trail clothes, which had been washed, mended and replaced where necessary. Hats had been provided, and stout walking staves, better than the sticks they had gathered on their way.

By the time they were done, Shilo returned. He, too was quiet. His clothes were a pale green color, and on the right shoulder there was a small embroidered silver sword. He pointed to it, wordlessly. Sheena looked at it, and smiled, and said, "So, the Guardians evaluate you as a Silver Warrior, of the sword at least. Well, who am I to argue. You acquitted yourself well, Student. I am proud to be your mentor."

419

But it was Kira who surprised them the most, perhaps herself most of all. She walked right up to him and gave him a long hug. "I'm proud of you too, Shilo" she said, "That test was not easy. You did well." And she gave him a kiss on both cheeks. He was surprised, and grateful. He relaxed. He said, "Thank you very much, Kira. Kal'Ton said, I should ask you about your test. But not today, not till it is all over. He said, I would be proud of you too." And a tension they had all been holding relaxed.

Sheena looked at her, proud and surprised. 'What an amazing girl' she thought to herself. 'Fifteen. And able to shoulder the burden of leadership, set off across the unknown world on a difficult and dangerous quest, able to postpone and possibly give up her first love for the sake of her duty to her people. Kind and caring, supportive, able to learn and change, and talented. I wish … all in all, I wish I had been more like her, and less like me.'

After Shilo had changed, there was little reason to delay. He assured them he was completely healed, and the amount of blood he had lost would not make any difference. Kal'Ton and Sha'La were waiting outside for them, anticipating they would leave soon, and they said they would walk with them to the end of the village, to the start of the path up the slope of the extinct volcano. Sheena looked at them in apprehension; her sense of foreboding was rising again. And with good reason. As they passed the boundaries of the village, a bright, glittering object became visible in the near distance, and she looked at the two Guardians. Kal'Ton nodded, and said, "Yes, Sheena. Your test. I am sorry."

Sheena looked at them, and at the shining thing standing by the path. "Oh, no. Not that … not that, to be a test for me. Please. Not that." Her face was pale, as pale as it had been in Intira's study, Bronn thought.

Kal'Ton shook his head. "I am sorry, Sheena. I have no choice, what I do is guided by the Angel. Your test is, you must walk with us and your group up to the statue and you must tell everyone why it exists, and why it is here. Or, leave and never return."

Sheena sank to her knees. She bowed down and rested her arms in the dirt, and lowered her head onto her arms, and stayed like that for a long minute. But finally, she rose, wiped her face (which did not do much good given her tears and the dirt on her hands), and with a dead expression on her face took one measured step after the other until she was standing by it. The others followed close behind. It could be seen to be a statue of a man, finely crafted, but coated in a brilliant mirror that blurred the contours and seemed to be without flaw. She stretched out her hand, and touched the statue's face.

She sighed, and turned to face them. "This is the last person I ever loved. Bronn, you have heard my story in Intira's study, and Kira, you've heard other parts of it. Shilo, you've been told much too, and Kal'Ton and Sha'La, you know as much as you need to, no doubt, thanks to the Angel. Well, here is the last part of my story."

"I fell in love with this man. I was attracted to him when I trained as a Warrior, but when I returned to Fire Hold he stayed behind, to study further. I never forgot him, however, and when I left, I asked him to come and visit me when he had taken his learning as far as he wanted to. It was hard to leave him, but I had my own burning desires."

"Finally, many years later, he did come to Fire Hold, to seek me out. I was of course Prime Witch by then and just beginning to make a move against the Ice Witches, though at that stage my plans were simple war. But still, I found time to get to know him again, and we re-kindled the love of our younger days in just a few weeks. But then, as I said, when I finally revealed my full plans to him, to have my revenge on the Ice Witches, he was appalled. He desperately tried to change my mind, pointing out all of the arguments a reasonable mind could throw up, but I wouldn't change my mind in any way. Finally, he rejected me, and said he would have no part of it."

"I was hurt and angry to have my selfish and unselfish love rejected, for there were parts of both in my feelings. With mind magic very similar to what Narn uses today, and what Shi'Kal'Tara tried to use on me a few months ago, I turned him into a puppet, a plaything that would sit by my side and do as he was told, bound by the compulsion of unthinking love. But as I have told, I couldn't bear it, to see him sitting there with no will of his own."

"I released him, and said I was sorry, but as I wouldn't change my plans, once again he turned away from me and went to leave. By this stage, I was working high level three, but in pain and fury for the first and only time I broke into level five. I do not know or remember exactly what I did, but I know that I created this level five shield around him. I'm not sure, but I fear that at that level, I did things that would leave him alive and aware inside that shield, his body suspended but his mind awake."

Sheena paused for a few seconds.

"When I came down from that peak, I was still in pain, still angry, but also sorry. Unrequited love still burned in my brain. I tried to undo my spell, but I couldn't reach that peak again, and the shield was impervious to everything I could do, even everything with as many Witches as I could meld together. My love, and the fear of what I had done to him choked me, and that was when I burned love out of my mind. And that then lead to my discovery of my evil mind control magic."

"After my revenge against the Ice Witches was complete and the world was mine, I made my first visit to this place. I was one of the very few who has spoken to the Angel before being tested, for I flew up to the cave rather than walking, carrying this statue. I asked for the Wand, but was refused. The Guardian Angel said there was no point. At best it would support me and perfect my level three magic – or level four, as I had just begun working on that, but that was not enough to breach the shield. It also told me that as I had burned my mind it was now lessened, and there was no chance I could do level five work again."

"While I didn't feel the pain of having hurt a loved one any more, still, I felt it was somehow wrong to leave him in the shield. The Angel confirmed for me that his mind was still active, and said that I had done well to make sure that he was kept in a place where he could see and hear, and that interesting things were presented to him, otherwise he might have retreated into insanity. I asked if there was anything that could be done for him."

"The Angel replied that there was little that could be done. The shield could be broken, but that would kill him, for sure. He told me that the best I could do was to leave him behind. Normally, the Angels do not interfere with the running of this world, but in this case as no-one else could possibly do anything for him, they would do what they could."

"I don't know what they did. I hope he has not been aware, trapped inside that shield for these last centuries. After my reign, my fall and my learning of compassion, remorse and sorrow, the guilt of this thing I did has been with me every day of my life. Of course, I know that it's only one person, and what I did to the Ice Witches was as bad or worse, and was for hundreds, thousands of people. But I remember how I felt about him."

Kal'Ton shook his head in sorrow. "You have passed this test, Sheena. To be able to confess it was one part, but the test has been going on longer than you think. Genuine sorrow over what you did was a part of it, too, as was learning."

"Oh, I've learned, Kal'Ton. Power, selfishness and thoughtless anger are not a good combination. I've learned that. Not as well as I would like. I have had two or three lapses in the past year. But Kira has been kind enough to grant me that changes happening in my mind may excuse them. I hope so."

They parted, and went on their way. The path was good and the climbing was easy enough. They were to some extent lost in their own thoughts. The tests that they had passed were all intensely real for each of them, and they were thinking them over. To be sure, they had some desultory conversation. Sheena could tell them that the cave was small, though easily large enough for the four of them. The Angel would be a vague outline of a person, softly glowing white, the cave itself unadorned and the Wand on the wall on a simple shelf. She could not tell them how they might get the Angel to give it to them, as she had not succeeded herself and knew of no-one who had been successful.

Finally, they made it to the top of the path. Unexpectedly, there was a sweet little garden outside, with golden flowers bordering a pattern in purple and red. "Well, this is different" remarked Sheena. Bronn squared his shoulders, drew a deep breath, and as the quest leader took the honor of entering first, then Kira, Shilo and lastly Sheena.

The cave couldn't have been any more different from Sheena's description. It was large and airy, with an indefinable sense of distance at the end. The walls were a pleasant light yellow, and lit by the same sort of artificial light that the Guardians used in their village. There was a comforting fireplace with a warm blaze, rugs on the floor and comfortable furniture. A small table held an assortment of little delicacies. The Angel was there, but no vague being. He was a solid looking man, bearded, looking in fact a little like Bronn. But he did softly glow white.

Sheena looked around, wonderingly. "What ... why ..." was all she could say.

The Angel smiled, and said, "Welcome, all! And welcome again, Sheena."

She turned to him, and said, "Are you the same Angel who was here last time?"

"No, indeed. We have tours of duty, we grow into other things and out of them. You should be able to tell, by the way I have re-decorated: the surroundings always reflect the inhabitant. Please be seated, make yourselves comfortable."

They hesitatingly sat down. Bronn cleared his throat nervously. "Ah-hem. We .. we are here to seek the loan of Alana's Wand."

The Angel nodded. In a friendly voice he said, "I figured that out all by myself, Bronn." He smiled. "No-one ever comes here for any other reason, you know, plus I am in constant communication with the Guardian village. Still, you are nervous. Relax! Everyone who comes gets their chance to convince me, and I listen without prejudice. We can talk a bit if you like, or you can begin your asking."

Well, Bronn at least knew what to do. He stood, and spoke the words he had dreamed. The Angel beamed, clapped his hands, and exclaimed, "Oh, well done! Very well done indeed, Seer Bronn! Beautifully pronounced. But I'm sorry, the answer is no."

Bronn sat down, aghast. "But .. but I Saw myself speaking those words! The whole quest has been to get to this point!"

The Angel replied, "Once again, Seer Bronn, I *am* sorry. Do you know what the words mean?"

"No ... in my Vision, they are words of command, but I don't know any more."

"Indeed so they are, words in the language of Angels – yes, we have our own. And they mean, 'Give me the Wand, for I need it'. That's all. I can choose to grant it you or not, and perhaps in your Vision I did. But things have changed since then. You made a decision in your test. Sheena has changed. Kira has changed. Shilo has become far more skilled. Your decision in your test was for the best probability of success, and my feeling – intuition – not quite right, there is a much more specific word in the Angel language – is that someone else should wield it. If, of course, they can convince me. Who would like to go next? Sheena? Do you have any words of command for me?"

Sheena shook her head. "I have nothing more than the last time. I want it for different purposes now, of course, but I can't see what good it would do me. I'm about as good a level one Fire Witch as one can be, I think, and I'm pretty sure the Wand can't heal my mind or even remove my self-limiting spell."

"Well, you're quite right. Its purpose is a simple one, though great and necessary. It was created specifically to help undo magic errors that could not be undone in any other way. But it has to be wielded by someone at the same level as the magic that was done. Your planned use of it is not what it was designed for at all. But worthy, in my judgment. Perhaps Shilo?"

"If it can help our cause in any way, then of course I ask for it. I demand it. But not otherwise."

"Your intention is good, Shilo. But that is not the way to get the Wand. You need a word of power, a word of magic. And, I agree with you. A perfect Warrior is unlikely to be what you need."

And that left only Kira. They all turned to her. Put on the spot, she did not know what to do. "I ... don't know what to say. I know no words of command. I believe our cause to be worthy, even necessary. Can we please borrow it? I'll promise to look after it, and bring it back?"

The Angel smiled at her. "You said, 'please'! Yes of course, my dear. Here it is. Look after it carefully, please. It is powerful, but it can be broken." And he reached into a pocket of his gown, pulled out a clear rod perhaps a foot and a half in length, and handed it to her."

Sheena looked at the Angel. "Please? That's it? She says 'Please', and you hand it over?"

"Yes, indeed, a powerful word. Children are taught, 'what is the magic word?' I don't know all of history, but I can tell you, in the last few thousand years many dozens of people have come to this cave with mighty demands, commands, needs, and great words of power. But Kira is the first in a long while to ask in the right way. Please. So simple. And yet, it shows a genuine need, not a selfish one. Of course, you can't just say it, you have to *mean* it."

Sheena put her head back and roared with laughter. Bronn, put out at first, eventually had to join her, and the Angel laughed himself.

"But please! Have one of these small cakes. Perhaps a glass of wine? There are things we should talk about, things you need to know. I will help you as much as I can."

Sheena was the first to accept some wine. As always she was willing, probably because she knew she would be the least affected. Bronn followed suit, it was dawning on him that he was well and truly relegated into a background role in what remained of the quest, and Shilo took a glass out of courtesy. Kira was given a small one. She didn't quite know what to do with the Wand.

The Angel saw that, and said, "Kira, you can put the Wand down if you want. It is attuned to you now; no-one else can use it until it is returned to me. And don't be afraid of losing it, you will find you always know where it is." And so she put it down on the table, took a small cake and a sip of the wine. It was a cool white, clear, slightly sweet without being cloying, refreshing and not too strong. Sheena sipped and then drank hers down, and accepted a refill. "Superb! Good enough for the Angels!" she commented, smiling.

The Angel laughed again, a pleasant sound. "Well, my successful group, I must tell you a few things. To some extent, you succeeded because the Angels are in favor of your quest. We do think it would be a good thing if Narn the sorcerer was stopped, though of course we will take no direct part. But still, it is our way that those who come seeking the Wand and are successful are rewarded, and not just with the Wand itself. Some of you now and some of you later I think."

"For you, Seer Bronn. You have chosen to give up fame and fortune to improve the chances of success for this quest. It was well done. As a reward, the Angels give you this Seeing for yourself. Your work is nearly done, but there is still danger. Your best bet to come back alive to your Kara is to avoid conflict. The quest is still important, but we see others carrying it forward now. You should still travel with the group, but choose your battles wisely." Bronn nodded his thanks.

"And for you, Sheena. Something serious."

Sheena put down her glass, and paid close attention.

"You have been working for a very long time, following the words of the Angels. You have learned compassion, sorrow, remorse. You have been forgiven by the Ice Witches. And, every day, you have prayed for forgiveness from God."

Sheena nodded.

The Angel paused. "Well, I am happy to tell you that you have been forgiven. Your repentance is genuine, your sorrow for what you did is real, and that is all that is required. Word has come down from the Archangels that you are forgiven. Normally, this is left up to the person to figure out, but this seems like a time for a small exception; you seem to need a bit of a push."

Sheena's month dropped open, and she trembled. "For ... forgiven?" she stammered. "Forgiven? I scarcely dared to hope ... Oh, am I worthy? Do I deserve it?"

The Angel shrugged. "Probably not. Who does? But God's mercy is infinite. Take it, be thankful, and sin no more, that's the Angels' motto."

Sheena sat back, tears in her eyes. "So much ... so much I never thought could happen. And now, if I can only find some way to forgive *myself* ..."

The Angel made a sound of annoyance and disapproval. "Pah! That is easy. Do you still have the ambition to join the Angels, to become one of us? You'll have to do better than that if you do, I'm afraid."

Sheena was genuinely puzzled. "What? What do you mean?"

"Look, the Archangels say God has forgiven you. That means, you must forgive yourself. If you don't, you're setting yourself up as having a higher moral standard than God. You can't do that, that's belittling God. It's a sin if you do it on purpose, there's actually a technical term for it. Let your shame go."

Sheena looked at him, her lips trembling. "So, you are saying I have no choice – I *must* forgive myself."

Kira sprang to her feet, and dashed over to her. Flinging herself down, she grabbed Sheena in a hug. "Oh, Sheena! I am so happy for you! That's everything! Everything achieved!"

Sheena looked at her and hugged her back. "Thank you, Kira. I'm still a bit overwhelmed. I think it will be

430

a while before it all sinks in. But ..." – the smile left her face. "No, not quite everything. I still have to rediscover love."

Kira smiled. "But, Sheena! I'm sure you can do it. Everything that the Angels said you would need to do! Done! And you thought it was all impossible." And she rose, and pushed in and sat next to Sheena.

The Angel smiled also. "Yes, indeed. One step more. And I can tell you something there, too, Sheena. Eight hundred years and more ago, the Angels feared you might never take that final step. Even we were not sure it could be done. But, you have tried relentlessly through the years and centuries. Now, we know it can be done. The potential is there. *But* ..." the last word was emphasized. "That doesn't mean it is certain. The last step is a big one. We cannot advise you on how you might take it."

Sheena mulled that over.

"And now, advice for you as a group. Is there anything you would ask?"

Shilo stirred. "Can Kira face Narn, now that she has the Wand?"

The Angel shrugged. "Face? Certainly. Win? No. She is making good progress in level two Ice magic. The Wand will help her there, if she uses it. But Tan'Nar'No is a very strong level three Fire Witch and a reasonable fighter. A level two can never win against a level three, Wand or no."

"Well then, what should we do? How does the Wand help us?"

"That is not fully clear at this time, even to us. However, I can suggest this: If you can make it back to

Fir'Caram, the Fire Witches have the capability to hold off Narn's forces. For a while. If you can recruit the help of the Queens, it is possible that with Sheena's help, you could continue training and make it to level three. And then, the Wand could help you. Then, you could win. You would have to make it there, of course."

"Or, you could stay with the Guardians. There, with Sheena's help, you could take as long as you want to study and reach level three. Sheena has the knowledge, but can't show you as the Queens could. Winning is more certain that way, because the village is mine. There, I can use what power is given to me to the full. Narn and the whole world could batten against it, and it would not fall. But it *would* be the whole world. It would take you longer, without a level three to show and train you. Narn would conquer everything and everyone. He is almost ready. Perhaps he would grow in power, take Nun's Hold and its knowledge and follow in Sha'Lin'Tra's footsteps and become undying. When you emerged, you would have to retake the whole world. Many would die. Very many, it would lay waste to the known lands. It would almost be better to just leave it, and hope for him to die, as Sheena suggested at Nun's Hold, or if not, get sick of life."

"So, you are saying, I can be safe and sure, but it will cost the world greatly. Or, I can risk myself and possibly save the world some pain. It seems to me ... I should take the risk. Will the Ice Witches be better off if I do?"

The Angel nodded. "I don't really know. But if you're asking my advice – and be sure here, it's just my personal advice – yes. Word has leaked out. Narn has discovered a clever thing, mini-Avatars. He can split an Avatar into pieces, and each piece has a very limited capacity. He can make it so that it can listen, and he can hear what it hears. He has mastered five Avatars, but he split one into twelve pieces, and planted them all over the world. He heard the Fire Queens discussing you, Sheena and Bronn. He knows a real Ice Witch still exists. I think it will not take him long to consider looking further north."

Sheena was impressed. "That's ... pretty clever. I never thought of something like that." The Angel acknowledged that Narn was both smart and ambitious.

"Couldn't you just lend the wand to one of the Fire Queens?" Kira asked. "She could defeat Narn, and the problem would be over!"

The Angel shook his head. "No. Three reasons. First, we don't interfere like that, in this world. Not allowed. We have to be asked, she would have to come here. Second, we can only lend the wand to someone with the right motivations. Someone like you, Kira, who will give it back when the job is done. Do you think, any of you, that one of the Fire Queens would give up such a tremendous source of power, when the immediate threat is over? You, Sheena?"

Sheena laughed. "No. The idea is ludicrous. You'd have to take it away again, by force."

The Angel smiled. "Exactly. And we're not allowed to do that. And thirdly ... the Angels aren't Seers in the same way as you, Bronn. It's more a matter of a feeling. We feel ... even if we did that, Narn would be defeated, yes, but only by putting another Sorcerer in his place. There would still be the tremendous, wasteful war that Narn is building up to now, just a different winner. But we feel ... we feel that, with you four, with Kira holding the wand, that somehow that can all be avoided. We don't know how, but the possibility is there."

Bronn stirred. "Oh, now I think I *understand*. I've dreamed, felt that our quest was important, but couldn't quite see why. I think I see, now. Narn could be stopped either way, but our way – a worldwide war could be avoided, with huge loss of life and destruction. We're making it *personal*." And the Angel nodded agreement.

Kira sighed. "I guess we should go, then. Back on the trail. Because, if we fail, well then, it can still be done the other way, after all."

The Angel agreed. "I think that would be wise. No huge rush though, you should let the village get things ready for you, tomorrow will be soon enough. I will walk down with you, I don't need to stay in this cave any more until the Wand is returned, so I will stay in the village. I will enjoy that."

And they walked down. The Angel seemed strange to them. Talkative, nearly human. He spoke a lot to Sheena, and she learned many things. An Angel existed as Avatars only, no physical body. It might have many on one world, or only one. On this world, there was not so much to do, Angels intervened very little. On others, more action might be required, on some, none at all, only observation. He explained that he probably seemed more human than the last Angel guarding the cave because he had been elevated relatively recently.

He said he felt able to give them further information. Besides taking over Fir'Alan'Atrah, Narn was making overtures to the Great Western Nation, and was making progress in his desire to raise an unstoppable army. The next plan would be to overwhelm the

Witches by sheer force of numbers, and use the vast forests of Fir'Alan'Cora to build ships. Discussing these matters and others whiled away the time walking down, which was less than walking up.

Eventually, they came to the silver statue, and Sheena sighed again, once more touching it on the shoulder. "I wish I knew for sure Bakaro didn't suffer" she murmured to herself. The Angel cheerfully reassured her: "Oh, don't worry – when you left him here last time, they got him out. Well, his mind and spirit, anyway. They left his body in there – they could have broken the shield by asking an Archangel, but we decided to leave it intact. We are going to put it into a special place – a sort of museum – where things that show the outstanding capability of human beings are shown and remembered."

"Outstanding? Outstandingly wrong, perhaps" Sheena replied wistfully.

The Angel nodded. "The reasons were not good ones, to be sure. But still ... to do level five magic! The Angels *were* surprised."

"And you say, you freed his mind and spirit? How does that work? What became of him?"

"Well, essentially the Angels asked him if he wanted to become one of them. And rather, much rather than stay in there for eternity, he accepted."

"Oh, my God. He's an Angel now? How wonderful! Where? What has he been doing? Does he have duties on this world?"

"Oh yes ... yes, he has duties on this world. For the last few hundred years, in fact, he's been guarding the cave of Alana's Wand."

Sheena looked at him in puzzlement for a second or two. And then she realized. "You mean ... you? You are Bakaro?" She looked shocked and fearful.

"Yes. Or rather, I was."

"Oh!" Sheena sank to her knees. "Oh, my Bakaro! Forgive me! I was foolish, arrogant, willful, evil. Forgive me, I beg you!"

"Oh, Sheena, get up!" The Angel lifted her to her feet as if she was a feather. "Of course I forgive you! I forgave you the minute you showed you were genuinely sorry for what you had done. And if I hadn't, I would have done so the minute I learned God had. You were stupid, though, to burn your mind like that. But I'm proud of you. Proud! I'm proud of how far you have come. Taken you a while, of course. But you have done well."

Sheena threw her arms around the Angel, and with tears in her eyes thanked him. She wanted to talk more, but he held up a hand. "I'm sorry, Sheena. But our time is past, and also not yet here. I love you, of course, that's the nature of an Angel. And if you make it through your quest and achieve your goals and become an Angel yourself, we can have a very special relationship. But you have other, more immediate goals to focus on."

And Sheena let her elation subside, and shouldered her burden of duty once more. But it was light now. Oh, how much lighter. Forgiven. Forgiven by God, the Ice Witches, Intira, herself (by order), and now Bakaro.

Chapter 13. Flight

For he who fights and runs away
May live to fight another day;
But he who is in battle slain
Can never rise and fight again.

Oliver Goldsmith (1730 - 1774)

The way around Utol'Afir'Astar was easy. There was a well-marked trail, kept clear for the Guardians to travel to the Witch kingdom and trade, or to Fir'Alan'Atrah if they wished. The Guardians went to both places, pretending in each case to have come from the other one to retain their anonymity. The going was easier also because the Guardians had repaired everything, and packed them easy to carry backpacks filled with food and everything else they would need. Kira was managing her two material Avatars easily now, and could even do it with both out of sight for a while. Sheena had one as well, of course, so that made seven packs but only four mouths. Of course, as Kira remarked Shilo wasn't pulling his weight there, for he carried only one pack but ate enough for two. However, he did carry the heaviest pack by far.

Shilo was beginning the first steps of Avatar projection himself. With intense concentration and focus he could, if not disturbed, just manage a wispy form standing in front of him. If he closed his eyes, he could see with it for a few seconds before he lost it. Sheena said he was doing just fine.

She got him to learn juggling, she had asked for a few sets from the Guardians. She explained again that Avatar control was a lot like juggling, and good jugglers were often good projectors, and training in one helped the other. Kira had been learning since an early age, and could manage three balls in almost any configuration, and five in a simple cascade. She was trying to learn how to handle four, which was actually harder. Shilo, clumsy at first, soon got to the point where he could keep three balls in the air in the basic simple pattern. Out of idle curiosity, he asked Sheena to show them what she could do, and they looked in amazement as she handled five, then seven, then all nine at once, throwing them in complex patterns over her head, behind her back, in chains, weaves, waterfalls and double cascades, four in each hand and throwing the last one back and forth alternately.

"How ... how many can you do? How many *Avatars* can you do?" Shilo asked in astonishment. Sheena smiled, and said that Fire Witches were sometimes better in pure numbers, but she didn't want to say, she could only project one at the moment anyway. "As to juggling ... well, when all this is over I'll train up again and try to show you."

Shilo was actually making far better progress in shielding. Unusually, because he hadn't managed a stable Ethereal Avatar yet, he was working on level two shielding – and doing very well. His was now stronger than Kira's – more layers - Sheena said it was because he was a Warrior, and their shields were often naturally good, and also he had been working on shields for a while, whereas he had only just started with Avatars. He was also improving dramatically with the bow, the Guardians had given them two fine strong ones and plenty of arrows. "I tell you what, Shilo" she remarked, "when all this is over, I'll take you back to Warrior's Hold. We'll get your other weapons work and hand-to-hand up to scratch. And then, if you can show a good level two shield, an Avatar or two – and given you're doing level two shielding you should be able to manage two eventually – plus Ice Magic, well, you'll be unique. I reckon they'll hand you your Gold badge on a platter."

And so they made their way along the trail. Winter was over, spring advancing and soon it would be summer. Even at this altitude it was getting warmer and Shilo shuddered to think what it would be like back in the jungle without Ice Witch skills. It would be hot enough at Fir'Caram even with the sea breeze. Bronn told them that on the other end of the world it was well and truly getting colder again. He told them Shira was expecting, which delighted them all. Kara wasn't, but there was plenty of time for that when they got back.

In the evening of that day, Sheena sat looking back the way they had walked. Bronn, looking to find her, walked back and watched her for a minute. She sat, unmoving, looking into the distance. He came over, thinking not to startle her, and then mentally tutted himself. Sneak up on a Warrior? Most likely she had heard him coming minutes ago, and indeed, she stirred, and said without turning around, "Hello, Bronn. Take a seat, if you want. Signs and portents, signs and portents indeed."

Bronn looked back. The sun had set behind the mountains, but was still over the horizon behind them. A stunning crimson sunset glow could be seen over the whole sky. "The sunset?" he hazarded.

"Yes, indeed. Utol'Fir'Ukania, the second volcano in the Great Western Nation is having a small eruption. I felt the earthquake earlier today, and of course the surge in power."

Bronn made an inquiry, and learned that Sheena had travelled with her parents before their fateful assignment in Iceland, on a diplomatic mission. When Sheena was first able to do some small Fire Magic,

Utol'Fir'Ukania was closer than the Witch kingdom volcano, and her mother had taken her there and let her bond to it.

"Yes, an earthquake, an eruption, and just a few minutes ago, a great shooting star. Biggest I've seen for a long while. I feel it, Bronn, I feel it. Our quest is coming to a close. Things ... are going to happen, and soon."

"How do you feel about it?" Bronn asked. "I'm glad, of course. I saw the quest, I put it together, I've had the visions ... but I'll be glad when it's over. Despite the dreams, I miss Kara so very much."

"Yes. Yes, Bronn, I'll be glad when it's all over too, one way or another. This last year has been astonishing. So much attained, so much realized ... forgiveness, where I despaired. Finding Kira and the Ice Witches. Getting to know you, and Shilo, traveling with you all. Great, wonderful privilege. And yet, now that the time is nearing an end, and so many burdens have been lifted ... I'm tired, Bronn. Now, more than ever, I need love in my mind, in my heart. Otherwise, I just can't go on. If we come to the end, and Narn is defeated – or he wins – and I haven't managed it, I just don't know what I'll do after I guide the Ice Witches home. Give up, maybe." She smiled. "Kira, our wonderful Kira, would probably say, I'm feeling the next step coming up. I hope so. I hope so, so very much."

"So many great things have happened, momentous things. World changing events are coming one way or the other. There's been more going on this last year than in the centuries before. And yet ... you know what moved me most, made me happiest, and yet made me realize how much I've missed? A young girl invited me to her birthday party."

440

Bronn, Master Seer and empath, knew what she needed. He sat down next to her, put an arm around her shoulders. She sighed, and leaned her head on his shoulder, and they sat, watching the last of the light fade from a dark red into black. A few minutes later, they walked back to their camp, Sheena guiding their way with light. As they came up to the others, Sheena murmured "Thank you, my friend."

They made their way along the ridges slowly and easily. No point in rushing and tiring themselves out if there was no need. Sheena worked with Kira and Shilo, strengthening their shielding. Shilo's Avatar slowly became a little more opaque, and Kira could do about as much with her third, as long as her two other Avatars were held to Ethereal. It was so hard, she complained.

"One, Kira, I doubt there's been anyone in the world in the last five hundred years that has made a start on her third Avatar while still only fifteen! Two, yes it *is* hard. Three, we're spending most of the day marching! Four, you haven't got anyone who can *show* you how it's done. Don't *worry*! Your fourth will be harder still, but I'll be amazed if you haven't got it together by the time you're twenty-one. Like juggling, the fifth will actually be easier. After that, we'll see."

"Oh Sheena, that might be good enough under ordinary circumstances – but what if we have to face Narn before I'm ready?"

And so, they worked on it as much as they could.

And then, one day, Narn's Avatar found them. They rounded a corner, and there it was. They stopped, dismayed. Eagerly, it walked towards them. Sheena

441

held out a cautioning hand as Shilo moved forward. "Steady, Shilo – it's an Ethereal. No need to worry too much just yet. Either Narn hasn't mastered the art of Switching or his Physical is too far away. It can't hurt to talk, but be careful, don't give too much away."

Narn nodded. He was a reasonably good looking man, in a somewhat gaunt way, the blue eyes were striking in the dark red hair. "Sensible! Why not talk, yes. And to show my good will, I will start. I've had my Witches scouring the trails for you, and every Avatar I can spare, and now you are found. Yes, I can Switch, but as you say not at this distance. My Physical is still nearly a hundred miles away. But I have horses, and a good trail. I can catch you. Why not give in now? I can promise you good treatment. I will not suborn you if you join me willingly."

Bronn scoffed. "Good will? Last time we met, you tried to kill me, and my Warrior companion."

Narn smiled, a genuine smile as far as they could see. "Yes, well. All's fair in love and war, no? I was somewhat irritated; you know how Fire Witches can be. You had just undone a major piece of work, something I had been building for a long time. But you beat me, though I have no clear memory of how you shattered my Avatar, and I hold you no ill will. You did it again, in Carm, and still I hold no grudge. No, I see you have skills and intelligence to be valued! They are all too rare in this world. I am *glad* I didn't kill you."

"But, on the other hand. I was extended on Seer's Island; my Avatar was far, far from my Physical. I could barely manage level one work. I'm much closer, here. I can have a Material Avatar or three here in a few days, and though my Physical will still be distant they will be solid level twos. And if I have to, I can get close enough for level three work. You cannot prevail, I can tell none of you are level three operatives. And even if you were, I'm a five Avatar man. Even the three Fire Queens, with nine Avatars between them could not stand against me."

"Look, I'll even swear under a truth spell if you wish. Seers are always useful. Another level one Fire Witch, a fine young Warrior. And the prize, an Ice Witch! When I rule the world, as Sha'Lin'Tra the Great did, I will let you rule your people. You cannot stand, what do you say?"

Sheena looked at the others, who all shook their heads. She stepped forward, and spoke calmly: "We will not submit. The Angels are not in favor of you ruling the world, and neither are we. It has been Foreseen that we will oppose you, and also that we have a fair chance of winning. But we are fair, if you will surrender to *us*, we will grant you amnesty."

Narn laughed. "Surrender? I think not. I have worked long and hard to get where I am. And Foreseen? Well. Let us speak honestly, at least. What odds have you Seen, Master Seer? Not certainty, I think."

Bronn answered uneasily: "No, not certainty. I think I can say that much without giving anything away. Things are never certain."

Narn turned his attention to Sheena. "The Queens say you think you are Sha'Lin'Tra, once known as The Great. Limited to level one magic, now. It sounds like nonsense to me. But, you either are, or you aren't, I will find out for sure, one way or another. If you are not, you fall under the protection of your group, I will allow you personal freedom, if you surrender. If you are, then you have much to offer. You could rule the world again, or at least a part of it. What do you say?"

Sheena shook her head. "It holds no attraction for me. If you are wise, you will let it go. What possible reason do you have for wanting to rule the world? It's a lot of very hard work for very little reward."

Narn smiled a hard smile. "Let us say, I will be vindicated, and proved. Fire Witches don't treat their men well. A man has to be twice as good to be considered as good as a Witch."

Sheena looked at him in wonderment. "You are a *five Avatar* Witch! You could walk into the capital and claim a rightful position equal to any of the Queens! What more do you want?"

Narn looked aside. "You wouldn't understand. A childhood of deprivation, submission, being told to keep my place. I never knew my father, and my mother died. A relative grudgingly gave me living room, but worked me hard for my daily bread. Never recognized for what I could do. When I managed level one Fire magic and was proud, I was beaten and abused for my presumption. When I reached sixteen, my great-aunt said she had discharged her obligation and I was on the streets. It took me a long time, a long hard time to begin level two, and rather than helping me, I was treated like a toy, condescendingly patted on the head. I and my uncertain Avatars were treated as a curiosity, nothing more – and I was told to keep my place if I was wise."

"I tried to enter the palace, and show myself to the Queens, and was thrown out. They said, go away, smarten myself up, put on some weight, get my hair cut nicely and find myself a real Witch, by which they meant a woman, to look after me. The fund that's supposed to support witches in need was denied to me as a man. When, because of my desperate poverty I stole, they threw me in jail and left me to rot, shattering my Avatars if I dared to send them out of my cell. I sat in there patiently for years, until I got to level three, not telling anyone anything until I was strong enough to escape. The jailers were not kind to me, a man daring to aspire to equality. Well, shallow though my goals may be, I want revenge. I want my place, given to me because none can deny it to me. I want what I consider to be justice."

Sheena barked a short laugh. "I wouldn't understand? I assure you, I understand only too well. I am sorry for your suffering. But now? Now, you could walk down to the city, and they would *have* to take you seriously. Five Avatars? That hasn't been seen for a *very* long time. You could change things. The Queens would recognize you, for sure."

Narn sneered. "Recognize? Certainly. And I could stand against them, if I had to. But what then? Would they let me be a fourth Queen, and we all play Happy Families? Well, you're a Fire Witch yourself. Supposedly a powerful one. Would they? Or would they distrust me, grudgingly grant me my deserved position ... and then quietly have me assassinated?"

Sheena had to concede he had a point. But still, she said, the risk of that was a part of "normal" Fire Witch life. He had the power and intelligence to manage that.

"No. I will take what was never given or offered, by force. They will concede me my place in their final surrender, I will be *prime* Witch. I will subdue them, I will control them with my mind magic. But you ... you have done me no harm. I bear you no grudge. If you are who you say you are, you could have a position beside me."

Sheena shook her head. "I know better these days. The game isn't worth the candle. No, I won't take your offer."

Narn looked at them. "Well, I expected no less. Always, people reject greatness. So be it. I will still win. Have at you. My terms will be less generous when next we meet. Think on that, think on what you have been offered and have thrown away. I was not granted the same courtesy."

Sheena turned to Kira. "Would you like to do the honors?" And Kira pointed and threw a bolt of the peculiar Ice Witch equivalent of fire. The Avatar, Ethereal though it was, shattered and dissipated.

"What do we do now?" Shilo asked. His Warrior nature naturally rose as conflict appeared on the scene; he wanted strategy.

"We run" Sheena said, briefly. "At a fast pace, Kira and I could just make it to the borders of Fir'Alan'Cara in three days, and another three to the capital. If we can make it, we'll be safe, safe for a while at least."

"Kira and you?" Bronn queried.

Sheena nodded. "Yes. I'm sorry, Bronn, but you just can't keep up that pace. And we would worry about you if we didn't leave Shilo with you. You've learned a lot, and you have your Seer's skills, but they aren't suited to survival on the trail. You will have to stay behind, and follow at a slower pace ... and Narn will come hunting. You may have to buy us some time. Together, I think the two of you and your firestaff will be enough of a barrier that Narn won't get past with just his Avatars. He could overwhelm you, but I think Kira is what he has set his sights on. He will take the time to go around you, recognizing that will be quicker. If we fall, he will come back for you, of course."

"But," objected Bronn. "I know you and Shilo could run the whole way there just about without a rest, but Kira can't. She can't go any faster than I can, really!"

Sheena shook her head. "She can. She doesn't know it yet, but it can be done. She has two solid Material Avatars now, and can be strengthened by the Wand. She's an Ice Witch. She can sleep, and have the Avatars carry her. Without the Wand, they could do it for perhaps half an hour, though I and my Avatar could help. But with it ... she can go on for a long, long time. Longer than I can, I think – even I will need one good rest between here and there, but she can sleep on the go. And we have a chance. He can send Ethereals to find us, but he can't switch till he's much closer. Materials can't move as fast, and Fire Witches can't do nearly as much with their Ethereals as Ice Witches. Even I, at the height of my powers, couldn't make an Ethereal cast a truthspell as Kira did to us on Iceland, Bronn. Talking is our limit, and even then you need to be at least a level two. Narn has to find us again, and then get close enough in his Physical. Or, find us with Materials. We have the edge, it can be done."

Shilo looked very uncertain. "I don't want to just let Kira go off. Surely there must be something I can do."

"Yes, indeed, Shilo. You can stay, fight, help Bronn. That is what the quest needs right now. *That is what your test showed you.* You can and will support the quest in the best way for everyone, not in the way that is best for any one person."

Shilo squared his shoulders, and nodded reluctantly.

"Do your best. Buy us some time ... but use your judgment. If and when you can't hold out any longer, if Narn Physical is there, or he's close enough to energize level three Avatars, *get out of the way.* Make a stand, but you won't help us any more by making a *last* stand. I rely on you, Shilo, to see when that time comes."

The four of them divided up their goods. Kira and Sheena would take some food, but little water, and only the most basic of weapons, a small knife each - if their magic couldn't handle something they encountered, a weapon wouldn't be much help. Kira would extract water from plants they encountered on the way, and also the energy replenishing honey from sap that she had learned to transform. It would have to do.

There was still a lot of the day left. Kira and Sheena set off, Kira with two Material Avatars to help carry, and Sheena ranging her Ethereal on ahead. They moved as quickly as Kira could manage. Bronn and Shilo moved more slowly – when Narn and his forces caught up, a distance between the two groups would be a good thing rather than otherwise. They made their way along the trail, evaluating every rise and narrowing as a possible place to make a stand, but nothing seemed suitable. When night came, they rested, but rose early in the morning when the moon came up. Bronn said that he had Seen them making a stand by a bridge.

And indeed, as they walked on and the sun came up, they found Kira had sent an Ethereal Avatar back to them to say that there was a bridge perhaps ten miles in front of them. She explained that she and Sheena were now a good fifteen miles past it, having marched most of the night. Sheena had built a stretcher, and Kira had rested as Sheena, her Avatar and Kira's two

448

had carried it with ease. She said she would dissolve her Avatar and reform it rather than have it run all the way back. Sheena was holding up well, and would keep on going for the whole of this day.

But they did not make it to the bridge, at least not without incident. A group of twelve people came up a side path towards them. Shilo's instincts told him something was up, and he spotted them, and also found the best place to stand. A narrow section with a little rise, and a good tree for shelter. As the group neared, Shilo saw they were ten men, a woman and yet another of Narn's Ethereal Avatars. They waited warily as the group came closer, and Shilo identified them as mercenaries by their garb, from Fir'Alan'Atrah by their size and coloring, which was darker than most Witches but far lighter than the Guardians. Shilo calmly stepped out from behind the tree, and loosed off three arrows in as many seconds, and went back into cover. They hit home – Bronn could hear the thud, and the gasps of the men who were hit. Two fell, and died within a minute with an arrow through the heart, but the third was only mortally wounded, and lay gasping and screaming. One of the others, keeping a wary eye out, stepped forward and put him out of his agony.

Shilo stepped out again and loosed two more arrows, but to no effect. One of the men had just enough time to jump to the left, while the woman leapt in front of another. She was clearly a Witch as the arrow hit her shield and stopped. The shield went down for a second, but she quickly reformed it. The group moved cautiously on, the Witch at the front. When Shilo attempted to step out again, she threw a firebolt and he quickly ducked behind. The bolt hit the tree, and a burst of heat made the bark crackle.

"We're going to have to take the Witch out of action" Shilo told Bronn. "I can't get two arrows off quickly

449

enough, and you're not a good enough shot to risk it ... what would be best would be, if you could use your firestaff. She's only a level one, I'm pretty sure. When you fire, I'll shoot at the same time. Can you do it?"

Bronn nodded, and armed his staff. "I can't guarantee I'll hit her first time, but I can shoot level one bolts quickly enough. But what about her firebolt?"

"Should have no problems with my level two shield in place. On the count of three, then? We step around, wait for her to shoot, then when I say 'go' you return fire. Ready? One ... two ... three!"

They stepped around the tree, from opposite sides. The Witch saw them, and predictably shot her firebolt at the most dangerous looking one, the man with the bow. It flattened into a wall of fire on his shield, and burned out. She looked stunned, Narn had obviously not told her she would be facing a Gifted man. Bronn fired from his staff. At the distance they were, perhaps fifty yards, he missed as he expected. But he corrected, fired again, just clipping her shield, and again, hitting it dead center and it went down. Shilo shot. Did he hesitate? Bronn though perhaps, but there wasn't much in it. The arrow took her high up on her right arm, certainly deliberate. With her standing stock still, Shilo could have put an arrow through either of her eyes at that distance. She screamed, and went down on one knee. She wasn't going to be lifting her right arm for another firebolt with an arrow in it, but she tried her left. Weaker, off balance and her left being her lightning side, it was wide and short. She slumped to the ground, in a faint, which surprised Bronn a bit. It was a disabling wound and no doubt she would be in shock, but Fire Witches were tough.

Some of the remaining men had bows too. Four of them loosed, and Shilo made an instant evaluation

450

that two would miss, and two were dangerous. Bronn ducked behind the tree as arranged, and Shilo put his shield up. The two arrows were stopped, and he dropped his shield. He fired four arrows in a blur, ducked behind the tree and waited. Then, he looked around to see the results.

Two more men were down. Shilo had judged the shots perfectly, the two targets had used small shields to protect themselves. Two fast, low trajectory arrows had been stopped. But the other two, slower, shot with less power and arcing down from above had struck home at exactly the same time. Both men were wounded severely. As the others were distracted, Shilo calmly shot another man dead, who had taken his eyes off the main danger.

That left nearly half the party dead or incapacitated, not counting Narn's Avatar. Being Ethereal there was not much it could do. Narn was clearly still not close enough to Switch it to Material, though it looked like he was trying.

The four remaining men clearly thought they still had the weight of numbers, and continued to advance. Shilo and Bronn together took a couple of speculative shots, but the men were well trained, and used their shields and reflexes to avoid them. And things took a turn for the worse: Narn's Avatar began to flicker, with the appearance they had come to know, having watched Sheena, of a Switch to Material at extreme range.

The men had begun to spread out, thinking to flank the two defenders. But suddenly, the Witch rolled over, awake again, and fired a lightning bolt at close range at Narn. His Avatar, being in a vulnerable state, shattered. She also managed a weak firebolt from her right, but it only had to travel a couple of yards and one of the remaining men fell. She slumped over, out cold again. The remaining three forgot themselves again, and turned to look at her. Bronn calmly fired another level one shot from his staff, and missed again.

That was enough for them. They turned and ran, leaving their dead and their wounded. Leaving Bronn to attend to their surprising ally, Shilo went over to deal with the two wounded men. Both were down, gritting their teeth in pain. Shilo, with Warrior training, saw that they would die eventually with the arrows where they were unless something was done. It looked like the men did too, for they waited in pain, but not in fear. They thought it was all over bar the mercy stroke.

"Bloody Hell!" one of them spat as he walked up. "A Warrior! Narn put us up against a Warrior, and didn't tell us! Curse him to hell!"

The other grimaced in his pain. "Come on, lad, we're done for. No way to get those arrows out where they are, and for us to live. Put us out of our misery."

Shilo knelt down. "You might yet be saved. If you were, what would you do?"

The first drew in breath as a spasm shot through him. With clenched teeth, he said, "We would owe you our lives. Certainly, we'll no longer fight for Narn. Not after that betrayal. Sending us up against a Warrior, without warning! If we can, we'll find the others, and switch sides. Maybe bring a few more. My word on it, Warrior."

Shilo nodded. "Good enough for me. Now, these arrows … there's a trick to them. I've never seen the like, but they are cleverly made. There's a lever that retracts the barb. I'm not saying it isn't going to hurt coming out, mind … so." He pulled an inset lever on the arrow, and then swiftly pulled the arrow out. The mercenary shouted in pain, for the arrow was deep in his shoulder. But it was out, without the ripping and tearing the barb would have caused if it had been possible to get it out at all. He did the same for the second man, who had his arrow high up, near his neck, dangerously close to the carotid artery – he had escaped death by a whisker.

"The arrows were clean, and plated with copper - you should have a good chance of avoiding infection if you clean, dress and bind the wound. Can you walk?"

The two slowly rose to their feet, gasping, with a little hand up from Shilo. "Aye we can walk" said the first. "Or, I can, anyway." The other nodded, though painfully. He let the neck wound bleed, a sound idea to flush the wound out, the flow was not too bad. "Our camp is not too far away. We'll return there; we have herbs and medicines and bandages." Shilo nodded. "Good luck to you, then." And he and Bronn turned to see what they could do for the Fire Witch.

She was still out. Shock, and the stress of firing energy out while in shock – and interference with the metal in her arm - had drained her. Shilo pulled out the lever and extracted the arrow. The wound bled freely, they must have severed a small to medium vein.

Shilo's meager healing ability was not up to doing much about it. He was glad she was still under while they took the arrow out, any tissue healing was way beyond him at the moment. Still, they had wine to wash it, for there was dust and dirt dangerously close, and a healing salve to keep it clean – and not just some hedge concoction either, made by the Guardians it had genuine effectiveness. They hadn't wanted to use it on the mercenaries as, after all, they had been enemies until recently and their supplies were limited. The Witch was a different story, she had genuinely helped them. Shilo put a compression bandage on, judging the tightness just right – Warriors made good field doctors.

They splashed some water on her, shook her a bit, clapped their hands and in general did their best to wake her up. It took a while, but eventually she was groggily awake, and then suddenly nearly fully awake. She lurched up onto one knee, but then fell back again. She winced and looked at her arm, and the arrow on the ground.

She seemed calm. "How bad was it? Will I keep the use of my arm?" She paused. "I suppose, thank you is in order. Thank you."

Shilo reassured her, showing her the retractable barb. "A simple hole. You should heal fully, in time. He gave a small smile. "It may twinge a bit in cold weather, if you ever manage to find some on this continent. And, we have used a powerful healing salve under that bandage, which is clean. With any luck, there will be no infection."

She nodded slowly, and flexed her arm. "It doesn't feel too bad. No doubt it will stiffen up tonight. But still. I thank you again. I seem to owe you my life ... and more than my life."

She looked at them in turn. "Narn used love magic on me, he hypnotized me. I would have done anything for him. But the shock of the arrow hitting me, and the interference from the metal while I was building a firebolt broke the spell. God!" she shuddered, still on both knees, looking down. "I feel violated, dirty on the inside. Eeeeough! Help me up, please."

454

Shilo and Bronn carefully lifted her to her feet. She was unsteady for a while as the blood flowed away from her head, but rallied. She seemed tough.

"A Warrior?" she asked Shilo. "You're a Warrior, for sure. And, though my time under that evil, horrible spell is a bit blurred now, I seem to remember a level two shield?"

Shilo nodded. "I am Shilo by name, a Warrior, yes, though only a trainee by rank. However, I've had a good teacher these last months. And this is Master Seer Bronn. And ... " he debated a second whether to tell her further, but as Narn clearly knew Kira was an Ice Witch, that cat seemed to be out of the bag. "And ... I have some Ice Witch talent, as well."

The Witch looked dubious at that, but Shilo reached out, and said, "Here ... that arm will be beginning to throb a bit now. Keeping it cool will help, and prevent some bruising too." And he exerted a little magic, and she felt the arm become cold. His control was far from perfect and he overdid it a bit, but muscle can take quite a bit of cold before being damaged.

She looked at them with widened eyes. "My name is Illa'San'Dra, Sandra for short. She laughed, a good sound to hear. "I was going to say in my condescending way, you have done well, for men. But you clearly outrank me; I'm only a level one Fire Witch. A strong one, I'm told, but still just level one. May I ask ... Shilo?" Shilo nodded, she had the name right. "Shilo, you could have spitted me through the heart at that range, as you did to those men over there. Why did you spare me? I'm glad, of course, but why?"

Shilo tilted his head to the left, acknowledging what she had said. "The mercenaries were one thing. They take their pay and their chances, they're fighting men.

I saved two, and they held no grudge – acknowledged their debt, in fact. Next time we meet, we'll probably be on the same side, though this time we were enemies. I killed the others without compunction, as they would have killed me, it was our job. But you ... I have been travelling with Witches, and one of them knows about this love magic. It seemed to me to be wrong to kill you for acting under compulsion. I would have done it if it had been necessary, of course ... but it seemed to me a disabling shot was possible. I'm glad it was."

Sandra looked down, and made a "Hmm" sound. Then she looked up again, and said in a matter-of-fact voice, "Well, I'm in your debt, and no mistake. Where are you going? What're you doing? I may be able to help you, I've lived as a herald and courier, on the road, for over five years. I know these hills and trails better than anyone, that's why Narn had me with him."

Bronn told them about their quest, and their hope of Kira and Sheena reaching Fir'Caram ahead of Narn and his forces. When she learned how far they were ahead, she thought intensely for a second or two, scowled and bit her lip. Then, reluctantly, she shook her head. "They'll never make it. Ahead of his forces, perhaps. But ahead of Narn himself? Not a chance. See ... how much magic do you know?" Without waiting for an answer, she continued. "Well, anyway, theory and history say, if you're strong enough, you can fly. It's something to do with level three shielding. None of our Queens are strong enough, the best they can do is to slow themselves if they jump or fall from a height. But Narn ... I've seen him. He can't fly, not quite. But he can glide. Now on this trail, there's a bridge ahead, and after that it winds up quite steeply. But after a while you reach the highest point, and it's all downhill to Fir'Caram. The trail winds a lot, and Narn will be able to cut out a lot of distance by gliding from one loop across the valleys to the next. And, when he's forced onto the trail, he can move at high speed, if he chooses. If it's really important to him, he'll pull in his Avatars and have them carry him."

Bronn and Shilo looked alarmed. Bronn said, "I've Seen us making a stand at a bridge ... perhaps that's what we need to do. If we cut him off there, can we stop him, or at least delay him to give them a chance?"

Sandra scoffed. "If Narn is there, in his Physical, how will you stop him from crossing?"

Shilo suggested, "Perhaps we can destroy the bridge, or burn it down?"

"Hmm" she said again, it seemed to be a habit. "Maybe. It's a very solid bridge. The wood is treated, and won't burn well, if at all. But if we had enough time, maybe something could be done. He could still project Materials over the gap, he's talented. He held two level ones stable over thousands of miles; he could have a few level twos down that trail like an arrow, quick as a thought. Level threes, if they are within a few miles, but perhaps it will buy them enough time. Do you have an axe?"

Neither of them did. A search of the bodies of the mercenaries came up with a small hatchet, suitable for firewood and light enough for easy carrying, which would be barely better than nothing.

They took it, and without further words went on their way. Clearly, their work was not yet done.

Sandra said the bridge was a good three hour's walk away. Based on Narn's ability to nearly Switch his Avatar, she guessed he and his forces were about thirty miles or so behind them. But they had horses, and were all tough, they could do it quickly if they tried.

As they walked along, she moodily lapsed into silence. Shilo tried to draw her out, but did not have much luck. Bronn, knowing more about people and being used to dealing with difficult cases, was more successful. When she would not talk, he told them about their journey and some of the difficulties they had had. Since she had chosen to live a life on the open road, he told her of some of their journeys in other lands. Her interest was raised, in spite of herself, particularly the details of travelling in the cold.

He asked her how the arm was feeling, and she shrugged. "Throbbing, painful. Just useable. I'll live, and I'll keep on walking." Shilo applied another burst of cold, which she said helped.

He drew her out about how she was feeling, what she was going to do next. She scowled. "I'll be looking for my revenge" she said simply. "Have you ... have either of you known real love?"

Bronn replied that he had, that he was in love with a wonderful woman who he had Seen in dreams for years, met, and loved in real life, and to whom he was looking forward to returning.

"Lucky you" Sandra said flatly. "Well, I've known love, too. One happy year, but it ended. Not too badly, it just turned out we wanted different sorts of lives, and we drifted apart, and I left the city and took up this job. But while it lasted, it was a wonderful feeling. And then I knew it again – when Narn forced it on me. Curse him. I feel violated, to the core of my being. To know that it's not real, that it has been *done* to you, manufactured in your mind against your will. I shudder every time I think of it, from the depths of my soul. And I yearn for it, too, because I remember it. It hasn't been properly ended and resolved, like my first. It throbs, like this arrow wound. I hate him for it. And yet, a part of me, a weak part, would have me go to him and beg for him to put me under the spell again. So, I hope to see him dead, so that can be let go."

Bronn asked, "And did he violate you physically was well?"

For the first time, Sandra's face softened. "No. No, he didn't. There was plenty of opportunity, and I asked him to, many times, in my state of utter infatuation. He had other women, unbonded, who hoped to get a hold on him that way – hah! No chance there, he's one of the most single-minded people I've ever met. But apart from the evil of the spell itself, he was considerate enough to us as people – he never overworked us, and he never forced himself on us – though as I say, it wouldn't have been forcing, we would all willingly have done anything for him. When I asked if I could go to his bed, he said no. He said, he had been forced to do many things in his life, and while he needed us, he would not do that. I cried, of course. Now ... now, I suppose I am grateful I've been spared that memory, at least. It would have been a double violation." Her face hardened again. "But I'll still see him dead for what he did."

They marched on, and came to the bridge. Bronn's heart sank. It was a small bridge, spanning no more than a dozen yards across a narrow ravine. But it was no rickety structure of slats held together by ropes that could be cut down with a sword in a moment. It was a solid construction of aged hardwood, bolted together by steel, and the bolts sealed away from the weather deep in the wood by pitch.

"You see what I mean" commented Sandra. "Here, watch this."

She lifted her right arm, somewhat painfully, but managed a creditable firebolt. Fire splashed out against the wood, which sparked a bit where splinters stood out, but was basically unaffected. She concentrated, and tried a thinner, hotter, more localized stream of fire, holding it for nearly a minute. The area she had aimed at glowed red hot and smoldered a bit before going out, but it was clearly not going to burn; it had been treated.

"That's all I can do. I won't be able to do it again for a while, either. Maybe I could burn through it in a couple of weeks, but we don't have that sort of time."

Shilo took their hatchet and made a light swing at a support. It sank a depressingly small distance into the wood. He tried harder, as hard as he thought the handle could take, and it made little difference. He had chipped a tiny fragment out of the stone-hard wood.

He shook his head, too. "A couple of weeks for me, too, assuming the hatchet doesn't get worn out with sharpening, which it would."

Sandra said, "I could burn the pitch out of the bolt holes easily enough, but without the right spanner to undo them it would be pointless."

While they were talking, Kira's Ethereal Avatar came running up. She stopped short, seeing Sandra, but came on. Quick introductions and explanations were made, and Kira nodded and said, "Sheena has had a thought during the night about the bridge, Shilo. The end of the bridge is resting on a shelf of rock. If you can use Ice Magic to cool it, Shilo, and then Bronn uses his firestaff, it might be enough to shatter the rock and drop the bridge."

Shilo said, "Brilliant! *Brilliant!* But …" he wandered over to the edge and looked at the rock a bit dubiously. "There *is* an overhang, otherwise it would be impossible. But still, that's a *lot* of rock. Can you help, Kira?"

Kira shook her head. "Not much. My Ethereal Avatar really can't do any work, other than the tiniest things. Just talking is hard enough. And we're a good fifty miles away, perhaps half as much as the crow flies. It's outside my range for holding together a Material Avatar, or at least one with any respectable power."

Sandra murmured: "As the crow flies … or the Narn glides." It was a good point, and Bronn told Kira what Sandra had said about Narn. She replied, "I've got my Physical to tell Sheena that, and she's impressed. Very worried now, too. I've got to go back and we're going to make double time. Good luck. And, she says, remember: do what you can, but when it's done, get out of the way!" And her Avatar vanished.

The rock was nearly solid, but they poured their water into what cracks there were. Shilo froze it, which would put it under some stress. "That's the easy part" he muttered. Cooling bulk rock was going to be harder. Fortunately, Utol'Fir'Cara was not too far away, Shilo had some contact with it, and that enormous fount of power would help.

He worked for a good ten minutes, under increasing strain. They could feel the area getting colder, even though he was trying to keep the cooling entirely in the rock. Kira could have done much, much more, because Shilo was still inexperienced and learning.

461

"Watch out!" Sandra called. A man came running down the road, towards the bridge. An Avatar, as it turned out. "That's no Ethereal Avatar, that's a Material projected and sent. At this distance, it'll be at level two strength. Whatever you're going to do, do it now!"

"Maybe we can buy a little more time" Bronn said calmly.

The Avatar came running over the bridge, a determined look on its face. Bronn had his staff at level two, and fired nearly point blank. It wasn't quite enough, the shield went down, but Bronn quickly fired again, and it was gone.

"Whew!" he said. "I wasn't sure level two would be enough, but I couldn't risk level three. We'll need everything I've got for the ledge."

"Will you have enough?" frowned Shilo. "I thought those things were only good for a few shots." Expertise in all sorts of weaponry was, of course a basic course for all Warriors. Bronn explained that the staff had been modified at Nun's Hold with a garnet extension, and fully charged by the Guardians. It would take some time for the charge to trickle out of the garnet into the rubies, but he should have one good level three bolt left.

While they were waiting, Shilo rested, they went through their packs and lightened them, and then he did what he could for further cooling. It wasn't much more, his capacity and speed of recovery were still building. Finally, he said, "I'm done."

Bronn had been walking around, looking for the best vantage point. He wanted to hit the overhang from below if possible. There were several good views, but all a long way away, and his past history with the staff suggested close by was better given the difficulty of aiming. Finally, they decided the best bet was near enough, but someone would have to hang over the cliff. Shilo volunteered. He sat down, and got Bronn and Sandra to sit on his legs. Holding the staff, he leaned over backwards, his knees pivoting at the edge of the cliff. Upside down, he calmly pointed the staff in the right direction and pressed the firing button.

The brilliant level three firebolt shot out, hitting the overhang exactly where he had intended. Warrior aiming. There was a terrific explosion and a backwash of heat. But the cliff did not go. Shilo sat up, his abdominal muscles lifting him back up with ease, and rolled himself back onto land.

"What do we do now?" he asked.

Bronn scratched his chin. "Well … we do what we can. There may be a bit of a charge left in the garnet. We wait a minute, then give it everything that's left from the top. And if that doesn't work, we did what we could."

They walked over as close as they could, and waited for whatever charge was left to trickle into the rubies. While they waited, there was a "crack!" and a large bit of cliff broke off. "That's good" Shilo remarked.

They didn't know how long to wait. But that was forced upon them. Sandra and Shilo felt the wash of magic, and another Avatar was coming up the trail. "May as well go now" Bronn said evenly. "On the count of three? One … two … three!"

He fired, and a weaker bolt shot out. A little stronger than a level two, but not by much. Sandra threw her firebolt, and then for good measure a shot of lightning.

For a half second they thought it was not enough, but then the overstressed stone finally gave way, and it and the bridge fell with a crash, falling, falling into the ravine, lost in the depths.

They stood, as the Avatar came up to the edge and looked down, its chest heaving in psychic reaction. It looked up at them, its eyes narrowed, and it fired its own firebolt. Shilo had stepped forward, and it shattered on his shield.

It looked across at them, and calmed, and finally managed a grin, more of a grimace. "Well played. You have delayed me again. But, I'll get across somehow, or, there is another trail, lower down. Harder, longer, but I *will* get there. I value your skills, and I shouldn't have fired that firebolt. The curse of a temper. But, fair warning, if you're still in the way, if you stand against me when my Physical comes to this point with all my Avatars I'll conclude that you are stupid after all, and I'll make sure you *don't* get in my way again." And it dissipated, dissolved and recalled.

Bronn and Shilo picked up their packs, and made to set off up the trail. They looked inquiringly at Sandra, and she shrugged, and followed them. "Will you come with us? We could look after that arm" Shilo asked. She shrugged again. "Hmmm. Might as well" she said. "I'd like to stay and wait for Narn, but it would be throwing my life away, or worse, risking him taking me again. I'll bide my time … and there's no other trail for a bit anyway. I suppose I might as well try to get back to Fir'Caram and do what I can there. I have useful knowledge."

Bronn agreed. "Yes, I can't see much more we can do here. Ideally, I'd like to keep out of Narn's way and get to the capital to meet up with Sheena and Kira if we

464

can. Or, catch up to them and help. But there's no way of doing that."

Sandra looked at him. "There's a way to keep out of Narn's path, and it might get you there quicker. There are many small tracks through the hills and the forests, if you know where they are. As far as catching up, it's risky. The way is much shorter, but it's not always passable with rivers overflowing, trees falling and the like. Narn wouldn't take them, he wouldn't take the risk of getting lost or delayed – once across that ravine and up to the top of the hill, his way is clear."

They walked on for an hour or so before Sandra showed them the first little track off down the side of the hill. Small and not easy to see, it was more like the idea of a track than a real one. But she assured them it was the way to go. They descended fairly fast, with a good view down the slopes – the forest was far lighter here than the jungle further west. They could see the river that went down to the city, Fir'Acual'Cara, curving in the distance, quite a fast running body of water. Shilo asked, "Is there any way we could get onto that? A village where we could buy or steal a canoe?"

Sandra stopped, frankly appalled. "Travel on *that*? Are you out of your *mind*?"

Shilo shrugged. "Why not? We've done it before. Look, from this height you can even see canoes on it, I can see two from here."

"Yes, but they're Ungifted villagers, they're raised to it! I'm a Fire Witch! I don't even know how to swim! A ship's bad enough, but a tiny bark shell on *that*? Water, fast running, crocodiles, God knows what! Even Narn wouldn't do it. He wouldn't ask *me* to do it!"

465

"Would you have done it if he *did* ask, while you were in that state of artificial love?"

"Well, yes. Probably. I suppose so."

"So, can you do it while you hate him? Remember, both of us *can* swim. We've been on a river many times, we'll get you out if it's humanly possible, probably with no more issues than if you'd decided to have a cold bath. With that, we've got a chance to catch up and maybe help somehow. Otherwise, with Kira and Sheena going flat out and with three Avatars to help, and Narn gliding all over the place, we haven't a hope."

As they spoke, Sandra looked up, feeling another Witch nearby, and sure enough they saw a shadow sailing above.

"I just don't know if I can do it. I'm sorry, the very thought terrifies me."

"Fair enough" Shilo said. "You've helped us far more than we could possibly have expected already. When we get to a village, help us get a canoe and we two will go on. You follow on foot, or go wherever you want of course."

"Hmm" was all she said.

They followed the trail for several hours, eventually coming to a large village. The people who lived there were more than happy to sell them a canoe; Bronn still had a few pieces of gold in his backpack. They discarded most of their food for fresh, and got drinking water – without Kira they couldn't use the river water, Shilo's skills were nowhere near advanced enough to do transformation work. Sandra, dithering in mild panic, finally got to the point where she screwed up

466

her courage enough to agree to going along. Her concerns were a little eased when Bronn thoughtfully asked for and got two sets of flotation bladders used to help young children who couldn't swim.

It wasn't a great vessel. It leaned a little to one side, which they offset with seating and careful positioning of their by now meager packs. It didn't smell good at all, and as they found out when they swung out into the current with Sandra gripping the sides of the canoe almost hard enough to splinter it, it tended to leak. Baling every hour would be a necessity.

They put Sandra in the front, tied around with the flotation bladders, so Shilo could sit in the middle – he would be the one paddling most of the time – with Bronn at the back, steering. They figured Sandra would be anxiously alert every second of the trip and more likely so spot any trouble coming up. And so she was. To have something to do, she nervously fed energy into Bronn's firestaff, one never knew.

They drifted downstream. The water was flowing rapidly, Shilo estimated a fast run, say fifteen miles an hour. Of course there were winds and bends, but they were there on the ridge and also so some extent the trail, which paralleled the river some way to the north-west. He thought, based on his best estimate, that Sheena and Kira might be going two-thirds as fast, but they had a good head-start. Based on Sandra's sketch map of the trails and where they thought Narn could glide across, some careful deductive reasoning, a half remembered Vision from Bronn and a couple of wild guesses, Shilo estimated they should travel downstream a day and a half, resting at night, and then they might be near enough to be of some use. He said that it was his duty to try to do something, but Bronn and Sandra should keep out of it. Bronn agreed he would keep well clear – his firestaff now almost completely discharged, he would more likely be in the way. Sandra said she would make her own decision, thanks very much.

There were two sets of rapids, and it took the three of them, Sandra's Avatar and all of Shilo's great strength and endurance to portage the canoe around them. For the second one, they had to leave everything behind and carry the canoe only, and counted themselves lucky not to have had any serious accident on the steep path around it. They lost hours doing it, and more when Shilo went back to pick up the rest of their gear. Despite the noise, Bronn and Sandra were dozing when he got back, and they drifted downstream just far enough to be away from the noise and find a landing spot. Sandra was literally too tired to be afraid.

They made a very basic camp on a dry patch of sand - the rain had kept off. Sandra baked the top few inches with fire to kill off any biting insects that might be living in it, and Shilo cooled it again, draining the heat into the river. They changed the dressing on Sandra's arm. There were a few small local spots of redness, but by and large the Guardian's salve had done a miraculous job. Shilo then kept watch with his shield over them. Three quarters of the way through the night, he woke Bronn to take over; he needed some sleep to be at his best the next day.

The following morning started off easy. The river continued on its relatively placid way. But almost before they knew it, it cut through a more rocky area and the flow was compressed between cliffs. The canoe raced on, now going faster than a man could run. They were lucky, sometimes when that happens the water can become 'white' and choppy, navigable only by experienced people in sound crafts. However, it didn't, not quite. They came out the other end after several tense hours, Sandra white and shaking with reaction. Shilo had done his best to reassure her: the villagers had told them the river never became so rough as to be a problem (except for the rapids), and if there had been any real danger, one would expect Bronn would have Seen it.

Nonetheless, she turned a pleading look at the two men and asked if they could go ashore. She was wrung out. Shilo said he thought that would be a good idea, and as well, with the faster flow they were about where he thought they should get out anyway. "Also" he added, "that sounds like another set of rapids in the distance to me." And there was indeed an ominous low sound of thunder in the far distance.

They kept to the left bank – the villagers had said there was always a landing spot on either side, but the left hand ones were better, and saw it as they rounded a bend. But Sandra called out, "Ware snags!"

They were only a few dozen yards from shore, and the water was moving more slowly in the lee of the bend, but they were too close. Shilo cursed and tried to back-paddle, but it was no use. The canoe hit a submerged tree trunk, throwing them all off balance – Bronn into the bottom of the canoe, Sandra nearly off the front, and only Shilo staying half-upright. The current slowly swung the boat about till the keel was parallel to the tree, and then unceremoniously tipped them over into the water.

Much was lost, although the water was barely chest deep. Bronn only managed to hold on to his firestaff. Shilo kept a hold of his sword and bow, and grabbed a couple of water-bags. But Sandra managed nothing. Although she would have been fine if she had tried to stand up, or even just float and let the swim bladders support her, she panicked. She thrashed her arms and

469

legs screaming wildly, sucked in a mouthful of water, and in her extremity fired both a firebolt and lightning. The firebolt went off into the sky, luckily, but lightning and water don't mix. Both Bronn and Shilo felt the jolt uncomfortably, but the effect on Sandra was much greater as it was right next to her – she was out cold, floating face down. Shilo reeled her in quickly, lifted her, and despite his other burdens and the oozy bottom of the river walked out with quite a bit less trouble than Bronn.

Time was of the essence. He turned her over his knees to get as much water out as possible, over onto her back, and breathed life back into her lungs. Fortunately she had not inhaled enough water to constrict her throat or do any damage. She soon coughed her way back into the world, wet, muddy, crying and unhappy. Bronn did the comforting, he was much better at it. Shilo went back into the water and tried some salvage. The canoe was gone. He found one small pack snagged on a branch. It contained food, much of which was ruined by the water, fire starting equipment (now totally sodden and probably no use; still, they had Sandra and she could light anything that would burn once she recovered), spare bowstrings sealed in wax paper. The bowstrings were useful, the one on the bow had got well and truly wet and was no more use. The bow itself might warp in a few days, but could possibly be saved.

Shilo gathered wood, while Bronn fetched water in one of the water-bags. He and Shilo had rinsed off close to shore, but Sandra wasn't going anywhere near the river just yet. She did thank Bronn for the water, and slowly pulled herself together. Soon, she was able to organize an Avatar to help with the wood, and light the fire. She showed her toughness by gritting her teeth and walking to the river. She stood there for nearly a minute, and then walked in up to her knees, and took off her outer clothes and rinsed the mud off, then modestly put them back on and removed her undergarments and did the same.

Shilo surprised her and Bronn by taking them, holding them up and running his hand along them. Water ran out in streams, and he handed them back to her perfectly dry and slightly warm. She pursued her lips, and said, "That's a useful skill!" He told Bronn that Kira had taught him, it was a first step to getting water out of plants, and much easier. She stepped aside, put them on, and removed the outer garments and he did the same to them, and then to their clothing in turn, and finally the boots. He made a creditable effort towards the process of keeping the leather soft and did make a difference, but could not manage the butter soft feel Kira could. Still, it was a remarkable performance given how new he was to Ice Magic.

They sat and warmed themselves by the fire, Sandra giving the odd shiver as she thought about her experiences. They ate what food was salvageable but would not last, which left very little indeed. Not enough for another meal, that was for sure. Finally, Sandra shuddered, and said, "God in heaven. Never again. You will never get me to set foot in one of those deathtraps as long as I live."

Shilo nodded and said he understood. He apologized that she had had such a bad experience. Sandra was actually quite gracious about it, and said she knew it had been necessary, and also that Shilo had saved her life. "I suppose I shouldn't just run away" she muttered, "but it's hard."

Shilo nodded. "I know what it is to fear" he said. "It's hard, hard indeed when it's something basic, like water to a Fire Witch."

"You?" she asked, amazedly. "You, afraid? I've not seen a moment's hesitation in you about anything! Afraid of what?"

"Insects" he replied. "Spiders, mostly. And yes, I'm over it now."

"Not a problem for me, of course" Sandra replied. "I don't like them, but I just burn them up if I need to. How did you get over the fear? What did you do?"

"I was lucky enough to acquire the skills I needed to handle it. It was when I learned Ice magic. I freeze them."

Sandra nodded. "I can see how that would work. But what can I do about water? There's always so much of it!"

Shilo shrugged. "Learn to swim. That would be the easiest."

"Learn to swim?" Sandra scoffed. "A Fire Witch, swimming?"

"I know of at least one other who can, very well." Shilo replied. "And a Fire Witch is a person first, and anyone can learn to swim if they put their minds to it. It's easy to say 'I'll never go near the water again', but you never know."

"Hmm. Perhaps you're right" Sandra mused.

And then both she and Shilo gave a sudden start and looked up. Even Bronn felt something. "What's *that*?" Shilo asked, disturbed.

"Someone's throwing fire energy about. A lot of energy. A *lot*! And not very far away. That has to be Narn, it's even more powerful than what I felt the one time I saw

472

a Queen in action. Wow. That's big, *big* time stuff. I ... I fear for your friends."

Bronn stirred. "Can you lead us there?"

Sandra nodded. "With that energy thundering about out there, I could lead you to it a hundred miles away. Whether or not it's safe to do so is another matter."

"Can we at least get closer?"

"Oh, sure, if *that* keeps on going we can get as close as we like as long as we don't get seen. He probably wouldn't even notice us if I threw *my* firebolt."

And so they set off through the break in the jungle next to the landing point, and into the forest.

Two days before, Kira and Sheena were on the trail, running. Hardened by long months of walking and climbing, and not carrying a pack, Kira did very well. She found her pace and held it, for five, then ten miles, rested and then went on at a slower pace. Sheena kept up easily, of course, despite carrying the pack. They stopped every now and then at a likely looking tree and Kira extracted water, and twice the sugar-sap. And then they walked for a good long time, stretched and jogged a little more.

Finally they rested and ate something. Despite her good efforts, or rather because of them, Kira was footsore and aching. Sheena cut two poles and built a stretcher with cloth brought for the purpose - one of their blankets from the guardians which had sewn loops for that use, and other purposes such as making a shelter. They ate, drank, and Sheena gave Kira a good massage; she would have to walk again the next day. She watched while Kira fell asleep, into a deep sleep of great tiredness, and then slowly, gently she and the three Avatars picked the stretcher up. It was asking too much for them to run through the night but they managed a steady smooth walk, with Sheena and her Avatar at the front projecting a light. It worked surprisingly well, Kira did stir occasionally but managed to stay asleep. Probably the Wand helped, certainly she had no trouble keeping her Avatars going. They walked through the night, Sheena resting occasionally.

Early in the morning, Sheena reckoned they had covered forty miles or more and were at the highest point of the trail. She asked Kira to send an Ethereal Avatar back to get status from the men and tell them about the bridge. Kira was able to run her Avatar along at nearly fifty miles an hour, and so it was soon back to Bronn and Shilo.

And they went on. Kira jogged when she could, and was carried when she could no more. They couldn't have done it without the Wand, even Avatars have their limits, based on what energy their Physical can muster. Sheena was a tower of strength, moving fast herself and often carrying half Kira's weight between herself and her Avatar. After a few hours, Sheena got Kira to send her Avatar back again, with her idea about the bridge. They learned the unwelcome news that Narn could physically catch up with them with gliding, and Sheena commented that he was surely the most talented Fire Witch of the age. But she was worried, frightened even. She told Kira to dissolve her Avatar, take the time to reform it and then they must be on their way

And they ran. They went all day, with occasional stops for water, and huge sickening swallows of the sugary sap Kira could conjure out of the right trees and plants, and ate unstintingly from the food they carried for energy and to lighten their load. Fortunately, they were often out of the sun and it was still cool at their altitude. They went on through the night, but finally both Kira and Sheena reached their limits. They had to stop, if only for a few hours. Sheena could have kept on going for another day or so if it was just her, but the effort to carry their pack and support Kira as well eventually took a toll on even her body. They stopped, and slept, exhausted, for three and a half hours till the morning.

When the sun woke them, Sheena forced them up. They ate sparingly, drank a lot, performed a basic toiletry and went on. Kira's muscles were screaming at her, and Sheena got the three Avatars to carry her on the stretcher while she worked her small miracle of massage and what healing she could do. Eventually Kira could rise and walk, and so they went along for hour after hour.

But even these heroic efforts came to nothing. While still a good fifty miles from the patrolled borders of the city-state of Fir'Caram, two of Narn's Ethereal Avatars came running along the trail and found the two women. Quick as a flash Narn Switched them to Material, and they ran on, more slowly. There was nothing else to do; Kira threw up a shield. A mighty, strong shield, strengthened by the Wand, multi-layered, but still a level two shield, and Kira knew it. Narn's Avatars, themselves only level two with Narn physically still too distant, knew it too. One of them threw a firebolt, which fractured a layer. Kira rebuilt it, but just barely before the next firebolt. She could only keep that up for a limited time, and anyway once Narn's Physical was close enough to use Avatars in level three it would last minutes only, if that long.

"What do we do? What *can* we do?" Kira asked in dismay. They could walk the sphere of the shield along, but at a pitiful pace. It wasn't worth the effort.

"I don't know. Nothing. Nothing but wait." Sheena sank to the ground, tears flowing. "Oh Kira, I have failed you. Failed! I should have told you to stay at the Guardian's village! I should have run on, last night! Oh, God! What will Narn do to us? What will he do to *you?*"

Kira moved closer, and wrapped her arms around Sheena. "You haven't failed!" she said urgently. "You've done everything you could! You have been amazing. *Amazing!* You've taught me so much, taken me so far. I've been places, I've seen things I could never have imagined! We gave it our best shot. And don't worry about me. Narn wants me, to rule my people. Well, one day he will die, and I will be free again. But you! What can we do for you? I *fear* for you. Should I dissolve the shield? Maybe I can hold off his Avatars, and you can escape into the forest!"

Sheena looked at Kira. She knew that would never work, a last ditch prayer on half a wing if there ever was one. But she looked at her in awe, scarcely conscious of the blows on the shield, stripping away layer after layer, and increasing in intensity. What a girl *What* a girl! Fifteen, in a strange place, with an uncertain future of possible death or enslavement only minutes away, and her thoughts turned to comforting her companion, to what she could do for *her!*

She felt the tension mounting. Trapped, no place to turn. Her mind felt full, to bursting. Make a stand? No chance, a level one and a level two against a level three, with five Avatars! What. *What?* She felt the desperate desire, the combination of her oath and the

476

emotional need to keep Kira safe tearing at her. She groaned in agonized desperation.

It was too much. Something had to give, she was under too much tension, filled to bursting with emotion and pulled harshly. And what gave was the weakest point, the scar across her mind. Someone watching with the visual overview the Gifts gave would have seen it stretched taut, and then suddenly rip like a piece of silk pulled too far. And what had been building up beneath it, across centuries of patient effort and growth flowed up into the space that was now there. It hurt. It was a joyous agony and ecstasy as emotions and feelings flowed across a place that had been quiet for so long.

Sheena cried out in extremis, and Kira looked at her greatly worried. The barrage on the shield continued, but Sheena did not notice at all. She looked at Kira with her mouth half open. Finally, Sheena said, wonderingly, "I … I love!" Her eyes opened wide, staring, and her hands shot up to clasp her face. In a voice full of shock and astonishment, she cried, "I *love*!" And then her arms fell lifeless by her side, and she said again, in a quiet voice full of aching, joyous surrender, "*I love* …." Kira was brought to tears herself by the intensity in the words.

The shield was nearly down; Narn had finally physically caught up to them and was energizing his Avatars to level three. But deep in Sheena's mind, the old and mighty limiting spell, its parameters met, quietly dissolved away and was no more. And her power and energy burst free, not into the old channels based on selfishness and hate that had been unused for so long, but into the new ones that had been being built so slowly over the centuries. They were untried, but they were strong.

477

And Sheena drew a shuddering breath, and said, "I love *you*, Kira. I love you as if you were my own daughter. I love you. I *love* you."

And she rose smoothly to her feet, and her aura burst forth from her head, a glorious crown towering in gold and purple and the red of righteous anger, trailing off down her shoulders and back like wings.

And she said in a clear, ringing voice: "And no harm shall come to you so long as I live and stand." And there was fire in her right hand, and lightning in her left, and she smote the Avatars through the nearly ruined screen, brighter and fuller furies than anything Kira had ever seen. They went through the Avatars' shields as if they were not there, and shattered them into a million tiny fragments.

Narn sank to his knees, the pain of close-by Avatar destruction overwhelming him. But he managed to project his other three, and incredibly, one more, and waveringly he slowly re-materialized his fifth. The three sped away, down the hill. He laughed, no mean feat given the terrifying apparition of Sheena enraged, with a towering aura shining brightly in front of him, and cried: "Too little, too late! You have power, but not enough! You have too many friends nearby, and I have five Avatars! Surrender and I will spare them. You *cannot* protect them all! *I am Narn the sorcerer!*"

He threw an intense firebolt, which hit her level four shield. No effect, no effect at all. The shield didn't go down, the bolt was not even deflected, it was quietly absorbed.

Avatars flashed from Sheena too quick to see. Seven flew downhill far faster than Narn's. Another five flew towards Narn and his two, crackling with menace. Sheena said, in a quiet voice, "And I am *Sha'Lin'Tra.*"

There were surges of power, nearby and down the hill, as the Avatars battled. A brief, one-sided battle that lasted no more than a second, and left Narn flat on his face with reaction after the destruction of all five Avatars, close up. But incredibly, he rose again, to his elbows. Kira couldn't believe his resilience; having had her two shattered by the fire Queen on the ship, it had taken her long minutes to recover.

Narn looked at her, nearly defenseless, his mouth open. "Wait! Wait!" He cried, for Sheena had raised her arm again. "Twelve? *Twelve Avatars?*" he cried in disbelief.

"Yes. Well, I'm out of *practice*" Sheena replied in a voice full of menace. "You threaten my friends, those who I love." Some of the anger left her voice, and her arm dropped, and she said, wonderingly, "those ... those who I love ..." And her voice firmed again, and she said, "It shall not be." And she raised her arm again.

"Wait! *Wait!*" Narn called again, barely rising to his knees. He raised his arms above his head, and said, "I surrender!"

Sheena looked at him. "*Surrender?* You? How can we trust *you?*"

Narn appeared at ease, now that the immediate moment was past. Kira had to admire him. He shrugged. "Test me. Ask me under truth spell. I am a quick thinker. You *must* be Sha'Lin'Tra, the Great. Even if you're not, it doesn't matter, close enough. *Twelve Avatars!* You must be using level four magic. Even if I had conquered Fire Hold and had the three Queens and all the Nobles on my side, we could do nothing. *Nothing!* I'm not stupid, I can see the obvious.

If you want to rule the world in my place, I couldn't possibly stop you."

Sheena shook her head. "I've been there and done that. As I said, it's a thankless task with little real reward and simply not worth it in the end."

Narn continued: "I wanted to try it, but as you oppose me there's no point. Me, a level three Witch against a level four? Five Avatars against twelve? I don't even know what you can really *do*, let alone how to fight it. And if you don't want to rule, you a Fire Witch yourself as you say, it must be so – it must be not worthwhile, and I will not aspire to it any longer."

Sheena looked uncertain. It was too easy, in some ways. "You will have to make amends. You have done much harm."

Narn shrugged again. "I will do whatever you ask. Whatever you say. Test me."

Sheena cast a strong truth spell, and quickly verified the simple fact. Narn had surrendered without qualification.

She said to him, slowly, "I will have to place you under restraint. If you don't resist, I can work a spell on you to limit you to level one magic. And attach a tracer spell, so I will know wherever you go. I'll swear to take them both off before we make a final decision on what to do with you."

Narn shrugged again, and Sheena entered his mind and bound him with the oh-so-familiar limiting spell, and then powered down her aura. It was over.

Kira walked over, and threw her arms around her. She hugged Sheena fiercely, and kissed her on both cheeks, crying with happiness. "Oh, Sheena! You were *magnificent!* I knew it! I knew you could do it! Oh, I love you, I love you too!"

A group came up a side trail, Bronn, Shilo and Sandra, wonderingly led by a procession of Avatars. Sheena merged a good number of them, the place was frankly getting a little crowded. She rushed over and embraced Bronn, kissing his somewhat dirty three-day-growth face. "Oh, Bronn! I love you!" and Bronn's face lit up with a smile, because he knew what her saying that meant. She had met her final test and passed it. She turned, and ran over to Shilo and hugged him too, saying "Shilo, my student, I'm so proud of you! And I love you too!"

And she walked over to Sandra, held out her hand and said, "Sister Fire Witch, Illa'San'Dra, welcome. I've heard how much you helped my friends ... oh, what the heck, I love you too!" and she embraced the surprised Witch too. She laughed. "Oh, I'm going to have to calm down sooner or later, but today, I'm going to love anyone who gives me half an excuse!"

The Avatars had told Bronn, Shilo and Sandra what had happened as they led them up the trail, and Bronn and Shilo laughed out of sheer joy for their friend. Sandra managed a half smile, though she was clearly in awe of Sheena, whose aura was only now subsiding, and it also soured a little when she looked at Narn.

Finally, Sheena looked around, and said, "Well, I suppose we'd better start making our way down to Fir'Caram. We've little to no food or water, but Kira can provide water and I can hunt easily enough."

Narn coughed, and said, "If you don't mind a suggestion from me, some of my men are following not far behind. And behind them is a group travelling more slowly who have plenty of food. They are at your service, of course."

And so, they decided to wait. After the initial exhilaration of Sheena's success, and the sudden abrupt end of their quest, it felt incredibly strange to be just hanging about, waiting. They moved under the shade of some trees, and Kira got water for them. They walked about, talking in groups. Bronn was anxious to get to sleep and tell Kara that he was safe, and it was over, but he knew there was no chance of his falling asleep right now. Still, he tried a trance, with no success.

Sheena and Kira healed the rest of Sandra's arrow wound. Kira was no better as a healer, but far more could be done now given the bond between them, and Sheena's vast capacity now that her limitations had been removed. Kira said she thought that with a talented Ice Witch healer working with Sheena, they could just about heal anything.

Sheena had a bit of a talk with Narn. She was fascinated by his quick recovery after his Avatars had been shattered; she said that was remarkable in itself. Since she had free access, she looked over his mind making an assay, and said it was most unusual. Perhaps as unusual as her own, though nowhere near as powerful. She told him he must release the Witches he had under his love spell. Knowing far more about it, she showed him how he could pass the bonds over to her. She would do what she could to release them without making another dozen mortal enemies for him.

He in turn was fascinated in a professional way about her abilities, as was Kira and also Shilo. He had picked up her saying she was out of practice and could only manage twelve Avatars. He and Kira were awed when she said that she expected to re-train fairly quickly up to her old level: fourteen Material and three Ethereal. He shook his head when she demonstrated some level four work. "And I thought I was the premier Fire Witch in the world, with my five Avatars. Compared to you, I've got nothing."

Sheena shook her head. "It's all a matter of degree. You have far more control over your actions and feelings, which is a good thing – a very good thing for one with power. For you to make amends will probably be much easier. I'm not competent to judge here, I'll be asking advice from the Angels when we return the Wand, but I think they will advise me to make much the same requirement of you: to go out into the world until you truly believe that, if not what you did, at least the way you went about it was wrong. To learn compassion for others, and how to forgive those who have done you wrong, to make amends for what you have done. It would be easy to execute you and have done, but ability such as yours is all too rare. And I'll be the last to say you should not have your chance."

She told him the story of her own rise and fall, and final rise again. He shook his head wonderingly again, and walked off slowly to think.

Bronn was just glad it was all over. Shilo was too, but was puzzled. He couldn't understand Sheena's ready acceptance of Narn's surrender, and why immediate retribution was not called for. Swift justice. Sheena explained.

"You see, Narn has actually done nothing that's unforgiveable, or even against the laws and ways of Fire Witches. Yes, he wanted to rule, but if we punished every Fire Witch for that, there'd be none left. Yes, he used his powers harshly and with little regard for others, but he's a Queen level Witch. They all do that, it's a way of life. The other Queens opposed him, of course – but again, that's normal. Because he threatened them personally, not as a matter of principle."

"No Queen since my time has thought of uniting Fireland. But it's more a matter of natural caution than lack of desire or will. I left notes, guidelines when I retired, and hopefully they are still read. Fireland is huge. It takes vast effort to conquer it, and vast effort to keep it conquered. There are a limited – very limited – number of Witches with real power, and having them all over the continent would leave Fir'Caram exposed. Certainly, any Queen left there would naturally take over and consolidate her position, disadvantaging those away conquering. They don't try to do it, out of natural caution and instinct."

"Taking over Fir'Alan'Atrah is against the treaties. But he didn't kill the rulers, he used mind magic and just moved in. He'll use it again and move out, and I'm sure they will be more than happy to get their country back. They could demand justice from the Queens, I suppose, but there's no law against using mind magic. It's too new a rediscovery. Shi'Mal'Tara was going to use it on us, after all! When he leaves, I'm sure one of the conditions he will ask for when he hands power back is a pardon. That's what I would do."

"He's interfered in other countries as well, of course, and that's against treaties too. But not with any success. Very little real harm done, and I suspect the Seers and the Nuns will just let it go, glad to see the end of it. The Warriors wouldn't, but he never got around to doing anything there."

Bronn understood, and Shilo haltingly so. Narn's ambitions and the opposition he had faced from the Seers and the Nuns and the Warriors were more a matter of policy than an absolute. He had been stopped before war could be waged, a major war which would have been unforgiveable. In a way, Bronn was the initiator and the group were the prosecutors of opposition, and it fell to them to judge and punish. And an outstanding level of Gifted ability should not be lost to the world if it could be turned around.

Finally able to do so, while they were waiting Sheena showed Kira three-Avatar work and techniques, and level three work. With her understanding of Ice Magic, one could see the light dawning on Kira's face as so many things became clear, better explained than the Queen Shi'Mal'Tara could, with only knowledge of Fire Magic.

They had not noticed Sandra walking towards Narn purposefully, and talking to him. They had bound her not to try to kill him, and Narn was not able to run away, so they were not really on watch. They didn't see her subtly lead him away into the shade of a tree, but no-one could have missed the cry of agony and loss he screamed for a long breath, rousing everyone.

Kira and Sheena rushed over, Sheena's aura flaming anew. Sandra gaped at it in astonishment, but quickly recovered and gazed down with considerable pleasure at the man lying on the ground. "Good!" she said with satisfaction. "Now you know what it feels like. And serve you right, too."

"What did you do to him?" Sheena asked angrily.

"No more than he did to me" Sandra replied with a grim smile on her face. "Since you so helpfully limited him to level one, I was able to put him under the same love spell he used on me. I know it's level two work, but having had it done to me I found it easy. And then,

I released him from it, so he can know the feeling of violation. I had the right."

"Perhaps, but you take too much joy in it" Sheena said slowly, letting her aura dissipate. "That is not a thing to be proud of."

Sandra shrugged. "Maybe. I certainly wouldn't do it to anyone else. But to him ... yes, I enjoyed it." And she turned to walk away.

Narn slowly rose, and then to his feet. "Again!" he pleaded. "Please, again! Make me love you once more!"

Sandra turned and gloated. "Yes! You know how *that* feels, too? Good! Suffer, you bastard. I am glad! *Glad!*" But as she looked at him, a troubled expression came over her face. And finally, she said, "No. No, I'm not. You should know how it feels to have the spell on you, to have your mind violated. But not how it feels to wish it again. No-one should have to feel that. I ... I am sorry for that." And she turned and walked away, her victory turned to ashes.

Narn stood unsteadily, staggered a few paces and sat down, put his head in his hands, and they left him to be alone with his loss.

He was a resilient there as he had been with his magic. When the first group of his men arrived, he was self-possessed again, and told them that the war was over. He sent most of them on the trail to Fir'Alan'Atrah, and a delegation of three on horses to Fir'Caram with a signed proclamation of cessation of hostilities. They waited for the bulk of his forces, some twenty men and two witches with mules, horses and supplies to arrive, which they did half-way through the afternoon.

486

With a camp being set up and everything under control, Sheena took Kira and the Wand the two hundred or so miles back to Utol'Fir'Astar (a much shorter distance as the crow, or in this case the Sheena, flies) which took her only a little over an hour. Landing at the village, they were greeted enthusiastically, but told the Angel had returned to his cave and was expecting them. "Call here on your way back, we will have something for you!" Kal'Ton called.

It was only a minute or two's flight to the cave, and Bakaro was waiting. "Sheena!" he laughed. "Oh, Sha'Lin'Tra the Magnificent!" and he picked her up and hugged her, and exuberantly threw her far up into the air, ten, twenty feet, with the strength of an Angel. She floated gently down, of course. "Oh, you have done so well! I knew you could do it! Just in time, by the skin of your teeth, but you did it! I am proud, so proud! I love you!" And he hugged her once more.

Sheena smiled, so happily. "And I *love* you too, Bakaro. Oh, it feels so good to be able to say that truthfully!"

Kira handed over the Wand, saying a thank you. "I'm not sure how much use it was, though. Sheena did most of the work!"

Bakaro nodded. "Yes, but she could never have done it without you. The need to keep you safe was the final stress that freed her. Under the scar in her mind, she loved you already. And she needed all the time she could get for the stress to act and her mind to finally give in. Without the Wand, your shields wouldn't have held up long enough. I didn't know all that at the time, but I see it now. Bronn's vision was good, and true, but incredibly finely tuned. You were all essential in the process. Great evil has been avoided by you and your Quest."

He turned to Sheena again. "And now, my dear, I suppose your time has come. Do you still aspire to be one of us, to join the Angels?"

Sheena said, "Well, yes, of course! To join the Angels, to rejoin *you* would be wonderful. But ..."

Bakaro spread his arms. "Well, the time is here! I can take you now, if you wish!"

Sheena said, stammering "But ... but I cannot! Not now! I am sworn, to help Kira get home, to help train her, to see her people returned to their home, to see her become their leader!"

The Angel frowned. "Bah! Trivialities! They will take care of themselves! Now is *your* time! You *must* come!"

Sheena said fearfully, "No! No, I cannot! Surely, it doesn't have to be now, not right now? What will a few years matter?"

"Now!" the Angel thundered. "Now, or never! An Angel commands you! *I* command you!"

"Sheena!" Kira said, urgently. "It doesn't matter! Go! I release you from your oaths! I'll be fine! We'll be fine! This is what you've been working towards for nearly a thousand years! *Go!*"

Sheena looked at her, trembling. After a few seconds, she slumped. "No." she said. "No, I can't just accept freedom from my sworn word just because it's convenient. And what about the prophecy? The Ice Witches will never return to Iceland unless I lead them."

"Then it is *never!*" The Angel said sternly and sadly.

Sheena bowed her head, and said sadly, "Then so be it." And she turned her head to go.

Bakaro laughed. "Oh, well done! You pass! I knew you would, again! Well done, indeed! You will make a terrific Angel when your time comes!"

Sheena and Kira turned, shocked and astonished. "But you said ..."

"I lied" the Angel said calmly. "It was a test."

"*Another* test? And I thought, Angels *couldn't* lie!"

"Oh, yes. There are always tests. There will be many. Most of the time, you won't recognize them till they are over. Even the Archangels face tests. They help us grow, and realize what we are. And, Angels can't lie? Well, usually we don't. And we can't, when we speak in the language of Angels. Nor can we, when we speak about God, or God's word. But we can, otherwise, if we have to. This was just a little one, for a test. *Some* Angels, who I won't name, thought you'd fail that one, but I knew. I knew. Take as long as you want!"

And they laughed together, and he blessed them, and they went on their way.

Before they did, however, he confirmed that the course of action Sheena proposed with Narn was a wise one. And he talked with Sheena briefly, in private.

Back at the village, they received another happy farewell. Sheena said she and Kira would visit by Avatar, and hopefully Shilo too. Bronn would have to visit by synchronized dreaming if he wanted to, which given the Seer talent in the village was not impossible, or make the long physical journey otherwise. They had packed a very large backpack, which Sheena thanked them for but winced a bit when she considered flying with that and Kira as well to carry.

Fortunately, Kira was light. When they set off, she lightened the weight of the pack by one bottle of wine. Sheena drank most of it, but Kira had more than her usual mouthful and was just a little tipsy when they landed. Still, it was a special occasion. The empty bottle landed on an unknown, unexplored grass bank on a ledge on a cliff at the back end of nowhere and broke in half, the last dregs and drops in the bottom being a welcome if unexpected drink for a large green lizard. And so more than one being had an unexpected celebration that night.

Sheena and Kira made it back just before sundown, sailing down to a gentle landing, which awed everyone including Narn. He, who had been proud of his gliding, once again shook his head over true flight with a passenger and luggage.

Narn's supply corps had the basics, but there was little in the way of wine or the little fresh delicacies in the pack, which were well received.

Nightfall came, and they settled down for their rest. Although the day had been clear, the evening had clouded over and it began to sprinkle with rain. The supply team was not burdened down with tents, though they had waterproof cloth that each person could use to make a more or less unsatisfactory lean-to. Those who could put up their shields, but before the rest had finished grumbling, Sheena casually expanded hers to cover the whole camp, causing general gratitude in those who couldn't shield and knew little about it, and slack-jawed disbelief in those who could and did.

Narn, in particular, was technically interested. As the person closest to Sheena in power and talent, he was bemused. "That must be level four work" he commented. "Yes, indeed" Sheena replied. "Some of it's not very hard, once you're competent at level three. Of course, I had to rediscover level four for myself, and if I do say so, that counts for something. But you could learn it, and Kira will. I will teach you, if you manage to achieve what we talked about today, assuming you do it while I am still in this life."

Narn became animated for the first time since his defeat. He had seemed cool and reserved since then. "I would like that" he said with raised eyebrows. "I was committed before, when you spoke of those conditions, but now I have an ambition again." And he went off to talk to his men, and nearly everyone went to their well-earned rest.

Sheena worked for hours into the night. With her abilities unleashed, there was much she could do. Following the eleven remaining bonds (Narn had suborned a round dozen Witches) with level four techniques, she worked with them in dreams. In the morning, she was able to tell him that three had simply let the whole thing go, shrugging it off. They had said they would have done the same thing, realistically, if they had had the power. Two didn't like it at all, but accepted it as Narn's right, because of the hierarchical nature of Fire Witch society. Level threes could do pretty much as they wanted. Three had been extremely angry and were prepared to hunt him down, but Sheena had simply bribed them; she had gold hidden about in one place or another. Two more, surprisingly, had chosen amnesia. They would remember nothing the next day, whole months would be missing from their memories. One was simply grateful. She said, she had never loved anyone or anything before, and now that she knew what it felt like, was planning and hoping to repeat the experience voluntarily.

Narn was amazed at that. "Grateful!" he murmured. "I didn't expect that. And yet, ..." he trailed off, thanked Sheena for what she had done, and wandered off to think while the group had their breakfast.

After that, there were decisions to be made. Sheena, bolstered by her talk with Bakaro, told Narn that he had been judged, and if he wanted to live he must abide by that judgment. He had to return to Fir'Alan'Atrah and hand control of the kingdom back to its rightful rulers, and disassemble his war machine. That would take time and need his full authority, and Sheena would remove his limiting block so he would have full use of his power. But once it was done, he would have to voluntarily re-impose that limit, adopt a disguise and travel, talk to the common people, learn to understand them. He would probably have to return to Fir'Caram. He would have to live as a level one for two years, but after that time if he was able to truthfully say he had no ambition to take and rule by force, that he genuinely saw that what he had done was wrong, that he had learned forgiveness, the spell would be lifted. Becoming a Fire Queen (which could be his title, even though a man) by *right* was not barred from him, nor was he expected to become weak or let compassion rule him when hard decisions needed to be made. He agreed to all these terms under truthspell.

And so the party divided up. Bronn, Sheena, Kira, Shilo and Sandra were left with enough provisions to take them the few remaining days past the border and to the city. The parting was awkward. Sheena respected Narn's power and ability, his cool-headedness, and his ability to change, to take his fall and his new path in his stride. Bronn was achingly glad it was all over, he was still alive and was returning to the far north and Kara. Shilo was glad it was over, but did not look so very happy. Kira was glowing, she was so proud and happy for Sheena, and glad to be going home, too. They all were pleased that the quest had ended so quickly and easily, without the need for an horrific war. They knew Narn was going, and why, and understood the reasons – but still, something as simple as a hand-clasp was hard. Respect was there, yes, and Narn was surprisingly likeable. But no-one liked him, not yet. There was too much history for that to happen in a few days.

Narn didn't seem to mind. Perhaps he saw the effect, but felt the cause was already in the past. He said goodbye, his thanks and his apologies to each of them in turn. He was more sincere with Sandra. She acknowledged his apology, with a brief nod of her head, but did not accept it. When he said his thanks with apparent sincerity, she was puzzled. "Thanks? For what?" she asked brusquely.

"Something Sheena said to me made me realize, something one of the Witches I suborned said. Your spell was painful and violating, and I am sorry that I did it to you, now that I know. But as you said, you had the right to do it to me. And ... well, I did not have an easy childhood, nor an easy life as a young man. I don't think anyone cared for me much, I got grudgingly granted living space and food by a distant relative, who worked me hard. I wasn't treated well; people resented talent and ambition in a man who wasn't prepared to live as a pet. I never had occasion to love anyone, and especially not as I began my rise to power. The love I felt under your spell was my first, no doubt that's why it affected me so much. It was a hard lesson, but I am grateful for it. Like that Witch Sheena mentioned, I hope to experience it again, under ... ah ... better circumstances."

Sandra looked at him for long seconds, but finally turned and walked away without saying anything. The other goodbyes were said, and there being nothing more to say or do, Narn's party turned and began their long walk on the paths back to Fir'Alan'Atrah.

Sandra came over to Sheena and the others. Abruptly, she said, "I'm going to leave you. I'll not go to Fir'Caram, though I'll give you the name of someone, I would appreciate it if you'd tell them I am alive and well." And she mentioned a name, and a part of the city.

"Where will you go?" asked Sheena, though she thought she knew.

"I'll join Narn and his group. I have the right, he owes me."

She paused, her somewhat grim face working uneasily. "Yesterday I hated him. I loathed him, I would have seen him dead in an instant. Today ... today, I merely dislike him, and I haven't forgiven him. But that's quick work, quick change. Who knows where it will end? I think I'd like to find out."

"And, I am a Fire Witch. I respect power, talent, drive, ambition. He certainly has all of those, though I'd like to see a bit more passion in him, a bit more fire, properly directed. And there is time, before he must go back to level one, he could teach me much. I'd like to be a level two, if I can."

Sheena nodded. A Fire Witch herself, she understood, more than the others possibly could. "Then fare you well, Illa'San'Dra. May your ambitions be fulfilling and fulfilled."

Sandra replied as formally: "Fare you well, Sha'Lin'Tra the Great. May your ambitions be fulfilling and fulfilled also."

And she smiled, the first genuine smile they had seen on her face. It looked good. "And you too, my friends. I am glad to have met you." And she turned around and made her way along the trail at an easy jog.

Sheena shook her head as Sandra left. "That Narn is surely one of the luckiest people alive. Talented, powerful, stopped before he could do too much damage to others or himself, and not nearly as stupid as I was. His redemption will not take long, I think, and now he has a companion."

"Not as talented and powerful as you were, though, Sheena!" Kira said.

She nodded somberly. "As I said, lucky."

"Still," she smiled. "Look how it has turned out! It took a while, but am I not one of the luckiest people alive too?" And she laughed, and said, "Come on, let's go!"

Chapter 14. Homeward bound

The keeper of the city keys
Put shutters on the dreams.
I wait outside the pilgrim's door
With insufficient schemes.
The black queen chants the funeral march,
The cracked brass bells will ring;
To summon back the Fire Witch
To the court of the Crimson King.

King Crimson

The remaining trail to the borders of civilized Fir'Alan'Cara, which quickly became a road, was a joy. Easy going, the surface was firm and clear. There were regular garrisons, and the weather was pleasant.

Travel in the backwoods was mostly on Queen's business, little that was productive was done out there. Horses were sometimes used if the matter was urgent, and the road kept clear for their travel.

Garrisons were well provisioned, keeping a fair sized farm about them. In time, as the border moved north-west, they might become the center of growth for a new town. But for the group of travelers, it meant they didn't have to worry too much about food, which meant less weight, and faster walking. Though to be sure, with sixteen Material Avatars available to them, they could probably have carried a banquet with them if they wanted. However, Sheena didn't want to advertise, she was planning to visit Fir'Caram, not take it over as ruler again. She kept her fire well-hidden, rarely used techniques enabling her to hide her talent in a similar way to when she had been under her limiting spell.

The garrisons were sophisticated enough to know a Witch when they saw one, but not so much that they would instantly see Kira and Shilo as being something different to the norm. And Bronn got his due respect, of course. As a result, they rarely had to pay for anything, and travelling was easy. Bronn asked somewhat plaintively if Sheena could not fly him home. She said no, he was a much heavier weight than Kira. It would have been within her abilities to fly to Iceland if she was by herself and took several stops, but not carrying someone. Still, he had managed to make contact via synchronized dreaming and at least Kara knew he was on his way, and was ecstatic that he was safe.

A week of easy travelling saw them at the walls of the city, somewhere near dusk. They were a long way from the main gate, but there was a smaller gate within easy distance. It was securely barred, however, and the Witch on the other side was not sympathetic to their needs. "Go away. Camp. No-one gets in without a truthspell so we know they're not with Narn" she said in the short, brusque sentences so typical of Fir'Caram Fire Witches. When they said they were happy for her to test them, she said, "No. Go away, come back tomorrow. Takes two Witches, just to be sure." She just laughed at them when they said it was urgent and she should go and get another Witch. "I could. But why should I? Tell you what, if you're so important, I'll do it for a bribe. One gold piece per person."

Bronn's funds had run low. Sheena could get money once inside; she visited Fir'Caram at least every fifty years to keep her accounts and letters of credit active, and make sure a few little caches had not been found, but that wasn't going to help them now. She offered double that the next day, but again the Witch just laughed. "Oh, sure, I imagine you'd be coming back for certain to pay that. Hah! No, I'll do it for a bribe, cash in the hand right now. My mother's sick, I can use the money. Otherwise, tomorrow. Don't care if you're a Noble. It's my job. Have a nice night."

And that was that. Sheena could, of course, have blasted the door off its hinges, or more simply just have lifted the veil on her talent. The door would be opened without a second's thought to someone of Queen level, but Sheena wanted to continue keeping a low profile.

She also seemed unconcerned, she was uncharacteristically calm at the out-and-out barely legal attempt at extortion, and just led them along the wall for a ten minute walk. "Right, this will do" she said.

"What, we're going to set up camp here?" Bronn asked. And truth to tell, it wasn't very inviting. There was a fair bit of rubbish around and it didn't smell too good. And, it was beginning to rain.

"No, we'll enter the city here" Sheena said. "It's simple, I'll just fly you in one at a time. This is a quiet area, Ungifted quarters, but conveniently close to reasonable inns."

And so it was. She lifted them one by one over the wall, swearing a bit at Shilo's weight. He was truly no longer the somewhat slender youth they had met over six months ago. He was still tall and athletic, but hard journeying and hard training (and a *lot* of eating) had bulked him up. Sheena said it looked like he was going to be as tall as Master Thirro, and as strong as Master Cordubo, and in another year she doubted she'd be able to get him off the ground at all. Even now, she lifted him alone – no pack, sword or anything else – and it was hard enough for the half a minute needed to get over the wall.

The walk to the inn was easy enough. All cities have good parts, bad parts and dangerous ones, and this was one of the worst – the slums of the Ungifted section. But still, no-one would think of accosting a party of four walking confidently along, with one of them showing a Witch-light to guide their way. A chancy business at the best of times to tackle even a lone Witch, it would need two good archers and at least one other, and even then the chances of all coming out alive were not great. And then, they had better be prepared to flee for their lives, because the other Witches would question every living soul in the city under truthspell, asking if they knew who had done it, or knew anyone who hadn't been questioned.

No such thing had happened in living memory. People didn't call the Fire Witches vindictive, not even in private – any more than they remarked that the ocean was wet. Vindictive and vengeful they were; also arrogant, willful, and hot-tempered. But they were also loyal to their kind, and supportive in their way. They were doers and achievers, intelligent, talented, passionate and highly creative. They made wonderful friends, great lovers, and bad enemies. There was a lot conflict, or even out-and-out fighting among them that sometimes resulted in injury or even death, but that was accepted. Violence by a non-Witch was a different matter. Seer's Hold was the most egalitarian of places, Gifted and Ungifted worked side by side, with no prejudice for or against either men or women. Warrior's Hold was two-tiered, but Warriors came from anywhere, and they often served Ungifted rich patrons. But the Fire Witches were the rulers of Fir'Caram, and the Ungifted were ruled. The Nobles ruled the Witches, and the Queens were on top.

Sheena knew all of this, of course, and had been bred and raised to it. She knew what to do. She asked a disreputable bunch which was the best inn, and received her due right of answer with barely a sniff of thanks. And so they made their way there. Witches sometimes, but relatively rarely (mostly travelers returning from overseas) stayed at the inns, but they expected premium service when they did. She didn't even comment when the innkeeper inconvenienced a party of five to give them the best suite of rooms available. Adjustments would be made, and if someone at the bottom of the chain had to leave and find another inn, well, too bad.

Bronn asked if all of Fire Hold would be like this. "Yes" smiled Sheena. "This is the way we are. You'll most likely see some fireworks tomorrow, too, when we visit the palace. Contentious, arrogant, often in error but never in doubt. That pretty much defines Fire Witches. To act differently to the way we did tonight would be to attract notice, questions and inconvenience. Prideful assumption of one's rights and privileges is the way it goes. Even I, who have learned a bit better after centuries of effort ... well, even I, I am sorry to admit, still enjoy it. A bit guiltily, but I do."

They made full use of the facilities of the inn – luxuries to them. They bathed, ate, drank and slept. Sheena woke early the next day, and made her way to a money handler. She took substantial funds from an account – all she needed was her token, which she had carried around the world.

She made her way down to the nearest gate, and asked the name of the Witch who had been on duty the previous night. She was truculent and not pleased to be woken. "What do you want?" she asked in a surly tone. She was surprised when Sheena handed her four gold pieces. "You said you needed these, because your mother is not well" she said. "What ... what ... that was *you*? How did you get in? And why are you giving this to me *now*? Not that I don't need it."

Sheena shrugged. "There was a time when *my* mother was not well. No-none could help. No-one should have to live with that, if aid can be given. But anyway, there's always a fund for Witches in need. Why didn't you use that?"

The Witch sighed. "Money is tight. Vast amounts have been spent readying the city for Narn, hiring mercenaries, Warriors even. Seers as well. There's just not enough to go around."

Sheena's lips tightened. "It should never get that tight. That will have to be changed."

The Witch laughed. "What can you or I do about it? That's the province of the Queens."

Sheena looked at her, and just for a moment let the veil slip a bit. The Witch gasped as a wave of power washed over her. "Oh, something will be done" Sheena said a bit grimly. "Don't worry about that. You go and see to your mother." And she left the trembling Witch behind her and returned to the inn.

Things had to be done. But there was really no tremendous rush, the danger of Narn's mounting army was over. The delegation of three Narn had sent should have calmed things down though some confirmation was probably in order. What was needed now was to make the Queens aware that the Ice Witches would be returning, and get some help. Fir'Caram was the logical place to hire a large ship or several smaller ones.

As there was no rush, they spent the morning buying fresh clothes, getting their hair cut and getting a feel for the tone of the city. There had been no general proclamation that the danger was over, which worried Sheena, but there was a feeling that things were about to change. Finally, she decided that they may as well make their move, and they made their way over to the palace.

The palace was impressive. It was designed and built to impress. It was a monument to arrogance and self-importance, built with great effort out of stone, lavishly carved. There was gilding, tiling and color everywhere; it only just escaped being gaudy because the intent was also to convey the presence of power, and power that the wielders were not afraid to use. But it was beautiful, too.

Sheena explained that the place was hierarchical, just like the society. Any Witch could enter the massive front door. Some Ungifted, too, if they had a pass – but all those were staff who did the bulk of the work. The administration of the country and the city was done in the many sections of the first level. All a Witch had to do to enter was display some form of talent, usually the sense one Witch had of another was enough.

The second level could be entered by any Noble Witch – one able to display level two abilities. These were sufficiently few that a simple facial recognition was usually enough. Similar to the first, any level one Witch with a pass could enter too; they did the work there. Important decisions were made, and management of the first level was done. The Ungifted were rarely seen, and could only be admitted under custody of someone with the right to be there.

The third level was reserved for the Queens. Nobles attended them and did a fair bit of the real work, though there were also some level ones with high abilities outside the field of magic. So few entered there that everyone was on first name terms and the passes were unnecessary, though issued. An Ungifted person could theoretically enter if taken there by a Queen, or a Noble was told to bring them there. The Queens made the strategic decisions, but mostly just enjoyed their rule.

They entered the first level without any problems. The security was nominal, a projection by Sheena and Kira of an Avatar was enough. The checkers were Ungifted; even in these difficulty times the likelihood of anyone who had no business to be there entering the palace was low, and the consequences potentially severe. And the other two were men anyway, and so of less concern.

They walked through an opulent, well lit entrance passage, wide and carpeted in red. Red was a predominant color, for its affinity with fire, but there was a fair bit of gold too. There were frequent statues and paintings of Queens past and present, and Nobles too. Corridors led off at frequent intervals, and doors could be seen along them, some open, some closed and people moving purposely everywhere.

The main passage led straight ahead, up a wide staircase to the smaller and even more impressive second floor. There were two Witches there, guarding the entrance. They viewed the party with interest, new faces were relatively rare.

"Your business, Fireladies?" one of the Witches asked politely.

"We are passing through, we have business on the third level" Sheena replied evenly.

"Do you, indeed. Well, if you say so, but the Queens are in a bit of a mood today. Still. Don't know either of you. Show us. And we'll have to truthspell you."

Sheena and Kira both projected two Avatars, and submitted to truthspell, saying that they did indeed have business on the third level, were able to do second-level work, were not in league with Narn the Sorcerer and had no evil intent.

"Good enough for me" shrugged the Witch on the left. "And you vouch for your companions, of course. Can I have their attributes for the register?"

"Surely" Sheena replied. "This man is Master Seer Bronn. I vouch for him. And this one is Shilo, a trainee Warrior though soon to be ranked. I vouch for him, too."

"Well, well. Men of talent. Interesting." She looked Bronn and Shilo over, paying real attention to them for the first time. She seemed particularly taken with Shilo. "My, oh my, the Warrior's a pretty one, isn't he? No chance he's unattached, I suppose?"

"There are two of us. And two men. What do *you* think?" Sheena said tartly.

"All right, all right. No harm asking." The Witch waved them through.

Kira said quietly and admiringly, "That was clever, Sheena ... you didn't lie because of the truthspell, of course, but you completely mis-directed her there."

"Thank you, Kira, yes I did. I suppose I hadn't thought of that aspect of Fire Witches much, we've had other concerns, but yes. Shilo is, as you said back at Warrior's Hold an attractive man, and Fire Witches are as ... well, as direct and sexist as men in other parts of the world. It wouldn't do to let him go wandering off by himself, especially after dark. Having him thought of as attached, particularly to a Noble, will help."

They wandered through the shorter display passage of level two. Care had been taken to show that the Witches on this level were more privileged, had more power and more leisure time. There were as many paintings and statues but they were of higher quality. There was more natural light, and there were many things on display chosen purely because they were nice, impressive or expensive. Large vases, smaller ones with flowers, carvings, places to sit and wait, tables with glasses and pitchers of water, people in strategic places looking to be helpful.

But Sheena strode through it all, leading them through an internal corridor and round to the staircase on the other side that led up to the third level. It was much shorter than the grand passage to the left of the building, she said.

There was a Witch there, obviously a Noble by her dress, with a patronizing and somewhat bored expression on her face, though she perked up a bit as they approached. "Well, greetings!" she said. "Level two admissions sent an Ethereal up to me to let me know you were coming, with descriptions of course. Good descriptions" she added, letting her gaze drift idly over Shilo. "Two level twos, and I've never seen either of you before. That's unusual. But still, not enough to get in to see the Queens today. They're having a bit of a .... discussion ... about the problem of Narn. Come back tomorrow. And ... if you'll take my advice, don't bring him" she said, indicating Shilo. "Queen Kil'Mar'Sha has recently dismissed her consort, and is not above pre-empting even a level two. Just a word to the wise, between Nobles" she winked.

"Well, thank you" Sheena said a bit impatiently. "But we need to see the Queens today. Now. It's urgent. What we have to say concerns Narn also. Let them make the decision."

"Hmm, well if you're so insistent, it must be important, at least in your own minds. On an ordinary day I'd risk it … but today, no, sorry, it's not worth getting my head bitten off, or losing my job. Two Nobles and two companions … no, you'd have to show me something a bit more impressive than that. Sorry."

Kira pulled Sheena aside, and whispered: "Can't you show her you're level three? That would get us in, surely?"

Sheena whispered back, "Yes, of course, but I don't want to reveal that till we're in there, and then not until the right time. They would detect it from inside, and be too prepared. We're going to need to catch them off-guard for the right effect. But it's allright, what she just said has given me an idea."

They stepped back to the entrance, and the Witch sat up, alert now but wary. Not one in a hundred would have ignored that dismissal.

"Very well, we will have to try to impress you" Sheena said. "Shilo, show her what you've got."

Nothing happened for a second, and Sheena turned slightly to look at him. Shilo was looking at her blankly. She suddenly realized what he was thinking. "Oh, for God's sake! Does no-one around here think of *anything* else? Shilo, I'm not talking about your manly charms! Show her some of your *other* skills! You know, your recently acquired ones?"

"Oh!" Shilo blushed. "Of course …" and he froze a bowl of water on the desk which had some fragrant flowers in it, and projected his level two shield for a few seconds.

The Witch picked up the bowl, and turned it over. "Ice Magic?" she asked, stunned. "Level two shielding? *And* a Warrior?"

She looked at the group again. "Very well. That's impressive. Impressive enough for me to at least get you someone closer to the Queens to talk to." And she projected an Ethereal Avatar, which went through the magnificent carved and gilded double doors behind her.

After a minute or two, another Witch came out, opening the doors this time. At last a face they recognized. "Hello, El'Lan'Tra" Sheena greeted her. "It is good to see you again. I know the Queens are busy … I can feel it, even from here. But could you tell them, or at least Queen Shi'Mal'Tara, that Sheena, Kira, Bronn and Shilo would like to talk to them on matters of urgency."

El'Lan'Tra stopped short. "Well! Welcome! I had not thought to see you here. You may enter, of course … Queen Shi'Mal'Tara has said you were to be brought to her if you were seen. But … I must warn you, she is not in high favor with the other Queens at the moment. When she told them about you, they said she was a foo … ah, wrong to have let you go. And they do not agree with her arguments about this proclama … oh, I'm saying too much. I'm just saying, you should not expect to be received kindly. You'd be better off waiting until Queen Shi'Mal'Tara is free and alone."

"Thank you, El'Lan'Tra, but I really think we should see them as soon as possible. We'll just have to take our chances."

"Very well, then, Sheena and Kira. I'll take you and Kira and Master Seer Bronn. Your young man will have to wait outside, of course."

"Ah, assistant El'Lan'Tra ... the young Warrior has just shown me a level two shield. And some Ice Magic." The Witch from the desk put in, deferential despite the fact that she was a Noble and El'Lan'Tra was only a level one.

El'Lan'Tra frowned. "Has he. Has he indeed. Ice Magic. Very rare. And level two, you say. Never heard of that. Come to that, I've never heard of a Queen saying a Noble and a level one" – she nodded briefly to Kira and Sheena – "should be sent to her any time of day or night. And if it comes to that ... I can't detect *any* power about you at all, any more" she said, turning to Sheena inquiringly. Sheena briefly lowered her power hiding spell, just enough to let some of her power show.

Both the other Witches turned and looked at her. "Shielding talent? Hiding?" asked El'Lan'Tra. "I've never even *heard* of that! How is it done? *Why* is it done? What level *are* you? Are you ... a *Queen?*"

Sheena calmly replied, "Oh, it can be done, if you want to. The technique is quite easy. Witches don't look for it or learn it, because usually they want to advertise their power, not keep it under wraps. But as to being a Queen ... maybe. The three will have to decide. Maybe they will let me be a minor power, but I think ... I think three Queens is enough for the moment. I think they will be happy for me to go away again, which is what I intend, and why I'm keeping my power hidden."

El'Lan'Tra was clearly a very bright and able woman, to be working with the Queens as a level one Witch. She shrugged. "Either you're Queen, in which case I can't stop you going in, or you're not, in which case you're going to have a hard time of it as I warned you. Still, Queen Shi'Mal'Tara's commands apply there. Please come in, all of you."

508

She led them through the doors and into level three. The reception room was at first sight less opulent than the level two rooms, but then one could see it was only less cluttered. There were many beautiful and ornamental things on stands and in cabinets, many of great age. But there was little time to look, for El'Lan'Tra led them quickly through, around a corner and though a large, dark wooden doorway into what was a sort of meeting room. There was a large and beautiful table near an enormous window, with three impressive but comfortable chairs. There were other, less impressive chairs to one side, rarely used, because only a foreign dignitary would be asked to sit in the presence of a Queen.

But what was in use at the moment was a large central space, and the three Queens were using it. They recognized Shi'Mal'Tara, of course. The other two were of a piece. They were both tallish, and had similarly red hair, though one was lighter and had it cut short, and the other was darker, the color called russet, and longer. She was younger than Shi'Mal'Tara, and good looking in a conventional way, while the other was older and stunning.

All three were arguing and had their auras up, and the room was half-lit by their flashing brilliance. By their relative sizes that Shi'Mal'Tara was the weakest of the three, but there was not much in it. They had clearly been arguing for some time, pacing, strutting and shouting at each other. The older and strongest of the three was saying in a loud voice as they entered, " ... and I say it would be foolish to accept this proclamation of Narn's at its face value! What if it is trickery and deceit? Send others out to verify and report, we're agreed on that. But release the heralds? Make a general announcement? No! The people would relax. Defenses would be lessened. We need to stay on the alert ! We need ..."

509

Facing the window, as she was, she had not seen or heard the group enter the room, but she noticed the other two were no longer listening, and she turned around.

"El'Lan'Tra! What does this mean? How *dare* you bring these people in? You were told we were *not* to be disturbed!"

"Easy, sister" Shi'Mal'Tara said. "I had left instruction that if these people were ever seen again, they should be brought to me at once, and El'Lan'Tra is *my* assistant so she is simply obeying orders."

"*These* are your four? The Seer, yes, the Warrior I see, the young Witch ... you said, Ice Witch, I'll want to see some evidence, but yes I feel her power, but *this* one? The one you say claimed to be Sha'Lin'Tra? Ridiculous! I cannot feel *any* power from her at all! Still, you are to some extent redeemed for letting them go, Shi'Mal'Tara, as they have returned. Let them be taken and held, we will examine them after this discussion is concluded." And she waved a dismissive hand.

But Sheena said calmly, "Sister Kil'Mar'Sha, I must tell you good news. Narn the Sorcerer has indeed abdicated. He will fight no more. Fir'Caram is safe, I give you my word on it."

The Queen looked at her in unbelieving shock. She fairly screeched. "You *dare* to talk to *me*? As if we are *equals*? God! If I had not said you were to be questioned, I would burn you right here and now! Down on your knees and beg forgiveness, or I swear I won't restrain myself!"

"Oh, I'm sorry, what was I thinking. I'm sorry, I should have thought to come out of hiding" Sheena calmly replied, at the same time partially releasing her

510

masking spell. Her aura flamed up too, but restrained. It was smaller, weaker, less bright than even Shi'Mal'Tara's. Everyone in the room felt the wash as her level three power became apparent.

The three Queen's auras flamed higher in reaction. The third queen, clearly of a calmer temperament, said wonderingly, "A Queen? An unknown third level? Welcome, welcome indeed. With four of us, we could face Narn ourselves. Well, with level two backup."

Sheena shook her head. "Thank you for your welcome, sister Tan'Ra'Sha. But there is indeed no need. Shi'Mal'Tara will have told you of our quest. We obtained Alana's wand. With it, we whelmed Narn."

All three Queens started talking at once, but after a few seconds Kil'Mar'Sha's voice won out. "Stop!" she shouted. And then, more calmly. "I welcome a new sister, of course. But I want some *proof*. Narn is dead? Show me his body! Otherwise, we must be careful. Sister Sheena here – how do we know she is not a dupe, under Narn's spell? Level three, yes, but a weak one. Narn could have suborned her. A five Avatar Witch, he could overpower *me*! Show me his body! Show me this fabulous wand. Show me this *Ice Magic*, even!"

"The last is easily done, at least" Shi'Mal'Tara said. She went herself over to the table and fetched a glass, and handed it to Kira, who half froze the water and then sloshed it around so it would not crack the glass, and passed it on to Shilo, who froze it the rest of the way.

"Allright, impressive, particularly in a man, but Ice Magic, poorly controlled, does spring up from time to time" Kil'Mar'Sha barely conceded. "But a colony of Ice Witches? Where? Iceland is *deserted*!"

Kira curtseyed, the courtesy going a way to calming the Queen. "We live on an island, unknown to the world, further north" she said. "We fled there nine hundred years ago, at the start of Sha'Lin'Tra's reign."

"Well, that at least we can confirm" the Queen said, still more calmly. "Ships can be sent. But that is not our primary *issue* right now. Narn is the issue. Show us his *body*! Show us this *wand*!"

Sheena shook her head. "The wand has been returned. And Narn is not dead. He is under a self-limiting spell, his talent now only level one, until he has made amends. But it is done."

"Well then go and get the wand again. If it is true. It will be useful. And we will check on Narn, as I have ordered. If it is so, well and good, we will bring him in and have our vengeance!"

"You will *not*!" Sheena said, her temper moving away from calmness. "I did not set all this up so carefully to have you ruin it, to drag him in and make him grovel! He *will* be allowed his chance at redemption. And you *won't* get the wand, that's for sure. And you *will* stand down your army. It is the only *sensible* thing to do!"

Witches, particularly Queens don't like being told what to do. The Queens, even Shi'Mal'Tara, were angered at her rough words, and flared up. They all began talking at once, voices rising, Sheena's often above all, she had a truly magnificent voice, clear and lovely even at top volume. She played them like instruments. She made subtle insults, never openly threatening. She played them one against the other, driving up their fury. Avatars were projected, and the Queens drew closer together. Finally, Kil'Mar'Sha screamed: "Enough! It will be done as *I* say! As *we* say! Because *we* say it! Who will stand against us? *You*? Queen

Sheena, the would-be? You, who had Sheemal half-convinced you are Sha'Lin'Tra? What a joke! Will *you* stand against us, and enforce your *will*?" And pushed beyond their fairly short tempers, two of the Queens and their Avatars raised their arms and prepared to strike. Shi'Mal'Tara held back.

Sheena dropped her final barrier, and Sha'Lin'Tra the Great stood revealed. Her aura towered up, making the Queens' look like candles in daylight. Her fourteen Avatars flicked out, faster than thought. Her firebolts were still restrained, but lightning crackled off her left arm and grounded itself menacingly. In the sudden silence, her voice spoke again with a steely ring: "I will if I have to. If you won't listen."

The Queens paled. Their auras subsided, and their lightning too. Sheena powered down a little herself, and added in a calmer voice: "I would rather have your co-operation."

The Queen's Avatars disappeared, re-absorbed. Sheena merged hers too, but Tan'Ra'Sha, who seemed a bit quicker on the uptake than the other two, had counted them. "Fourteen?" she said weakly. "*Fourteen Avatars?*" she shook her head. "If I hadn't seen them with my own eyes, I would call anyone who said it mad. Legend speaks of Sha'Lin'Tra the Great and *six* Avatars. Even that I dismissed as exaggerated legend until I heard of Narn and his five!"

Sheena shrugged and smiled, her temper cooling. "It never pays to boast. Always keep something in reserve; you never know when you will need it."

Kil'Mar'Sha said, awe in her voice, "It shall be done as you command, Queen Sha'Lin'Tra. It's obvious you're either her, or greater than she was. We will stand down the army, pass word not to arrest Narn on sight, and tell the city it has a new ruler, now that you have returned."

Sheena shook her head. "The first two, yes. But not the last. I have no desire to rule again, Fireland is in good hands. Many will rule better than one, I think."

Kil'Mar'Sha said again, "But *why*? You *could* rule. You could rule the world! You *did*! And you could do it *again*! The Fire Witches could be the pre-eminent Gifted people in the world!"

Sheena shook her head again. "You forget. I have done it. I don't expect you to understand or even believe, but it isn't worth it. The world is not meant to be ruled by one person, or one Gift. Remember the phrase, 'may your ambitions be fulfilling, and fulfilled?' Well, it's a nice thought. But fulfilled ambitions leave you very little, it's actually the journey that is satisfying. My ambitions don't include ruling the world any more, I have moved on to something better – ruling myself. That's an ambition with no limits and no end. So, no proclamations. No announcements that I'm here, I will just quietly go my way. But leave Narn free."

Kil'Mar'Sha and the other two bowed. "As you command."

Sheena shook her head a third time. "No, as I request. I have no right to command the Fir'Caram Queens. Well, as I very strongly request and suggest, yes, alright, I *do* want to see it done that way. I am a Fire Witch, after all." And so it was decided.

"Something else. Narn was the way he was because he was poorly treated as a talented young man." Sheena recounted some of his story. "It's worth considering if that's a good way to run things. The Warriors have recently decided to change their ways, and train women once more. You might want to think about that. I think Narn's redaction will come fairly soon, years rather than decades. He has a companion by now, I suspect, and if that works out long term then well and good, but if not ... if not, in a few years there might be another level three person in Fir'Caram worthy of Queen status, though a man. A highly talented one. Quite a good looking one as well, if he were fed up a bit." And the Queens looked at each other a bit speculatively over that one.

Kil'Mar'Sha nodded. "Unacceptable. I know our society is different to others – I like it that way. And life is no doubt hard for the Ungifted. We rule, we look after them up to a point, but they are mostly left to themselves. They can always leave, if they don't like it. But we look after our own. Talent is the one and only criterion by which a Witch should be judged. Male Witches are rare enough as it is without beating them down. And no Witch, man or woman should have to steal. Didn't know it was that bad. We'll investigate and root that problem out. Changes will be made."

The next part of what Sheena wanted went easier. The news that the Ice Witches would be returning to Iceland was hard to swallow in one lump, but the idea of balance returning to the four gifts was surprisingly easy to accept and hope for. The instinctive longing for it was present, if not understood, in all Gifted people. And Sheena's revelation that Ice and Fire Witches working in pairs could be surpassingly good healers was simple fact, not exaggerated legend, was good to hear. The Queens agreed to send three ships, to be at Ice Island mid-summer (locally) or thereabouts. The expense would be high, but not unbearable given the lessening costs of the army as it was disbanded.

Also, Sheena said they could use Sha'Lin'Tra's cache from the treasury, which was a small vault supposedly reserved in case she ever returned. "Spent" Kil'Mar'Sha said gloomily. "Spent hundreds of years ago. No-one ever thought you would be coming back."

"Such is fame" laughed Sheena. "Still, I doubt it's all gone. If you lift the central flagstone, you might find a helpful surprise."

They were offered accommodation in the palace, of course, fine rooms on the second floor – the third had little in the way of such things. While they were waiting for their packs to be brought from their inn, Bronn quietly said to Sheena, "That all went exactly as you planned and wanted, didn't it? The anger, confrontation, shouting and over-aweing I mean."

Sheena agreed. "Yes. I know my people. Unless they could see that I was powerful enough to confront them, powerful enough to have confronted Narn, they would never have believed anything I said. They would insist on waiting and verifying everything. And unless I showed myself to be like them – prone to anger, willing to subdue them, a bit arrogant and demanding – they would have considered me weak of will, insipid. They would never have listened to what I had to say, considered change. And getting those ships out of them would have been impossible."

"And, you enjoyed showing off." Kira added.

Sheena laughed a little. "Well, yes. After all, as I've confessed before, I'm one of my people, too."

Over the next week, Sheena raided her various accounts and caches, and called for funds from the store under the vault. Time was of the essence, and she spent money almost recklessly. She bought a square rigged clipper, very fast – the owner said, driving due north now that the winds had started to rise, it should be able to manage a good twelve miles per hour during the day, and the night too in the open sea; two hundred miles in a day might be achievable given good weather. She hired Sim'Bo'Lo and his picked crew to sail it, being open about the destination, paying his outrageous price without a murmur and saying he could keep the ship into the bargain.

This meant they could make the approximately 5,000 miles to Ice Island in around a month. Theoretically. In practice, they would be stopping several times, probably on one of the islands in the Lute's Chain, certainly at Nun's Hold, for fresh water and supplies. It would be advisable to go around Iceland to the west, skirting 'The Toes' and stopping once or twice on Peace Island. And the likelihood that the weather would co-operate perfectly was low. They would go as far north as they could until it was clear the freezing seas put the ship in danger, and they would leave it as close to Ice Hold as they could get. Bronn, Shilo and Kira would be dropped off, and Sheena would see the ship safely back to somewhere it could winter – probably Peace Island again – and simply fly back to meet them. They would walk across however much of Iceland was left to cover (Ugh! thought Bronn, snow and freezing cold again), and pick up their sled-boat and sail it back across the ice to Ice Island.

That was the theory. In practice, Sheena said, they had two Ice Witches this time, and herself, to get them safely across. Given her vastly greater power and capacity than the last time, she said it should be relatively risk-free.

Shilo kept quiet most of the time Sheena was organizing, paying and talking. Finally, when these travelling points came up, Shilo said privately to her that he would prefer not to go with them. If Sheena would release him and give a recommendation, he would return to Warrior's Hold and train there. Sheena raised an eyebrow. "Really. I thought you would want to come with us, to be with Kira and help her."

Shilo sighed. "It's complicated. Even if ... well, she drew apart from me at the Guardians."

"And if I tell you that you are still my student, and must go where I go?"

Shilo bowed. "I will do so, of course. It is my responsibility. But ... I beg you to reconsider."

Sheena said "Oh, I wondered when this would come up. You poor young man. I know what's going on in your mind and heart. Well, let us talk ... and then, if you are still set in your mind, I will grant your wish."

By 'us', she meant herself, Kira, Shilo and Bronn. Shilo was reluctant. Kira was looking anywhere else, once the subject was explained. But Sheena had something else in mind other than words. She took two white crystals out of her pocket, and said, "Kal'Ton gave me these the last time Kira and I were at the Guardians' village, when I flew her there to return the Wand. He says they are not magic, though even with everything I know, they look like it to me ... still. They're Kira's and Shilo's business, really, but I know what they contain. And, Bronn, Kal'Ton said you should know too as you were part of all of the tests."

She picked one of them up, and breathed on it. It began to glow with inner light, and a beam shot out of it, a few inches, making a small pool of light on the table. Sheena adjusted it so the light shone nearly straight ahead, and amazingly, it formed an image,

518

tiny yet perfect, a couple of feet high. It was a record of Kira's test. The figures, Kira and Kal'Ton replayed the scene from the Guardian's village, with small yet clear voices. The detail was amazing; it was all too easy to see the anguish on her tiny face.

Kira looked down at the table. There were hints of tears in her eyes; while it had been some time ago the memory being brought back was hard. Bronn felt embarrassed for them both, he didn't understand why he needed to see this. It was too personal. After a few seconds, she made to get up, but Sheena said gently, "Wait! There is another, another side."

And she breathed on the other crystal, and positioned it carefully when it began to play. It was a record of Shilo's preparation for his test. Kal'Ton was speaking to him.

"Shilo, you will be one of the first tested, and I am sorry, it will be a hard test."

"I am ready sir. I have trained; I feel I'm ready for anything."

"This will not be that sort of test. Tonight, at dinner, you will be sitting with people we think you will like, for conversation and entertainment. A very beautiful girl, a fighter in her own right, will be seated next to you, and you must allow her to seduce you. This is not, I must carefully say, a duty for her against her will. We are far freer than Warrior's Hold on such matters, and she has seen you and is very attracted to you. Dozens of girls and women were offered the opportunity for this test, but she was the one who spoke up earliest and most firmly. You must say nothing to Kira, you must behave as if her feelings in this matter are unknown, or unimportant."

Shilo spoke in a hushed, horrified voice: "What?" What is the purpose of this test? How does it benefit anyone? All it will do is hurt Kira. And me."

Kal'Ton spoke in his melodious voice, sadly. "Shilo, you must understand that right now Kira loves you. She loves you too much. We think – and it is not just idle thought – that if she is too close to you, your quest may fail. She will be too concerned for you, and not do other things that are necessary in the same way and to the same effect."

"But I can't hurt her! I can't bear to! I would do anything for her!"

"Then do this. Duty is hard, I know. Your duty to the quest. Better to hurt her now, than see her dead later."

Shilo looked at him for a long time. After a while, a long while, he bowed his head. "I will do it" he whispered. "For her. Will she ever know? Will she ever forgive me?"

"Perhaps. But you can never tell her the details."

The image faded, and all except Sheena though it was over. But there was another scene, the next day before the fight. Shilo was angry.

"Did you see the way Kira looked at me?" he asked in anguish. "As if it meant nothing. As if she didn't care."

Kal'Ton nodded somberly. "I did. But still. There are compensations, surely. Kal'Tia is a wonderful person."

Shilo nodded. "She is" he said, bitterly. "And I went with her, as the test demanded. I did my best not to insult her; my body did its duty, but my mind and heart were not in it. I would have done anything to give that duty to someone else. At one time, I would have

520

thought it a dream come true, but I now know I am over that part of my life. I want nobody. Nobody but Kira. And she doesn't care for me." And tears were in his eyes too.

Kal'Ton said, "The test shows you that you can, and will, do your duty. And you can rise above your feelings. It is hard, but now you know you are strong. But there is one more test today, a simpler one."

Shilo nodded without interest. "Something simple would be a good thing."

And the scene faded.

Shilo and Kira looked at each other. They spoke as one. "You love *me*? I love *you*! ..." and they both said they were sorry, and should have known ...

Sheena smiled smugly. "And *that's* why I think you should come with us!"

Shilo looked at Kira with joy, and then at Sheena. But a shadow crossed his face. "No." he said, heavily. "No, ... I still think I should return to Warrior's Hold. The age difference is still there. But I will wait there, train and hope."

Sheena laughed. "What, you couldn't bear to be with her, knowing you can't touch her? You can't wait *two months*?"

"She'll only be sixteen in two months! But the age of consent is eighteen! Two years!"

"Sixteen, for Ice Witches. They grow up earlier, you know."

"But *I'm* not an Ice Witch! I am a Warrior!"

"You *are* an Ice Witch. You could freeze that pitcher of water in an instant. You're getting very good at controlling your body temperature, and have made a start on your first Avatar. Oh, technically, you would need to be adopted into an Ice Witch family, that's tradition when talent comes from outside for both the Ice Witches and the Fire Witches. But there will be no shortage of people willing to do that. And then, you're an Ice Witch. Still a Warrior, of course, and needing training in both areas. But as long as you're on Iceland, there's no problem. So ... do you think you can keep your hands to yourself for two months?"

Shilo radiated joy. "Oh, *yes*! Can I be with her? Talk to her? That's allowed, isn't it?"

Sheena nodded. "Certainly! As long as you don't neglect your studies, either of you. You can even kiss her, as long as you have a chaperone. Within reason, of course."

Chapter 15. Closures

O for a draught of vintage, that hath been
Cooled a long age in the deep-delved earth,
Tasting of Flora and the country green,
Dance, and Provencal song, and sun-burnt mirth!
O for a beaker full of the warm South,
Full of the true, the blushful Hippocrene,
With beaded bubbles winking at the brim,
And purple-stained mouth;
That I might drink, and leave the world unseen,
And with thee fade away into the forest dim

John Keats

Sheena sat in her study, legs up on a comfortable little couch, resting, with a good bottle of seaweed wine. She had been granted a suite of three rooms: a bedchamber, living area and a small entertainment or reception room. She needed the space; people often sought her out for help with one thing or the other, though they would give her breathing and resting space. The past year had been hard, taxing even her deep energy reserves. Only now did people feel they could take a day off.

The trip to Ice Island had been relatively uneventful. They made five stops along the way, one of nearly a week while a storm blew itself out. However, that one had been with the ship in the safe harbor of Nun's Hold, and themselves in the solid walls of the Hold itself. Intira had been glad to see them, delighted that Narn was no longer a problem and glowingly joyous over Sheena's redemption. She nodded in a highly satisfied way, saying, "There! Our fundamental principles are sound, you see?" And then she laughed at herself, remembering that they were in a sense Sheena's fundamental principles.

The nuns arranged for Sheena to give lectures on the nature of level four magic, and everyone took notes feverishly. She spoke more openly and freely about who she was and what had happened in her life, and Intira released the small personal library Sheena had given her to general access.

Just before Nun's Hold, they had a small run-in with pirates, déjà vu for Sheena. There are always opportunists, and a few crews had sought to cash in on the general uncertainty of the war with Narn, and the resultant fewer patrols of ships with Witches on board. There were none around Warrior's Hold – only a madman would attack a ship with a reasonable chance of a Warrior being on board, there was no-where to run! And near Seer's Hold, the chance of being Seen was too high. Sheena simply flew over, and had a highly enjoyable show-off. In their panic, the crew attacked her, and she just let it all bounce off her level four shields for a bit, and then released her Avatars, disarmed everyone on board from the captain down to the cook, zapped them with low-level lightning till they stopped trying to fight, and told them they could all make the choice: swear under truthspell to never do it again, or swim to shore. It was a long swim, they took the oath.

After that, the winds had unfortunately been a bit contrary. Inconsistent and sometimes stormy, the crossing to Peace Island had not been easy, and had required a lot of tacking to and fro. As had been practically inevitable, they were later than they had hoped, and it was already starting to get very cold. Their first stop at Peace Island had to be longer than they wanted too, the ship needed some repairs. Fortunately nothing serious enough to warrant having to get it out of the water. But the whole crew worked hard to get it done, and they hired whoever they could from the island, though most of the men there were busy battening down for the winter. The only way everything got done was because they had additional hands: sixteen Avatars, Sheena herself and Shilo, and of course Bronn and Kira.

Then, they hugged the coast under unfavorable conditions and made second port on Peace Island, loading fresh water, provisions and just waiting things out for too many days.

Finally, reluctantly, they had to make the hard decision: they were never going to make it to Ice Island in the ship, the seas would have frozen there already. They would sail north-east as far as they could, and land somewhere on the coast of Iceland, and trek a hundred miles or so across the land. Hopefully there would not be too much snow. In the final extreme, Sheena could fly them to the Hold one by one.

They aimed for the point where they had last seen the Hold Tribe, figuring they would have settled down for the winter. Even that they only just made, it was a close thing. The bay was freezing, but not frozen yet.

A fair number of the Tribe was waiting for them, curious as to why a ship would come there. Practically no-one ever did, there was little in the way of resources and no reason to go there. The Tribe was known to be hostile or at least acquisitive, the only reason to go there was if a ship needed shelter, water or had been blown off course. They recognized Sheena, Bronn and Kira, of course. Johnno came forward, and was clearly at a bit of a loss. Tribe tradition required him to make an attempt on the ship and claim it as salvage.

Sheena spoke in a clear voice, saying that they were heading north and were going to be bringing the Ice Witches back to the island. She spoke of ancient prophecies fulfilled. She revealed herself as Sha'Lin'Tra the Great, which was taken rather doubtfully, but a manifestation of her aura and a level three firebolt were enough to show the Tribe that the world was changing – had already changed, in fact. Accustomed to adapting to the very real forces of nature that ruled their lives, they clearly saw the futility of opposing Sheena. She was pretty much a force of nature in herself.

Sheena spoke to Johnno in private, and was delighted to find that he had been able to move on, and had taken a wife. She spoke to him at length about how having the Ice Witches back would mean both an increase in responsibility for him and the tribe, a change in their way of life, and a great series of benefits. He seemed a bit dubious, but they did still have their legends.

She left Shilo and Kira and Bronn in the Tribe's care – their first new responsibility to the Ice Witches – while she went with the ship back to Peace Island. It was just as well she did (as she had thought). Three times the vessel got stopped by the ice freezing over, and the only way they got free was by Sheena blasting a path through it. The third time, the ship's crew thought there was no chance, but Sheena jumped over the side of the ship, hovered just above the ice, and let fly a full strength level four firebolt, which as Sim'Bo'Lo said, 'shook the ship, the heavens, the sea and probably the underworld too'. They sailed for a mile through shattered ice floes to clear water, and made it to port. The locals were not pleased to have a ship there for the winter, but were mollified when Sheena explained that they had some provisions, a fair bit of good Prosperity wine, gold to pay their way, and the crew would be well behaved – otherwise she would have something to say about it.

Then, she simply flew back.

Collecting the others, they began the three day walk back to the Hold – three days in summer. In the days of the approaching winter, with the days shortening rapidly and everything starting to freeze with only brief thaws in the middle of the day, and slowly deepening snow, it took longer. Kira was perfectly comfortable, and Shilo only felt the very coldest hours of the night, and could easily warm himself up when he woke at that time. He was becoming a very real Ice Witch. Sheena managed, but Bronn was steadily getting more and more miserable. On the second last night of the journey the weather really set in and it got bitterly cold, the wind turning around and blowing from the north. Always trying something new, Sheena set up a shield shaped like a tent over them and kept the snow off. She warmed the ground first, and they kept just comfortable.

But the next day, with the snow settling down to a fierce blizzard, she gave up and airlifted Bronn to the Hold. It wasn't easy. For a start, Bronn was no lightweight, and she had to keep a shield up as well, and press against the force of the wind. She had to rest several times. Then, in the snow, even the massive Hold wasn't easy to find. However, she flew straight into the wind until she reached the end of land, then back a bit and along the coast until they came to it. Resting only long enough to open up their apartment and carry a good load of firewood in for Bronn (a dozen Avatars made that easier work) she set a good blaze, and left him with just enough food for one good meal.

Flying back was easier – she was alone, going with the wind, and she knew where she was flying to – she had left an Avatar with Kira and Shilo, so she would be able to find them. She had left another with Bronn, so finding the Hold would be easier next time too.

The night was intensely cold. Even Kira felt it a bit, and the three of them huddled together around a fire built from wood Sheena had carried from the Hold, and then under the coverings they had, with a double shield over them. In the morning, Shilo wanted Sheena to fly Kira to safety, but she overrode that. Kira would manage with her shield and her greater Ice Magic talent to keep her warm, and an Avatar for company. Shilo was going to be the problem, Sheena was not sure she could lift him and manage a shield at the same time, into the wind. Still, she had an alternative. Using a fourth-level shield, which she could shape any way she liked, she carved the two longest pieces of wood, which she had reserved from the fire, into very passable skis. Having lived on Peace Island, which was nearly as cold as Iceland and where there was ample snow in winter, Shilo had the skill. They had to be tied onto his boots with rope, but they managed. Then, she had to build a complex shield about him. A simple sphere would have been impossible to drag and besides would have cut the ropes she used to tow him. But it was done, and she dragged him over the snow for the forty or so miles they had to go. It wasn't easy, especially the uphill parts, but it was doable.

It took many hours, but eventually they made it. Shilo settled in with Bronn, with a grateful sigh, and Sheena thought about returning to Kira. She was frankly ravenous, and they had not brought much food – as Sheena said, pulling Shilo's great hulking carcass was quite enough to be going on with, thank you.

After a brief rest, a sudden thought came to her, and she sent an Avatar off, down into the cellars. Ice Witches were always careful to have reserves 'just in case' and there were a few things down there still useable including a crock of crystallized honey and quite a few bottles of brandy, lead sealed. Sheena mixed brandy and honey and gave some to Bronn and

Shilo, which laid them out for the night, and drank as much of it as she could stomach herself. She flew off to Kira, more than a little under the weather in both senses of the word, though she was mostly sober when she arrived. Still, she was exhausted, and ate hugely and fell into a deep sleep for the long night, letting Kira do the shielding.

The next day, she realized with dismay that she had overdone it with the honey brandy, and had lost the Avatar during the night and she would have to re-find the Hold. But that could be done. There was still Kira and five packs to get to the Hold, so she ate another enormous meal and flew Kira and one pack off north, leaving an Avatar as before. Although the blizzard raged unabated, and it was barely possible to tell day from night, she did a better job of guessing where it was, and had them in the Hold in a few hours, and the packs by the end of the day. It would all have been impossible without flight - the snow was now deeper than Shilo could reach.

And then, they waited. Slowly, the blizzard howled itself out and the wind swung around to blow towards the north once again. They passed the time talking, practicing both Ice Magic and Warrior training. Kira was now competent with two Material Avatars and one Ethereal, even with both Materials out of sight. Shilo had firmed up his Ethereal, and could send it out of sight briefly too, and Sheena and Kira said he surely had the mental structure needed to progress further and make it Material, and begin a second. No hurry, there was plenty of time.

Sheena said his Warrior skills were getting better every day, and he could easily best her with sword and bow, could win hand-to-hand mostly because of his great strength, and would manage it with the quarterstaff soon enough.

The sea was frozen solid now, quite a bit earlier than expected thanks to the blizzard. Sheena flew herself down to the beach, and melted down the snow over a broad area till she found where they had left their sled-boat, then blasted a channel through the snow down to the water's (or rather ice's) edge, and another up to the Hold. The marched in triumph down the rather slippery re-freezing path, to the sled. They made up a reasonable sized sail using all their Guardian-supplied bedding and blankets tied together by means of those so very useful holes and loops, designed for just such purposes. They had no mast, so they made a kind of kite. It probably wouldn't have worked except that Sheena could fly up and keep it airborne and stop it from dragging on the ground.

They made rapid progress when the sled moved, especially when they came to areas with little to no snow. But they lost time when they ran into drifts. Having nearly twenty pairs of hands (counting Avatars) did help get it dug out and moving again, but Sheena had to resort to blasting and melting several times. Still, it was only forty miles and they made it easily in five hours rather than the days it had taken to go the other way.

Bronn, via synchronized dreaming, had told Kara they were coming home, and everyone who could project an Avatar had sent one out to find them and guide them home. They couldn't know that Sheena could fly up for a bird's eye view and spot the island from afar, of course, still, all those extra hands made it easy to handle the last few miles.

The homecoming was joyous ecstasy.

Bronn and Kara absented themselves from general company for several days again, surfacing only for meals, and no-one minded a bit. After that, they still wandered about the Hold rarely separated by a distance greater than an arms' length.

The old rituals were dusted off, and Shilo was adopted – by Marko and Shira as it happened, which technically made Kira his cousin, but only very technically. There would be no issue about him and Kira having a relationship. That was still a few weeks away, however, they had arrived well in time for Kira's sixteenth birthday.

On a related note, Shira was definitely starting to show her pregnancy, and looked as happy as person could be. Marko was a much easier man to get on with, too. Besides their relationship, they had been working on their healing techniques, to good effect. Shira had practiced her Fire Magic diligently, and Sheena said she would get even better when she could travel to Fireland to bond with a volcano, whenever that might be.

Shira was completely secure in her relationship, and had no problem letting Marko work with Sheena to do some emergency healing that arose over the months that followed. With Sheena channeling level four energy, Marko said he reckoned he could probably heal the fish in the stew they were eating. A joke, but not by much.

Marko was proud of his niece, with her two solid Avatars and the third on its way, already more than he could do and he said he would happily hand over leadership of the tribe whenever she or Sheena thought the time was right. He also remarked, when he saw Sheena's array of Avatars, he understood what she meant about it not being a good idea to challenge for the leadership! Sheena said, about twenty or twenty-one would probably be the right age. She thought that first the Ice Witches should move back to

Iceland and consolidate there, then when Kira was eighteen she and Shilo should make a trip to the three Holds with a couple of other Ice Witches and Sheena, as envoys and heralds to really establish proper diplomatic relationships, and so that Shilo could complete his training at Warrior's Hold.

Work began in a low-key way for the move to Iceland. Mostly planning at first – they still had to get through winter and spring before the ships from Fireland would get there.

Everyone was awed by Sheena's abilities, but charmed by the unaffected way she used and spoke of them. While she thoroughly enjoyed showing off at Fire Hold, that wasn't the way of the Ice Witches, and she felt no need or inclination to act that way at Ice Hold.

The only exception was when Kira's sixteenth finally arrived. A formal and public ceremony was held to acknowledge Kira's coming of age. However, for her private celebration, in her thoughtful way, Kira held much the same sort of party as last time, inviting only Sheena and the same handful of girls. They *made* her show off, which she did for them, with firebolts, fireballs and shields, level four magic and of course her Avatars. In some ways, however, they were more awed by Kira's two and a bit Avatars. They expected amazing things from Sha'Lin'Tra the Great, but Kira was one of them, they had known her all their lives. Nonetheless, one of the big hits of the evening was Sheena's promised juggling show, with nine balls in the air, two behind her back being bounced by her heels, and one on her head.

The other was when she flew each and every one of them in turn up through the sky to see the beauty of the full moon reflecting on the top of the clouds, and the stars shining oh so brightly above. Wrapped up in preparation, the cold meant nothing to them for a few minutes, of course. Only one of them was too afraid of heights to go up, and even she changed her mind when the others were landed either silent and enchanted, or crying with joy and wonder.

They begged her to show them how it was done, and she smiled and showed them as best she could, describing the energy flows. It wasn't a technique that came naturally to Ice Witches; it required a very different type of thinking and direction of the mind, and Sheena thought it was quite impossible, of course. If Narn, with the power to drive five Avatars, could only manage a glide, how could a group of adolescent Ice Witches possibly hope to fly?

But Ice Witch minds are quite different from Fire Witch minds, and almost unbelievably, they all grasped the technique and three of them could do it straight away. One could just lift herself off the floor for a few seconds, one could rise, and touch the roof – and Kira flew right over the Hold and onto the cliff, and then back after a short rest. And most of the others started to lift off with a bit of practice. It looked like many Ice Witches *could* fly, once they were shown how to do it. It was just that a Fire Witch *able* to fly was only born once every few thousand years, and no-one had ever shown them. And, very likely, their magic and minds had changed, living isolated on Ice Island. Sheena's best guess was that pretty much any Ice Witch able to project a Material Avatar – and that was *all* of them – might be able to do it with practice. Kira's first efforts were as good as Sheena's had been, and that was when she had mastered her eighth Avatar!

And so the evening ended, and the girls hugged her again. They were a year older and more reserved, and perhaps they might not have done it on their own, and Sheena suspected Kira had primed them. But they meant it, it had been a wonderful night – and all of them leaving as potential fliers, certainly determined to try to master it.

The next day, the technique spread like wildfire throughout the island. The sky was full of flying Witches, and there were a few unfortunate accidents. Some overreached themselves and had to struggle not to fall out of the sky. Others didn't pay attention in all three dimensions and ran into each other, or inanimate objects. A few tried to project an Avatar at the same time, and found out that *really* didn't work. There were cuts and bruises, and one broken bone – and Shira and Marko handled most of them, and Sheena and Marko handled the worst. Two or three who really went too far and would have died, Sheena plucked out of the air and saved.

Shilo managed to learn how, too, although it took him longer, partly because he was now quite heavy.

Over the next few days, things settled down. The Witches got better and better; only the very young were left gazing wistfully into the sky as their brothers and sisters or parents soared about. But they knew their time would come, at least. People learned to look above and below as well as side to side and Sheena had to learn a bit there too as she wasn't used to having company in the sky.

Shilo and Kira were absent during all the chaos in the clouds. No-one minded; she was over sixteen now and free to make her own choices, and everyone was very happy with the choice she had made. Of course, she knew the Ice Magic method of contraception - Sheena had firmly reminded her the day before her birthday that the last thing they needed right now in the middle of training and preparation for the move back to Iceland was a pregnant Ice Queen, which had made

Kira blush – mature though she might be physically, and experienced beyond her years by the travels of the last twelve months, she still had the rather endearing notion that she and Shilo were being very discreet about their developing relationship, and no-one really knew what was going on, or really understood.

And so the Spring slowly passed, with the business of the Hold going on nearly as normal. As always, there was a lot of spare time as even the Witches didn't go outside much in the worst of the cold. It was too cold for most level one Ice Witches. The best of them (and the level twos of course) could take it, but there was little need or point, it was dark and everything was frozen. There was a lot of time devoted to entertainment - stories, theatre, endless games for the children, craftwork, plus of course the needs of everyday living. It seemed utterly pointless after a few weeks to pretend that there was anything short-term about Kira's and Shilo's relationship, and so they had a short formal engagement and were married with the full traditional service and feast a few months later.

They made an impressive couple walking down the aisle; tradition required them both to show their Avatars. Kira had stabilized her third, and Shilo had progressed his to Material – Sheena had not let either of them slack off during their courting - and it had been a long while since a couple had got married that could show four Avatars. And Kira was stunning in the dress she had made for herself, "made" being the operative word, given she had constructed it from the ground up (out of seaweed, of course!). Shilo had finally stopped growing, and with the physical development of the Warrior he was, could only be described as a beautiful man. Handsome just wasn't enough.

Sheena gave them a week off for a honeymoon, and resumed their training.

And the plans for the return to Iceland matured. Sheena suggested to Marko, Kira and the elders that they should not abandon Ice Island. She explained that as it was further north than Iceland, but still directly on the north-south Ley line, that children conceived and born there would on average be more powerful Witches and less likely to be born Ungifted. The North Pole would be best of all, but a quick exploration by Sheena had shown there was no more land further north. So, quite a lot of things that would otherwise have been moved were chosen to stay.

They presented the ideas to the tribe, and they were all enthusiastic. Few people are fully happy about deserting a home, however harsh or humble, and the idea that the Hold would persist and remain useful caught their enthusiasm. Rosters were proposed for the number of people who should stay, and for how long. Someone was worried that the trek over the ice would be dangerous, and over the water possibly more so, until Sheena gently pointed out that given their newly discovered abilities in flying, on a good day with the wind behind them they might manage it in less than half an hour.

And that caught their enthusiasm too. Someone proposed that there was no need to wait for the ships from Fireland. They would wait for a good day when the weather was clear, maybe a bit nearer to spring, and the wind low or in the right direction, and just fly across. The best fliers could carry a pack of helpful and necessary things, and of course they could return and repeat the journey as often as they liked. Everyone agreed, and Sheena thoroughly approved. Knowing Fire Witches as she did, she said it would give the Ice Witches far more recognition and status to manage the migration themselves, with the ships being a convenience rather than a necessity.

And so, one fine day in very early summer, a cloud of Ice Witches rose from the island. Kira, already with the eye of a leader, asked Marko to organize everyone to leave in the morning, while it was still nearly dark – the sun having only just begun to think about approaching the horizon. She said Sheena should be in the lead, and got her to project light so that everyone could see her, and follow her easily. And so, a bright, shining new star appeared in the sky, and a new legend was born as the old prophecy was finally fulfilled. Sha'Lin'Tra the Great had relented, and led the Ice Witches home.

It made a great story, one that grew with re-telling. In practice, it was a bit more complicated. Some people had over-estimated how far they could carry a pack, and three caches were left on the ice as they lightened their load. Some had over-estimated their flying ability, and had to stop for rests (Shilo was one of those, and no wonder, Sheena said – it was a good effort for him to even get his body weight off the ground!), and some even turned back, to try another day after more practice. But most of those who were going made it reasonably easily. The best fliers waited with those who had to rest, and one or two helped the ones who couldn't make it go back. Kira insisted that Sheena go the whole way to the Hold, but then allowed her to go back with a handful of the best fliers to help and protect the rest and pick up the packs. There were bears on the ice, of course, and best not to take too many chances.

Only two people carried their children in the first wave, and they were very young babies. The rest came in the much smaller wave, where Sheena and the more talented fliers pulled their trusty sled. After that, one or two flew over, one or two came in the sled, and a few went back and forth to keep operations under control at both places.

The first few days were chaos, with people and Avatars everywhere, cleaning, making things safe, opening up windows and shutters, organizing the kitchens, the toilets, the chimneys, bedding and everything that needed doing for a Hold that had been shut up for a hundred years. Sheena asked Marko organize it, and Kira to help – to learn how it was done. She herself acted as second in command, and was able to help tremendously as firstly she knew the Hold far better than anyone else, and secondly, she could be in eighteen places at once, with all fourteen Material and three Ethereal Avatars out. But even she was amazed at how well the Ice Witches worked together, with almost no friction. Fire Witches would have been in arguments, if not in out-and-out physical conflict, every five minutes.

On the third day, Sheena suggested a quick flight over to the Hold tribe by a dozen flyers, and that impressive landing and re-introduction well and truly made the point that the Witches had returned, and life was going to be different. Kira suggested a swap, three Witches for three Tribesmen. The Witches could explain how things worked with them, and the Tribesmen could see that the Hold was safe, and the Ice Witches powerful but human.

It all worked out surprisingly well. The Witches loved their new land. As summer started and progressed, they explored everywhere (a lot easier, when it's done by air), found the best spots for seaweed and fishing, and good soil close by for their summer crops.

A little later, Shira's baby was born – back on Ice Island. While it was far too early to tell her level of talent normally, Bronn showed how useful a top level Seer could be, predicting she would be medium-high powerful, a solid two Avatar Witch, which made both parents very happy and proud.

Finally, the ships arrived, carrying many useful items and luxuries Sheena had purchased. They unloaded, and followed the retreating ice to Far Ice Island, loaded up those heavy items that were to be brought over, and a few people who preferred to go by ship – some children and some of the elderly. Sheena bought one of them outright, the Ice Witches needed a ship for a variety of reasons including transporting seaweed – there was no good bed very close to the new Hold, and their needs would be as great as ever. And, they would want to trade with other Holds.

The other two sailed back, to stop at Nun's Hold and Fir'Caram. Bronn and Kara went with them, a bittersweet parting. Everyone was happy for them because they were going where they wanted to be, but Kara was family for many at the Hold. Sheena, Shilo and Kira were sorry to see the group being split up, of course.

Still, they took a great gift with them.

Sheena had been puzzling over Narn's new magic – splitting up an Avatar. It had taken her a long while, but she had finally figured it out. She didn't want to split it up as much as twelve times – she chose four pieces, which could see as well as hear, and speak, but not move. They were simple spheres, glowing softly. As long as Sheena didn't fall into the deepest of sleeps, she could keep them 'alive', and she could communicate with people wherever they were. She asked Bronn and Kara to drop one off at Nun's Hold, Fire Hold, get one sent to Warrior's Hold and take one back to Seer's Hold. She documented the technique, and it was set to revolutionize communications about the world – there would be good pay for any Witch who could master it, because part of one of their Avatars would be fully occupied, of course.

And so, Sheena sat at her couch, resting. Thinking about how the Hold was now thriving, and how the world would be changing, with Ice Witches flying everywhere and sub-Avatars being used, no doubt in ways she hadn't even thought about. And Warrior's Hold training women again, and Fire Hold having put polices in place to secure the rights of men, at least among the Witches. It would be a long time before things were as egalitarian as at Seer's Hold or Ice Hold, but perhaps a new age of equality was beginning.

It was all done. The quest was over, the Ice Witches had returned. She could move on, and join the Angels, once Kira had taken over from Marko. That would still be a few years, of course, but it didn't matter. She had one Ethereal Avatar wandering about the Hold, and she focused on that, seeing the bustle of activity. And a quick peek to Nun's Hold, where Intira was still Mother Superior, a little older but still with life in her. And over to Seer's Hold, where it was still early morning, but she caught a glimpse of Bronn and Kara, looking about as happy as two people could be.

No, it didn't matter. She would happily wait, while Kira matured in her skills, while Shilo consolidated his, and when the time came she would take him to Warrior's Hold and get him that Gold ranking. She would keep in fond, if distant contact with Bronn and Kara, and help the Ice Witches as much as she could. It would be easy to wait. She loved them. She sighed, took a sip of wine, and luxuriated in the wonderful, mind filling, achingly beautiful feeling. She loved them all.